Anne Marsh writes sexy contemporary and paranormal romances—because the world can always enjoy one more alpha male. She started writing romance after getting laid off from her job as a technical writer—and quickly decided happily-ever-afters trumped software manuals. She lives in North Carolina with her two kids and five cats.

Cara Lockwood is the *USA TODAY* bestselling author of more than twenty-six books, including *I Do (But I Don't)*, which was made into a Lifetime original movie. She's written the Bard Academy series for young adults and has had her work translated into several languages around the world. Born and raised in Dallas, Cara now lives near Chicago with her husband and their five children. Find out more about her at caralockwood.com, friend her on Facebook, Facebook.com/authorcaralockwood, or follow her on Twitter, @caralockwood, or Instagram, Instagram.com/cara_lockwood.

If you liked *Hookup* and *The Sex Cure*
why not try

Hotter on Ice by Rebecca Hunter
Slow Hands by Faye Avalon

Available from Mills & Boon DARE this month.

Also by Anne Marsh

Her Intern
Inked
Ruled

Also by Cara Lockwood

Double Dare You
Hot Mistake
Look at Me
No Strings

Discover more at millsandboon.co.uk

HOOKUP

ANNE MARSH

THE SEX CURE

CARA LOCKWOOD

MILLS & BOON

First Published in Great Britain 2020
by Mills & Boon, an imprint of HarperCollins*Publishers*
1 London Bridge Street, London, SE1 9GF

ISBN-13: 978-0-263-27751-7

MIX
Paper from
responsible sources
FSC C007454

This book is produced from independently certified FSC™ paper
to ensure responsible forest management.
For more information visit www.harpercollins.co.uk/green.

Printed and bound in Spain
by CPI, Barcelona

HOOKUP

ANNE MARSH

MILLS & BOON

CHAPTER ONE

Maple
#goddessofwar #eraser #accidentalpornstar

I MAKE MY grand entrance, bursting through the doors of Kinkster in San Francisco's gritty, dirty, fabulously alive Mission District. Kinkster is a hookup app for people who preferred nonvanilla sex, but you wouldn't guess it from the office space. It's all bland start-up chic, a wide-open, minimalist stage of tables and laptops ringed by a jeans-and-T-shirt-wearing chorus staring at me with varying degrees of shock. *Yes, look at me.*

Righteous anger surges up in me again, temporarily swallowing the too-familiar sense of shame. I wish I weren't here, that Madd Dixon was every bit as perfect as he had seemed. Hot and poetically sweet, he wrote me an honest-to-God card after our first night together, swearing I'd reformed his bad-boy self. Charming, rugged, downright dirty in bed? Yes, yes, and oh you betcha please. We'd been an instant couple from our first date, sharing sleepovers and late-night laptop sessions as we built our respective online businesses. While I built my influencer kingdom, he'd sourced a paper goods supply business, delivering monthly subscription boxes of pretty notebooks, pens, and sticky pads to thousands of home offices across the country. We'd planned to adopt a rescue puppy and last weekend I'd cheered from the sidelines as he played rugby with a brutal, ferocious masculinity that melted my panties right off and made me think, *He could be the one*. Right now, however, I'd settle for taking his head off—the big one *or* the small one.

God, he's a liar.

Madd Dixon also turned out to be a cheater and a bastard, his decision to post our personal video on Kinkster being the cherry on the shit sundae he'd served me. For your eyes only, I'd texted when I'd sent the video I'd made of myself with my phone. Ours, he'd agreed with a winky face and a kiss—and I'd stupidly believed him. Now a gazillion Kinkster subscribers have watched me pirouetting in nothing but my birthday suit and ballet slippers. My inadvertent show-and-tell has already garnered me five hundred hookup requests.

A blue jeans–wearing engineer pads toward me, eyes widening as he takes me in. Sure, he might recognize me from my successful five-year career with the San Francisco Ballet—but I'll bet he remembers me naked and dancing in that stupid video. Him and everyone else in San Francisco.

He's willing to play nice, though, asking, "Can I help you?"

No, no you can't, I want to scream. My picker is irredeemably broken given my recent man choices. My pre-Madd pick was equally a disaster, and the guy before that…let's not go there. My feet settle automatically into first position, no longer poised to leap.

"Yes," I lie. What I really need is a brain transplant or a lobotomy. Some kind of drastic intervention. "Someone's posted a video of me on Kinkster without my permission. I want it taken down."

"There's a take-down form on our website for reporting copyright violations." He volunteers this information cautiously and I bet he wishes he hadn't stood up because, hello? Helpful, nice people get handed a shit sandwich from the snack cart of life.

"I don't want to fill out a *form*." I inhale deeply, centering myself because otherwise I'll do something even more stupid than dating Madd. "I want this fixed. Gone. Deleted."

Lola, my best friend and wing woman, tried to warn me about Madd. Over the years, I've razzed her about her broken man picker, but it turns out that I'm the one who needs "Remember: Guys Are Assholes" tattooed on my forehead because over and over I pick the assholiest asshole of the bunch. And my stupidity matters more now than ever because one of my post-ballet career moves is my Instagram brand. Being an Instagram influencer has much in common with a circus seal juggling a bright red ball on its nose. If I serve up the cute, perky and well-balanced version of me and create super popular online content, I'll not only be able to promote my own athleisure line, but I'll score paying gigs promoting other products. The downside? I'm always on; the curtain never falls on my performance because I share my personal life with a gazillion insta-friends.

"Take me to your leader." I stab a finger toward Hot Nerd, who nods nervously, spins on his (bare) heel and marches toward a glass-walled office on the far side of the building.

"Max?" He tosses the name over his shoulder for confirmation, although clearly he's already decided that Max Whoever-He-Is gets the pleasure of dealing with me.

"Is he responsible for Kinkster?"

Welcoming-Committee-Nerd nods vigorously and the mental soundtrack in my head picks up steam. Today's theme song is "Ride of the Valkyries." What kind of guy codes an app specifically for kinky hookups? And what does it say about me that I've spent hours scrolling through it? When Hot Nerd pauses in front of an office door, I barrel through it before nerves can get the best of me. No script? No worries. I'll improvise.

Sunlight floods the office, silhouetting a big, rangy guy sprawled behind yet another laptop. They must pass those things out like candy. The iron-and-wood shelves bolted to the exposed brick walls house an impressive collection of *Star Wars* figurines outnumbered only by stacks of books. I register dark hair just long enough to run my fingers through and suntanned skin. Head Nerd clearly gets out of the office. A lot. Long lashes sweep up as I storm toward him. God, he has the most gorgeous eyes I've ever seen. I might accidentally fall into them for just a second before I recover and continue my self-righteous advance.

He certainly doesn't look like a geeky code genius. He wears faded blue jeans, work boots and a battered UC Santa Cruz T-shirt, with nary a pocket protector or a button-up shirt in sight. When he crosses powerful forearms over his chest, I catch a glimpse of ink. Worse, his eyes crinkle up as he shoots me a cautious smile. *Stupid,* hot *bastard.*

I look at his handsome, arrogant, knowing face and I throw my phone at him as hard as I can. It's a dramatic gesture—and a futile one. I should have thrown the coffee I held in my other hand. My phone bounces off his shoulder, hits the trendy concrete floor of this stupid, stupid loft space and makes an audible cracking sound. It's not his fault that Madd is a first-class asshole, but the "Ride of the Valkyries" soundtrack blasting in my head thankfully drowns out logic, because I need to blame *someone* for my own stupidity. He'll do.

He shoves effortlessly to his feet, making himself an even larger target. "Max O'Reilly."

"Asshole," I counter.

He lifts one broad shoulder. "Guilty as charged. Or were you introducing yourself?"

A hint of a smile still plays about his gorgeous mouth. Stubble roughens his jaw. He hasn't shaved and I suspect he simply can't be bothered. His gaze drifts down my body and I wait for the moment of recognition. Sure, I'm fully clothed *now* but naked ballet makes an impression, as the number of hookup requests I've received attest.

"We haven't met." He sounds certain, although now he frowns. "But you look familiar."

He shifts those killer hazel eyes to my phone as he bends to pick it up. Thanks to the unlocked screen, he gets an eyeful of me dancing, a graceful *Swan Lake*-esque solo that's all pirouettes and graceful leg extensions. If only I'd bothered with a tutu. A leotard. *Something.* Since I'm wearing only my favorite pink ballet slippers in the video, however, there are *many* less-than-PG moments. When Asshole Ex and I broke up because I wanted an exclusive relationship whereas he desired a harem, he'd had the last laugh. He'd created a whole fake fucking profile on Kinkster for me (you really couldn't call it dating). He'd then shared our video and my favorite dirty fantasy with the entire world. I love being watched and I thought I enjoyed the risk of being caught, but this is next-level risk. This is the difference between getting busted by the mall cop making out with your boyfriend and waking up naked in bed with an entire SWAT team surrounding you, guns drawn.

Max studies the cracked screen for a moment before turning it off and setting my phone on his desk. Hazel eyes sweep over me. "You dance really well."

So not the point. "Take it down."

Give him credit. He keeps his eyes on my face. "Why?"

And just like that he plunges into negative territory for those of us keeping score—and yes, he's earned a penalty.

"Are you insane?" I extend my arm, lean over his desk and pour my coffee on his keyboard. The queen of impulsivity—that's me. "Why would I choose to share my private video with the world?"

That devastating hint of a smile returns. "Why would you take it down when you look gorgeous?"

Sadly, I'm still reeling enough from Madd's betrayal that Needy Me laps up the compliment. Bitter Me gets right on his ass, however. "That was a private video."

"And that was an expensive laptop." He sounds calm. He doesn't leap to clean up the coffee carnage. "Your video has 2,348,992 views and it's trending."

Maybe I should club him with his hardware? "Take. It. Down."

"So you're Maple." He gets this little puzzled crinkle between his eyes as if I'm a math problem and he'll have me worked out in a minute.

"Like the tree." I wave my hand impatiently. I've heard all the jokes before.

"That's not it." He thinks some more, taking his goddamned time when my entire life is slowly imploding before my (and a million other) eyes, then he smiles. A full-on, sun-wattage-worthy grin. I want to kill him. "You're Lola's friend. I know Lola."

Okay. So if he knows Lola, he's likely one of those dot-com wealthy boys that hang around her new billionaire boyfriend. They're like frogs or mosquitos spawning and where you find one, there's bound to be a whole bunch. It also certainly explains why he's not outraged at my violation of his hardware—not only does he have loads of money, but he's probably also in possession of some new, shiny insta-backup system and hasn't lost so much as a second of work. I think I could hate him. *After* I kill him.

"Look," I say. "I've had a shitty, shitty day. It kicked off with discovering that I was dancing a naked solo on your Kinkster app because Asshole Ex decided to branch out into the revenge porn business. Then it escalated because it's not just me being embarrassed that you and a million billion other guys have seen more of me than my gynecologist. This threatens my job, okay? Companies won't hire an influencer to pimp their products if she's cavorting naked on the internet, because they figure she's too busy pimping her personal assets to be bothered with theirs. And since I happen to like electricity and eating and all those other useful things that a girl has to pay for, I need to *keep* those contracts rolling in—which means you need to take the video down."

Max studies me some more. Thinking maybe, but it's hard to tell. "Work here. For me."

WTF? I have a job. Plus, he's seen me naked.

"Pass."

Apparently, he misinterprets *pass* as a different four-letter word, one that rhymes with *duck*, because he counteroffers. "A new job to replace the old one, thirteen hundred stock options, and a date. With me," he adds, lest I think he's being overambitious and asking me to take on the entire engineering team.

"Who let you out of the cave?" I step into him.

My new Neanderthal acquaintance stands firm, but I've already figured out that Max O'Reilly lacks the boundaries most people possess. And because he won't back up and I won't back down, we end up thigh to thigh, our bodies brushing as if we were dancing. I'm far too aware of the heat of his body, the controlled strength concealed beneath his clothes. He isn't a professional dancer—I'd know him if he was—but he does far more than code all day.

"Why did you make the video?" God. That *voice,* low and smooth, perfect for phone sex, and parts of me demand that all of me pay attention, especially since when he lowers his head, his mouth ends up so very close to mine. His lips demand kissing. Nibbling.

Maybe even outright biting.

Except he's seen me naked.

He's watched my video.

This is totally, absolutely crazy, even for me. There's no way on God's green earth that I'd work for him or go out with him. Plus, I have the whole broken man picker thing to work on. It's the shame talking, I decide. I'm embarrassed that I fell for Madd's lines, and now I want to prove to myself that other guys like me just fine.

"It was a surprise for my boyfriend." Max O'Reilly works in an office that has windows rather than walls, and I'm certain we have an avid audience. I can feel my cheeks flush, my body heating up because I have a dirty little secret of my own. *Hi, my name is Maple and I love being watched.* "He wasn't supposed to share it."

"How did you know he wouldn't?" Max looks genuinely curious.

"Because we were in a relationship? Because I trusted him?"

Max shifts, and for a moment I think he's giving up. But then he leans into me. "I don't have relationships."

Of course he doesn't.

"I have hookups," he continues. "For sex."

I give his announcement a moment of silence because wow. This man either has no filter or he's entirely too honest—which he proves with his next words.

"It's more satisfying, yeah?"

It certainly explains why he's used his coding skills to develop a hookup app rather than, say, curing cancer through genome sequencing. I intend to explain the joys of a committed relationship (again, *liar*), but something entirely different comes out of my mouth. "Did you jerk off to my dancing?"

"Yes." His lips quirk, as if he's maybe trying to rein himself in but can't quite manage it.

"Fix it." I stab my finger into his big beautiful chest. Obviously, I'm not on the dating market at the moment, but he *is* muscled. *You, sir, are definitely more than just an engineer.*

He looks down at me, that slow smile curling his mouth. "How?"

"How should I know?" I throw my hands up in the air. Yes, I'm being dramatic. No, I don't care. "Take it down. Make sure there are no copies anywhere and then forget you ever saw me."

I turn and storm out of his office, ready to bring down the curtain on this particular performance. No one stops me as I march past the tables of software engineers and through the front door. No one knows that I'm silently replaying what happened in that office, the way our bodies brushed, the way Max O'Reilly *knew*. He knew what I liked. He recognized the heat that curled through my body at the thought of him watching me dance. Maybe he even knew about the freedom in exposure, in dancing wide open and free. Or maybe he's just a dirty pervert—a pervert who still has my phone in his possession.

CHAPTER TWO

Max

DON'T SUE ME but my eyes are glued to Maple Washington's dramatically exiting and truly spectacular ass. I keep it discreet, but I'm a huge, huge fan of the yoga pants. She came, she spoke, she gave me a boner despite my legitimate, good faith efforts to listen to her. In under three minutes, I'm six thousand dollars poorer (the laptop) and my balls are Smurf-blue (the boner). What the fuck just happened? And how do I fix it? I pull out my phone and start a new list of Things I Learned Today:

Item: Ms. Washington's parents shouldn't have been allowed to name a child because adding anything to a birth certificate from the *Acer* genus is wrong.

Item: Bad breakup + revenge porn = most popular video ever

I can't remember a more successful share on my app and I have an excellent memory for numbers.

Leaving the video live is tempting. Naked, dancing Maple is amazing *and* she's making me cash—but since the word *yes* has yet to come out of her mouth, it's a no-go. I believe a hundred percent that consent is nonnegotiable—plus, she'd just come right back here. And while my dick definitely votes for a repeat visit, my brain suggests that angry hate sex will never, ever top Maple's to-do list. She's more likely to kick me in my Smurf-colored balls.

Still, she hasn't lawyered up to hit me with a lawsuit—she's just demanded I fix her problem, and even if her timeline and expectations are unreasonable (the internet is forever, ladies and gentlemen, until or unless a gigantic EMP wipes out the world's electronics), she hasn't bullshit me, either. Unhappiness is inevitably and directly proportional to monetary demands, so I would have expected Maple's demands to include a mountain of cash. Instead, she's all righteous indignation. I half expect her to take a flying leap over desks or an engineer as she barges out of Kinkster. Energy crackles almost visibly off her, along with something else, some charisma or star power, a secret charm I've never mastered and that has me—and everyone else at Kinkster—staring after her as our front door bangs shut.

She barely skimmed my shoulder, putting her at five feet four inches tall in shoes. The blond hair piled on top of her head added three more inches. The yoga pants, a cropped shirt and a long-sleeved drapey thing (San Francisco is notoriously damp and chilly) completely covered up what was on display in the video—and before you insist that people don't walk around naked and gyrating, remember that this is San Francisco. We host annual parades devoted to sex and naked people. I allow myself a minute to imagine Maple leading a parade down Market Street. Fantasizing is inadvisable, but since she won't work for me and she's flounced out of my life, imagination it is.

I have her phone, so it isn't even as if I can call her. Which would have been inadvisable idea number two. She's gone, making her dislike clear—ergo, I don't get to fuck her. Ever. I add that to a new list, the list of Things that Suck—Get Over It. Having had her within touching distance, I know the real Maple has brown eyes. And even though she wore flats rather than pink ballet slippers, she moved through my office as if she were dancing. Just thinking about her feet makes me swallow. She has small tits and the lean build of a dancer, a sexy, flexible package that drives every remaining thought from my head.

I need to let it go.

Let *her* go.

Instead, I watch her dance one last time on my phone, staring at the screen where she spins effortlessly in beautiful loops and spirals, her right leg extending and flashing me as she whips through a series of beautiful, obscene kicks. I'm both turned on and resentful that I can't stop watching her.

When my lead engineer sticks his head in my

door, I trigger the script to remove her video from our servers, shove my phone back into my pocket and silently hand him my coffee-soaked laptop. I keep spares on the shelf in my office. Stockpiling avoids downtime. Returning to the code I was working on when Maple busted in seems anticlimactic, however, so instead I amuse myself by looking up my guest. I stay respectful, though, and stick to Google and stuff found online. I do no digging into her personal life, but I still add the following to my Things I Know about Maple list:

1. Maple danced five years for the San Francisco Ballet. They have awesome photos of her dressed as a swan princess (white feathers everywhere) and a hot corsair's date.

2. A year ago, Maple left the ballet and became an influencer in the athleisure space. This means she works out in fancy clothes eighty hours a week and lives on either ramen noodles or air unless she has a new supply of free energy bars from a partner. In which case, she lives on those. In all cases, she takes pictures. An insane number of pictures.

3. Her Instagram is vibrant, colorful and loud—and full of pictures of Maple in the aforementioned athleisure wear, with food, and in places like the beach, the gym and the airport.

4. She loves puppies.

5. And kittens.

6. People pay her to do photoshoots and spend time in yoga pants. She smiles often, she's a bit of a goofball, and I'd bet she sells a *lot* of clothing. I'd buy whatever she's selling.

7. She's always on the move—running, dancing, twirling, twitching. It's entirely possible we could run together and she'd keep up with me. Or beat my ass. She'd certainly look better doing it.

8. There's a photo of her in a big, poufy fuchsia skirt with a white T-shirt supporting Alzheimer's research. She's doing more twirling, along with smiling and standing up for what she believes in, and it's hard not to smile back because she's just that passionate.

9. Number seven promptly makes me imagine what Maple would be like in bed.

10. I need to stop this.

It's child's play to trace the account that originally uploaded the video. I hack into the owner's laptop and discover that Madd Dixon didn't bother to cover his trail or delete the original video. Given his demonstrated lack of ethics, I don't limit myself to publicly available data, instead going for a deep dive into his cyber life. Just call me Miss Marple. Or maybe Poirot. Mustaches and suits are a better look for me than cardigans and pearls.

When a paper cup and straw materialize in front of my face, I reach for them automatically. The cup retreats. My first thought is that Maple has come back. It's illogical because she hates me. Still, when I look up and realize it's just Jack, I'm disappointed if not surprised. We have a standing Thursday taco truck date and I've worked through my alert.

"You stood me up." Jack waggles the cup just out of reach. "And yet here I am, putting out."

"You're easy." I take the cup and hit Save. "And I was busy."

"Eat." A paper bag thumps down next to my laptop and I smell cilantro and cumin.

"Thanks, Mom."

Jack says something else, but I'm no longer listening. I'm planning the next step in my Madd campaign.

"What're we doing?" He leans against my desk, tearing into his first taco. Jack's a big guy and he requires a constant fuel supply. He's also much more observant than most people give him credit for.

"Getting even."

His brows lift in amusement. "Turned white knight?"

"You don't have a Kinkster account." Which means he's likely the only adult male in San Francisco who hasn't seen Maple's video. And while I'm unexpectedly glad he's a Maple virgin, it also makes asking his advice harder.

"I'm married, remember?" Jack wads up the tinfoil from his taco and lobs it into my trash can in a perfect two-point shot.

I attended his wedding, so I definitely remember. There are, however, married people using my app—and not all of them are hooking up with each other. I note, not for the first time, that Jack doesn't sound one hundred percent happy. Maybe 70 percent. Sixty even. It could be a bad day, week or year in the venture capital world he rules, but I suspect money's not the problem.

I look up and engage in some wishful thinking. My people skills are minimal, whereas Jack is a great guy. Everybody loves him, and not just because he's a big muscled guy and outstanding eye candy. I've heard him labeled teddy bear, lumberjack and Thor. Whatever. He's one of the few people I care about, and so for him I make an effort. We've been friends since freshman year at Santa Cruz when we shared a dorm room and terrorized the computer science department. When we graduated, we went in different directions. He married on the beach and founded a venture capital company. I coded dating apps and had hookups. We also each made a billion dollars along the way but, to be fair, we're still fundamentally the same people we were back in our college days. We know when the other is full of shit or having a bad week or just needs to get out on the ocean and surf. I'm sure a surfboard is enough to fix Jack this time.

Jack steals a second taco from the bag. Right. He's waiting for an answer.

"I was at your wedding." I snatch the bag back and assess. Ten tacos plus the two currently residing in Jack's bottomless stomach make six each since California is a community property state and dividing shit in half is legally mandated. I pull four foil-wrapped tacos from the bag and pass them to Jack. "Don't worry, I'll bear witness that you're married."

Jack is suddenly very interested in his taco.

Item: Jack isn't a hundred percent good.

He points his half-eaten taco at my laptop and even I recognize a brilliant diversionary tactic. "What are you really working on?"

"Revenge. True story."

Naturally, Jack slides my laptop around to see for himself. The picture of Maple is downloaded from a cached version of the San Francisco Ballet website. In it, she balances on the toes of one foot, her other leg extending into space behind her. Her arms are flung wide as if to hug her audience, and despite the solemn look on her beautiful face, her eyes smile at us. Sparkly white fabric fills the frame around her and there's something on her head that looks as if a tiara and a peacock mated and produced feathery diamanté babies. I prefer the naked dancing.

Jack returns his attention to his taco. "Who is she?"

"Lola's friend. She paid me a visit this morning."

"And you decided to get to know her better?" Jack raises a brow. It's one of his innate talents and it drives me crazy that I've never mastered the move myself.

"She was upset. Her boyfriend posted a video of her on Kinkster. It was our number one video."

Jack sighs and knuckles his eyes with his hand. "Kinkster doesn't post cute puppy videos, so I'm assuming there's a connection between her upset and the boyfriend's video."

I'm never a complete ass, not on purpose. "It's down."

"But how many people saw it first?"

"It has 2,348,992 hits. It turns out that Maple is a very talented naked dancer and she's totally uninhibited."

Jack groans. He's always been Mr. Rules, while Dev and I are a little more flexible. Dev was the third guy in our freshman suite at UC Santa Cruz, the first of us to earn a billion dollars, and the member of our friendship triumvirate most likely to use his coding skills for evil. His is a wicked taste for revenge. Steal his ecommerce software and you'll wake up one morning to discover that you're unexpectedly selling dildos or other hard-to-explain items. I admire the effort he puts into keep our world fair.

Jack clears his throat. *Right.* He believes we're

having a conversation in which we take turns talking. Honestly, it's more like a one-way sermon—as his next words prove.

"Which is 2,348,991 people more than Maple intended."

Is it?

I'm not so sure about that.

I feel my mouth curve up in a smile as I repossess my laptop.

"I can't make people unsee her," I say when the silence stretches on too long. *Duh.* Even I don't possess superpowers. "But I can get even with Madd."

"What kind of a name is Madd?" he mutters. I don't say anything because the answer is obvious. Stupid, pretentious, owned by a man with a small dick and no brains—take your pick. According to Madd's website, he was born in Orange County, California, but I'd bet five bucks his mother didn't put *that* name on his birth certificate.

Jack's eyes shift up and to the left. Now he's thinking, too, which means Madd is totally screwed. Jack's brain is scary good when it comes to revenge and diabolical plots. "Public access records?"

"Mostly? This is why it's important to beef up government security. Since I'm using my powers for good, however, you can save the lecture."

To be fair, there will undoubtedly be a next time and the next time might not be motivated by a belief in justice and fairness. I'm a big fan of rule breaking for any reason, plus I'm nosy.

"And the public good is somehow best served by stalking Maple's boyfriend?"

"*Ex*-boyfriend." Five fun facts about Madd?

1. The password on his voice mail was 123. I add fourteen decimal places and record a new message announcing his move to Siberia to seek a natural cure for his STD.

2. He's either unaware that his phone automatically saves the photos he takes to the cloud or he's the ultimate narcissist because his cloud storage includes 129 dick pics. I make picture 116 his avatar on all his social media accounts.

3. Madd isn't into charitable giving. I help him out by rerouting the contents of his checking account to an erectile dysfunction research group and a save the gorillas campaign. Personal growth is important and this way he's covered literally *and* metaphorically.

4. Madd's inbox is a busy, busy place after I run a handy little script that signs his email up for every known newsletter on the planet without an unsubscribe link. He currently has 19214 welcome emails.

5. He uses the same insecure password on his dating profile, his bank account, his rideshare

apps and multiple online shopping sites. Naturally, I change them and his security questions to a twenty-seven-character password complete with arcane punctuation in random spots.

6. His real name is Raymond. I haven't decided what to do with that yet. I'll save that dessert for later.

Jack shakes his head when I close the lid of my laptop three minutes later. *Mischief managed.* "I hope you have a good lawyer."

This is a rhetorical question since we have the same firm on retainer. You get what you pay for and we pay a lot. I flip him the bird. "I won't get caught."

"This isn't college," he says, and I hear the warning there.

"I know." I do, too. Sometimes I miss those days. Not the broke-and-starving part, but the freedom to do whatever we could get away with. Having a company of people who depend on me for their paycheck and health insurance took some getting used to, but so far I haven't let them down and Kinkster makes good money. Still, I'm standing on the steps in the pool of life while Jack and Dev splash around in the deep end. While the number of married couples in the United States with kids is currently at an all-time low, it's still not unlikely that Jack and his wife procreate in the none-too-distant future and then things will change even more.

I finished inhaling my first taco. "How's Mrs. Jack?"

Jack shoves the remainder of his taco into his mouth and chews methodically. I count to freaking forty before he swallows. I'm never quite sure when people are legitimately acting weird—maybe he's on one of those diet quests where you chew twenty times and commune deeply with your meal so that you enjoy more, consume less and magically shed weight. It's equally possible, though, that he's avoiding answering my question.

"You killed her and buried the body," I deadpan, going for my second taco.

He frowns. "She's traveling for work."

Huh.

Mrs. Jack travels a great deal. I'd share that comment or make a joke, but Jack's face takes on a closed-off look I process while I consume tacos three and four. He doesn't want to talk about Molly, I decide. Usually Jack's an open-book guy, happy to share and either tell you all about the awesomeness that is his life or bitch about the work-related stuff. Sometimes, though, he gets in a mood and slams the book shut. I've had my fingers pinched more than once, so I back off. I'll ask Dev and then we'll figure out how to fix whatever is wrong with Jack.

"Maui?"

"No."

"Mexico?" Molly's work takes her mostly to tropical destinations. She's visited Mexico, the Bahamas and Thailand in the last year. I had no idea that being a pharmaceutical sales rep was so much fun, but Jack claims she's really, really good at it and that these trips are often company-sponsored rewards for being a superstar employee. While Jack tries to remember where his wife is this particular week, I briefly debate with myself whether or not my fellow Kinksters would be more or less productive after a week in Mexico.

Honestly, we'd probably single-handedly destroy trade relations between Mexico and the US. At the very least, some of us would end up on a first-name basis with the consulate and since I like keeping my vacation options open and my engineering team intact, I finish off my fifth taco and reluctantly scratch "group tropical vacation" off the mental prize list I keep. When I was a kid with a reluctant acquaintance with toothpaste, my dentist used to motivate me with postcleaning visits to a cardboard treasure chest he kept underneath the receptionist's desk. I'm the dentist now in this scenario and my employees are fishing for prizes. The most popular is cash, although Prada bags and Harleys come in second and third.

"Iceland," Jack announces.

What?

Right.

Mrs. Jack.

"They sell drugs in Iceland?"

Jack takes a sip of his drink. "Molly went to Iceland."

Iceland has never struck me as a hotbed of industry, but I'm pretty sure that's where the northern lights are and it sounds really cool. And then I have a moment of sheer genius.

"Why don't you join her for the weekend?" My fingers are already flipping the laptop open, pulling up my favorite travel site, and plugging in dates and airport codes. Wow. If you get bored having hookup sex, you can stare out the window at glaciers *and* lava fields. Or go fishing! Or have sex in geothermal pools! (Actually, I'm not sure of the effect of what is essentially superheated bathwater on the male penis, but kissing has to be possible.)

Jack frowns. "She's working."

24/7?

I open my mouth and close it. Don't go there.

Plus, Jack's already off onto another topic.

"Are you planning on hooking up with Maple?"

Quickly finishing my last taco, I protest, "I'm not interested in her."

Jack just snorts. "Sure you aren't. She's a girl and you haven't hooked up with her yet. That makes her your type."

I shrug. "Clearly, she's attracted to asshole idiots and I only qualify on one count, not both."

Jack laughs, which was my plan.

The thing is, Maple and I might have something pretty important in common.

I love to watch.

And she clearly lives to perform.

I'm not Mr. Relationship—hello, I wrote a hookup app. Can I be any clearer? Hookups are short, expectations are agreed upon in advance, and everyone goes home with the fabulous parting gift of an orgasm. Plus, when I open my mouth I run everyone off. I'm blunt, I love numbers and I'm the nerdiest billionaire ever. Yes, I own a Jedi lightsaber and I'd have levitated out of bed and through my day if I could. I have two PhDs, I type at light speed but my handwriting is shit, and I remember everything in numbers: miles, seconds, URLs or IP addresses. The ladies not on Kinkster frown on numbers unless they're the number of zeroes in my bank account. Maple is obviously creative (very, *very* creative, particularly at 1:12 in her video), so there's no way we could ever work. Plus, she's more than a little crazy—and (let's be honest) I'm an engineer at heart. A dirty, filthy rich billionaire engineer, but she's way too unpredictable for me. Code does exactly what you tell it to do, with no surprises, no messy emotions and no drama.

Fifteen minutes later, Jack abandons my office for his and I go back to stalking Maple online. Ten minutes more and then I'll stop. I promise. From their respective Facebook timelines, I learn that Maple and Madd had been seeing each other for eleven months. In dog years, that's fourteen years. In human years, that means hundreds of cute couple photos. There are so many that I skip counting them because I'm burning through my minutes and I already know that Madd is a total dick.

I'm not sure I've done enough, to be honest. A quick check in Kinkster's databases reveals Maple currently has an impressive 937 hookup requests. I send her 937 lavender roses as an apology because purple is the color of royalty (I google it) and she's a fucking queen.

Deleting her video from our online storage takes even less time. A few keystrokes and Kinkster no longer has its very own dancing ballerina. Removing her performance from our backups requires a few additional steps and documentation, but five minutes after I start, I've erased all traces of her. No breakup was ever quicker or more thorough.

Goodbye, Maple.

CHAPTER THREE

Maple
#cheatnight #notsohealthy #betterthansex

"He sent you the flowers?"

The *he* is one Max O'Reilly, hot, sexy, frustrating-as-hell, impossible-to-read billionaire bachelor. Yes, there's an entire app devoted to dating financially successful San Franciscans. Yes, I looked him up. Yes, despite his weird dating-and-job extra value combo meal proposition, he's as commitment averse as any of the guys I've dated before and the only relationships he seems to have embraced have been brief connections between his penis and a handy vagina. He's like public transit in San Francisco, rushing from stop to stop and predictably overcrowded, while I've always been more of a Trans-Siberian Railway girl, in it for the long haul and the memories.

Lola stares at me, nail polish brush hovering over my bare feet in her lap as she waits for my answer. Or possibly she's just dizzy from the overpowering scent of roses in full bloom. I've been walking around in a rose-scented cloud since they arrived three days ago. I hum a few bars from *The Blue Danube* waltz. Strauss wrote it to cheer up the Austrian nation after they got their butts kicked in the Seven Weeks' War and went broke, so it seems like a good post-Madd-breakup theme song. Plus, it's catchy and the ultimate earworm.

I'm hosting our monthly girls' night in my San Francisco studio. Despite the limited space (made even more limited by the addition of 937 roses in full bloom), I love my tiny, closet-sized living quarters. Said quarters are at the very tippy-top of a house fronting a square that's alternately foggy, hot or just outright grimy, and inhabited by trees, pigeons and the occasional homeless guy. Everything in San Francisco is short on space and so the house is tall and gangly like a twiggy, sun-starved plant reaching for the occasional spot of sunshine when it breaks through the inevitable clouds and fog. The outside is all decorative bric-a-brac and a real-life turret with a wind vane sitting on its red-tile top. I had a choice of living in the turret or the unit next door, which has a balcony. If I'd been a billionaire, I'd have gone for both and knocked down the wall between them, but instead I chose the balcony. I do a morning barre routine there, fingers curled around the balustrade while San Francisco trundles sleepily below me as I plié.

Lola alternates pink with white polka dots and

pink stripes on white, which means my toenails are as cheerfully pretty as the rest of my feet are not. Years of dancing *en pointe* have changed the shape and look of my toes, and even though they're no longer blistered and bloody from hours of daily dancing, they'll never look the same again. Doesn't matter. I love them. They're a reminder that I really can do anything if I try hard enough and long enough.

"He sent 937 roses when he returned my phone." At least I'm almost certain they're from Max. The handwriting on the florist's card was really bad, to the point where if you'd told me the note was in Cyrillic, I'd have believed you. The one person I know, however, who did not send those flowers is my ex-boyfriend. Madd never sent me roses. In retrospect, I'm lucky he didn't gift me with an STD. Part of me wants to laugh or find a way to rub my ex's face in my flowers (starting with the thorny bits), but the rest of me is still a sad, angry llama that appreciates expensive flowers. And the quick phone repair job. I definitely wasn't offended by that.

"Wow." Lola caps the polish. "That's random."

"It's very precise," I counter. "I think he sent one rose for each hookup request I had on Kinkster."

Frankly, that number is obscene. Literally. I need no more dick pics in my life, so flowers and a free phone repair are a welcome change even if the only "message" was Max's name scrawled on the florist's card in black Sharpie, bold and impatient. The picture I snapped of my new floral accoutrements already has a thousand likes on Instagram.

Lola just grins. "That sounds like Max actually."

I try to sound cool, as if hot, smart guys send me the contents of a florist's shop all the time. "He sends flowers wantonly and indiscriminately?"

Lola considers this for a nanosecond. "Max is not a flower guy."

"His mother? Dead coworkers? Nada?"

"You'd have to ask him, but flowers are for the well mannered. Max is blunt." She makes a face. "Wrecking-ball blunt. He tends to put people off. It's the *precision* flower-sending that makes perfect sense. He wouldn't send a dozen roses, but 937? Absolutely. That number means something to him and he loves numbers. He's equally likely to send you 937 truffles or 937 thong panties or 937 of whatever else pops into his dirty mind."

"Tell me more." The smile stretching my own face is as big and goofy as, say, a bouquet of a thousand purple roses. I only want to know *more* because he's seen me naked, I tell myself. And never mind that by that standard I should be holding mass meet and greets across the foggy, fine city of San Francisco. "Is he seeing anyone?"

Lola snorts. "Not for more than an hour at a time."

I don't have relationships.

I have hookups. For sex.

Doesn't he realize that relationships are special? Any two people can hook up, but it takes effort to maintain that connection. It's the difference between a salad of edible flowers and growing a garden from seed. It's what makes Madd's betrayal so much harder to stomach, because not only had I almost decided that he was my forever man, but I'd invested a considerable amount of time in us.

"He's a billionaire," Lola says. "That makes it harder, if you know what I mean."

Now it's my turn to snort. "Because not having any money makes everything so much easier? Pardon me if I'm not feeling sympathetic."

"People date him for the experience or because they want stuff from him." She turns my foot, admiring her handiwork.

I'm not stupid. I'd connected a few dots even before flouncing out of his office on Monday and then promptly checking him out on the Billionaire Bachelors app he created, an app that's apparently the best way to meet the love (or lay) of your life. Think about that for a moment. He's the CEO of a company that hooks people up for kinky sex and DIY porn. It doesn't take a genius to figure out that's a moneymaking idea; but *billionaire* conjures up images of hot, cut guys (or old, fat guys) in expensive suits. But maybe that's like assuming all dancers run around in tutus 24/7?

"That explains how he could afford all the roses." I can't remember the last time I dated someone who was financially solvent enough to purchase a dozen roses, let alone almost a thousand apology flowers.

Not that Max and I are dating. Or hooking up. Or even remotely interested in each other. Although I *do* appreciate the fact that he did what he promised to do and took my dirty dancing video down. Madd had definitely set the bar low in the promise-keeping department.

"Do you want me to cut Madd's balls off? Or send Dev to perform the amputation?" Lola grins, clearly enjoying her mental revenge fantasy.

Frankly, it appeals.

"That would be a career-limiting move," I say finally. "I think I'm going to have to take the high road here and avoid a recreational stay in San Quentin. I'm holding out for the round-the-world tour."

"Madd's a dick." Lola waves the nail brush for emphasis. "I never liked him. Next time, you should listen to me."

"Duly noted. Walking away from a long-term relationship sucks. Madd and I were a couple and I invested time in us. I thought I knew him."

Does that sound plaintive? Yes, it does. I make a note to kick myself in the butt.

Lola's already shaking her head. "How many times have you gone out with a guy just for fun?"

"We had fun," I protest.

"You go from zero to sixty," Lola says. "You move him in and then it's all future plans and serious talks because everything has to be a milestone and a step forward and special."

"Lola."

She leans her head against my shoulder. "You need to slow down, Maple. You don't think about what's happening right now because you're so busy planning for a future that never arrives."

"The future never arrives because I pick shitty men," I say.

"You don't *know* them, Maple. You just fantasize them into being right. I think you need to take a break."

"From life? From sex? Or just the entire male gender?"

Lola sits up and slaps my shoulder. "Just have fun the next time you go out with someone. Use him for sex. Don't go plunging into another long-term relationship five minutes after meeting someone."

I make a face, willing someone to knock on the door or a telemarketer to call. Now would even be a good time for the upstairs neighbor to do the galumphing walkabout she usually saves for 3 a.m. "No more relationships. Just fun. And business. I'm still trying to get offered that contract from the Live Your Best Life people."

I'm not ashamed to beg. Please, please, please pick me to be the face of your yearlong campaign because there is nothing I'd love more than to spend twelve months touring the world on your dime and shooting fabulous, yoga-and-dance-related content. Can you imagine what that would be like? Jet-setting from one tropical island to the next? They just fired the influencer who was the social media face of their campaign for drunken scooter driving in Thailand, so they need to find someone fast.

My phone pings, alerting me that dinner has arrived. Saved! I lever myself off the bed and walk to the door on my heels because it would be a shame to spoil Lola's handiwork. I haven't had pretty toenails in years—it's one of the downsides to being a dancer. Nightly ice baths, gauze, blisters—none of those scream "pedicure." Even now that I'm no longer dancing professionally, my feet are still tough and I love them.

When the intercom buzzes, I let in the delivery guy and carefully walk over to the door on my heels to retrieve our dinner.

Lola frowns at me. No, at my *feet*. "How do you do that?"

I look down automatically, but those are the same feet she was painting seconds ago, albeit slightly dustier. I need to up my housekeeping game. "Do what?"

"Walk so gracefully," she says. "It's not fair."

"Years of practice." I dig into the bag and pass her a set of wood chopsticks. While anybody can dance, ballet requires a commitment. In relationship terms, it's a monogamous, twenty-five-year marriage rather than a fun hookup. And while I think I like my new life, it feels strange not to be spending sixty-plus hours a week dancing. "How are things with Dev?"

She grins. "He's amazing."

"Out of bed, too, I hope?" I arrange my food on

the table and snap a picture then ten more because the lighting's not quite right. #cheatnight #notso-healthy #betterthansex. Which, I discover when I dig into the first carton, isn't an exaggeration at all. Mmm. Chow mein with those bright red chunks of pork.

Lola launches into a Dev story, something about a romantic weekend up in Napa. I think there were supposed to be wineries and maybe a romantic picnic surrounded by grapevines, but Lola's story meanders from a really cool-sounding lunch in a restaurant that even I've heard of to a roadside pit stop (kissing) to finding a stream surrounded by wildflowers (where far more than kissing happened).

Her face glows when she talks about Dev. She met him by crash-landing in his lap at a networking event, and then followed the introduction up by hiring him as her new summer intern. Of course, it turned out he'd *really* come to her office to find out why she was illegally using his software (a completely innocent mistake on her part) and then they'd had hate-sex before agreeing to mutually use each other for orgasms. Or so Lola tells it.

Because there's that glow that says their relationship is far more than crazy hot sex in some pretty kinky places. They're happy together rather than angry and I think they may be working their way toward that long-term monogamous thing sooner rather than later. Like picking-out-a-puppy-together territory or possibly even a permanent move to the

Kingdom of Happily-Ever-After. I've heard they have engagement rings and killer ceremonies there. Lola's Dev stories are pretty freaking amazing, but I hope he realizes just how lucky he is. Lola may not have a billion dollars, but she's worth the world to me and I'll kill him if he can't see that.

The Kinkster app on my phone pings and I can't stop myself from giving the screen a quick glance. "Max owes me a rose—I have another hookup request."

And eww. This guy also sent a picture and my eyeballs are burning. There are things you can't unsee, no matter how small the phone screen.

Lola grabs a carton of kung pao shrimp and digs in. "I thought you deleted that app."

I shrug. "Just keeping track of my fans."

At first, I kept the app on my phone to make sure Madd hadn't uploaded anything else. Then, I kept it just because. Just because I'm curious. Just because the kink other people get up to is amazing. Just because it reminds me of Max and then I can't focus, imagining the way his mouth curled into a grin and his legs brushed mine. Maybe just because part of me wonders if he *really* deleted all the copies of that video—or if he's still watching me.

CHAPTER FOUR

Max

SATURDAY IS THE crown jewel in a week that went rapidly downhill after I met Maple on Monday. It takes twenty minutes to find a place where I can pull off the Santa Cruz highway because the sandy stretch fronting the Pacific Ocean is busier than an In-N-Out drive-through after a pot festival. And then, when I finally battle my way to the surf break, rookies clog the water, battling for a shot at the waves. Secrets have a way of getting out. The whole time I'm out on the ocean, my brain keeps rewinding my encounter with Maple. Did she really believe her boyfriend would keep her video secret? Does she think about my watching her video? Does she imagine, even for a second, what I look like fisting my dick as I watch? *Watched.* After an epic wipeout on what should have been a good wave, I abandon my surfing attempt and head in. The sun is setting and tomorrow is another day. Just call me Scarlett.

My board bumps against the backs of my knees and I adjust my grip, towing it to shore and up onto the sand. Splashing behind me indicates Jack and Dev are following my lead.

I lob the usual no-brainer over my shoulder. "Tequila and tacos?"

Jack, Dev and I always hit up T&T after our Saturday surf. Not only is it just down the road from our favorite beach, but the bartender makes all sorts of weird margaritas and there's a taco al pastor that's the best this side of Cabo. This time, however, no one rushes to agree or joke about whose turn it is to pick up the bar tab. Instead, the silence stretches out between us. I turn until I can see their faces. Nope. I'm still clueless.

Jack finally shrugs. "Sure."

He doesn't sound sure.

A frown puckers his forehead. When did he get so distant?

Dev's not even looking at me because he's head down in his phone. "Lola's in."

This is supposed to be our time together, but things have changed since Dev met Lola and our Saturday nights have changed.

"The more the merrier," I say because I can't let him know that I mind. I'm the laid-back one in our group, the one who bounces from hookup to hookup because anything longer than twenty-four hours is too long.

Dev shoots me a look and I bite back a wince.

Right.

Lola's a default setting now and not a user preference.

After four years at UC Santa Cruz and then flopping together in a crazy small San Francisco studio while we got our businesses off the ground (and I finished off PhD number two), old habits die hard. It's always been the three of us. Four, I guess, if you count Jack's wife, Molly, whom he married six weeks after graduation. But things change.

Items one and two: Dev and Jack have changed. Is it terrible that I feel a little bad about that? We'll sort it out, but right now I feel unsettled. I don't like not understanding the rules.

By the time we're seated on the deck at T&T, the sun's down, it's dark, and I'm feeling better. T&T is the best beach bar in the world. The thatched roof talks back to the near-constant ocean breeze, whistling and flapping and filling up any silence not handled by the waves crashing on the shore just yards away. The furniture's a comfortable, mismatched set of wooden Adirondack chairs (not Mexican but I cut the owners some slack) and swings suspended from the palapa roof so that you can rock gently back and forth while you belly up to the bar. There's no better place to unwind and analyze the day's waves and rides. It's so good, in fact, that I've given serious thought to buying a beach bar of my own on some fun tropical island in the South Pacific but ownership laws for noncitizens are draconian and I suspect I'd get tired of listening to drunk people whine because they won't own their shit.

For the first hour, drinks flow steadily as we break down the waves and our rides. We complain about the rooks crowding our sand, and for a few minutes, it feels like it always did.

But eventually Lola pops in, making a beeline for our usual table in the corner. She's wearing a tank top and a pair of athletic leggings like the ones Maple wore. I calculate the distance between her San Francisco place and here, and come to the obvious conclusion that she's once again spent the night at Dev's Santa Cruz place. At some point, the two of them need to just move in together, if only to cut down on the carbon emissions.

Item: They have no qualms about kissing in public.

In fact, Lola launches herself at Dev and they end up wrapped around each other, arms, hands and tongues going all sorts of places. This isn't a bad thing, although I prefer watching strangers go at it rather than one of my best friends. Dev also tends to be possessive and private, so I'm not sure what to make of this change.

Lola waves a greeting at Jack and me when she comes up for air, and for the next half hour we chat about the easy stuff—which companies have IPO'd, who's seeing who, and who's gone bankrupt since the last time we caught up over nachos. Silicon Valley is tough. We tease Jack about being Silicon Valley royalty, but he always counters that he's more pirate than prince. Nice people get eaten alive.

"I hear you're sending girls flowers now." Lola digs her elbow into my rib cage. Is she being friendly or is she pissed off?

"One girl." I stare at her for a moment. "And how do you know about those?"

"Maple's my best friend?" She makes a face. "Plus, it's really hard to overlook a gazillion purple roses in a San Francisco studio."

"Nine hundred and thirty-seven roses," I correct automatically.

Lola's grin widens. "You owed her six more by the time we finished dinner last night."

It takes me three seconds to work out that she's joking, although my fingers itch to order the missing flowers from my phone. "She didn't delete the app?"

Lola slurps her margarita. "Nope."

Oh. I try to figure out what that means. Is Maple interested in kink? I remember the heat in her eyes when I said that I'd watched her dance. I think she liked that.

Lola stares at me speculatively. "Why did you really send her flowers?"

"I wanted to," I say truthfully.

Jack looks up from inhaling his beer. "You like her."

I certainly like specific parts of her—and is that such a terrible thing? She's lovely. A whole list of adjectives pops into my head and I let them filter through my head. *Funny, talented, tenacious, vibrant*. Plus, I'll bet she's unbelievable in bed. Her eyes give away what she's thinking and she's super bendy thanks to that ballet career of hers. I suspect she'd surprise me, and in a good way. She's completely unlike anyone I've had sex with before, and not just because she can touch her head to her toes.

But the thing is? We'd never work. She's the queen of relationships, scouring her kingdom for The One; I'm the king of hookups. She has a wholesome business brand to manage and preserve, whereas I'm all about the dirty and the not-so-secret fantasies. After scrolling through her Instagram, I get why she's not so happy about her Kinkster stardom. Everything on her Instagram is the kind of pretty polished that makes you wonder why your life doesn't look that way and if buying a pair of leggings and doing a session of hot yoga might be the magic answer.

Maple's selling fantasy, just like me, but hers is a clothes-required world.

Lola's phone erupts, an entire troupe of Polynesian drummers banging and whooping it up in her purse. She pulls it out, looks down and frowns. Since I'm sitting next to her, I look down, too, so I can read along.

Rude.

Obnoxious.

Effective.

Sticks and stones—call me whatever you'd like but Lola has a text from Maple. I know this because the picture of the sender is Ballerina Maple, complete with crown. She looks like a wholesome, pink, sparkly princess, which just goes to show that you should never judge a book by its cover. I pluck the phone out of Lola's hands so I can double-check the message for myself.

HELP

My inner fixer revs, begging to go into overdrive, and I remind myself to step back. Assess. Maybe she's just got a shoe emergency or needs help picking out dish towels or forgot the name of the awesome Chinese restaurant they ordered from last night. Maybe it's nothing.

Bubbles dance across the screen as Maple texts.

And dance.

And dance.

No words appear—just more stupid dots. Even Tolstoi handwrote *War and Peace* faster than this. Lola makes a grab for her phone, but no way I'm giving it up. Instead we (she) compromise: I let her squeeze up against my side and angle the screen so we can both see. Finally, Maple finishes her text and hits the send button. A riff of Polynesian drums announces its arrival on Lola's phone.

Calling it in on the girlfriend code. Send troops ASAP. Need rescue before this guy cums on my butt.

And then nothing. I nudge Lola, slapping the phone into her hands. "Text her back."

I should try to be nicer. More polite. Something.

And if Maple wasn't asking for help, I'd try. Maybe. Lola opens her mouth to speak, then shuts it and starts tapping away. She texts even more slowly than Maple. I resist commiserating with Dev because sexting is clearly not going to play a part in their future life together. Finally she settles on: Where r u?

That's the wrong question. "I can find her."

Jack groans. "We've discussed cutting back on the felonies."

"I won't get caught." I never do.

Maple saves me from any felonious behavior by responding: Club XYZ.

The photo that pops up on Lola's screen is both slightly out of focus and badly lit. I think Maple's on a dance floor. Looking down over her shoulder. Where some guy is grinding on her ass and I see red.

Think.

I grab my own phone and bring up a little app I wrote. Five seconds later, I have Maple's GPS coordinates (south of Market in San Francisco) and a plan (drive there faster than a speeding bullet, kill the creep, rescue the girl—hot thank-you sex forming an optional epilogue). Fortunately, I've had a quarter of a beer so I'm good to drive. I stand up, registering the surprise on Dev's and Lola's faces. Jack just looks resigned.

"Going" is all I say.

I'm no one to Maple. Of course it's none of my business. Do I care? Not really.

Lola bolts upright. Nachos fly. "Not without me."

"Keep texting her," I order Lola. "Let her know help is on the way."

I don't deny that I'm going after Maple, but I drive a Porsche that's far faster than the piece of crap Jeep Lola owns. I'm going to get there first, and from the way Lola bellows after me as I stride away from our table, she knows it, too.

I execute the first part of my plan—the speeding bullet step—successfully, arriving in record time at 10:07. Club XYZ is indeed deep in the warehouse district. The surroundings are sketchy enough that I don't like the idea of Maple walking around here on her own. I bound out of the Porsche, toss my keys at the valet parker along with a generous tip and head for the front door. From the quantity of bandage dresses and sparkles decorating the line of people already waiting to go in, I'm seriously underdressed in my post-surfing uniform of jeans and a T-shirt. Fortunately, cash is always the perfect accessory and the bouncer happily lets me skip the queue when I share a little sartorial wealth with him.

The music's so loud that it's more vibration than sound, the kind of mind-numbing decibel level that entirely rules out conversation. A DJ spins in a cage above the dance floor. It reminds me a bit of my last launch party. I'm downright terrible at interacting with people, and the closer I get to the dance floor, the harder it becomes to avoid my fellow clubbers.

The outsize price of admission included a private table and bottle service in the VIP section. Eyes follow me as I'm led to my table. Having a table makes the next step in my find-and-rescue-Maple plan easier because I simply jump onto the table, searching for the dance floor. Spotting Maple is easy.

She's shockingly beautiful. I stand there a moment too long staring at her face—if only because I can.

Her hair falls around her face in a silky, flat curtain as she moves. Her part is a perfect white line down her scalp. I don't know if she came here alone or not, but three men crowd her. They likely think they're dancing with her but instead they fill up her space, throwing off the line of her dance, forcing her to either move backward or dance thigh to thigh with them. She's wearing a fabulously short dress with wide straps and a scoop neck. The whole thing is covered with silver sequins. Flowers? Spirals? Pi? Whatever the pattern is, I like it.

She dances all out, body moving fast and sure to the beat. Her cheeks are flushed, eyes sparkling, as she thrusts her hands over her head as if she's reaching for the moon or the stars. *God, she's special*, I think, wishing I was the one dancing with her. Not that I dance. People crowd the floor, bodies brushing, arms touching, everyone moving together for as long as the song plays.

Maple's skin glistens beneath the heat of the lights

and one hand traces the line of her collarbone, dipping down. I'm staring at her and I don't want to stop. My fingers itch to touch her, to kiss her and learn the salty-sweet taste of her. Dev was right when he said I was the hookup king and bad news for Maple, but he forgot to factor Maple into the equation. She's a new variable and that could change the entire outcome of the problem.

I like to think that when she looks up, eyes roaming over the watchers crowding the edge of the dance floor, she spots me.

That she's dancing for me.

She stares up at me, at someone, for a beat. Another. Her head falls back, hair spilling everywhere, and her lips move. Does she sing along when she dances, make up words when there are none? Is she smiling that secretive half smile for me? I look down, she looks up, and there's something between us.

Item: She makes me crazy.

Item: I don't mind.

Item: She needs rescuing.

Each step dances her farther away from one particular asshole who refuses to get the memo. He follows her relentlessly, gaze lingering on Maple's tits and ass. He doesn't look her in the eye and he's definitely not interested in her smile. He's missing out and he doesn't deserve a single second of her attention. *Be smart about this. She's got it. The SOS was a girl thing, a joke, not an action plan.*

And then he says something, Maple stops dancing and I see red. It's not a pretty color.

That's it.

No more.

I launch myself over the narrow wall separating the private tables from the dance floor. I'm no superhero, not even close.

Maple exhales, her eyes digging daggers into the stupid fuck who's now touching her arm. I agree with her. The guy's got a death wish, and tonight? I'm happy to play the tooth fairy and fairy godmother to his stupid.

He's going down.

Down.

Down.

CHAPTER FIVE

Maple
#nightlife #vip #sexydance #lifesituations

When I'm clubbing, I dance all out. I throw my body into the techno music, finding the pulse, the beat, the rhythm that perfectly fits each measure and note. The heat of the lights overhead is a familiar weight against my skin, as is the burn in my muscles and lungs, the beat of the music in my body. Tonight I'm dancing solo and it feels good, even if I sometimes miss the intimacy and trust of a pas de deux. You have to trust your partner to be strong enough to lift you high above the stage, to know his part in the dance and support you in yours. Those were good nights.

Someone puts his hand on my ass.

I don't think so.

Shift onto my left leg.

Jeté.

I'm reaching back with a sharp heel when strong

hands close on my hips and lift me off my feet. For a brief moment, I'm flying through the air, connected to the ground only through the man dancing with me. I should pull away but I can't stop myself from smiling; I miss dancing with a real partner. I land gently, my knees automatically bending into a plié as the hands let go.

I turn my head but he's behind me already, big body leaning in, eliminating any distance between us. Somehow, even though it's been five long days since we meet, I'm not surprised it's Max. For a moment, I tense in anticipation, wanting his hands back on me, lifting me, partnering with me in this dance. This is what I miss most about my ballet days, this connection, the disciplined intimacy between myself and another dancer. He breaks the silence, though, and with it the spell or whatever it is.

"Holy shit, Maple." He growls my name. Possibly, he yells it because the music is loud and we're on a dance floor after all. He's staring at me, his eyes full of emotions I can't sort out.

I noticed his eyes when I stormed his office, dark and watchful but a deceptively sweet, rich hazel with flecks of green like little secrets that you have to get close to discover. He's just as gorgeous tonight as he was then and no happier, either.

I look again. But no. So much unhappiness.

"Problem?" I lean back against him, resting my head on his chest as I slide my arms up around his neck. My hips move to the beat, teasing his with dirty circles. The poor baby's not feeling playful, though. He stands there like the Colossus of Rhodes, a big, broody, expensive statue just daring me to topple him.

Okay, maybe he didn't come here to dance.

Maybe he doesn't see the challenge he poses.

"Dance with me."

Hazel eyes hold mine. "I don't dance."

"You're not dancing right now," I correct. "But we can fix that. Move your feet."

"I saw your SOS."

And…still not moving.

SOS doesn't compute until I think for a moment. Right. The text I sent to Lola—and *not* to him. I narrow my eyes at him.

"Breaking some more rules, Mr. Bigshot Billionaire?"

He outright laughs, a devilish smile playing over his pretty, pretty mouth. It's a miracle I can hear his laughter over the music but we're pressed close together, so I definitely *feel* it. His chest shakes so hard he almost throws me off. I press my ear to his chest, grinning up at him. His breath feathers over my cheek, my throat. Laughter looks good on him.

His head dips. "Did you like your flowers?"

"Dance with me and I'll tell you," I suggest.

He shakes his head but then one hand settles on my hip, pulling me tight against him as he tries and fails to find my rhythm. His front bumps awkwardly against my rear and one thing is immediately clear:

Max was first in line when God handed out penises and he got the biggest, widest dick of them all.

"See? Anyone can dance." I tilt my head back, grinning up at him. "One foot, two feet, no feet, you move what you have."

He frowns now, his mouth curving down. I reach up and gently tap the corner. "You're so *sulky*."

He jerks back. I'll bet billionaires don't get much constructive criticism and that's okay. I'm a dancer—I live for that shit. "I don't know how to dance," he grumbles.

Right on cue, his jeans-covered hips bump my ass as he loses our rhythm again. He's not kidding. He really can't move. I dance with exaggerated slowness until he finds me, us, again.

"You don't dance well." I shrug. "I don't care."

He snorts. "Says the professional dancer."

The other guy, the one who wouldn't leave me alone and kept trying to grab my ass, hovers a few feet away. He's stupid enough to believe he still has a chance. The delusion is strong with that one. Max's other hand, the one not cradling my hipbone, splays low over my stomach, his fingers brushing dangerously low. Awareness heats my skin where he touches me.

"I like this." I close my eyes, the better to feel each shift of his body behind me. I think he may say something else, but words don't matter right now. We're dancing and the whole world could be watching and that just makes the moment better. I curl a hand behind his neck, setting the other on his thigh. As if he's fucking me slow and deep from behind, each roll of his hips making my panties wetter even though I'm almost certain I don't like him.

When the song ends, however, he stops. I pout, not ready to stop, but his hand on my lower back steers me toward the edge of the dance floor. Eventually we push through the crowd and lock in on the VIP section. Of course he'll have a table there. I'm sure throwing money around must be a membership requirement of the Billionaire Bachelors club.

People watch us. It isn't just that I enjoy dancing for an audience—which I do—or like cuddling up against Max—which is a hell yes despite his rather prickly personality. It's the way he makes me feel as if all of his attention is focused on me and that he's okay with my taking the lead if that's what I want. I feel safe with him, especially in a club crowded with drunken assholes, because he'll step in if and when I want, but otherwise it's my dance.

He doesn't so much as pause when he reaches the stupid velvet rope the club uses to separate us masses from the wealthy special snowflakes and sure enough, bouncer dude unclips it with a respectful nod. Max sails straight through, headed for prime real estate loaded with unopened bottles of champagne and one of those dark-chocolate-colored whiskeys that scream money.

I'm not a big drinker, so I pass when Max waves at the bottles. You have to pay for bottle service to sit in the VIP section, but clearly he doesn't feel the need to actually consume the alcohol.

"Phone," he demands.

What?

"Didn't you just go to a whole lot of trouble to return it?" I plant my backside on the already crowded tabletop because my feet are too antsy for full-blown sitting and this way I can swing them back and forth. "That seems like wasted effort."

"Phone," he repeats, leaning in. God, he smells good. "Please."

I imagine his face if I asked him why he smelled like cedar and spice and everything nice. Does he smell like this every morning or only when he makes an effort?

Back off, Maple.

Don't scare the nice man.

This could be why Madd left you.

Did I sniff Madd? Did I come on too strong, too fast, too much? Funny how I can't remember now. I give up and I pull my phone out of my bag slung across my front. The bag's awesome, all silver, beads and tassels. Lola swears I'm either a reincarnated Vegas showgirl or a disco ball wannabe. Whatever.

Max plucks the phone from my hand, taps in my passcode and frowns. "You didn't change it."

"What?"

"You should have immediately changed your passcode when I returned your phone." He shakes his head. "You can't trust random strangers."

"Are we strangers? You've seen my vulva."

The grin he gives me is crooked. "True, but if that's your criteria, then you should trust most of San Francisco."

"I probably could have Sharpied my passcode on my stomach and they wouldn't have noticed. Or maybe on my boobs." I cup them in their sparkly dress-nest and consider the available real estate. "I could fit a four-digit ATM passcode on my left tit, but the phone's eight-digit number is gonna get cramped. What do you think?"

He gets the cutest little crinkle between his eyes when he's confused. "What?"

"Are my boobs big enough to hold eight numbers?"

The idea of knocking Max off balance makes me oddly giddy. He's so logical. I stare at him expectantly, while the crinkle grows to Grand Canyon proportions as he stares at my chest.

He's actually considering it.

Or he's really, really checking out my rack.

Finally, he says, "How big are the numbers?"

"Max!"

He grins, and oh my God, I'm in trouble because it's a total panty-melting grin that sparks joy in my southern regions. It starts in his eyes, crinkling up the corners deliciously, and then spreads to his mouth.

"Gotcha." He returns his attention to my phone. "I'm putting my number into your contacts."

"Why?" Max doesn't strike me as the kind of person who randomly texts pictures of his cat but I've been tricked before. "Do you have pets? Because no more than three cute kitten or puppy photos or I'll initiate the autodestruct sequence. Also, no bathroom selfies. Or gourmet food pictures unless you're standing on my doorstep about to share."

"You have a lot of rules." My phone explodes into song in his hand, pealing out a rousing bar or six of Handel's "Hallelujah Chorus."

Madd's calling.

Max hands me the phone and I decline the call because I'm not stupid. He's a stupid, bad-news cheater but he was *my* mistake and it's hard to let go of the potential I saw in him. Madd gave great fantasy.

Madd is also persistent. When I don't answer, he texts a picture instead. In the photo he's cuddling a brown-and-white puppy in a big white tumbled bed. I bought him that duvet cover and now it dips artistically, teasingly, beneath the sharp, sexy line of his hipbones. I think he's naked. I can almost imagine that's the thick line of his penis beneath the sheet that's slipped beneath his lean belly.

Dreaming of u and our fur family.

I swear my heart stops for a second because this is the way I've imagined him for months and, now that he's walked out on us, he wants to be my dream man?

Max growls something so profane that I revise my opinion of his creativity upward.

"I thought he was a dick but puppies are a new level of clickbait," he says.

I cock my head, trying to figure out the man in front of me. "Wow. You truly don't have a filter, do you?"

He shrugs, his give-a-fuck either as broken or nonexistent as that filter. "I don't lie, if that's what you mean."

Madd did. Does? I look down at almost-naked Madd again. Is that Madd's puppy? Ours? A prop for his insta-life? Responses to Madd's text tumble through my head.

It's too late.
Why are you doing this to me?
Why don't I care more?

"Not-lying is good." My fingers skim over the phone screen, but I'm not going to answer Madd. Not tonight, not ever. "I realize you're just being honest with me, but I don't think I'm ready to discuss my ex-boyfriend with you."

He tucks my phone back into my bag. For just a moment, I feel the weight of his palm brush against my stomach and I fight the urge to lean in. "If you need me, text me."

"Why?"

He lifts me down off the table while he thinks

about it. I'm used to being lifted and moved about, although usually I've agreed beforehand and there's a well-established script. I wouldn't have predicted that Max's high-handedness is sort of sexy. Part of me wants to explore what else I might find sexy about him, but that's just madness. Or maybe horniness. Unfortunately, the guy attached to the very large penis isn't particularly likable even if he is eminently sex worthy.

His hand settles on the small of my back, fingertips brushing my bare skin. Unlike the creep on the dance floor, I don't think he even realizes he's touching me. He's just there and I'm here and somehow we have this bizarre connection. I should step away but instead I let him steer me in the direction he wants to go.

We're moving toward the exit before he answers me. "For whatever you need. Because I owe you. Because you clearly need either a fake boyfriend or your own personal bouncer until your San Francisco fans forget about your video."

If you had asked me earlier what I wanted, forgetting would have topped my list. That's why I Ride of the Valkyried his ass and issued a personal takedown notice.

I look over at him. "I lost a campaign today. I was supposed to shoot this big dancer, little dancer number with a pink-tutu-wearing mini-me, but now some other influencer will land it."

"They saw the video?"

I try to be fair. "They claimed their budget was maxed out so they weren't going to move ahead with the campaign after all, but my agent heard through her network that they booked a different influencer because I was trending for some very unwholesome reasons."

I'd been so excited to be scouted for that campaign because I'd always loved that brand. They were my first shoes and I still have them in my box of dance souvenirs.

There's a handful of paparazzi waiting outside the club in the hopes that someone shot-worthy or famous will exit and they perk up when they spot Max. Questions fly: *Who's the date tonight, Max? Are you and Hannah through? How about Melissa? Alice? Are you seeing* anyone*?*

"No comment." He frowns, his hand at the small of my back urging me toward the waiting car.

Nothing to see here.

Move along.

CHAPTER SIX

Max

A MISSILE CRASH-LANDS on my chest. Instinctively, I roll, cradling my laptop. Everything's backed up but replacing hardware is inconvenient and I've already done so once this week. For a brief second I'm airborne and then I fall, my shoulders hitting the floor hard as the rest of me slides off my sofa. The laptop slides to a gentle landing beside me. Fuck me, but I should invest in carpet. Maybe one of those shaggy rugs or a faux sheepskin.

I haven't slept in a bed since moving into my Santa Cruz place as I prefer to work until I pass out. The couch is the only piece of furniture in the big empty living space. It came with the house and has three legs; the missing fourth has been replaced by a stack of books. The Realtor described my style as postmodern. My housekeeper has declared it "easy to clean." I crack an eye, but the only thing on eye level is a Roomba slowly gliding over the floor. The black wood shows every piece of lint and dust. It drives me nuts, hence the Roomba army. There's a scratch in the floor by my nose that I need to get fixed.

Sun pours in the floor-to-ceiling glass windows. I don't own curtains. If you want to watch, watch. The sofa creaks a warning and I tense as the missile hammers my rib cage. I grab it with my free hand. *Danger*. Did I hook up last night after rescuing Maple and forget? Because that's a *female* hand. I let go fast while my brain catches up with the rest of me and I pry my eyes open.

Lola crouches over me.

No.

Scratch that.

She's straddling me.

"You suck," she bellows.

Given her lack of an inside voice, I decide she's talking about the way I abandoned her last night to go after Maple and not about any kind of sexual activity, but… I'm not sure. *Houston, we have a problem.* It's not that she knows the passcode for my alarm system—using the first fourteen places of pi was predictable—but that we're touching in ways a guy should never, ever touch his best friend's girl.

Oblivious to my dilemma, she glares down at me. "Maple deserves more than a hookup."

"What?" Despite my multiple PhDs, I sound less than intelligent but I require three hours of sleep to be functional and I'm now operating on less based on the angle of the sun on my floor. Rescuing Maple took the better part of the night.

"Do not mess with my friend." Lola punctuates her words with additional and vigorous rib poking. I turn my head to check my laptop while trying not to move because grinding my morning wood against Dev's girlfriend—even accidentally—would be disastrous.

"Can we discuss this over breakfast?" It's not unusual for me to stay up all night, but this is the first time Lola's paid me a solo call. Usually she's attached by some body part to Dev and I'm busy trying not to perv on them.

Lola bounces, I grunt, and she must figure out what my problem is because now it's her turn to freeze.

"Right," she says, staring out the window. Pink flushes her face. "This is awkward."

"Generally speaking, women don't attack me or try to ravish me," I offer. "In fact, I can remember zero instances. So I'm assuming I'm misinterpreting this situation and you're not trying to get me killed by Dev or offering yourself up as a substitute for Maple. Which is a very friendly overture but one I'm going to have to pass on."

Lola groans and pounds her head into my shoulder. I think. Honestly, I'm not sure what she's doing, but she'll have to do it by herself. Dev is a big motherfucker and I know exactly how hard he can hit. She climbs off me, however, which is progress.

I stand up cautiously, considering next steps. It seems likely that everything will become clearer after I caffeinate, so I head into the kitchen. Rather like my relationships, I have a policy of getting in and getting out of my kitchen. The room channels a Siberian snowstorm, all white subway tile, white marble and big-ass stainless steel appliances. You practically need a parka or snowshoes to fight off the pristine chill. I pull the fridge door open and check the contents. I need to place a grocery order. For all my dollars, I appear to own no more than a can of Coke, a bowl of Mini Moo's and an unidentifiable white take-out container.

Fake milk it is.

I get busy with the Mr. Coffee, shoving an espresso pod in and cranking on the buttons.

"Why are we talking about Maple?" I hope I'm not smiling like a jackass.

Maybe I am, because Lola holds up her hand. "Your app shared her naked nudie dancing with most of San Francisco."

She folds down a finger.

I think she might be really mad at me.

"She confronted you." Another finger.

"Instead of simply taking down her video, you made offers that included a job, stock options and sexual intercourse."

There's a brief pause. I suspect Lola is waiting for me to confirm or deny, but I settle for a noncommittal shrug.

"You sent her roses."

Finger, finger, finger.

"You rode your big, sexy white horse to the rescue."

"Am I the knight in that analogy? Or a cowboy? Because I drove my Porsche to that club and I'm confused."

Lola stabs her middle finger in my direction. Point made. "Poetic license. Either way, you don't seem to be keeping away from her and you need to rethink that decision, big guy."

"I didn't realize that she was off-limits." The coffeemaker finishes filling my lucky mug with tarry black goodness.

"You are the hookup king." Lola peers in the cup and shudders. "That is so gross."

I think she's referring to my personal life and not the coffee, so I hand her the cup and Mini Moo's and start drink number two. What does Maple drink when she gets up? Does she like her coffee milky and sweet? Dark and bitter? God. What if she doesn't even *drink* coffee? She could be one of those weirdos who starts the day with hot water and lemon or a hit of matcha. Whatever that is.

"Executive summary." Lola dumps a handful of fake creamers into her cup and then lobs the empty plastic cups at me. "Don't mess with her."

I redirect her missiles into the trash. "Do I look like a total dick?"

She looks around instead of answering. "This

place is almost completely empty. You should buy some furniture."

I look around, too.

I have a trash can, a fridge and a sofa.

I think she might be right. I should invest in something to fill up the space.

"They have people for that," Lola points out. "You could support the local economy and hire out."

"Dev hired a decorator, but I don't want some random stranger waltzing into my place and making decisions that I have to live with."

"Wow." Merriment dances in Lola's eyes. "And yet you're totally good with random hookups?"

"Sure?" I guess it sort of is the same principle, picking out what I'll live with based on the outside packaging. On the other hand, I'd have to pay a decorator and I've never paid for sex unless you count dinner and drinks. Which I haven't because I've never expected a girl to sleep with me because I've fed her. That's all kinds of wrong. You don't drop a bag of canned goods off at the local food shelf and expect the recipient to put out.

"There's nothing wrong with hookups." Lola takes a sip of her coffee and makes a face. "Although your taste in coffee is bad. Sometimes you don't want forever." From the way her mouth curls, though, she's thinking about Dev again. I'm pretty sure both of their hookup days are behind them.

"But you don't think I should hook up with Maple."

"Not really, no. She's no good with short-term rentals."

"So I'm not allowed to take her out and then get down on my knees, run my hand up her—"

Lola grabs my laptop. "Shop. Buy a room."

I think I understand why Dev likes her so much. She's fun. Since she's taken and we've already established that I don't do long-term anyhow, I do as she suggests and go online. I choose one of those mattresses-in-a-box for my bedroom, but after that I'm stumped. *Houston, we have a problem.* There are 11,298 furniture options and more filters on the website than the user interface for the space shuttle. I try a few sample searches before giving up and attacking the problem from a different angle.

"What would Maple like?"

Lola makes a face. "Maple is a hoarder."

"More words." I try to decide if I know what size my mattress is but I draw a blank. It's big.

"Maple loves keepsakes. Or she's a collector. Possibly a shopaholic." Lola leans over and taps a few filters. My possible choices narrow to 1,456. I suppose I could just order them all and then donate the ones I don't like, but then I spot the dreaded words: *assembly required.*

"She has lots of stuff?" I'm not exactly sure what Lola's getting at, but now I sort of want to see Maple's place. I'm also certain she'd hate mine because the only word to describe it is *empty.*

"She went to Bali." Lola dumps some stuff into

my cart. "When she came back, she re-created her hotel room because she'd had such an awesome time. Most people take photos or buy a T-shirt. She bought a Balinese bed. In Bali. It required a shipping container on a cargo ship to bring it back to San Francisco."

"So?"

"She could have bought a cheaper, look-alike bed here, but she wanted the real deal. A Bali bed from Bali. Maple is an overcommitter."

And again…so?

Lola sighs, so clearly I'm the problem here. "She's all in when she loves something—or someone. Her bed is the biggest, most ginormous, out-of-place bed I've ever seen crammed into a studio. She had to drag it up the stairs one piece at a time. She didn't quit."

"Is that the kind of bed with posts?" I mime the sticking-up bits. "Because if so, I want one of those. Think of the promo shoots I could host for Kinkster, with tied-up people."

Lola groans. "Never mind. Don't share your dirty thoughts with me."

"Right. No talking business." I save the cart to look at later.

Lola waves toward the ocean. You can't see it until you're leaning over the edge of the minicliff where my house perches, but there's a staircase to a private beach. "Are you coming down?"

"Maybe later."

Lola sticks her tongue out at me. "Rapunzel."

She darts out of the house so that she can have the last word, disappearing down the staircase to the beach. She's the silver lining to a bad piece of business for Dev. When his hookup stole his software and illegally posted it on a freelancing site for five bucks, Lola bought it. Dev went rampaging after her of course, determined to exact vengeance, but then he fell in lust—and now he claims to be in love. Jack's been off the market for years. Out of the three of us, in fact, I'm the only single guy left.

She's right. It's funny. I've always been happy hooking up before. I've never wanted more. And I don't now, I tell myself. It's just *Maple* I want. I kind of, sort of want to know more about the nonnaked parts of Maple, the parts she's never, ever shown the world.

CHAPTER SEVEN

Max

ADRIFT IN WONDERLAND, Alice chose to believe in five impossible things before breakfast.

I'm an engineer.
I believe in facts.

Fact #1: Maple has never asked me to text her. Not once in the twelve days since I met her.

Fact #2: Maple has never texted me herself—and she has my number.

Fact #3: I suck at texting.

Fact #4: She just broke up with her long-term, rat bastard boyfriend and she deserves the unicorn of the dating world.

That unicorn would be Mr. Perfect, a Ken doll and happily-ever-after rolled into one hot, muscled package that adores her, her family, her pets and every quirky thing about her. In other words: not me.

All I have to do to remind myself of my inability to string together words is scroll through my non-work-related texts from the last week. There aren't many—a pizza coupon and a reminder to put out the trash cans on Tuesday for pickup. Am I up for tacos? Yes. Surf Saturday? Where? I prefer communication to be both short and clear. Why waste time when you could be *doing* instead? Instead of taking a girl out for dinner and then forcing myself to engage in small talk, I hook up.

Still, I can't stop myself from imagining what Maple might be doing right now. In *fact* (har har), I don't even have to imagine her because I have the video of her dancing in the club saved on my phone. I replay it for the seventeenth time because watching Maple move is making this my favorite Sunday morning ever. I know by heart each dip her body makes to the music pounding around her. The way her hips find the beat and her arms rise as she turns. Something started between us when she exploded into my office a week ago. She may be ignoring the chemistry between us, as if the lack of words can put out what we feel or make us into friends or fuck buddies or some other neat label. Somehow my fingers fly over the screen, pulling up her contact info and tapping out two little letters: Hi. As soon as my thumb slides off the send button, however, I know I've made a mistake.

Hi? Why don't I just text *hey* while I'm at it?

Embarrassed, I stare down at my phone, mentally willing Maple's cell phone provider to have some kind of catastrophic server meltdown that will erase her messages from the last sixty seconds. The odds of that happening are low, so I'm weighing the odds of hacking in when my phone pings.

What's up?

Okay. That's a question and a question deserves a response, right? Not much. Lying on couch.

A long pause follows, during which I suspect she's lost interest, but then she types back: Pretty tame for a billionaire?

Gave the private pilot the night off, I text back.

She responds almost immediately: You have a private plane for real?

Timeshare.

This time the pause stretches out until I get tired of waiting for her response. Fuck taking turns. Does my partial plane ownership mean you no longer respect me?

I haven't checked my personal Kinkster app in a while. I pull it up while I wait for Maple to respond. I have 312 hookup requests, but strangely I don't feel like looking at any of them. Or maybe it's an abundance of riches. Or laziness.

Is it possible to be too lazy for sex?

The ping of an incoming text has me drooling like Pavlov's dog.

Does that mean you get tipped out a third of the way to Paris?

I grin down at my phone.

Come with me and find out?

There's a pause, and then: HAHA. Goodnight Max.

One text leads to another, and then somehow over the next two weeks we fall into a pattern. I don't know what's happening between us. We're not hookups. Are we friends? Maybe. I mean, clearly we flirt and give each other shit. She's funny. She teases me about her star status in the hookup world even though I know she's still worried about her professional reputation.

Plus, it's good to not be the odd man out anymore. My friends have all paired off, and while I don't want happily-ever-after, I'm not a fan of awkward, either. Dev and Lola. Jack and Molly. That just leaves me. Do I want to hang out with Maple?

Maybe. I mean, she's sexy as hell and I'd get naked with her in a heartbeat. Maybe.

Because I don't want her to stop texting me, either,

and that's what happens when two people hook up. Maple's on a man diet, or so she assured me. She's just barely broken up with Madd and now he's begging her to take him back, making promises and doing the woo. I could tell her that once an asshole, always an asshole, but she doesn't want to hear that right now. That's another reason I haven't hit on her, not really. Madd's holding out the fantasy of their perfect future together, and believe it or not, naked, spread-eagle me isn't such a tempting counter offer that she's rushing over to my place to drop her panties on my floor and rip my boxers off with her teeth. I figure there's always tomorrow or next week—whenever Madd shows his true colors.

In the meantime, I get free decorating advice because it turns out that Maple really likes furniture and she's willing to choose non-Balinese pieces. She also adores pillows and pictures and a million other pieces of crap, the absence of which marks me as a total barbarian. I spent a weekend making *mood boards*, which is way less kinky than I'd hoped. The best part about it was Maple's snort-giggle when I asked her if a mood board was the Christian Grey, X-rated version of pin the tail on the donkey. FYI? Totally not. Drawing my favorite sexual fantasies on a piece of poster board with a handful of crap markers would have been cake.

I am acquiring a houseful of furniture, though. Maple has an unhealthy love of floral prints and faux fur. Leather also has to be of the faux variety because sitting on dead animals is inhumane. Today I'm considering a vegan leather couch to replace the hand-me-down in my living room. In the plus column: ninety-six inches long, twelve inches of Roomba-approved clearance between the bottom and my hardwoods, and the color of a high-end Cuban cigar or an apple-cider doughnut. In the negative column?

Max: Legs look like gold paper clips

Maple: Hairpin legs

Max: WTF?

Maple: Very trendy

Max: On a scale of 1 to 10, my give-a-fuck has achieved negative numbers

Maple: Think of how impressed your hookup will be ;)

Max: More worried about banging her on the couch. Too slippery? What if we break it? Think I should buy two in case there's an accident? Do you want one for your place? I owe you.

Maple: TMI and no thank you. I have a big bed.

I ask for pictures but no go.

* * *

Maple is an early morning texter. Not the predawn hours when normal people are coming home from a wild time out at the clubs and bars or getting up to get ready for work because when you live in California, you're going to spend hours commuting to the office. And before you go getting all judgmental, I'll just point out that I'm usually up all night coding. Sue me if that means I like a nap at seven or eight in the morning.

Still, when she hits me up, three weeks after we started texting, I don't see it coming. Partly this is because I'd just gotten vertical on my bed, pillow over my head, because I've just committed a huge check-in and there's not enough Red Bull in the world to keep me up. I'm crashing hard when a herd of demented bumblebees erupts a few inches from my head.

Shit.

I grab my phone.

Maple: How's your day going?

Max: Maple?

Maple: You forgot my name already?

I can feel the stupid grin stretch my mouth. Not that there's anyone here to give a damn if I look stupid. She's so cute.

Max: Right. Oak. Crepe Myrtle? I'm in bed.

I snap a picture of myself. Not *that* kind. I know better than to send Maple crotch shots. If she wants to see my dick, she'll ask. I send her a perfectly lovely shot of my head. Yes, the big one. My hair's sticking up on end, my jaw's rougher than a cornfield after mowing and I'm naked. Not that she can see my goods, but I stripped off before dropping into bed and not even for Maple am I getting up to find a shirt.

Maple: Lazy bastard. They made me wear pants with buttons today at work.

Since she's working, I suppose taking her pants off isn't an option.

Max: What's up where you are?

Maple: Wanna buy a blender?

She sends me a picture. *Score.* It looks like she's standing in some kind of conference or exhibition space. There's a ton of people around her selling crap and networking as if their lives depend on it. That's just background music, though. Maple's front and center, beaming at me. I take in her goofy smile, the tight white T-shirt with the name of a nutrition drink company scrawled over her tits. Must be one of her influencer gigs and I briefly wonder how much they're paying her. Whatever it is, it's not enough. Her phone's aimed over her shoulder, which means I can't see her ass in the picture, but I imagine it just fine.

Max: I'll take a dozen

Maple: I need an honest guy opinion, okay?

Max: Hit me

Maple: Madd wants to meet for drinks tomorrow night. Bad idea to go?

Max: Don't want to be a dick about this but—

Maple: Uh-huh

Max: No, seriously. I've got one, he's got one, and that gives us a special bond, if you know what I mean.

Maple: Be serious?

Max: Delete and block. He's playing you and it's not the kind of game you're gonna win. He wants a hookup. He wants your panties on his floor because he's either got nothing better going on or he's got nothing.

She goes silent after that. I try shoving my pillow over my head, but my brain's awake and there's no going back to sleep now. Since I don't feel like getting up and adulting just yet, I take advantage of my naked, happy-to-see-Maple state and fist my dick. Whacking off alone in bed isn't my first choice but Maple's working and there's no one else I want to call, so I keep my hand beneath the sheet and get busy. When my phone vibrates, I groan.

Max: Interrupting, Palm

Maple: You know anything about Madd's sudden purchase of not one but two Mexican timeshares? He says he's locked out of his online banking app so he can't shut it down.

Maybe it's because I had so much fun texting Maple about blenders earlier today, but tonight's dinner meeting is excruciating. It's like a hookup gone bad where you know before the main course ever arrives that you're cutting the night short and nobody's scoring. The guys pitching me are eager and they've mastered all the right buzzwords, but the deal they're pitching isn't one I'm interested in. In fact, it's safe to say I'm bored, so when my phone buzzes, I look down discreetly. I have a message from Maple: What are you doing?

Dying, I promptly type. Business dinner. Send naked picture immediately to salvage day.

And even though I'm a firm believer in going for what you want in life, I'm surprised when Maple actually does send me a picture. She's ever so slightly sweaty, mostly undressed, and there's a railing behind her that I've learned is called a barre (preferably in a French accent). She's wearing pink tights and I swallow. It's not as if she's naked, but… Fuck. Me. Pink toe shoes peek out beneath an enormous pair of wooly leg warmers. The black cotton of her leotard skims her breasts, hugging the curves. She's leaning forward on her elbows, legs spread wide as she stretches, the phone held out in front of her. Better yet, since she's in a studio, the wall behind her is all mirrors and I can see the heart-shaped peach of her ass. A mischievous smile lights up her face. Fuck, she's gorgeous.

Hot and sweaty Friday night fun, she types.

I can't resist. No hot date? Is this me-time?

Her reply is almost instant. Sex right now would be awesome. I need a boyfriend stat.

My dick tents the front of my Armani dress slacks, demanding we go help her out with her abstinence problem. I excuse myself from the table. Hiding out in the men's room seems too clichéd, so I head outside to the restaurant's private terrace. Forty stories below, San Francisco lights twinkle around me. Those stupid rosemary balls on sticks and other perfectly manicured plants line the deck. I feel like I'm in a zoo but I take a picture anyhow (of my face because I'm not stupid) and send it to her.

At your service.

We've flirted with each other the last couple of weeks, our teasing veering between the dirty and the playful. Sometimes it's the kind of shit friends give each other, while other times I don't know what we're doing even if I want to do it all the time. I can almost feel her laughter shaking her phone. Maple loves dirty puns, bad jokes and having fun. I bet she fucking rocked that stage and lit up the room. I wish I could have seen her dance in the theater. I wish she were here. I wave off the waiter who approaches me.

Have a drink with me, I write back. To myself. Because even though she hasn't responded to me, I'm all in. I text her directions and wait. I may or may not be holding my breath. I've hooked up dozens of times through Kinkster, but that was easier. I didn't care about the women reading my texts; I just cared about having sex.

This is Maple and she makes me wait long enough that I suspect she's actually seriously considering my invitation. Haha. People will think I'm after your money.

I type back: My dick's even bigger than my bank account. I'm sure you can prioritize correctly.

Of course she's not going to let that go. Ask Guinness out then and go for the world-record.

Right. I'll get right on that. I fire off: Record is 13.5 inches. How do you think they measured that?

I love numbers. Yes, I measured my dick when

I was twelve. And then again when I was fourteen, sixteen and seventeen. If your boner clocks in at less than three inches, you've got a less-than-average problem—so I have nothing to worry about.

Maple's still going to give me shit. She types: Pfft. That's the official record. Unofficial guy in the UK is claiming almost nineteen inches. He can't work because his dick is so huge. He might actually get Disability.

I make the mistake of googling this, thus burning the images of a pants-less guy with his massive schlong covered in what looks like panty hose into my brain forever. Def a future as a porn star there. I reply, You're right. I can't compete.

Maple sends me a smiley face emoticon. Emoticons are tricky. They're not, as I've pointed out more than once, actual letters. They form no words. It's an interpretive dance where you can't hear the music and I hate the ambiguity. Is she smiling because she's imagining *my* dick? Or is she being sarcastic because she wouldn't be getting off on a foot and a half of panty hose? Maybe she's just in a random good mood. Or messing with me.

I take a stab at answering anyhow. No boyfriend doesn't have to mean no sex.

I'm sure this has occurred to her, but I feel the need to point it out. While I wait for her response, I abandon the pitch guys, settle our check and catch the elevator. It takes fourteen seconds to descend forty floors, and most of that time I spend imagining exactly what Maple could be doing with her boyfriend. Or to him. For him. Then I swap the pronouns around because I'm an enlightened kind of guy. I could do her. I know her feet get tired and ache. She claims that's the dance tax, for slamming them into the stage floor over and over again, but I don't think TLC would hurt. I'd be happy to rub them.

Or do other things.

There is a time and a place for a nonsexy, it's-all-about-you-babe massage, but personal experience says that it's also foreplay. Don't lie. You know that when you're naked and oiled up and I've rubbed all the places that hurt and the tension's leaking out of your body like helium from a balloon, you're going to start thinking about other things.

Jesus.

I come to a decision as I step out of the elevator and stride over to the valet parking podium. First, my hard-on's reached ridiculous proportions and I'm in serious danger of snapping my dick in half if I move wrong. Second, the guys there either remember me or, more likely, my car. One of them darts off to retrieve my darling and I return my attention to my phone.

Maple hasn't answered, but I totally think we should have sex. It's practically a public service on my part. Sexless Friday nights should be illegal. While I wait for the valet to return, I make my pitch:

We could hook up.

Dirty sex.
Multiple orgasms.
Lots of fun.
Say yes.

I'm still waiting for Maple's response when the valet hands me my keys. I slip him a twenty and slide into my Porsche. My music's already pounding, the beat vibrating through my seat. I don't flat out sing along or seat dance, but it's tempting. I had a poster of this car on the wall of my bedroom growing up and now she's mine. Of course, I also had a trio of sexy, naked ladies cohabiting in that same space. Hope springs eternal. I drive through the city while I wait for Maple to decide what she wants to say to me. Or, hopefully, do with me. I give her five more minutes to respond before I tell Siri to text her again:

Too blunt? I take feedback.

The highway here runs along the ocean. The road falls away from the shoulder in a steep, stony roll to the water. Waves break on larger rocks a few hundred feet from shore. I find a pullout and bring my Porsche in for a safe landing. I need both hands for this shit.

Ping. Two days ago, I decided that Maple required her own ringtone, so I assigned her the opening measure from "Flight of the Bumblebee." She'd told me a story about trying to do fouetté turns to it as a five-year-old and I'd almost peed myself laughing.

My phone buzzes with her response: How do I know you're not all talk? Prove it.

I'm Mr. Show, but clearly she's mistaken me for Mr. Tell. I'm grinning like an idiot at my phone when she texts again.

Chicken.

The squawking, clucking bird emoji needs no interpretation on my part, although it looks more like an ostrich laying an egg to me. She's on.

You want a menu? Am I a drive-through?

Her answering text is almost instant: Quit stalling.

Uh-huh. She thinks I'm bluffing.

If I give you a menu, you have to rank the options.

I don't give her a chance to disagree. Instead, I start texting.

A. The gourmet foodie option. I'll cook you a meal. Asparagus, oysters Rockefeller, licking your crème brûlée. A four-course meal on my table or my private yacht.

Not that I own a yacht, but I could. If that's what Maple fantasizes about.

B. The trip to a strip club option. I can buy the club out so it's our private place, or we can invite the whole world in. Lady's choice. You dance for me and I'll strip for you.

C. Blindfolded. You can imagine what's coming next. I might even take orders.

D. Stairwell quickie. Your workplace, mine or whatever building you've fantasized about your boss in.

E. Can you be quiet? I'll share my toys with you—and I have a great remote controlled one. You know where it goes. You wear it and a pretty dress, I take you out to one of those fancy crystal-and-china places, and then I see how many times I can make you come before dessert.

F. Sex in a hotel room with the curtains open and you up against the glass. First floor, fortieth, four hundredth. How many people do you want watching?

G. Get your Fabio on. We'll have sex in a meadow. I'll pretend to be the big, bad duke. You can be the milkmaid, the misbehaving duchess in need of a spanking or the Queen of England.

That last one's a little over-the-top but I'm all in if that's how she likes to play. My phone slips in my hand as I wait for her to respond. To choose one. I try not to imagine Maple over my knee while I turn her butt hot pink. Spanking's never been my kink but I'm willing to broaden my horizons for her.

I tap my phone.

Nada.

No texting bubbles, no message, no naked selfies.

Usually, I make an offer and then I'm out. I don't have to beg and I certainly know how to take *no* for an answer. I'm not San Francisco's biggest manwhore but I love sex and I love taking care of my temporary lady. Something about Maple makes me want to push, however. I can't let this—*her*—go. Before I can overthink it, I call her.

"Hey." Her voice is husky when she answers, or possibly she's ever-so-slightly breathless. Or I'm indulging in wishful thinking—stranger things have happened.

"At least tell me what you're wearing."

"You saw. I've added pants."

"Pants are overrated," I murmur.

She pauses. "I'm headed home. Pants seemed prudent."

"Alone?"

"Are you up for a ménage à trois?"

I drop my phone and have to retrieve it from the passenger-side seat. "Jesus, Maple. Play fair."

"You've never had a threesome?" Laughter fills her voice. "Because it's very, very popular on Kinkster. Don't tell me no one's offered."

"They've offered," I say mock gravely. "But I'm not a fan of eating family-style. I don't want just a taste—I want the whole thing."

"Wow." She takes a moment, possibly to process what I just said. I didn't think she was shockable, so she's probably working on the perfect comeback. Sirens wail in the background, followed by a string of car alarms. She's walking on a San Francisco street somewhere.

"So you're selfish?"

"Focused," I counter. "I prefer to give my undivided attention."

She hums a bar from a jaunty tune. "*Please.* I bet you've fantasized about two women together."

"I have," I admit, "but I'm watching them. I'm learning what they like, how they make each other feel. If I got in that bed with them, then I'd be thinking about my dick, too, because he's a selfish git and he likes having his turn. And then I'd also need to keep track of who I'd touched last. Or licked. Or finger-banged."

"Wow." Maple sounds breathless. *Score.*

"I'm not sure I'd have enough coordination to keep both my ladies happy without some serious one-on-one practice," I say thoughtfully. "Which is why I'm calling you to follow up on that menu."

"Oh?" She's definitely laughing now.

"We had a deal," I point out. "I give you a list of choices and you rank them from 'omg yes let's do that now' to 'only if it's my last chance ever to have sex.'"

"What's your favorite?"

I don't have to think. "You."

"I'm going into a tunnel. I'm losing you." Laughter threads through her voice. She's lying, she's teasing. We both know it.

"There are only eleven tunnels in San Francisco. Is this a wormhole?"

She's laughing when she hangs up on me.

CHAPTER EIGHT

Max

I EARNED MY first billion dollars with a dating app: Billionaire Bachelors. It's a digital shopping list for all you out there who prefer Prince Charming with a generous side of cash. You punch in your zip code and then the app gives you the down low on all the Prince Charmings who meet your criteria. Billionaires are one of our most popular options, although you can pick your future mate based on other important qualities like good looks and favorite winery.

I whipped it up in the Santa Cruz dorm room I shared with Dev and Jack, spending every second we weren't surfing with my head down in my code. I launched the app the day we graduated and I haven't looked back since. Both Jack and Dev have bitched repeatedly about being two of Billionaire Bachelors' leading men, but they weren't willing to bankrupt themselves to lose their starring roles, so screw them.

My second app is Kinkster, and it's equally popular (and unpopular with Dev and Jack who are adamantly vanilla in bed). One of the downsides, however, is that my PR team wants me to host a series of glamorous, sexy parties that sell the brand. Glamorous pool parties scream fantasy hookup, so tonight we've invited hundreds of celebrities, influencers and pretty people to my Santa Cruz pad to dance and get drunk on my dime. The music pounds away, drowning out the ocean and the buzz of dozens of conversations as my team puts the final touches on the event.

My fingers itch to text Maple and invite her over. It's not that I think this party is her scene, but I'd like to see her again. I'd like to hear her laugh and just… hang out with her. Even if we don't ever hook up, she's fun. When we first started texting, our messages were purely functional. She said thank you for the roses. And then she asked something, or I did, but we fell into a rhythm. Question and answer. Rinse and repeat. Yesterday, though, when I gave her a menu of kinky sex options to pick from, I wasn't joking. Not really. Something's changed between us as we text. I stare at my phone, willing it to show me a clue. A sign. A multistep, results-guaranteed plan. I think I went wrong when I sent the menu.

I removed myself from the friend zone and went—

Somewhere.

Limbo sucks. I stare at my phone, willing it to buzz with an incoming text from Maple. Since it's Saturday night, I don't think she's working.

Outside, the PR team continues birthing a party. Everyone's focused on the infinity pool that spills over into the ocean, adding the little details that will make tonight one Instagrammable moment after another. Citrus trees in terracotta pots sourced from Italy. A pop-up bar with themed cocktails. White lights. White lotus flowers floating on the surface of the pool. The only thing missing is the kinky sex—but that will come later, after my guests have had time to settle in.

Those guests arrive thicker and faster as the night progresses. I watch from upstairs as they come. They're allowed to roam downstairs, but the second floor is my haven and it's off-limits. Two hours after the party officially begins, I've made a grand appearance and the music is so loud that I feel rather than hear my phone buzz in my pocket.

I step behind a particularly impressive citrus specimen and pull it out. Maple's texted me a picture of take-out Chinese on a floral melamine plate balanced on the edge of a small tub, but it's her words that have a smile tugging at my mouth.

Fancy a swim?

I do a quick volume calculation. You'd have to sit on my lap and even then there'd be no room for water. Immediate displacement. Need to know if downstairs neighbor has flood insurance?

My phone buzzes again, Maple's picture flashing

across my screen. Before I can overthink things, I answer.

"Hey, Maple."

She launches into rapid-fire speech the way she does everything: bold and certain. "Do you like Chinese? Do you want to come over for dinner? We could watch a movie."

"What kind of movie?"

She tells me all about the romantic comedy she's Netflixing and the unlimited potential for happy endings. I mean, who doesn't like getting his happy ending? I'm seriously considering ditching my party when a deafening series of shrill screams erupts from my pool. Water hits my back and I instinctively hunch to protect my phone. It's water-resistant but that's a *lot* of water. I'm enjoying our conversation and I don't want to have to stop it in order to retrieve my backup phone.

"Are you killing someone?" She sounds cheerful but…

"Would that make you more or less likely to come over?"

"Less," she says eventually. I like that she stopped to think about it.

"Then I'm hosting a pool party." I lean against a convenient palm tree and eye the tangle of girls being fished out of the pool. From the size of the guy they crash-landed on, I suspect the football team I invited has shown up.

"Do I have to wear a swimsuit?"

I smile at my phone. “You should always feel free to swim naked in my pool.”

“Be serious.” Water sloshes on her end of the line. Is she *in* the tub?

More important: is she *naked*?

“You can do whatever you want, Maple. Wear a swimsuit. Don’t. Yoga leggings work fine, too. It’s a party, not rocket science. I’d just like you here.”

“So your pool *isn’t* full of bikini-wearing hot girls?”

“Truthfully, no.” I snap a picture of my pool and send it to her. “You’d be the hottest person here any-how, especially if you showed up naked. You owe me a picture of your pool party for one now.”

That makes her laugh. My phone buzzes a sec-ond later and I fumble it. Jesus. There are a whole lot of white bubbles above the soft, sweet curve of...

“Did you just send me a boob shot? I thought you had a no-bathroom-selfies rule.”

She snorts. “I thought you lived for naked boob pictures.”

“I like them,” I say solemnly. “But I’m not sure I can commit to them being my *favorite* body part. I’d need to see all the parts first so I could make a fair assessment.”

Maple hums a bar of something. It’s a church hymn, which is kind of weird, but she says it’s just autopilot because she did a lot of zoning out in church as a kid (her dad was a minister) and that’s what she associates with tuning out the world. It’s her thinking noise, though, so I hope she's making me a list of candidates for Max's Favorite Body Part.

"Come over," I say.

"Why?"

Because as much fun as playing word games with her is, I want to see her?

"We can play twenty questions in my pool." I don't know why I want her here, just that I do. "I'll send a car."

CHAPTER NINE

Maple
#glamlife #datenightgoals #ideas

THE RIDE TO Santa Cruz isn't short and it's tempting to nap on the posh leather seats because I've been burning the candle at both ends, but Max's car is too amazing to waste time on sleeping. Not only is there real French champagne on ice (and not the kind they sell at Target, either), but there's a box of chocolates and a cashmere throw. I spent the first two blocks pretending I was the queen of England and then another four after that pretending I was a film star.

Now I'm just me, but that works, too. The ocean at night looks painfully, promisingly perfect. When I roll the window down, salty, fresh air fills the car. It smells amazing. If I could, I'd live on a beach. We glide past dramatic seaside cliffs and creamy strips of beach until the dark, white-tipped ocean gives way to a charming jungle of houses and bougainvillea. What's not to like about Santa Cruz? It's peaceful and serene until we get close to our destination.

I hear Max's party before I see it. When the town car turns into a narrow street, the music bursts over us, pounding through the delicious, luxurious silence of the BMW's expensive leather interior until I swear my butt is vibrating. I have no idea how he got permission to hold a party like this, but I assume money was involved. Lots and lots of money.

Max's house isn't quite what I expected. Sure, it's big and it's oceanfront, and it's undeniably expensive—but it's also pink. With bonus *turrets.* Frankly, it's more suited to Cinderella than a hot geek billionaire. It's also lit up like an airport landing strip, an honest-to-God red carpet stretching from the sidewalk to the front door. Valet parkers wait to whisk cars away to who knows where because Santa Cruz is very much lacking in elbow room and all these people had to get here somehow.

Wow. The people. I try to get out of the car nonchalantly, as if I attend launch events all the time, but I'm seriously underdressed. Or overdressed, depending on how you look at things. Max hadn't mentioned a dress code—when we said goodbye, he was still making a case for arriving *au naturel*—so I'd opted for a blue, thigh-length Spell & the Gypsy Collective dress. The gauzy embroidery floats around my thighs in deference to the summer heat. I'm even wearing a pair of thong sandals with pink and white seashells on them because I was going to a beach party, so I assumed there would be sand. The red carpet is unexpected. Plus, it's Santa Cruz, which is a beach town, so I didn't expect people to be dressing as if it were Oscar night.

Mistake.

Big mistake.

Two waiflike women, one in pink sequins and the other in white, twine around each other, pouting and posing on Max's stupid red carpet. I make a mental note to give him shit. Most people go for petunias in a hanging basket or maybe an urn if they're feeling pretentious, but he's decided to re-create the Oscars. Photographers snap away, calling the waifs' names and demanding they "look this way." I've walked a few red carpets for press events for the San Francisco ballet, but this is in another league. It feels ridiculous. As soon as the path is clear, I sprint for the door.

The ground floor of Max's house is stuffed full of people, although he's still decidedly lacking in the furniture department, but I recognize the huge L-shaped sofa we picked out together. There's no Max, though.

I fish my phone out and type: Marco.

A waiter in black tie wanders by, offering champagne. Clearly, I'm out of my league. When my phone buzzes with a set of GPS coordinates and POLO, I'm almost relieved. This is just my goofy, number-loving friend Max who's frequently more engineer than bad boy.

I plug his numbers into my phone and start hunting for him. Two Marcos later, I step outside and find myself at the top of a staircase that's perfect for losing a glass slipper on. It glides and swirls its way down to the garden and that magical pool. Someone's twined white roses and jasmine through the railings and for just a moment I flash back to dancing in *Swan Lake*, surrounded by dozens of downy, betulled swans. That must be why my heart is pumping.

I spot Max striding past the pool—lit up with millions of fairy lights—and frowning down at his phone. Dark hair curls haphazardly over his forehead. He's wearing a white T-shirt, faded blue jeans and a black tuxedo jacket that's rolled up to reveal strong, tanned forearms. It's like he got half dressed—or half *un*dressed—and then stopped. Or forgot. Or—most likely—just didn't give a shit. He cares about lots of things, but clothes don't make that list. People watch him anyhow. Some of them reach out as if to touch him, to make him stop and look, but he just keeps heading for the house.

And me.

He pauses at the foot of the stairs and grins up at me. It's both weird and familiar at the same time. Something shifts inside of me, making me feel like glassware in a box, so close to breaking or falling out. Falling, I decide. I'm definitely falling.

"You didn't tell me you owned a stage set," I call down to him. The temptation to break into the port de bras of infamous swans of *Swan Lake* is strong but this isn't my audience.

"All the world's a stage, and all the men and women merely players." Max twinkles up at me. He's even cheesier than his pool lights. "Are you coming down or shall I go up?"

"You're a bad influence." I have to yell to make myself heard over the music. Nevertheless, we both know my words don't matter. I'm totally going to do it. Indeed, I toe my sandals off, toss them down to Max and whip my arms up into the familiar position. And then I'm descending, whipping through the familiar fouetté turns, my dress belling out around me. Not Odile's full thirty-two spins, but just enough to make my heart race, my left leg burn as it bears me around and around until I reach the bottom.

He meets me there, swinging me up and off the final step. I've put on some weight since leaving the ballet, but he lifts me easily, flying me through the air, around and around, until I curl an arm around his neck.

"Hey, Sassafras."

For a moment, I think he's about to kiss me when he trots out that stupid nickname.

Not a European cheek kiss or even a friendly peck on the mouth, but a full-on kiss with lips and tongues and all my favorite parts. But then he pulls back and flicks my nose before setting me down. *Friends don't kiss.*

"I'll introduce you around," he says. "There's tons of people for you to meet."

I believe him. If his living room's full, his pool

deck is a fire marshal's nightmare. People are crammed side by side until it's almost impossible to move, let alone dance. Or breathe. Still, a path always seems to magically open up for Max as he leads me from one knot of revelers to the next.

It's overwhelming, frankly. He makes introductions, I nod and smile, and somehow there are always new people and faces. The volume rises steadily, the level of champagne consumption is unbelievable, and the pool is a sea of naked beautiful people bobbing up and down. Max, however, just watches it all from his tiki bar, a slightly bored expression on his face as I work my way through my third cocktail. I have no idea how I fit in here.

"How did you get permission for all this?" I mumble-shout my question, which I blame on my cocktail consumption. It's stupidly easy to get me drunk.

"Permission?" Max winks at me.

I roll my eyes. "They can probably hear your pool party on the moon."

I swivel on the bar stool and stare at him, waiting for him to answer. Not just to put the pressure on but because his face is absolutely gorgeous. He hasn't shaved in at least a day, and stubble roughens his jaw. He looks strong, but in a natural way. He spends a lot of time outside, surfing and rock climbing, so his body screams *I can do this* rather than being a walking billboard for a gym. I slip my phone out of my bag and take a close-up of his jaw and throat.

"Afraid you'll forget what I look like?"

"Souvenir." I wink at him. Because, oh man, I sort of want to remember what he looks like right now. His eyes have that warm smile lurking in the back, the one that doesn't quite reach the grumpy line of his mouth because he's bored and doing something he doesn't like but he feels he should. "Are you going to answer my question?"

He snags my drink, takes a sip and makes a face. "(A) Dev and Jack are my neighbors. (B) I invited them. (C) My financial generosity is directly proportional to the volume of my music, and my neighbors bring many worthy charities to my attention."

Since he's blasting music at midnight loud enough to make his Cinderella castle shake, this must be a million-dollar party. I try to act as if it's no big deal to be that casual about money, but I suspect I need more practice.

"I want to show you something," he says.

"Oooh—a collection of etchings?"

He winks at me. "I don't have one of those—should I?"

"Well, a good etching collection can be an excellent investment." Keeping a straight face is harder than I thought it would be. "Do you even know what an etching *is*?"

He grins at me. "Let's go find out. You can quiz me."

He lifts a bottle of champagne from the tray of a passing waiter. The waiter doesn't blink an eye—just reverses direction to reload. There's probably the champagne-equivalent of a beer truck backed up to Max's house. Maybe Veuve Clicquot makes house deliveries? Max threads his fingers through mine and I lose my train of thought.

I've had a little too much to drink. Not so much that I want to lie down and sleep. Not enough to make the world spin. Just enough that I feel like I'm floating and happy. That nothing really matters other than Max's fingers mixed up with mine. I was worried about coming here, but everything seems perfect now, thank you, Dr. Cocktail.

Deep down, I know that nothing's changed. Max is still filthy rich and his dick is still not monogamous. Or even semimonogamous. A player? Yes. Hookup king? You betcha. But I tighten my grip on his hand anyhow and follow him into the shadows beyond the pool. When we get to the edge of a steep staircase, he tugs his hand free and drops to one knee. Strong, warm fingers wrap around my foot and tug.

"You need to lose these."

"I'll bet you say that to all the girls," I say lightly.

"But I say it well." He pulls off my sandals, tossing them to the side, and then stands up. He's so close that his body brushes mine and I do my best to pretend that it's just casual contact and no big deal. That my heartbeat isn't skipping just a little faster. That my breathing's as steady as ever. NBD, for sure.

"Come on." He's already barefoot as he sets off in the direction of a gorilla-sized man who looks suspiciously like private security and who is blocking a staircase on the far side of the pool. Somewhere beneath us, the ocean waits.

We climb down in the near dark, my hand in his, the other on his shoulder for balance. Broken necks aren't sexy. I pat his shoulder, savoring the warmth of his skin seeping through the thin linen shirt. Muscles flex as he moves. There are about a hundred billion steps but each one brings us closer to the beach.

My feet sink into damp sand as we step off the staircase. Moonlight illuminates a broad strip of creamy sand studded with small rocks. OMG. Tidal pools. I run over to take a look. It's too dark to see past the surface but I skim the top. There's something that looks like an anemone and slippery, darting black shadows that must be fish. Or leeches. Do they have water snakes in Santa Cruz and do they spawn in the shallows?

Max strolls up behind me and Drunk Me yanks her hand out of the water (sprinkling his blue jeans with tiny wet spots), panics a little and pretends to be amazed by the scenery. Which is really pretty freaking awesome. The gnarly-looking rocks bookending the little bay seem like something out of a fantasy book. "They look like dragons."

Max squints in the direction of the index finger I've stabbed at the dragon rocks. "Wrong. Clearly that's an excellent likeness of General Grievous."

"The *Star Wars* character? Are you nuts?"

"Are you blind?" He shoves the champagne bottle

into a nearby tidal pool and then strides toward the waterline. When I follow, my toes come in contact with the iciest water I've ever felt. Even the ice baths I used to soak my feet in after a day of dancing were warmer than this. I look down. Nope. No icebergs.

"What?" He frowns, his gaze following mine.

"I'm looking for ice cubes."

He snorts. "It's California. Anything's possible."

We trade jabs about each other's rock-spotting abilities (he'll never convince me in a million years that those rocks are George Lucas–worthy). Somehow we end up sitting cross-legged on the sand, just above the tide line. Max pops the champagne open, looking like a suave James Bond billionaire. No, wait. With his hair rumpled by the breeze, shirt open, back against the rock, he might be a pirate. I sort of like that.

His party pounds away up above us, but down here? Down here there's nothing but us and the ocean and all that dark stretching away.

"Let's play a game. Truth or dare." I grab the bottle from him and chug. My palate may be as broken as my man picker because I'm having a hard time telling the difference between Max's expensive stuff and the three-dollar-a-bottle crap I stockpile for New Year's. Or maybe I just need more practice?

He repossesses the bottle before I can practice too much. "Tell me the rules."

"Well, since there's just the two of us, we'll take turns. You have to choose between answering any question I ask truthfully and performing a dare of my choice. If you fail, you have to pay a forfeit and drink. Ladies first?"

Naturally, he deliberately misunderstands me and grins. "Truth or dare, Maple?"

"Thank you for being a gentleman." I blow him a kiss. "Truth."

I'm way too tipsy for dares.

"What's the shortest amount of time you've known someone before having sex with him or her?"

"Four days." I don't even have to think about it. "He was a Czech dancer I met on tour. My company was only in Prague for a week. We pas de deuxed on stage and then we did some private dancing."

"No drunken one-night stands? No hookups with a stranger or hot, tanned strangers on a beach holiday?"

I drink. Yeah. Not going there. "Your turn, hotshot. Truth or dare?"

"Truth." He stretches his arms out along the rock. I'd be worried about crabs or other sea creepy-crawlies, but he's completely relaxed.

"Oral sex or penis-in-vagina—you get one for the rest of your life, but the other is forever off-limits. Which do you pledge your undying love to?"

He frowns. "Am I giving or receiving?"

"Receiving."

"Do I get Sundays off for good behavior?"

I wink at him. "No exceptions. No cheat days. Pick one."

Now the corners of his mouth turn down. "Let's try them both right now so I can be sure of my answer, 'kay?"

I extend the bottle. "Are you refusing to answer the question?"

He leans forward and lets me press the mouth of the bottle to his lips. "Sex with a partner always wins. Truth or dare?"

"Truth." There's a bead of champagne caught on the corner of his mouth.

He winks at me. "Has anyone ever caught you having sex? And how turned on did that make you?"

I've had sex before. I've had vanilla sex, dirty sex, all kinds of sex. But nearly getting busted? That definitely gets me going.

"Yes."

"That's it?" His hands cover mine so I can't repossess the bottle. "Three letters don't merit thousand-dollar champagne."

Jesus help me.

"Are you kidding? Shouldn't we at least pour it in a glass?"

He winks and catches my wrists, guiding the bottle to my lips. "Have a drink and tell me all about the time you got busted having sex."

The alcohol is crisp and tart, but now I feel like I'm drinking liquid gold. His thumb brushes a bead of leftover champagne from my lower lip at the same moment I try to lick it away, and my tongue tastes Max instead. Now would be a great time for divine intervention, but instead I yank my head back and start babbling.

"We were in the bed of his truck in a state park. We were too broke to afford a hotel room and I thought doing it under the stars would be more romantic anyhow, so we loaded up the truck and drove a couple hours north of San Francisco." Now that I'm working on my new-and-improved man picker, I have to wonder that Tim had money for gas but not for the hotel room. "We'd piled the blankets and pillows from my bed in the truck bed, and Tim—my boyfriend—pulled over at this spot where you could see the ocean. We made out with an oceanfront view and all these stars overhead. I kept telling him to hurry because we'd passed a sign miles ago that said the park closed at sunset and so I was pretty sure we weren't supposed to be there."

The truck bed had had ridges and weird, mysterious dips. I'd had the faintest shadows of bruises for days and practicing lifts with my dance partner had sucked because his hands inevitably found every sore spot on my body. Max didn't need to know that, though, so I continued.

"He'd just got my panties off and his penis in when we heard gravel crunching."

"And?"

"The park had indeed closed hours before and we were busted."

Max groans. "You're a terrible storyteller. You're leaving out all the important bits, like whether the good park ranger saw your boyfriend fucking you and if he took his sweet time walking over to your truck. Maybe he ran the light down your bodies so that you knew that he'd seen you. Work with me here."

I get the idea. The sound of Max's voice, hungry, rough, *curious*, makes me wet. Remembering the hot, shaky thrill of that stranger approaching the truck as I tried frantically to shove Tim off and pretend that we were just doing some perfectly innocent stargazing? That makes me wetter and I suspect Max knows it.

"The park ranger turned out to be a girl."

"That's a good story twist." His knees brush mine and I'm on fire. I feel like I need to touch someone—touch him—and yet we're on the beach. An only semiprivate beach with a party raging away overhead.

"Truth or dare?" I gasp out. Do I want to do this? *Can* I do this?

"Dare."

"What's the sexiest part of a woman's body?"

"That's a question," he protests. "Not an action item."

"So picky," I tease. Although if I'm going to tease… "Let me help you out here. Why don't you show me? Mouth?" I run my fingertips over my bottom lip. "Boobs? Ass? Somewhere else?"

My hand moves lower.

Yes, I touch myself there, too.

"Do I have to choose?" His voice is rough, as if

he's on fire, too, when his hand covers mine on the slope of my boob.

"Dare." It's a challenge, so when he holds the bottle to my mouth, I lick the rim. I don't look away. I don't want to stop. He feels… *God*, I don't think I've ever felt this way. I don't remember all of the details of all of the nights I've shared in my life but I remember the worst—and the best. This night on the sand? This is a circle-the-date night, a red letter, marquee kind of evening.

He's whispering things, dirty dares I only half hear but I know what he wants. It's what I want. Pleasure. A connection.

Kiss my neck for thirty seconds, he says.

And then when it's my turn to dare him again, I whisper *Kiss my nipples for thirty more.*

Thirty is my new favorite number because half a minute is all it takes this man to make me feel everything I've ever thought and it's so much better, so much more *real* than I ever imagined. It can't just be the dark and the beach. It can't just be the dirty, secret fantasies that we trade back and forth.

Suck my finger and pretend you're going down on your guy for thirty seconds, he says.

And I do it. I can tell our thirty seconds are growing longer, and our bodies more reluctant to move apart when one of us calls time.

Dare me, Max.

Drink champagne from me. I dare you.

I can't tell if I've said that out loud, or if it's even

my turn. Someone had emptied the champagne bottle, though, so that last dare was off the table. We'd drunk it all. No—I had. He had? I only really know that I'm sweetly dizzy, the world making a slow-motion twirl around me as if I'm riding a merry-go-round. I should ride something. Some*one*…

Max makes a rough sound when I straddle his lap and slide my hands up his neck. I don't know why I haven't touched his hair before. "Be my horse?"

He blinks at me. I think I've finally surprised him. "You're into pony play?"

"God, no." That's me giggling. "I mean, if that's what works for other people, great, but I don't think I could do that."

"Okay." Does his mouth brush mine? I'm not sure. "Then explain it to me."

So I do. My voice gets dreamier and dreamier as I talk. I tell him about how the world's spinning as if we're on a carousel ride. He shifts beneath me and somehow I'm riding him. I'm tipsy, falling over the edge into sleepy drunk, but I know what I'm doing and, oh God, I want this guy. My not-friend friend. My Max.

"Sex on the beach?"

"Is that too vanilla for you?" I rise up on my knees so I'm looking down at him. "I know you like variety."

I'm dying for him. On fire. My body's like melted wax from the champagne and from him and I need him to do something about it. Somehow I'm on top of him, spread-eagle, and his amazing wonder dick is right *there* so I wiggle to say hello. And because it feels good.

"Jesus." He pants something, leaning back on the sand. I think it might be my name. "You may be overestimating my need for kink."

"I love your penis. Do you think I can come on you?"

He curls his fingers around my hips, guiding me lower. "I think you can do whatever you want to do."

"Good answer. I like getting whatever I want." *I like you. I want you.* I brush my lips over his. He feels slightly sandy, tastes slightly salty. Would his dick taste like this? Do I want to find out?

Yes, I think I do.

I rock against him and his amazing, not-naked, huge penis presses against my panties as my dress billows around us. It's so arousing. His hands shift to cup my butt and I close my eyes as the world swims gently, slowly around us in a haze of lust and champagne.

"Maple?" Max's voice. Hoarse, a little rough. He's asking me a question, he's—

"I'm not there yet." My eyes drift open as if looking could somehow put out the fire that's burning me up. "Help me?"

"Yes." He groans something else, a handful of words, something that doesn't matter because he curls his fingers in while he talks, his fingertips brushing the edge of my panties. Oh God, he knows what he's doing. The heat's spreading through my body like a forest fire and it's so good, better than I'd imagined until he slips beneath the cotton and I discover a new favorite touch. Maybe practice does make perfect? I open my mouth to ask him, but all that comes out are little needy moans that almost but not quite drown out the slick, wet sounds we're making together. I think he wants to hear me because then he's kissing me again and all the moaning and panting I do is into his mouth.

When I come, grinding against his impressive hard-on, it's still a sweet, sudden surprise. I rest my head against his shoulder. "Wow. They should bottle you."

I think he's saying something.

Daring me.

But—

Someone's attached weights to my eyes and they close.

CHAPTER TEN

Max

JESUS. I HOLD Maple tight because she feels good and I can smell her when I breathe in. There's the perfume she likes, the vanilla one that reminds me of cookies, and a trace of roses because she "hydrates her face" with a rosewater spray. And then there's the sweetly salty scent that lets me know louder than any words or porn-star screams just how much Maple enjoyed what she let me do to her. It makes me want to lick her from head to toe.

"Maple?" She shifts against me, her mouth pressing against my chest, and I need to be naked with her. "Dare me to hook up with you?"

The seconds tick by, one after the other. The ocean comes in and goes out. Her breathing settles into a gentle rhythm. I should regret that last dare, but I don't. This isn't a game of spin the bottle or even a tease. I know Maple isn't a hookup, but I'm not ready to let her go yet. So instead, I smooth my hand down her amazing hair. It's all looped and twisted and tucked into itself like an infinity symbol or some deliciously complicated bit of highway and overpass.

"Maple?"

She breathes out, soft and steady, deep and oblivious against my chest. She's asleep. I guess that's a good thing because I shouldn't be asking her to hook up. It's just that we've both had a few drinks and we're on a beach—and we've touched each other.

I know the sounds she makes when she comes.

I know—

Math.

Shit.

I calculate the number of cocktails she's drunk since she arrived (four) and the better part of a bottle of champagne. For just a moment I wish she'd been taller, bigger, less tired, had a full stomach. Anything so that we could keep playing our game. I want her so badly.

Instead, I shift her so I'm holding her with my left arm, leaving my right arm and hand free to text. Two texts later, my team is shutting the party down. I forgot that she'd worked this week and now it's late and she's tired. Of course she's going to fall asleep after she comes.

My pop-up parties are notorious for their abrupt endings. One guest described them to all of Instagram as "wham, bam, thank you ma'am" parties and it stuck. I get mine, my guests get theirs, and then everyone goes their separate ways. There's no hanging around or hanging out, so no one up there will care if I pull the plug and send them home.

Maple mutters in her sleep, shifting, and I stroke her hair, her arm. It's probably the hottest thing I've ever seen, the way she lets go. First she let me make her come and now she's letting me hold her while she sleeps. I can't stop touching her even though it's not going to end up with me inside of her driving us both mad. Her arms are toned and strong. I noticed them when she waved from the top of my stair earlier tonight. She was fucking gorgeous then, and now—now she's even more so.

When the noise finally dies way above us, I stand up, shifting her in my arms. She settles in as if she belongs there, and I file the sensation away. I'll analyze it later. Right now, I need to get her somewhere she can sleep. Plus, the tide's really coming in now and we'll be out of beach soon unless we pull a *Survivor* and camp out on the rocks.

Tomorrow I'll tease her about having to carry her up the stairs like Sleeping Beauty or one of those movie princesses who always needs rescuing by a prince in disguise or a white knight. Not that I'm either of those things. I'm fairly certain I don't know how to be. Turns out I can climb the stairs holding her just fine, though, even if I don't have my knight errant license and no one would ever mistake me for a hero.

Security nods at me when I reach the top. For a moment I wonder what he may have heard or seen, but it doesn't matter. He's signed an NDA and I've learned that Maple *likes* being watched. The possibility of getting caught gets her off.

Since I'm not getting off tonight, however, I carry Maple upstairs to my bedroom. She'll have to spend the night with me because it's not as if I can send her home in the car like a package. Or a hookup. I feel off-kilter, but I like having her here, so I decide not to examine things too closely.

I gently kick the bedroom door open. A quick scan reveals that my housekeeping team has done its job and everything is in its place. The white cotton sheets are folded neatly back on the enormous bed, and the gray duvet Maple talked me into is folded into a neat rectangle at the foot of the bed. And then there's the ocean. I open the French doors that lead out onto a small balcony, so that the ocean air can pour through the room. The ocean smells amazing. Like salt and something wilder, freer and less permanent.

When I set Maple down on the bed, she curls into a ball and buries her face in the mattress. Okay. I can figure out a plan. Just because I've never had a hookup put the brakes on before we finished the date doesn't mean I can't do this. Whatever *this* is.

Just don't panic.

Two minutes later I'm still clueless and Maple's even more soundly asleep. Her position doesn't look comfortable to me, but maybe dancers are more flexible than us mere mortals? And suddenly, even though this isn't a date and we haven't quite had sex, I feel like tonight might just be okay. I want to wake her up and tell her how much fun I had. How much I'd like to do it again and is she busy tomorrow?

Or the day after. I'll take any day she gives me.

But Maple sleeps on, oblivious. It would probably creep her out if I stripped her down and put her in one of my shirts, so instead I set out a pair of clean sweats and my favorite UCSC T-shirt where she'll see them when she wakes up. I also put a spare toothbrush on the bathroom counter, along with three towels and a new bar of Irish Spring in its bright green wrapper.

I realize she has sand on her feet when I make a round-trip back from the bathroom and QA my handiwork. Sand I can fix. I lift first one and then the other while I run a warm washcloth over them. Getting sand in the bed sucks and I think she'd like it better this way. It's not as if I have a foot fetish—I think—but my dick didn't get that memo. Maple has the most fucked-up feet I've ever seen. High arches, calluses, a permanent arch that's both unnatural and strangely beautiful. For most of us, hard work maybe makes itself seen and felt through ulcers. Or gray hairs. Or a honking big bank account. All of Maple's hard work, however, is written right there on her bare feet. She's not afraid to let her passions change her.

Eventually, when her feet are clean and I can't think of anything else to do for her, I tuck her into my bed and then I lie down next to her. I don't quite wrap myself around her, but I want to.

CHAPTER ELEVEN

Maple
#morningafter #oops #thiscouldwork

SUNLIGHT POURS INTO the room, tap-dancing on my eyeballs and working its way beneath my skin. I stretch into the warmth because I'm surprisingly cold. Maybe the landlord finally fixed my AC? There's a second sun pressed up against my leg and over my rib cage. No. Wait. Not a sun but a someone. Last night's memories filter back slowly, one moment at a time, like water dripped from a tap. The town car. Max's party. Our private party on the beach. And maybe something more. When he'd touched me it had been a dare and a challenge and part of me had decided to take him up on it. I didn't care then that he was a player and a rich guy, someone with whom I had absolutely nothing in common. I didn't care that we'd fuck and move on and that I'd probably regret his passing out of my life even though that was stupid. Maybe. Or maybe we'd meet, in weeks, in months, in years to come and the thought would just flicker through the back of my head: *I know what he looks like naked.* A quick sliver-shiver of a thought like fish in a stream, here and then gone.

I open my eyes without really intending to and there he is.

Eyes closed, lashes brushing the tender skin beneath his eyes. I have no idea what I thought would happen, but thinking clearly wasn't part of last night's plan anyhow. Max breathes deeply, and I let my gaze roam over his face. His lips part slightly, dark stubble roughening the line of his jaw and cheek. Awake, he's always so focused and intent, but asleep he seems softer and somehow vulnerable. My eyes drift over his face, seizing this chance to commit him to heart. He's the same Max who invited me over, who took me down to the beach, who licked my neck until I came. The only thing different is that now I don't have to imagine him naked—or mostly naked. Max likes specifics and I still haven't seen his penis.

He's sprawled on his side, one leg over mine, an arm draped over my ribs. My temporary dark-haired Adonis. At some point between the beach and bed, he's lost his shirt. Broad, capable shoulders crowd out the morning sunlight. His chest is muscled and lightly dusted with dark hair, narrowing to a delicious six-pack that demands my attention.

There are no visible tattoos, no jewelry, just almost-naked Max in a pair of ordinary red plaid boxers. I think I'd like him even better all naked. He's pretty much the hottest man I've ever ogled, let alone shared a bed with.

I don't think we had sex last night.

Mistake. I run a questing finger over his hip. I haven't been able to stop thinking of him since I barged into his office. That was weeks ago. It wasn't romantic or sexy or even remotely hookup-y. But then he started texting and I answered and now here we are. A thick ridge tents the cotton of his boxers and I want… I want…

I look up and his eyes are open. I love his eyes. Up close they're more gray than not, framed by unfairly thick lashes. I race to find words to say but nothing feels right, so I just draw my finger over his cotton-clad hip. Back and forth. And then again. He made me come last night. He put me in his bed. He wakes up looking like a Greek god while I'm undoubtedly rocking a case of bed head and morning mouth.

"Morning," he rasps. There's a question in the word, a question I think I want to answer. *Should we have sex? Do you want to hook up with me? Is this a mistake?*

My finger traces the line of his hip bone, down, from one small cheek to the next to something so much bigger and harder. I brush the tip of his dick with my finger and he jerks. *God, you're big,* I think, wishing I knew what he wanted. Are we friends who drank too much and passed out together? Am I the party guest who just wouldn't go home? Or—

Are we a little something more?

No. I'm not doing *more*. I've learned that lesson.

"Max?"

My voice sounds hoarse which makes sense. My throat feels as if I tried to eat sand for dinner.

He stares down at me for a long moment. I can feel his eyes moving over the top of my head and then down. I slide my finger along the length of him again. "Should I go?"

I feel rather than see him shake his head. And then he licks the side of my neck. It tickles and it's a little weird and it feels so freaking amazing because you don't *do* that to friends unless maybe you're both cats. Or possibly dogs. Or—

I pretend the sound that comes out of my mouth is a moan. Something sexy, something husky or rough or anything but the raw, ugly, *needy* sound I make. I'm going to fuck him.

I leap out of bed, pressing my hand against his chest when he leans up. "Stay here."

He blinks at me. "Maple?"

"I'll be right back." I toss the words over my shoulder as I sprint toward the bathroom. Thank God for billionaire McMansions and en suite bathrooms. I rush in and slam the door. How fast can I do sexy? Or at least satisfy basic hygiene requirements? I map out a strategy while I pee but apparently Max is impatient—or has no boundaries—because he's knocking on the door before I've magically transformed myself into a sexy glamazon.

"Maple?" My name again, more insistent.

I pop the door open, holding a strategic hand over my mouth. "I need a toothbrush."

He points wordlessly to the precise pyramid on his bathroom counter. Toothbrush, toothpaste, dental floss, mouthwash. Behind them is a neat row of miniature beauty products. The man is a Boy Scout.

In unison, we move to the double vanity. He pulls open a drawer and retrieves his toothbrush. I tear into the stack of oral hygiene goodies he's left for me. And then we stand there next to each other, brushing and rinsing.

It's like we've just fast-forwarded our lives thirty years and now we're an old married couple. It's awkward but cute. I can smell mint toothpaste and then he reaches for the mouthwash.

"Five minutes," I tell him with a smirk. "And then I'm getting the party started without you."

I saunter out of the bathroom, pulling the dress over my head and tossing it onto the floor. I'm reaching for the clasp on my bra when I hear the bathroom door click shut. Yep. He's got it figured out. Just in case he needs any additional clues, I ditch my panties, sprawl on his bed and start taking care of business.

Just because he got me off last night doesn't mean I'm completely willing to trust my happy ending to him—plus guys love the show-and-tell and it gets things off to the right start. The wetter I am, the better tab A fits into slot B, if you know what I mean.

It never takes me long to come when I concentrate. My body's tightening, warming up like a runner hitting her stride right before she rockets off for a victory lap around the park. My legs tense, fingers dipping deeper, because right there, there, *there* is today's magic happy spot.

And of course that's the moment the door opens. "You were serious about not waiting."

For a moment, I think about stopping. Just waiting for him to come over here and take over. Or better yet, ordering him. I don't have any problems putting in requests when someone asks what I want. But this feels good, too. Truth is, I'm so aroused by the way his eyes heat up, following my fingers, that I'm a heartbeat away from coming.

It feels so, so good.

My hand slides down my panties. "Sex is always better when I take care of myself."

"So you don't need me at all." The dirty boy leans against the wall, his gaze trained between my legs.

"You bet I do." I wink at him. "I've decided to take advantage of you just as soon as you join me."

Touching myself in front of Max doesn't feel awkward. He tilts his head, watching, and we both know he's memorizing the way I do it. That he notices exactly how I like it. It's not just that he's an engineer. It's just that he's Max and he cares about details and he loves to learn shit—and, since he's supersmart and even more competitive, he therefore needs to be the very best at whatever he's learning.

So I'm a little surprised when he doesn't rush to join me. Instead, he reaches into his boxers and fists his dick. His hand mirrors mine, stroking up. Down. I've got an obstructed view of his penis and that's a waste because what I can see is spectacular. He's long and thick and if I were comparing, which I'm totally not, he's far more gifted than my boyfriends have been.

"I didn't expect that." I gesture toward his crotch.

He looks down. "What? You thought I'd have a carrot-sized dick?"

"Fruit of the Loom. Isn't there, like, a billionaire's code that requires you to wear Gucci or Balmain?"

He shucks his boxers. "Better?"

And then, while I'm still staring at him (because now I have a ringside seat and there's a *lot* of Max O'Reilly to appreciate), he launches himself onto the bed. His fingers find my ribs, gently tickling as he rolls me on top of him. I've never liked being tickled but his fingertips scrape over my skin, dancing, teasing, playing. I snort-laugh and grind against him. He's not getting away from me now.

His hands cup my butt, lifting me up. I plant my hands on either side of his head, bracing myself so I don't fall off. Not that there's any chance of that, because my mouth's stuck to his and we're kissing, his tongue in my mouth, mine in his the way he's going to be inside me real soon. Turns out Max really knows how to kiss.

The rough, hungry pressure of his lips against mine makes me dirty moan.

He's naked, I'm naked. Could this morning get any more perfect? And could I be any more screwed? Hooking up with Max is the best worst idea I've ever had.

He pulls his mouth away from mine, staring up at me with hot, hungry eyes. "Yes? We're doing this?"

His penis isn't as polite. It pulses against me, hot, hungry and deliciously eager. Rational decision-making is overrated. I also part my legs as I come to this happy conclusion.

"Hurry up." I may bounce ever so slightly because the man is taking forever. He makes a rough sound as the tip of him slips inside the first inch of me.

I squeeze because I shouldn't be the only one suffering here. Plus, I've got him where I want him, so letting go would just be a waste of time. He groans something, so I do it again.

"Condom, Maple." He throws out an arm, yanking open the drawer of the bedside table. While he looks for the condom, I admire my view. His chest is a work of art, all muscles and sun-bronzed skin. He must spend a lot of time outside without a shirt. There's also a gorgeous line of muscles and the best ever happy trail arrowing down to—well, let's just say I really hope looks aren't deceiving.

"Scoot," he growls, slamming the drawer shut. "Either come up here or let me get this on."

He flexes beneath me. Choices, choices.

I snatch the condom out of his hand and move back to give myself some room to work. His body is a delicious distraction, and even though I'm a big believer in safe sex, I can't help wondering what it would feel like to take him bare. What the hell is happening to me? I promptly drop the condom on him.

God bless a man who does his crunches because he levers up so he can reach the condom and hand it to me. He doesn't even seem to notice my unusual gracelessness, but maybe that's because his hands are skating down my arms and sweeping over my breasts. I'm not an overachiever in that department, but I've got enough. His fingers find my nipples and do a stroking thing that makes me arch.

"Do it again."

Apparently Max is good with taking directions, because he does. Plus, he palms my boobs, cupping and rubbing and generally driving me insane. "How about this?"

His mouth discovers my nipple.

"Yes?"

I'm grinding on his massive, Vlad the Impaler–worthy penis, so that's all I can manage. I don't know how some people manage to call out all the stuff they're enjoying most or recite epic poetry. I'm just trying not to moan, because I feel like I should retain a modicum of dignity.

"Aren't you supposed to be doing something?" He sounds downright happy for a man who's doing all the work.

"Can't reach," I mumble. Scout's honor. It's true.

"Problem solved." Before I can squeak out a protest, Max turns me around effortlessly. Sure, I have a perfect view of his penis, but this also means that my butt—and other parts—are right there in his face. He pauses, just a beat, as if he's waiting for me to greenlight him. When his hand strokes over the curve closest to his mouth, I moan again.

Fuck talking. My brain just stops. If the man wants a conversation, he'll have to hold it with himself. Talking with my mouth full would be rude, right? I've always been flexible, so I do a sort of downward dog and take him into my mouth. He lets out a hoarse shout, but I'm a busy woman. Plus, he started this, so I don't think he should be doing any complaining.

Just to make sure he's one hundred percent satisfied, I show my appreciation to his penis. Plus, I may have had one or two (dozen) fantasies about him fucking my mouth, and this is my chance. I lick him from the base to the tip, sucking hard. At some point, when his breathing grows rougher and the hands in my hair tug harder, I add the edge of my teeth and my palms. As blow jobs go, it's slightly rough—and trust me, he definitely appreciates it. Max may be a nice guy most of the time, but he likes that bit of edge with his sex.

Clearly, he finds it motivational, because he doesn't hold back. His mouth seems to be everywhere at once, licking and kissing a soft, dirty path.

The man may be shit on a dance floor but his tongue flies over me and I swear I'm hearing the "Hallelujah Chorus" with each decadent stroke. I manage to keep my end, fisting and sucking, but little noises escape me. Whimpers, goddamned moans, an entire yes-please chorus—it all erupts from my throat in full stereo, porn-worthy volume. The bastard chuckles and then he picks up the pace.

I need him in me. I maintain just enough control to snatch up the condom from where it's fallen on the bed and tear it. The foil packet goes somewhere—as if I care—and then I'm wrapping a hand around him. One more good, juicy lick to ease the way and then I'm smoothing Mr. Condom down his penis. For a moment, it almost doesn't fit. He's truly enormous. I rise to the challenge, though.

I reverse my position. Dancing has made me really flexible. On top, underneath him, spooned up beside him—so many choices. I decide I need to see his face because he's staring up at me as if I'm the center of his universe and we both deserve a reward. I brush my mouth over his. Being the giver he is, his hands keep right on touching me.

"How?" He grits the question out.

"Do you need a menu?" Honestly, I'm not picky. *In* works for me. I lick my palm and wrap it around his dick. My fingers don't meet. He's big and I'm going to need all the lube I can get.

God. I can't believe I'm about to pop my hookup cherry. On the other hand, I've always been way into monogamy and I'm suddenly certain I haven't changed my position on that. Who would want to share this amazing penis?

He lifts me up and I sink down. Oh. Forget Bora Bora or the stage spotlights or all those other times I thought I was hot. Heat pebbles my skin, and I can feel the warmth pouring off Max. He feels this, too. I throw out my hands, trying to find some traction or something to hold on to. My nails dig into his shoulders while I bury my face in his throat. This has the added advantage of letting me scream without alerting the entire world to what we're doing.

He grips my butt, maneuvering me down and then somehow his thumbs are grazing my clit, pushing me open as he moves inside me and the orgasm train is barreling into the station. He does something else with his fingers and his magic penis is slamming into me, and *hello.*

I scream into his throat. My whole body gives it up, trembling and shaking as I see white and light and a whole galaxy of the sexiest, hottest stars ever. Keeping still is an impossibility. I bump and grind, milking him for all he's got because if I stop to think for even a second, reality will creep in. None of the guys I've slept with in the past have been players like Max and I hate, hate, hate not being the best.

He flips us over, shifting forward, and I think I groan his name. Or "More." I could just call him that from now on. I wrap my arms and legs around him just in case he's thinking of going anywhere, and then all I can do is hold on.

Max O'Reilly is fucking me. One big palm cradles my head which has apparently grown nerve endings or something overnight because the rasp of his fingertips against my scalp has me shivering. The other hand cups my butt and holds me still for his next thrust.

Works for me.

I force my eyes to stay open because missing any second of this isn't an option. Max thrusts deeper and my eyes may roll back in my head. Just for a moment because then I'm watching him again. His face is fierce, all of his attention concentrated on the place where we're joined together. His hands hold me close as he moves, finding our rhythm until his strokes get harsher and there's no more gentle.

Which works for me.

God, it works for me.

I lose track of the details after that, but that's okay. Max is a detail man. He's got me. I run my hands over his shoulders and down his back. I palm his butt. And I taste every inch of his silky, sun-kissed, salty skin as if he's my very own mansicle and if I don't hurry up and lick him good, he'll melt away. He tastes amazing, so good that I have to lick him over and over because if once is great, a thousand times will be even better.

He kisses me back, his mouth working down my jaw to my throat. I love what he's doing, as the noises

I'm making attest. He's big down there, making me stretch for him, and I love that, too. He's thrusting deeper and deeper, and we're both more than a little out of control, because I don't know about him, but this feels amazing.

It's almost a shock when I come, squeezing him hard, my thighs trying to strangle his waist. I lock up, chasing that glorious heartbeat, as the bed, the world, everything ignites in a blaze of heat and all I can do is feel and yell because he needs to be here with me.

"Max, Max…ohmygod… Max."

And I think he is. He thrusts once, twice, and then he's coming, too, making Max noises that I hear dimly through my happy, postorgasmic bliss.

CHAPTER TWELVE

Max

"You have an amazing dick. It's a dozen inches of pure magic. Do you think you're just naturally talented or is it practice? Some kind of hookup magic?" Maple drills her head into my shoulder, trying to wiggle into my side. Apparently sex makes her talkative.

"Twelve inches is an overstatement." My dick's happy to make the effort to live up to her expectations—it perks right up.

"Wow." Her gaze dips downward. I can feel her lips curve up into a smile. "You could have fooled me."

I'm not sure what she expects me to do. Or maybe it's what she expects *us* to do? I've never had sex with a friend before. The friend in question snuggles into my chest, recovering from her own orgasms. I know she came at least three times, because she told me so. We could have sex again. I could get up. Or maybe she wants a shower, a good exit line, compliments? This is why I stick to hookups.

Except…

Item: Best. Sex. Ever.

Item: Maple is still talking.

I listen while she babbles on, stroking my hand through her hair, sorting it out because we've totally messed it up. When she slows down, I slide my question into a pause.

"What do you want to do now?"

She hums a bouncy measure as she gives my question some thought. This isn't so bad. We've had sex, we both came and no one's made a mad rush for the door. Maybe this can work.

"There's one thing that could make this better," she says.

I'm more than willing to take suggestions. "Just one? Hit me."

I run my hands down her hair while I wait for her answer. I've restored order. Mostly. I've never stuck around after my hookups. Yes, I'm the little kid who spots a giant Lego tower and goes all "me smash!" on it and then walks way because the fun part is the crash and the way the Legos spray everywhere. I'm not a fan of picking up the pieces. But I don't think twice about kicking Maple out of bed or finding an excuse to go. Instead, I tug a long section of her hair toward me. Ginger maybe? It smells as pretty as the rest of her, all sunshine and spicy.

She hums a little, a tune I don't recognize yet. "Biscuits and gravy would be heaven on earth. Can you cook? Or are you just a pretty penis?"

"Hmm." I pull her on top of me. "Pretty sure there's a sad lack of pork products in my kitchen. Ditto on baked goods."

She makes a face, eyes laughing down at me. "I'll have to downgrade your star rating, Mr. O'Reilly."

"That's bullshit." To prove my point, I lean up and kiss her. I know exactly how she likes to be kissed now.

I take my time, even though my dick's ready to go again and I think Maple could be convinced. Our kiss is slow, a sleepy, sweet press of our mouths. We're just sitting in the Porsche, keys in the ignition, motor idling, rather than tearing up the highway balls-out. I can't remember the last time I kissed someone like this. Her stomach growls, though, so I break off our kiss. Priorities, right?

"I just lost another star, didn't I?"

She giggles. "You gonna fill me up, hotshot?"

"Was that the best dirty joke you could come up with?" I reach out an arm, patting around for my phone on the bedside table.

"Is that a challenge?" She rolls her eyes, her body shaking with laughter.

There's a little hole-in-the-wall mom-and-pop place on the other side of Santa Cruz that caters to the college crowd. The cook there makes the best gravy ever. They have chocolate gravy and biscuits the size of hubcaps.

"I can see I'm going to have to work to stay number one in your fantasy list." I send my fingers flying over the screen. The restaurant doesn't deliver, but the car service I use sometimes is happy to pick it up and bring it here.

I turn the phone around so she can see. "Twenty-seven minutes. Want to see what I can do in twenty-five?"

We're in the shower.

I'm on my knees, doing some not-so-Sunday worshipping.

Maple moans my name, while her fingers tear at my hair. I volunteered my head when she complained about being off balance. My face is between her thighs, her right leg over my left shoulder, and let's just say we're not playing Twister or yoga for adults.

I lick up her slick, sweet slit. We established five minutes ago that she *really* likes this, and sure enough, she starts making those whimpering noises I fucking love so much.

Or maybe it's English. Can't tell, don't care, because she's coming on my face and she's definitely thanking me. Moments later, I stand up, kill the water and lift her out of the shower.

Best twenty-two minutes ever.

After we consume our cumulative weight in biscuits and gravy, we wander out to the kitchen because Maple has repeatedly mentioned wanting *to murder a cup of coffee.* That answers my earlier question about whether she was a matcha-drinking freak. She's not. Instead, she's a full-on caffeine monster and that's something I actually stock in my kitchen.

Much to my regret, she's wearing clothes again. I pointed out that this was both a shame (no one should cover up a body as hot as hers) and a waste of time (I'll just have to strip her after we're done refueling), but she refuses to give in. Instead, she steals my favorite UC Santa Cruz T-shirt and slips on what she calls her "emergency panties." Apparently smart girls keep a spare pair of panties in their purses just in case the night's date turns out to have a Conan the Barbarian side and rips the first pair off with his teeth. Or in case, you know, there's an impromptu sleepover and she wants to not do the walk of shame pantyless the next morning.

We take our coffee outside, but when she goes to perch on a lounge chair overlooking the ocean, I have a better idea. "Sit here."

I pat my lap. I know what she's thinking, but she's safe. I'm wearing a pair of ancient navy blue sweatpants that dip dangerously low on my hips, and so the suggestion's not as obscene as it sounds.

She sets her coffee mug down and straddles my legs, leaning back, arms arched over her head in a perfect, round circle as she stretches. Or something. Fuck if I know what she's doing but her thighs grip mine and I can't stop myself from running a hand up the toned, taut lines of her stomach.

"So?" She arches further until her ocean view

must be completely upside down. "Are we really going to do this?"

I've never had anything but temporary hookups, so I'm not sure what *this* is. "Give me more words."

"Have sex."

"News flash." I pull her upright and hand her the mug. "You've already had your wicked way with me."

She buries her face in her cup. "I meant, are we going to do it more than once?"

I lean in and nip her ear. "Once again? Already checked it off the list. I'm hurt you don't remember."

She stares back at me. "Do you want to do it again?"

"Do you?"

She mock-sighs. "I do have hundreds of guys pinging me for a hookup."

I want to go all caveman on those guys.

"You didn't delete the app?"

That can't be true.

She's not looking for a hookup.

Is she?

"I don't want to have to hide in the house," she says. "I want to get out, to live a little. Maybe Madd was a bad choice. Maybe I can do better. But if I'm being honest, just the idea of dating makes me want to scream. I'm tired of putting in all the work. I just want sex. And a friend. Are you taking applications for friendship?"

"You want to hook up with me? Are you fucking with me?"

She shrugs. "No. Well, yes. I totally want to fuck you. Do you have a girlfriend?"

"Jesus, Maple. No. Do you think I'd lie to you?"

"No. I don't. It's one of the things I like about you."

At her words my brain gets a little dizzy, as if there's not enough oxygen in the room. Which is impossible. Maple's breathing just fine. Maybe I'm having a heart attack?

"Don't have a panic attack." Maple leans in, pressing her fingertips against my mouth. Not sure how that's supposed to encourage me to breathe, but it works.

"I'm not proposing to you," she continues. "I'm just saying that—if you have no plans for a hookup with a random, sexy stranger—maybe you'd like to make plans with me."

Hell, yes. Play it cool, I remind myself.

"What makes you think this could work?"

"Item one, hot sex." She winks at me as she uses my favorite phrase. And honestly, having sex with her again is a no brainer. She's freaking gorgeous, her smiles and constant motion pulling me in. The way she hums her own soundtrack as she dances through life, the way she picks herself up when life hands her a shit sandwich, the way she goes balls-out when she decides she wants something, it all makes me want more. Naked more.

"Item two, I looked your profile up on Kinkster. We like the same things."

She slides that in there, as if it's no big deal. You like country ballads? Me, too! Tacos on the beach, margaritas with salt on the rim, and sex in public? You bet. Right there with you.

"Item three, it's your fault my phone's blowing up and since there's no way I'll come by a date honestly for the foreseeable future, you owe me."

"I want to fuck you again," I agree. "And you know I don't do boyfriend/girlfriend gigs. I don't know how."

"So we hook up exclusively. The best of both worlds. Awesome. We're agreed. I'm glad we had this conversation." She swings off my lap. "I need to head back to the city now."

A few minutes and a whole lot of kisses later, she's fully dressed and headed out the door. I sort of want to pick her up and throw her over my shoulder. Let my caveman act out because he's feeling… possessive.

I'm sure that's why I follow her out the door to the waiting car.

Because I can't help it.

Because I sort of miss her already.

"Call me," I say.

She winks as she hops into the car. "Maybe."

CHAPTER THIRTEEN

Max

I FIND MYSELF having a hard time focusing. The week after I make Maple come on my beach and in my shower is a long one. I jog from meeting to meeting. I stand to make a phenomenal amount of money this year, as do the members of my team. My engineering team plays the *what-if* game every day. *What if the stock goes to forty? What if it goes to eighty? What if we hit triple digits?* My what-ifs are different.

What if Maple and I hooked up again?

What if once wasn't enough?

What if once is all I get?

Maple is conspicuously silent despite the multiple orgasms I gave her. She doesn't text. Or call. Or barge into my life, my office or my bed.

As if having sex had been my idea.

Naked Maple was amazing. My brain replays over and over the moment she yanked her dress over her head. She tossed it aside like she didn't give a fuck.

That was hot. Her body? Also hot. The way she rode me and made sure she got her happy ending? Hottest. Fucking. Thing. Ever.

I don't know how often Maple likes to have sex, so when Monday passes without a call or text, I'm not particularly alarmed. A twenty-four hour no-text window after sex isn't *that* unusual. Okay, so maybe I'm not as calm as I pretend I am. And I look at my phone more often than a normal, sane person should. I blame the sex. You ladies are right. We guys should call when we say we're going to. This is the first time it's happened to me and let me tell you: ghosting sucks.

By Friday, I've written an app that automatically checks my Maple messages for me and intones *nada, boss* after each unsuccessful poll. We've officially gone 123 hours without contact. I'm touring a penthouse condo in a new San Francisco high-rise when I finally cave to this inexplicable need I have to see Maple again. I've been thinking about buying a place to crash at when I don't feel like driving back to Santa Cruz. Part of me wonders if Maple would like it. I walk through a living room—big enough to park a small plane in—that is accessorized with sweeping views of the San Francisco business district. There are more city views from the bedroom, while the dining room offers a peek at the Bay Bridge. I suspect that if I go out on the terrace, I'll be able to finish my sightseeing with Alcatraz Island or something equally postcard-worthy.

The bathroom is the only private place. When I flick on the lights, I discover it's all gray stone and maple wood. Chic, upscale, contemporary. Check, check and check. It's also more than a little boring. In fact, the only thing colorful in the entire condo is the powder room where the designer went nuts. One entire wall is covered with these little gold triangle tiles and there's a gold faucet. The hot and cold water taps are gold loops. I can just imagine Midas taking a shit here.

I'm still not sure what to say to Maple, so I text her a picture of the bathroom. It's not the sexiest thing (I'm not stupid enough to include my naked dick or any other body part), but I'm genuinely curious to hear what she's got to say. I shoot her a quick text.

Too much?

At first, all I get is radio silence. Then typing bubbles. More bubbles. When her text finally hits my phone, it's entirely unsatisfactory.

Why?

What does that even mean? I send her a close-up of the gold tiles. It's like King Midas was set loose in a decorating showroom. I'm half-scared she'll love it, half-worried she'll think my own taste is suspect. Whatever. It's the stupidest text ever, so of course I have to push it.

Thinking of buying a place in San Francisco. You think we need one bedroom or two for the kids?

This time her response comes much faster: What if we have triplets? Do they have to share? Are you going to play favorites? One bedroom—three teenage girls. Do the math.

She makes a good point. I wander out of the bathroom and text: We should take parenting classes. I'm free tomorrow.

Like the guy I am, thinking about babies makes me think about making babies. Except for Maple, I haven't hooked up with anyone since she busted into my office.

I feel like I'm wearing a goddamned chastity belt.

I check out the bedroom while I consider my next steps. Like the rest of the condo, the bedroom's tastefully decorated in modern minimalist chic—whatever that is. As far as I can tell, it means gray. The view from the floor-to-ceiling windows is awesome, though, so I snap a picture of that and hit Send.

Max: See that window? Me too. I have some thoughts.

Maple:?

Max: You. Naked. Legs spread, tits on the glass, me taking you from behind. Hands over your head, my fingers laced through yours. How many people see you come besides me?

This is what the listing agent should have included in the property description: *luxury penthouse condo with great views and six rooms to have sex in. Do it outside on the terrace, up against the windows where the world can watch or move inside for some soundproofed fun. Bonus room for use as wine cellar or sex dungeon.* No one cares about the two bedroom, three bathroom parts—it's all about how you're going to live in the space. Square footage? Does it matter?

Maple must be reading my mind, because she doesn't make me wait.

Maple: Forgot class. You busy tonight?

Max: Might buy the furniture too. You like this table?

Maple: Answer mine first.

Max: Greedy girl. Tell me where you want me and when. Can start in any room, but definitely recommending the bedroom.

The link Maple texts me leads me to the home page for the San Francisco Opera. Apparently, four-million-dollar penthouses aren't her thing—she'd rather spend Friday night surrounded by Doric columns and designer evening gowns. She's bound to get bored, so it's a good thing she has me.

Max: You want a mausoleum for Christmas? A life-size replica of the Greek Parthenon for your front lawn?

Her response is some kind of emoji. I can't tell if the yellow happy face with the pink tongue and the manga eyeballs is happy, sad or about to vomit. I make a note to ask my engineering team on Monday—one of them will know.

Dress code is black-tie, she texts.

She's so narrow-minded. Naked is better.

She fires back right away. Charity event. Clothes required. Come with me?

In my experience, charities are interested in the size of your checkbook. Give enough and showing up naked is on the table. Also? She's left the door wide-open to jokes with that last question. I imagine her cradling her phone, that impish smile lighting up her pretty face. I don't think that question was an accident. On the other hand, she's also just asked me out on a date.

I try and fail to remember the last time I went on a second date.

Max: I'm a giver, you've got that right, but I prefer to do my giving one-on-one. I'm a special donor. Tell me where to come.

Too much? I couldn't resist. We spend a few more minutes hammering out the logistics for our date night. Maple wants to meet up in front of the opera house, while I'd like to pick her up and am willing to go as far as to meet her in bed. For the moment, we compromise on door-to-door service.

The Realtor sticks her head in the door. She's a young redhead with legs for miles and a sleek gray suit that matches the bedroom decor. She's already offered to program her number into my phone so I can call her anytime if I have questions about the property. When I pointed out that all her contact info was on the listing, she countered with an offer of special services. A month ago, I would have suggested we discuss the property details over drinks, but now I just text my financial team to handle everything.

"Are you interested?" she asks.

In her? No.

I take a moment to let that sink in.

I turn my gaze back to my phone. Yes or no?

Maple: I don't know what I'm agreeing to.

Max: Live a little. Pick one.

Maple: Then yes.

Have I mentioned that *yes* is my favorite word? I nod at the Realtor. "We'll take it."

CHAPTER FOURTEEN

Max

BEING A BILLIONAIRE has its perks.

Yes, yes, I started as a code geek and a software engineer, but I didn't get where I am today by being pretty or by not pushing. You do it this way? I'll find a better, faster, cheaper way to do it and then I'll sell my way. Knowing when to dig in and when to let go is critical. Case in point? I started both Kinkster and Billionaire Bachelors in my college dorm room. The dot-com world works from anywhere—some of our most famous success stories were birthed in garages and spare bedrooms. Where there's electricity, hardware and a whole lot of will, there's a path to better software engineering and millions or billions of dollars. We can make shit happen from a manger in Bethlehem—we don't need Herod's palace.

What does a software engineer do? Well, on the days I'm wearing my halo and am a good boy, I figure out how to make a computer fix a particular problem you've got and I do that by translating your commands into bits and bytes. The brake lights on your car and the ice maker in your fridge, the streetlights that come on when the sun sets, proactive parking meters that give you shit when you've overstayed, and shoes that talk to your smartphone—that's the superhero code, out there saving the world and making life easier.

Some days, though, the devil's sitting on my shoulder and I like to mess with things. The felonies teenage boys can get up to? Trespassing, vandalism, petty theft, joyriding and some old-fashioned underage drinking? There's a computer version of that, too. Some hackers like to use their powers for evil and exploit whatever vulnerabilities they find in a system, running amok in other people's systems. The best part of being older and smarter, however, is realizing that now people will pay me to do this stuff. White-hat security hackers figure out how to breach a company's software defenses and identify their weaknesses.

Does Maple have a weakness? A small one. She's nice.

She watches carefully and figures out what other people like—and then she serves it up.

You want to argue that's a good thing?

It can be. She's the neighbor you want, the one who will water your plants and feed your demon puppy when you decide to make a last-minute trip out of town and all the reputable dog sitters are booked or you're broke. She likes making people happy and she's good at it.

Why does this matter?

I'm so happy you asked. Because I want a second shot—and then a third and possibly a fourth—with Maple, so I need her to trust me. To let me come around. Come in her. On her.

Bottom line? I plan to be the best hookup she's never had so that she'll keep calling me.

A few hours after making an offer on the San Francisco penthouse, I arrive at the address she texted me. I've opted for a car service tonight and I'm ready to make a good second-date impression. I'm wearing black-tie and I look good. No, I'm not that arrogant. Every guy looks good in a tux. If we were smarter as a species, we'd opt for dress blacks instead of jeans and T-shirts.

I hop out of the car because I need to get on top of this date. It already feels like the grown-up version of high school prom. Which I skipped because not only did I graduate two years early but I was a stretched-out, skinny kid and it wasn't a good look. A six-two, 120-pound teenage boy doesn't exactly rock the high school dating lists.

When I get to the front door, however, I realize I don't have the access code. I work around it by punching the button for the intercom. Maple answers and we're back in business.

"Rapunzel, let down your hair!"

"Why?"

"I can come up," I offer.

There's a reason most hookups happen somewhere public. You know what it is—your place, whether it's a full-blown mansion or a tiny studio you share with three cats and a potted plant, is *yours* and who likes sharing? And even if you're trusting a random stranger to bring the orgasms, do you really want to trust him with your stuff?

I didn't think so.

For hookups, I generally prefer a nice hotel room. Having sex in a hotel is also scientifically proven to be better than at home. Don't believe me? I read a study once that claimed our bodies put out more endorphins and dopamine when we are having ourselves an adventure. Orgasms and hotel points—it's like the ultimate two-for-one. Maple tempts me to try something different, however. I'd like to see where she lives and hold her in her own bed. I'd like to think that then she'll remember me when she goes to sleep or does whatever it is she does when she's home alone.

"I'm coming down." Maple disconnects and I wait.

There's a homeless guy camped out in the tiny, sloping slice of driveway in front of her house. San Francisco has a huge problem with homeless residents. Shit happens, life happens, PTSD happens, drugs happen—and sometimes it's all of the above, but it's a problem. No one should be sleeping outside on the sidewalk unless it's truly a choice and most of us would pick a mattress, four walls and a ceiling. I hand him a twenty, which is like slapping a Band-Aid over an amputated limb, but it's also a start. We strike up a brief conversation while I wait, during which I learn that Lieutenant Bob served in the US military (he won't say which branch), he's got a brother in Toledo (we both agree that's nuts), and he keeps an eye out for Maple when she's coming home late or taking out the trash. He's a good man.

Maple is standing on the steps behind me when I turn back around, a smile lighting up her face. Her hair's scooped up on top of her head in sleek, smooth loops, and her eyes are smoky dark and mysterious. She's clearly dug deep into her makeup drawer and she looks fabulous.

My gaze automatically drops down to appreciate the rest of her and that's when my mouth pops open and gets stuck. A lemon yellow sparkly dress hugs her rack and hips, stopping a few inches south of paradise. The skirt is made out of this see-through gauzy stuff that floats around her long bare legs as she dances down the stairs. And because I must have been a very, very good boy (in a previous life, obviously), she's wearing heels, a pair of three-inch strappy shoes that I'd like to see wrapped around my waist next.

I meet her at the bottom, settling my hands on her waist and twirling her in a slo-mo circle. Her skirt flies out around us. "You look fantastic."

Let's be honest. She looks all the things.

"Hey." She curls an arm around my neck and lets me whirl her around. "I look like a hot dog with mustard."

She hums a few bars of "Take Me Out to the Ball Game." Maple's always playing a soundtrack.

"Did I mention I love hot dogs and that mustard tops my all-time favorite condiments list?" I drop a kiss on the end of her nose. "I brought you something."

"You already donated 946 roses to the cause." Maple turns a little pink as she says this and looks uncertain. It's the cutest thing ever.

"It was 937, but this is more fun."

I want to kiss her for real when I hand her the bright blue box. So badly.

Instead, I watch her pop open the box. She looks surprised—and pleased. I went with the gold charm bracelet so that I have an excuse to keep giving her little souvenirs. The first charm is a tiny, diamond-studded car. I slip it on her wrist.

Lieutenant Bob shouts after us. "Bring back dessert!"

Maple flashes him a wide grin. "Two of everything!"

Frankly, I think Lieutenant Bob deserves to eat everything twice.

When we reach the curb, I have a brief debate with myself. Do I slip in next to her? Perch on the opposite seat? Or just cut to the chase and pull her into my lap? Out of respect for her pretty dress, I slide in next to her. During the ride to the San Francisco Opera, I show her pictures of my new penthouse. It's fun but it's also awkward. That's why I stick to hookups. Relationships with a clearly defined expiration date are so much easier. I thought about giving her a key charm or even a real key, but that would be weird.

"So hit me with the plan for tonight?"

"It's a charity performance," she says. "Members of the San Francisco Opera are going to reprise Puccini's *Madame Butterfly*."

I wave my phone at her. "You want to give me the highlights, or should I figure it out for myself?"

She makes a face at me. "Butterfly is a fifteen-year-old geisha who is 'married' off to a visiting American naval officer. He promises to return for her when the robins nest, even though he really sees her as a hookup—he's got big time marriage plans involving a real marriage to the right kind of woman, an American woman. Needless to say it all ends badly, particularly for Butterfly, but the music's amazing, the fundraising cause is important, and it's an opportunity for me to meet a few people."

Yes, it's a free performance where at the end of the night, after watching a tragedy unfold onstage where no one gets a happy ending, you're expected to write a check that's hundreds of times more than purchasing actual tickets would cost. It's a good thing I'm loaded.

I wink at her. "So you want me for more than my dick."

She winks right back. "I'm in it for your pretty face."

I like this girl.

What? You find that hard to believe? You think I'm just planning the best way to get her out of that dress and bouncing on my lap wearing just her heels? I'm an excellent multitasker, so sure. But I do like her. She's funny, she's tenacious and she returns any shit I give her with interest.

Her gaze flicks toward the front seat. There's a panel separating us from the driver, but it's closed. Plus, he gets paid to pretend that the backseat of my car is Vegas—and what happens here, stays here. Maple doesn't have to worry that she'll wake up tomorrow to find herself splashed all over the gossip sites.

Her hand wanders over my thigh. Then she leans in and squeezes my dick through my dress pants. "I'm thinking of this as a two-for-one special."

"Are you?" My voice comes out as a growl.

"Mmm-hmm." She's humming something else now while she makes free with me. "Or maybe a three-for-one special. I'm hanging with an athleisure wear company that's looking for an influencer, plus I get to give back to the arts in San Francisco."

"That's two," I point out. "You want a seat on the board for a ballet nonprofit and you can meet the right people to make that happen."

She pats my thigh. "You're number three. I get to hang out with you."

The opera house is lit up like a Christmas tree, except we're the presents. When our car pulls up in front of the steps that sweep up from the street to the main entrance, someone opens the door and I get out first. I know the drill. My job is to help Maple get out without flashing her panties to the waiting photographers and then make sure her dress is still covering her ass before she hits the red carpet. Flashbulbs explode everywhere. The knee pop, the ankle cross, the cute-couple-glued-together-at-the-hip—we pose our way up the carpet.

Okay. Let's be honest. I totally hate this part, but it matters to Maple. This is the other kind of exposure she enjoys, the less sexy, more commercial kind. Plus, when a photographer asks us to kiss, I'm happy to take one for the team and swoop Maple backward over my arm. When I'm asked to comment on the status of my relationship with Maple, I just wink and say that I'm a very lucky man.

Once we finish running the gauntlet, we hit the open bar, and then Maple's talking people up, so I lean against the wall and observe. I learn four new things about her.

Item: She loves those bright red maraschino cherries the bartender floats in our drinks.

Item: She's into something she calls *house porn.* This apparently involves lusting after online pictures of expensive houses rather than guys. Or girls. Or both.

Item: The stuff she puts in her hair smells like coconuts. Coconuts manage to be a fruit, a nut and a seed—there's probably a bad joke in there but Maple failed to warn me that on a scale of one to ten, tonight's boredom factor would rate a hundred.

Item: Okay. Maybe ninety because apparently I like making Maple happy—and she likes feeling me up when no one is looking.

Eventually we're ushered into our seats, which are box seats. Naturally. Neither nature nor the opera is a meritocracy, and only the best people make it to the mezzanine and the box seats. You have to be either very, very rich or a super donor to sit in one of these spindly, gold-gilded seats.

"I think we got upgraded," she whispers, running a finger over the red velvet that covers the edge of the box.

"Or Christmas came early," I say with mock seriousness as I nod to the occupants of the box to our left. There's a senator sitting there, along with two mayors, a representative and three foreign dignitaries. If this was political bingo, I'd be yelling, *Bingo!*

But let's be honest. We know what's going to happen: I'm going to be making a very large donation to the opera.

Maple

"You sit like you're on a throne." Max's amusement tickles my ear. I think I had too much champagne before the opera because my stomach is warm and full of happy tingles that spread through my body like ripples in a fountain when you toss a quarter in for luck.

"You can pay me homage later." I know how I sit, but I still look down anyhow, as if something might have changed. Thanks to years of ballet training, my spine is straight, my legs together, bent to the side, ankles crossed. It's how the British royal family sits and it guarantees I don't flash my panties at anyone in the theater. But as soon as I think that, my brain tumbles down the rabbit hole. I'm aware that there are hundreds of people here, most of whom are at least pretending to watch the performance onstage. I squeeze my thighs together, pretending to myself that I'm not imagining a different scenario, one where I ease my legs apart. One where strangers are staring at me, their eyes tracing down my body, over the shadowed space between my legs. I'm wet just thinking about it.

Max tugs on the charms that slide against my bare wrist. "Earth to Maple."

"Sorry." I flash him an apologetic smile. "I'm paying attention."

It's true, even if I'm not paying attention to what I should. The lights go down and the gold velvet curtain that's hidden the performers rises. Show time. I'd forgotten how performing made me feel, the hot, warm nerves, the delicious tension that I release into the dance. It made me feel alive, and I miss it. I read a book once where the main character had her first ever movie audition and came from the heat of the lights and all those gazes on her. There's probably some disturbing Freudian explanation, but all I could think was I know that feeling.

At some point during the first act, Max nudges my shoulder with his, holding out another flute of champagne. He's like the alcohol magician, producing it from nowhere. Usually, I limit myself to two glasses, but I'm tired of rules tonight. I'd rather have the ticklish prick of the bubbles in my nose and the warmth of hundred-dollar-a-glass champagne sliding down my throat. And even while I know I'm lucky—I could be Lieutenant Bob or a million other people who don't have even a fraction of this moment—I'm missing something.

Max says something. It's under his breath and the tenor is letting the whole theater know in no uncertain terms that the woman he's serenading onstage is his everything. At best, my Italian is rusty. Other than food words, my conversation is limited to cursing and place names, so I should be concentrating on the singers. I should lose myself in the music. But I'm too aware of the man slouched in the seat beside me. Max has no boundaries. His body bends and flows and takes up all his space and some of mine. Our arms touch. Our legs brush.

Honestly, I'd crawl in his lap if it wouldn't be some horrible breach of theater etiquette. Max's fingers tap and his leg fidgets. Not in time to the music, but as if he's hearing something uniquely his in his head. Or maybe he's bored? I did drag the man to the opera after all. I partially blame him, though. The man is just so appealing in a tux. Or half a tux. He's undone the first few buttons of his dress shirt and the bow tie he has yet to wear is half-stuffed into the pocket of the jacket draped across the back of his chair. Instead of wanting to do him back up, however, I want to finish the job and strip him down right here. In public.

I snort before I can stop myself. We'd never be invited back, no matter how big of a check Max wrote. Sitting next to me, he's somehow teasing and frothy, as expensive as the champagne that's a perfect complement to the evening and I'm lucky. So very lucky. Stupid tears prick my eyelids. I won't be sad. I shouldn't be. I have so much.

"Maple?"

I hear him whisper my name as his big, warm palm covers my forearm and strokes. His voice, pitched low because we do not, ever, yell in theaters, is both rough and hungry. When I slide a glance at him, he's staring at me and not the stage. Instead of looking away, I watch him back. He's right. This is so much better. The more he stares at me, the warmer I feel, as if something's filling inside of me with each breath I take.

"I'm okay." I motion vaguely toward the stage. "We should watch that."

He nods and pulls a face. He knows I'm lying. We really do have the best seats in the house. It's the kind of box that seems like it should belong to royalty. A shoulder-high wall separates us from the next box and we have six gilded, red velvet chairs all to ourselves. Despite the tiers of seats above and below us, it feels as if we're alone.

I do my best to lose myself in the music, which is glorious. I know Puccini's story ends tragically, the American naval officer betraying his geisha bride and irrevocably breaking her heart, but right now there is nothing but beauty and pleasure. The geisha bride and her new American husband sing about how they'll be reunited when the robins nest and they're just so happy that you have to smile. I sway in time to the music, bending toward the performers like an open flower in the sunshine.

Max trails his fingers down my neck. I love his hands. Like the rest of him, Max's hands are sure and confident, his hands callused and roughened by hours on a surfboard. If I close my eyes, I imagine I smell the sun and salt, the ocean and the wax he rubs on his board for speed.

He leans in more, his mouth brushing the sensitive spot behind my ear. "You smell amazing."

I whisper the words before I think. "Make me forget?"

Max doesn't miss a beat, doesn't ask why or what or how. He simply leans in more, his weight pressing against me, his mouth kissing my ear. I don't have the theater any more, but I have this. With a rough sound no one can hear but me because poor little Butterfly's husband is making more promises he has no intention of keeping, Max slides his hand over my knee.

The box to our right is empty.

The box to our left is rapt, their attention focused on the stage.

Max's hand skims further up my leg. I don't even know what I want. I'm afraid to demand specific things, to tell him this or that or more or even right now. When I look at Max, his eyes are dark, the lines of his mouth hungry and intent. He has a plan or a fantasy, and either is good enough for me. This is how I want to feel—alive and eager, my body anticipating the next move in our dance. What would he do? What could we do in a darkened theater? Max has an excellent imagination.

"May I?" he whispers.

"Hurry up."

Warm fingers wrap around mine and he takes my hand, pressing it against the front of his dress pants. He's hard, his dick arching against the fabric. I measure his length with his palm, squeezing gently. "You like me."

"Yes," he growls.

Yes.

This is a bad idea, the best worst idea ever. We're in a public theater for a highly publicized charity performance. There are photographers, guests, a thousand reasons I shouldn't do this—and two of the best reasons. Max. Me.

I meet those brown eyes that seem to see me in a way no one else ever has. He pays attention as if there's no detail too small or too silly about me. Everything matters. Madd never looked at me like this, as if I were interesting. As if he wanted to talk with me, touch me, be with me. As if just sitting here were enough. I know we're just friends with benefits, a casual hookup, but it feels like it's enough. As if I'm enough.

I move my hand, wrapping my fingers around his wrist, and pull his hand higher on my thigh. He lets me, his mouth easing into a smile that warms his eyes and turns up the corners of his lips.

"Touch me here."

I whisper the words, not because I'm ashamed but because the tenor onstage is crooning passionate words to his soprano, their voices filling up the immense space of the theater, and yet somehow even as they reach the back of the stalls, singing, soaring, they're quiet too. I move to their music, my body finding their rhythm as Max strokes the curve of my upper thigh with his thumb.

"Like this?" he asks. "Or higher?"

"Make me come."

His mouth brushes my jaw in a soft kiss. "Then watch the show."

My heart soars, leaping about my ribcage as if I'm about to take flight, to leap across the stage. This is a new piece for me, a dance I've never rehearsed, but the trick is to trust your partner when he lifts you. Max won't let me fall—or fail.

His hand moves higher, fingertips grazing the edge of my panties. When he slips beneath the lace, the ache between my legs grows worse.

"You like this." Max's voice is a low, whiskey growl in my ear. "Do you like the way I touch you? Or that all our neighbors have to do is stand up and they'll see you riding my hand in the theater? Or that no one knows, not really, what we're doing and that it's our dirty little secret?"

There's nothing to say because it's all true and maybe that makes me greedy, but it feels too good when Max touches me for it to be wrong. His arm presses against mine, his body shielding me from the audience on our left. I unbutton his pants, easing the zipper down. I take a brief second to be grateful for cotton boxers that open in the front and then I'm curling my fingers around him and stroking his bare flesh.

He eases my thighs apart, spreading me open, shoving my dress to my waist. Velvet brushes my bare skin like a thousand tiny, hungry tongues. I think I moan. I need more. I'm a swing pumping up toward the sky but there's still so much further to go.

He pushes a finger inside me and heat spirals through me, my body tightening around him. He makes me fly and I don't want to stop. I want everything he'll give me—and Max is infinitely generous. He explores me leisurely, slowly, surely. His fingertips glide up and down my slick folds, finding spots that make me see white or whimper or clutch at his dick as if it's the joystick for this wild, mad ride.

I forget to wonder who might see us. Later, I'll tell myself that it's okay if someone saw. I'll tell myself I love the thrill of being watched. But right now, I can only think about Max and how he makes me feel as he fingers me in the theater exactly right. I clutch his hand between my thighs, squeezing, riding him because we're both coming more than a little undone and it feels so good. Little sounds escape me and there's the unmistakable sound and scent of wetness. I'm not sure our dirty little secret's such a secret anymore because someone's head turns in the box next to ours but then I'm whispering words again. I'm coming. Right now. You too.

I know this is just a single moment, and I know that Max is as off-limits for me as Butterfly's naval officer is for her. Max will never be a forever man, but when he comes, his dick shoving against my palm as I squeeze, I feel happy.

Max

After the performance, we mingle in the lobby, where the caterers have set up a dessert and champagne bar. While I distract the event organizers from our opera box shenanigans with a generous donation and newfound passion for the opera, Maple loads up her clutch with a selection of finger pastries for

Lieutenant Bob. Apparently, she's come prepared and stashed empty plastic baggies in there.

Bob's properly appreciative when we deliver the goods, and then I walk Maple to her door. She's humming something I don't recognize.

I hum a bar with her. "Do you always have a playlist?"

"I like music, Max. Do you have something against *Romeo and Juliet*?"

"Isn't that the one where the guy loses his virginity and then promptly kills himself in a crypt because the dumbass can't tell that his girl isn't dead? Because that one makes me wonder just how bad our hero was in bed. I think you should pick something happier."

Maple laughs. "Do you have a suggestion?"

"My all-time favorite movie in high school was the one where Bo Derek does some naked horseback riding. I was too busy staring to pay attention, but if that scene had a soundtrack, that's the one I want."

Maple's still laughing when I kiss her.

FYI? I outkiss poor stupid, dead, cockblocked Romeo. Our mouths come to rest on each other gently and then we're kissing. It's sweet and slow, like one of those dreams where you're running but getting nowhere, the air a thick, sweet tether—but without the stress. We're getting somewhere, but neither of us is in any rush. I breathe in, she breathes out, and our kiss grows rougher as tongues and teeth come into play. I cup her head, holding her still so I can take her mouth, and she grinds up against me, doing some taking of her own, and fuck Romeo—we're going to have our very own happy ending right here, right now.

I tear my mouth free. I think I might be panting. "Can I come up?"

There's only one way this ends, right?

"I—"

"Maple?" Someone clears his throat. Loudly. Or maybe that's just Karma laughing her ass off at me.

Maple jerks back like she's been stung by a bee, except it's dark o'clock and bees prefer to shack up in their nice, cozy hives at night. It's a simple phototactic response. They gravitate toward the light.

Maple's brow furrows as she peers at the shadowy throat-clearer. "Madd?"

Of course she can identify him by basic biological responses, the cockblocker.

"I think we should talk," he says as he comes forward.

Talking is highly overrated, unless it's the kind of *yes please give me more* conversation Maple and I shared in our opera box tonight.

But Maple is staring at Madd and Madd's extending a plastic-wrapped, supermarket bouquet of pink flowers. I size up my competition: he's three inches shorter and wearing stupid chino pants and a green-and-white-checked shirt. He's pretty, though, with blond hair and ink covering his forearms and throat. That must have hurt and I'm glad. He deserves to suffer.

I stare at him, willing him to leave. Or to drop dead. I'm really not fussy. "What do you want?"

Madd doesn't take his eyes off Maple, which is a smart move. He's showing her that she's the focus of his world, which makes him a smart dick. "A second chance."

I swear I hear miniature violins playing a har-de-har-har chorus as he speaks. Is she really going to fall for this? When she and I could go upstairs and take our kissing to its logical conclusion?

In short: yes.

She pats me on the arm. "Thanks again."

And…that's it?

"Madd and I should talk—" she continues.

"Who's he?" Madd cuts her off.

I smirk. "Her date."

"My boyfriend," she says at the same time.

CHAPTER FIFTEEN

Maple
#plottwist #shakespearewouldbeproud #choices

LAST NIGHT WAS—well, I'm not exactly sure what to say about last night other than that it pretty much turned out *exactly* like Romeo and Juliet. There was gorgeous music, some fairly memorable speeches, orgasms for all, and then it all went to hell and no one ended up happy.

After Max reluctantly left, I dragged the box of Madd's leftover stuff down the stairs. Dealing with him feels like the dream where you suddenly realize it's the end of the college term and you haven't been to class once—but now you need to pass the class. I'm lost and running to keep up, but then I wake up and realize that it was just a dream.

We're not going to get back together.

We'll never be a couple.

I'm not going to score an A—and I don't care. I don't need to be who he wants me to be anymore.

I wake up—alone—the morning after my Madd showdown and wait to feel regret. It's like poking at the tooth that was sore for days or weeks and now there's no pain and it feels a bit like a miracle. Madd's flowers are in a vase on my bedside table. Which is also my kitchen table and my coffee table but… details. Perhaps I should have tossed the flowers in the dumpster, but I'm a sucker for hot pink stargazer lilies. Their gorgeous scent fills my studio. Someone's even snipped off the orange stamens that stain your fingers and clothes so that there's nothing to mar the pretty.

Madd himself? Well let's just say that I suspect his harem was about as happy as I was with his unwillingness to pick a partner. He's come back because I made him feel good and who doesn't like that? Plus, now that his new girl's kicked him to the curb, I'm useful again. Whatever. He may have traveled for business or been unhappy with his life or decided that I wasn't Ms. Perfect, but that didn't excuse his choice to cheat or to post our private video. This time, I want someone to choose *me.*

And speaking of choices?

Max has been a busy, busy boy. His latest text reads like the top ten from Kinkster, and let's just say he knows how to make his case. There's a reason (or nine) why he's the king of hookups.

Hey girlfriend. Choose the one place you'd really like to have sex:

1. Redwood Park. Big-ass Redwood trees, Jurassic Park-worthy ferns, and all the suits in the Transamerica Pyramid watching from their fancy building.

2. Greenhouse in the lobby of an office building.

3. Golden Gate Park. They've got a park, a conservatory and a beach.

4. Coit Tower. Come on—the name begs for it.

5. Muir Woods. Pick a tree. Any tree.

6. Quickie in the Japanese Tea Garden.

7. Baker Beach.

8. Sexy times walk in the Marin Headlands.

9. The Sutro Baths. No idea, but anything that rhymes with Kama Sutra has to be good.

I stare at my screen for way too long, imagining him writing this. I can see his face, intent on the screen, the little crinkle he gets between his eyebrows when he's working through a problem. Is he in his office even though it's Saturday? In his enormous bed in his even bigger, emptier Santa Cruz beach mansion? I've seen him naked now, so it's far too easy to dress him in a pair of faded blue jeans, feet bare, T-shirt gone so that I can mentally ogle his chest and remember what it felt like to anchor myself on his biceps.

Is he *serious*? I don't even know what some of those places are, but already I feel like we share a little secret. That I'll never see or hear those names again without thinking about having sex there. With *Max. God, he drives me a little crazy.*

Before I can remember the dozens—and dozens—of reasons why public sex is a bad idea, I'm committed.

Tell me about Golden Gate Park. Show me a secret part.

He texts back a map pin. Meet me at 3.

Living in San Francisco, you learn quickly that so many things are less romantic or glamorous than you believed. Fog is cold and damp. You have to step over passed-out alcoholics and the homeless in order to exit the train station, and there are so many of them that it gets harder and harder to remember that they're people, not obstacles. You see people doing things in the street—personal, private things—and sex is the least of it.

I know that meeting Max in a public place for sex isn't romantic. It won't be comfortable.

But I do think it will be exciting—and excitement is something that's been missing from my life for a long time. I've spent years dancing to other people's scripts, and while I couldn't see myself making a habit of hooking up in a public park, I want to do it. Maybe just this once or maybe twice or however many times we feel like it. I don't know how it will end, but it feels right. It feels like I'm finally embracing some part of myself that's been hiding in the wings, waiting for her cue to come center stage.

I roll onto my back, letting the phone slip beneath my covers. I can feel the broad smile stretching my lips, but there's no one here to see me grinning like a loon.

Light slips in through the windows, along with street sounds. San Francisco's awake even if I'm not. Sirens blare over the muted roar of cars; Bob's sorting cans in the alley between my house and the next. There's music from downstairs because my neighbor likes to salsa while she housecleans. Later there will be the rumble of delivery trucks and the barking call of the food vendors who trundle their carts up and down 16th Street offering churros, corn on the cob and lime-and-chili-flavored slices of watermelon.

Not ready to move yet, I trace my ribs with my fingertips, stroking up over my breasts and then down. Max O'Reilly is funny and he goes for what he wants. Not in a greedy, I-have-to-have-it-all way. It's more like he simply plans the shit out of his life and therefore gets more done than others.

Case in point? He has not one but two PhDs. Who needs more than one? Who has the *time*? He did his graduate work at the Berkeley campus of the University of California, where someone told him he could only enroll in one program because no one could possibly complete the dual coursework, let alone write two dissertations. Max's reaction was pretty much *watch me*. He lived on Red Bull. Lola says he never slept more than two hours in a row, so he didn't bother renting an apartment—he just moved from lab to library and back. Now he has PhDs in computer science and philosophy.

Three o'clock seems far away. To kill time, I force myself to get up. Max loves my "bendiness." I suspect he's had the usual fantasies about dating a gymnast but has decided that a ballet dancer works, too. He's right. As he's seen for himself, I can indeed put my leg behind my head.

I work through my usual morning barre routine on the tiny scrap of balcony in front of my studio. Since my apartment sits on a bit of a hill, I have a view of the opposite hillside and acres of pastel-colored houses and roofs. The BART train snakes through it all—and since I overslept this morning, the fog has mostly burned off already.

As I launch into a series of pliés and tendus, Lieutenant Bob waves up at me, off to do whatever it is he does when he's not sleeping in my driveway. Driveways are small and steep in this part of San Francisco. We curse the rare days when it rains because the water rolls down the eight feet or so of asphalt to decorate the garage floor. Bob doesn't seem to mind the slant, though, and since none of us has a car, everyone in the house has decided not to mind Bob.

He and Max seemed to hit it off. There's lots of lip service about the homeless in San Francisco, but few people go hands on. It's too easy sometimes to just think of Lieutenant Bob as part of the landscape rather than as a person. Not that I'm shooting for saintliness or anything remotely like it.

But Max took the time to chat with Bob, and I like that. Sure, Max is still the elusive, sometimes cranky, often filthy billionaire who likely has a higher IQ than all of NASA combined. He prefers watching, but he also likes to fix things and I suspect that he's slowly coming around to the idea that he and I are not a one-time thing. Not that we're a real couple, but I almost thought, given enough time and dirty texting, that we could be friends.

I bring up the last picture I took last night. In it, Max is leaning against the edge of our box, his hands in his pant pockets. He looks like a Silicon Valley James Bond in his expensive tux, rich, powerful, but still rough around the edges because he doesn't play by other people's rules. I'd been trying to play it cool, but it had been tough. Billionaires aren't part of my daily life, and just scoring the invitation to the charity performance had been huge. How I ended up, even temporarily, with a guy like Max is one of life's fabulous mysteries. I'm not sure he even realizes just how much of a unicorn he is. He knows he's good at his job and he has a pretty good idea of what he can do with that magic penis of his, but people look up to him for other reasons, too.

I want to reach right through the picture and lick him. He makes me laugh, he makes me come, he makes me feel as if when he looks at me, he sees *me*. I'm struck by that the most. I've spent all of my adult life dancing on stage, so I'm used to people watching me, but they saw only the character I was dancing. Between the costumes and the makeup, the sets and the lights, there was no way they saw me.

I think Max does.

Or at least as much as I've been willing to show him.

My finger hovers over the picture. I should post it to Instagram. My followers like frequent peeks at my personal life, and I follow the general rule of thumb of posting three parts promo to seven parts content. I show them what I eat, what I wear and how a ballerina works out. I let them follow me backstage, onstage—pretty much everywhere. That's life in the influencer fishbowl and I have no reason to think Max isn't aware of what I do. It's no secret.

And yet I sort of don't want to share him with my world. Max is mine. I scroll through the photo album on my phone. I don't have many pictures of him, but Max isn't the kind of guy to strike a pose. His poise on the red carpet last night surprised me.

He gave me a present—for no reason—and while I've never been a jewelry girl, I love my new bracelet. I feel my heart pick up its pace a little remembering the brush of his fingers against my wrist, his thumb tracing the pale blue veins beneath the fragile skin as he worked to do up the clasp. The car charm is to remember the opera, he'd said.

As if I could forget.

I'm humming a made-up tune patched together from my favorite ballets when I head into the steamy bathroom for a shower. It's silly, but I take a picture. Of me in my towel.

And I send it.

To Max.

I'm not completely naked because I've learned that lesson and I really don't know Max. Even if I am having fun *getting* to know him. I text.

See you at 3

CHAPTER SIXTEEN

Max

I spot Maple before she sees me. She's focused on her phone, following the map pin I texted her. Golden Gate Park covers more than a thousand acres. In addition to a network of roads and trails, there's a carousel, an aquarium, a museum and multiple flower gardens—all teeming with San Franciscans determined to enjoy a Saturday outdoors. She'd never find me without a specific point to meet.

The July weather is a sticky, humid weight against my skin, but Maple makes everything better. Her yellow sundress with the white polka dots is like a walking, bouncing ray of sunshine, although she's caved to the practicalities of a park meetup and chosen practical white canvas sneakers. An enormous straw tote bag bangs against her hip as she walks and she's pulled her hair back in a high ponytail that swishes from one shoulder to the next.

She has the exotic walk of a dancer, legs turned

out ever so slightly. I almost forget to breathe watching her. She's strong, the skin exposed by her dress sun-kissed and lean. Dancing burns a ton of calories, plus the girls are encouraged to keep themselves skinny because their partners have to hoist them overhead. That's one thing Maple said she didn't miss about the ballet world, the constant focus on how much a dancer weighs. I don't get it because she looks amazing and I think everyone should eat, but she just said that I'd never had to leap in circles while holding another dancer over my head and that I'd feel differently about those five pounds if I did.

She looks up from her phone and spots me, her face breaking into a smile. She looks so happy that I pull out my phone so I can relive the moment later. And when she swats my phone away, I pull her into me for a slow kiss. We have hours. I don't have to rush.

"Have you done this before?" I ask when we come up for air. Her pretty mouth is pink and swollen, her lips parted and damp. I've left my mark on her.

And then I realize that I've been so busy staring at the visible signs of our kiss that I've entirely missed her answer. I lean down and brush a kiss over her cheekbone. She has a freckle there, half-hidden by her hair. "Tell me again?"

She pinches my ass. "I'm a park virgin."

I know she hasn't had as much sex as I have, but even if it makes me a caveman, I like the idea of being her first. *And best.* I table that thought for later. Right now I have a fantasy to deliver.

"Would you rather have a bed?" She shouldn't do anything she doesn't want to do. Or, rather, she should do as *much* as she wants. It's like the eating thing. She's never going hungry again on my watch.

She pinches my ass again. "You promised me a fantasy." Apparently she's determined to drive me crazy, because she leans up on tiptoe, her mouth brushing my neck. "I'm not wearing any panties. I figured that would make things easier."

Well, fuck. I grab her hand and pull her across the grass and toward a clump of Monterey pines on the far side of a duck-filled pond. There's tons of cover here, including a faux Greek ruin, a genuine folly like the kind you find in a Jane Austen novel. Cover seems important because while lots of people have sex in Golden Gate Park on a regular basis, I don't think Maple truly wants to get caught. The possibility might be exciting, but getting busted by a cop and then dealing with a ticket or worse? Not so fun. Ask me how I know.

Or don't.

That's okay. I don't want to think about anyone other than Maple today. When I unfold my brand-new picnic blanket, Maple's watching me, her cheeks pink, her smile growing. I can almost see the happy, dirty, playful thoughts tumbling through her head. *She's so gorgeous*, I think, and wonder why we're out here, about to have an afternoon quickie instead of taking our time in my bed or hers. I could strip her down if we were alone. I could make her scream. I could break through that ever-so-slight reserve that whispers to me that she's still on guard and that she still doesn't trust me, not one hundred percent.

Her smile gets broader when she pushes me onto my back. It's a game, obviously, because I'm a big guy and she can't force me, but I take her love tap and flop down obediently.

"Taking charge, are we?" I give her a mock-stern look and open my arms wide. "So come and take me."

She drops down onto me gracefully. I wonder if she was ever awkward when it comes to moving and knowing how to propel her body from one point to another. Is it something they teach in ballet schools or was she born that way?

Laughing, she leans down, planting her hands on either side of my head. We did it like this at my house, my brain reminds me. I should make this different. Make it better.

"You're the expert," she whispers. "Now show me what you like to do outside."

We kiss for a long while, my hand sliding up underneath her dress. She wasn't lying—she's not wearing panties. I'm content not to rush at first, stroking the soft curves and then delving deeper. She's just starting to make those happy moans I love so much when there's a suspicious rustling in the bushes. Maple jumps to her feet, her hands abandoning the buttons of my jeans. A black Lab bursts through the shrubs. A guy calls in the not-so-distant distance and the dog abandons us.

When she laughs, I stand up, lifting her into my arms so that her bare legs are wrapped around my waist. We kiss like that, swaying together to some music she can hear and that she's making me feel. I'm not really into dancing, but this is good.

Except then the homeless guy wanders through. He's not quite all on planet Earth—based on his one-sided conversation with invisible alien overlords—but he notices enough to give me a thumbs-up.

Maple buries her face in my throat, shaking with silent laughter. "I can't. We're going to end up on *America's Funniest Home Sex Videos.*"

It's funny and awkward and strangely hot. I've never laughed with any of my hookups before. Or with a lover. Maple is dying as she points out a very suspicious pile of trash in the bushes. I don't think our hookup spot is as exclusive as I'd thought.

But the day's fucking gorgeous and the sun's warm. It would be a shame to waste it. I can smell roses somewhere, and the ocean. There are palm trees not too far away, and some tall, pink and white spikey plants that I'll google later because they'll have a name. The dog reappears.

"Plan B," I tell her, dropping us down onto the picnic blanket.

As my fingers fly over my phone, she leans back, one arm braced around my neck, the other arched over her head as if she was trying to hold a balloon. Sunlight dances over her face.

"You could take over the world with your *hardware*." Her voice sounds dreamy and sun-drenched. There's an unmistakable note of happy laughter beneath the words.

After I've made a strategic donation and pulled some strings, I dash with her across the park and into a back entrance of the conservatory. The conservatory has glass windows and hothouse heating for all the flowers it nurtures. Plus, it's a popular spot so as I make love to Maple, there's always a murmur of voices and the erotic threat of discovery. She likes it.

A lot.

CHAPTER SEVENTEEN

Maple
#f #beachgoddess #sunsetlover

"SUNSETS ARE DAMNED inconvenient. Always on a schedule." Max has only just rolled out of bed, which he blames on me jumping him. I blame his bizarre sleep schedule on too much work *and* too much fun. Two weeks after our park tryst, we've managed to have sex in a Porsche, christened every room in the swank penthouse he just purchased, and made an acrobatic attempt at sex in the penthouse's elevator (Max should have picked a taller building because we ran out of time).

"It's your fault we're late." I resist the urge—*just*—to smack his butt as he tugs me down the steps to the beach below his house. Honestly, his butt's a thing of beauty in faded blue jeans but I've already left scratches on said ass because the man is insatiable and said insatiability makes me crazy and one thing leads to another and…

Naked things.

Lots and lots of naked things, which now puts us at risk of missing the famous Santa Cruz sunset. I'm not sure whose idea it was to watch it armed with champagne, but Max isn't giving up easily. He's stubborn.

"I'm not the one who took fourteen minutes to come." Nope. He's not willing to let it go. He'd chased down my third orgasm with the same delicious tenacity when I'd claimed I was too tired to come anymore without permanent injury to my vagina. He may also have promised to kiss everything better later if it turned out I was right and certain parts of me were sore.

"Once again, I blame you." True story.

He swings around and has me up against the railing before I can squeak. Not that I'm complaining. Max has a gorgeous body, and his front is every bit as drool-worthy as his back. I hook a bare leg around the back of his thigh and pull him closer still because maybe I'll have found my second wind by the time we get back to his place. Undoubtedly, I'll be ready to jump him again. The man is more addictive than online shopping.

The gleam in his eyes is all the warning I get before the cold champagne bottle brushes against my boobs. My nipples pebble. I shove it away, but then he leans down and kisses me, which is a problem because once he starts, I never want him to stop. He presses his mouth to my lips, tasting me, and I breathe him in. Our lips slide over each other, nipping, pulling, making room for ourselves because this feeling between us never stays small.

I pull, he tugs, and I forget all about standing on a staircase and the ocean at our feet. There's just Max and me. I want to eat him up and make him part of me. I want to freeze this moment in time so I can hold on to it and bring it out and relive it in the years to come. A seagull screeches overhead and the moment winks out of my grasp like soap bubbles from a magic wand.

"Come on." He tugs me down the steps. "We're almost there."

I'd follow you straight to the gates of hell, I think.

Which is stupid because that isn't what Max wants from me.

So instead I tag along on his heels to the beach below his house. I cradle our champagne in one arm and hold on to him with the other, our palms touching, our fingers entwined. It's the perfect recipe for romance except that we aren't alone.

In theory, the beach is private, but this is California. Both water and sand are public access up to the high-tide line, so this isn't the first time we've discovered random strangers on the sand or riding the waves. My gaze flickers to Max. I think I want him to be disappointed, too, but I also suspect that he's making this romantic gesture for me because he thinks it's what I need. He'd have been happy to stay in bed having hot, dirty sex over and over again.

"Someone stole our idea." I pass the champagne bottle to Max. He has all those delicious muscles—he can carry it.

"What gave it away?"

I expect him to make a dirty joke about the remnants of someone else's romantic picnic spread out on our beach. In addition to a sandy, rumpled plaid blanket, there's an empty wine bottle spiked in the sand and abandoned shoes. When I look closer, I spot a familiar bikini top. I gave it to Lola when I was sent a box of swimwear to promote on Instagram. A girl can only wear so many.

I look around but neither Lola nor Dev are anywhere in sight on the beach. The two of them are cute, almost permanently joined at the hip like Japanese beetles or bunnies, so they must be here somewhere.

Laughter floats across the water—*bingo.* They've paddled way out, presumably on Dev's surfboard, and now they're wrapped around each other, doing who knows what. Okay. I suspect I know *exactly* what. The board rocks wildly, followed by more laughter.

"God. Tell me they're not—"

Max assesses the situation. "Not."

Thank God.

I walked in on Lola and Dev once. Part of it was my fault. I was used to doing the knock-and-enter when I stopped by Lola's. It had never been a problem before, but on that particular occasion I'd seen more of Dev than I should have. And let me tell you: the man had a mighty fine ass and absolutely nothing to be ashamed of. I'd pretended an immediate and highly specific case of amnesia and vowed to wait for a hearty "come in" after that. I'm not sure what they expected when they decided to have sex on the beach.

Not that Max and I have pure intentions ourselves. Since the night of his pop-up party, when we dared each other into hooking up, I've had fond memories of this beach. I usually come down whenever I spend the night—or the afternoon or the morning—at Max's place. The ocean is amazing, even if the temperature never seems to get much above freezing. Max says I exaggerate and that the average temperature is a refreshing fifty-seven degrees Fahrenheit.

Something flares to life on the surfboard and, no, that's not a euphemism. It looks like Dev has somehow transported a sparkler out there, the kind of cheap but fun firework that you can buy year-round in the groceries in the Mission District. I wonder why he'd be doing something that seems doomed to failure—water and fire not mixing well—but the shrieking and rocking distract me.

I definitely don't want to know what they're doing.

Since I deserve a consolation prize, I grab the bottle from Max and plop down on Lola's blanket. We've missed the best part of the sunset anyhow and the sun is dropping rapidly now beneath the horizon, pink and yellow streaking the sky in broad, colorful bands. I lean back against Max, using his legs as a backrest while I try to sort through my feelings.

His hand plays with my hair, finding all the stress points in my scalp. Or maybe they're chakras? Whatever, it feels good. The man is talented. But with the pleasure comes the usual doubt. He makes me happy, but do I do the same for him? Am I doing enough or am I just taking, taking, taking—and eventually he'll have had enough and leave?

Lola and Dev reach the shore before I achieve any sort of epiphany. They wear matching black wetsuits, although Dev has unzipped his and tied it around his waist. I try not to stare too hard but the man is seriously built.

"You need to model your wetsuit for me," I whisper, leaning harder into Max's touch. I'll do something nice for him when we get back to his place. A blow job or some sexy naked dancing. Something memorable. Max's low grunt of amusement floats down to me.

Because…

Dev is grinning like a madman as he leaps off the board, swinging Lola around in an ungraceful little circle. She's shrieking and Dev's victory pumping her fist, turning it so we can see what he was really up to out there. It's so obvious that I'm almost blinded.

Lola has a diamond. A big, canary yellow diamond surrounded by the cutest baby diamonds on a gold band. They're *engaged.*

I bolt off the blanket because engagements call for hugs and champagne, and I have both to offer. Lola and I might do some happy dancing as we hug it out, too. Not that I'd want my man to pop the question on a surfboard—that seems super risky. What if he dropped the ring? Or a fish bumped the board? Or a seagull crapped on them? These things happen all the time.

Max and Dev exchange good-natured jibes and backslapping hugs. I know Max isn't one hundred percent happy with the way his friends are settling down around him, but you wouldn't know it to look at him.

"Your turn." Lola points her ring finger at me as if she's gained a magic wand rather than a ridiculously expensive piece of jewelry. I'll bet Max is making sure Dev has it insured. "I know you said you weren't ready but—"

I'm still not. "I'm not interested."

"You don't get to be not interested when the right man shows up. You could take Max." She waggles her eyebrows in his direction.

"Please," I scoff. "He's the hookup king. The only ring he's going to put on it is a cock ring."

"Why not?" Lola frowns. "You guys are the only ones left except for maybe Jack's business partner."

It's like being the last kid picked for dodgeball.

"You think he wants to get married?"

"Have you asked him?"

"We're opposites," I protest. "It would take a year just to sign the prenup!"

Plus, I'm totally not interested in marriage.

Lola looks mulish. "I think you guys would be great together."

"Right. Let's imagine how this would go. I drop to one knee and I say, 'Max, will you marry me?'" I hit the sand on my knees to make my point—dramatic embellishments always help sell the story. "And then he reminds me that he's all about the hookup. Why on earth would I want to go there?"

Lola bites her lip.

Oh boy.

I turn my head, and sure enough, Max is standing on the sand behind me. Is this where I say I didn't really mean it? Do you think his feelings were hurt?

No.

Me, neither.

Jack steps off the stairs and onto the beach. "What did I miss?"

"Lola's trying to sell me to the highest bidder," Max says drily. "But she set the opening bid too high."

CHAPTER EIGHTEEN

Maple
#rockyroad #guiltypleasures

IN THE WEEKS that followed Lola and Dev's engagement, I expect something to change, but nothing does. Max and I spend most of the nights together. We may have started out as a hookup, but now? Now I don't have a clue, although it doesn't take a rocket scientist to figure out that Max has never had a relationship in his life.

Item: He wrote a hookup app so an algorithm picked out his perfect match.

Item: He let a million billion strangers use it.

Item: And then when he was filthy rich because everyone wanted to throw cash at their dating problems, he had women (and men) throwing themselves at him because filthy rich plus mad bedroom skills makes Max a very, very popular boy.

It's hard not to resent that, even if he claims he doesn't even notice it happening anymore. When he attends industry events, business meetings or even the Whole Foods grocery because he needs beer, bread or toilet paper, women come up to him. They give him their numbers or offer to send pictures, all while making dirty suggestions in the produce aisle. He dismisses it as the side effect of the billion dollars. In Max's world, money is the ultimate aphrodisiac and if he was broke, he'd be able to pick out tomatoes unmolested.

I'm not sure he's right, but a controlled, scientific A/B study isn't possible. Max is super careful with the billion dollars. This is a guy, after all, who plans everything, up to and including an orderly, aisle-by-aisle assault on the grocery store. There's no way he'd lose a fortune...and *that* is why women hunt him down in public like he's the last lion or bear or unicorn. For all his bad boy, dirty sex outside, the Max inside is safe. More important, he keeps the small handful of people he cares about safe.

I, on the other hand, barely have a nodding acquaintance with *safe*, as my dating history bears witness. My high school boyfriend loved dirt bikes and race cars. He sped through life, and giving him my virginity was simply another speed bump he flew over with reckless disregard. We had sex on the hood of his car, and I was pretty sure he was already thinking about his next race and his next track bunny before he pulled out.

My second boyfriend was a fellow dancer I met as an apprentice at the New York City Ballet. He up and left when he got offered a company position in Moscow. I maxed out my credit card to pay him a surprise visit, but the surprise was on me as I discovered him in bed with not one but two dancers. My dreams of monogamy and happily-ever-after dashed, I raced back to New York.

And then there was Madd.

Madd who I'd been ready to propose to and who'd also decided that I wasn't enough.

My man picker clearly needed a reboot, so it was a wonder that I'd hooked up with Max. Or maybe that was why we were together—because he'd made it perfectly clear from the very beginning that he never, ever did long-term relationships. He hooked up. He moved on. I was the one tempted to linger.

Max and I? We aren't a real couple.

Someday soon, he'll stop texting or I will, and then we'll be done, too.

I don't know who he is, not really, not any more than he knows who I am. I know the superficial things, like the drink he's most likely to order (or not) from a bar menu. I know the names of his favorite beaches and that if there was a surf competition, he wouldn't be in it but he would be part of the security patrol zipping up and down the waves on Jet Skis and keeping things safe for everyone. I know he buys Fruit of the Loom cotton boxers and white Champion tube socks in a twelve-pack because that's what he's always worn and if it isn't broken, he doesn't fix it.

I know *exactly* how he likes his sex—and that I love it the same way, too.

But I don't know the big things.

Or what goes on inside his head.

What scares him.

Or what he loves.

It isn't just that we come from different worlds, or that his bank balance has far, far more zeroes than mine does. He lives his life shields up, shutting everyone and every intimate emotion out, and I understand that—even as I want to get inside him while keeping myself private. I could have feelings for him. Like greedy, greedy Icarus, not content to fly, I have to soar higher and higher, closer and closer to the one thing I've been told repeatedly is off-limits.

But—even though I know our breakup is coming more inevitably than Monday morning after Sunday—I am still glad when my phone buzzes with an incoming text. Are you free tonight?

Yes, I am.

CHAPTER NINETEEN

Max

THREE WEEKS AFTER Lola and Dev spring their engagement on us, Maple informs me that she has a charity event and that, as her faux boyfriend, I'm obliged to be her date. It's one of those dinner-and-silent-auction nights, the kind that requires an entire ballroom full of crystal-and-flower-heavy tables seated with a guest list of San Francisco's most influential and charitable. Maple's table is hosted by a company that designs yoga leggings in fun prints for jet-setting around the world, and tonight is apparently Maple's in-person audition to partner with their brand. If I think about it too hard, I sort of want to sabotage her success—because there's no question that she wins them over—because at some point she won't need a faux boyfriend anymore. People will forget about the video, they'll remember all the amazing, awesome things she's done, and then we'll be over.

No doubt I'll be glad to have my old, carefree life back, but right now I curse the yoga people.

The event has a faux red carpet so guests can feel special while hired paparazzi snap hundreds of pictures, most of which will go unused. As soon as I help Maple out of the car, the flashes start going off as the photographers call our names. *Maple, Max—over here please. Max, this way. Max, do you have any comment on your relationship? Are you planning to propose?* I ignore the questions because responding is like tossing chum into a boiling sea of sharks. They'll run with whatever I say—and by tomorrow at the latest, Maple will have married me in a Fijian elopement because she's pregnant with my triplets. I've seen it happen too many times to subject her to that kind of scrutiny. Plus, then her dancing video will definitely resurface. Someone will have made a screen capture, Madd will have another copy, or someone will hack Kinkster's backups.

Instead, I concentrate on where my hand rests on the small of her back, in a polite, public touch. My body can't forget the feel of hers, the lightning connection we have, the smell of her skin on mine, on my sheets, on everything. *God, she's amazing.* If I don't start thinking about unpleasant things like tax returns and trying to get through to my airline's online call center, my hard-on will be immortalized by the paparazzi forever.

So naturally, I just have to lean in and whisper, "Are you wearing panties?" You never know with

Maple. The answer is sometimes *yes*—and sometimes *no.* I've been looking forward to finding out ever since she waltzed down her stairs to join me in the car.

Going all in because, hello, *job interview*, I'd also arranged for a stylist for tonight. The woman had called in five dresses from high-end local designers. Maple claimed it was just like every *Pretty Woman* fantasy she'd ever had, except that she'd be putting out for me and not Richard Gere. The dress she'd eventually settled on is actually a skirt, a blue, floaty number with layers and layers of tulle net that filled up the car and conveniently hide my boner from the photographers. The top is a close-fitting bandeau that leaves teasing glimpses of her belly on display. Her blond hair is pulled up into a long, sleek ponytail that brushes her shoulders and calls attention to the fortune in loaner diamonds the stylist arranged to borrow. When I told Maple she didn't have to give them back, she announced I was crazy, which really meant *hell, no.* But Maple and diamonds need to happen more than just this once. My new favorite mental image is of her naked in my bed, wearing a diamond tiara. Or one of those dog collar things.

She did let me give her a new charm for her bracelet, which I put in the win column. I'd picked out a diamond that belonged once upon a time to a Russian empress. When I think of Russia, I think of ballet—and ballet always makes me think of Maple.

The charity dinner itself is stuffy and loaded with

pretentious people. While Maple networks, I do my best to smile and look like I'm not bored while I mentally draw wireframes for a new app. It has to be able to handle hundreds of thousands of simultaneous users because delayed gratification is only fun when we're talking orgasms. Occasionally, I glance around the table. The pair from the yoga company hang on Maple's every word, which I take as a good sign.

Getting into the limo to go home is a relief. I tug her into my side and slip an arm around her shoulders—*nice*—since she ruled out sitting on my lap in a moving vehicle weeks ago—*safety hazard.* I can still kiss her like this, but I've barely pressed my mouth against the soft skin of her throat when she starts talking. From her point of view, it's been a great night already. The yoga legging people loved her and have hinted they'll be sending a contract for her to review. She's not sure whether it's the international travel gig she covets the most, or if it's a smaller campaign, and she doesn't want to count unhatched chickens and yet... Excited words spill out of her mouth one after the other, so block after block slips by while she talks—and yawns.

"Sorry," she mumbles eventually. "Too many late nights."

I know she's been working hard to rebuild her influencer gig after the video catastrophe. She signed with a new agent last week and already booked two smaller campaigns for something called a "bag spill" that sounds suspiciously like tipping out the contents of her purse and snapping pictures of the artistically arranged mess. Whatever. It doesn't matter that I'd personally rather stand naked on a BART train during rush hour than prance around a studio letting a photographer take shots of me. Lots of people find programming mind-numbingly boring, so if your passion also pays your bills and you aren't literally prostituting yourself, it's all good.

"Do you want me to take you home?" I'd been planning to take her back to my new penthouse condo and break in the dining room table, but I'm up for a change in plans.

"Do you mind?" She snuggles down into my chest.

"Your wish is my command." I can hear her breathing growing slower and deeper as she relaxes into me. I run a hand down her ponytail, fisting the soft length. "Are we playing *Sleeping Beauty* tonight?"

She hums something that might be a bit of the music from dinner but we're already turning on to her street. I'd hoped we could spend the rest of the night having sex together. Actually, I'd looked forward to round two of truth or dare but I clearly have to rethink that plan. I get out of the car and hold the door for her as she gathers up her monster skirts, finds her feet and gets out.

I steer her to the door, kiss her one more time, and then force myself to let go. We still have time left before we fake break up with each other and go back to our regular lives. I want to spend all of those hours with her, however many or few there are. I don't want to go back to being pre-Maple Max.

I think she's about to head up the stairs like she always does, but then she hesitates and turns brown eyes up to me. "Do you want to come up? You're welcome to crash and then I'll make it up to you in the morning." She leans up and brushes her mouth over mine. "No pressure if you want to get going. I can go up and go to sleep."

I thread my fingers through hers. "Lead on, Macduff."

She winks at me and opens the door. The house is a San Franciscan Victorian, so there are a *lot* of stairs. Plus, Maple's designer dress isn't made for a narrow stairwell. She finally settles for hiking it almost up to her waist, which is downright cruel. I follow her, eyes glued to her ass. She's wearing panties—almost. I'm not sure the green thong with white polka-dots qualifies as underwear.

When we reach the top of the house, she hesitates. "The housekeeper comes never. Because I don't actually have one."

"Uh-huh." I'm not interested in sleeping with the housekeeper.

She doesn't move. "So I'm a bit of a slob."

"Okay?" How bad can she be?

"If you promise not to judge me, I promise to wake you up with a blow job tomorrow." Maple gives a jaw-cracking yawn and shoves her key in the lock.

As if I care about her housekeeping skills. I close my hand over hers and turn the key. The door opens and I get my first idea what she's on about. Maple has a lot of…stuff. Not that she's a hoarder (yet), but she has piles and piles of things stacked up around the room. Because it's a studio, what you see is almost entirely what you get.

The bones are good. The room has a high, vaulted ceiling and a tiny French balcony with big glass doors. It's just that you don't notice those things because…stuff. Clothing racks line one wall and black lacquer bookcases with crystal doorknobs front the other. There's also a miniscule galley kitchen and a door that must lead to the bathroom.

She jumps onto the bed with a groan of relief. Or at least I assume it's the bed—whatever it is, it's buried in faux fur blankets (because I've yet to meet a lavender mink) and pillows. Her heels go first and then she starts wiggling her way out of her dress. She's asleep halfway through, so I finish undressing her, tuck her in and crawl in beside her.

I wake up to find Maple curled up in bed beside me, eyes glue to her phone.

"They offered," she says, turning the phone around so I can skim the email.

Remember when I said I only wanted the best for her? Yeah. Me, too. There's only one thing to say, so I say it. "Congratulations."

"I'm going to travel the world." Maple flops back

on the bed. At some point during the night, she's gotten up, because now she's wearing my dress shirt. It looks far better on her than it ever did on me, or maybe it's the deep V that frames her breasts. She scissors her legs into the air, kicking gleefully.

"They're going to *pay* me," she continues. "I'm going to design a capsule collection for them."

Ask a question. Show interest, you idiot. "When do you leave?"

"Next week."

She rolls over onto her stomach, her fingers touching the screen of her phone as if she needs that contact to believe it's true. Her voice is happy. Excited. She's looking at her perfect future and there doesn't appear to be a place for me in it. It's not that I was expecting forever or promises or a ring. I'm not that man, even though she's definitely that woman, and I know this is the end for us. I should say something, but I don't know where to start.

So instead I show her how I feel.

I straddle her butt and legs, running my hands down the length of her spine to work out the knots.

Say something.

Don't let her go.

Selfishly, I want one more memory, one more time. So I lean down and kiss her neck and shoulder. The straight, proud line of her spine and the dimples just above her ass. And then I go lower, giving her the very best, very dirtiest sex I can think of.

Giving her memories.

And when she's moaning face-first into the sheets, my face buried between her legs, I show her everything I'm feeling, everything I have no words for.

Give it to me.

Let go.

Let me—

"I love this." She gasps the words out and that's my greenlight to give her more until she's hollering my name, fingers digging into the sheets, and I slide into her from behind.

We don't have to say goodbye.

Not yet.

CHAPTER TWENTY

Max

I DON'T FEEL RIGHT. I wander from room to room in my Santa Cruz place. I could assemble some of the furniture that's still in fourteen boxes in my dining room. Maple left before we could put that stuff together. If I'm not in the mood for some Allen wrench action, I could change up the line of orderly soldier pillows marching across my ten-foot leather couch with the stupid hairpin legs. The blue pillow could go next to the new brown pillow. Or the white with the crocheted lumps on the front. I bought two leather pillows, as well. So many choices. Life's exciting at Chez Max's. Noise, noise, noise.

You know what's wrong with me?

Not the flu.

Not Ebola.

Nothing that antibiotics can cure.

I have a bad case of the Maples. That's not me, this mopey, sad llama who works a record number of hours and doesn't even bother to count them. That's not my life. The one where I work ten-hour days and divide the rest evenly between sleeping, surfing and fucking, with the occasional well-timed break for personal hygiene. I'm the Jedi Master of productivity—or I was.

Maple.

Maple Maple Maple Maple. If I say it fast enough and often enough, the words blur together until I sound like a drunk. I'd never understood what made two people decide that they were it for each other, that one person was enough—more than enough—for the next sixty, seventy or infinity years. Maple and I agreed—we were just a hookup—so why did I want to change the rules of the game now?

How long until I'm over her? Two hours, two days, two months? I don't think I can handle much more. I have deadlines, a company to run, a life to get on with. And yet, I'm moping around my house, online shopping for pillows I don't need, doing nothing. It's annoying.

This is why I'm out on my board, in the dark. Surfing in the daylight is too easy. Sharks? Jagged rocks? Skull-cracking meet and greet with the ocean floor? Pfft. Bring it on. Surfing at night is risky, but so is life. There are variables in the ocean—shifting light, rogue waves, a rock I didn't know was there. But since there's a full moon tonight and I can't sleep and don't want to code, I'm out here. Frigging moonlight spilling over the water makes it almost too easy.

I blame all that light for Jack showing up beside me. So much for hiding out. I ignore him and sit there on my board, rocking gently up and down. A tsunami would be good right about now. A hurricane. Anything to stir things up and get them moving.

"Hey," he says finally.

I eye the ocean, but there's nothing worth the risk of riding, not yet. It's all baby waves when I want a huge, epic wave, the kind that hammers you into the ocean floor if you make the wrong move but that also promises the ride of a lifetime.

"You want to talk about her?"

Notice that he doesn't say *it*. He goes straight for the jugular and the elephant in the room. Ocean. Whatever.

And… I cave.

"How did you know with Molly?"

"That we were in love?" Jack sizes up the wave rolling toward us. It's not bad, but not worth riding.

"Sure." I shift on my board. "Tell me your firsts. The first moment you knew you loved her. The first time you asked her to marry you. The first time you realized that forever didn't seem like too long."

"You know how we met." Jack glances at something swimming beneath us. It doesn't come equipped with a dorsal fin, so no worries. "College keg party. She wasn't a fan of cheap beer in a can, so I volunteered to fetch her something else. Since I wasn't of legal buying age, it took a couple of hours to hack a fake ID. She'd left the party by the time I came back, so I tracked her down and convinced her to drink mimosas on the beach with me and watch the sunrise."

It's silly and probably cute, but I don't understand what made it work. Clarification is in order. "And that's when you knew?"

He rolls his shoulders. "It's not a checklist kind of thing, Max, or an array that you feed numbers into to get the predicted output. We met and then there was just something about Molly that made me look twice."

"I looked twice." Still waiting for that tsunami, FYI.

"At?"

"At someone else." No wonder Catholics go to confession in those booths. There's no way I look Jack in the eye right now. "I fell in love with her. Maybe. How do I know?"

He doesn't give me shit, but he doesn't start laying out a ten-step plan, either. Jack fixes things. He takes broken, inefficient, jacked-up companies and he turns them into first-class performers. I'd appreciate it if he could work that magic on me, but instead he just stacks his hands behind his head and gives me a once-over.

"Give me the list," he says. "The Ten Things I Love about Maple."

I can give him the first ten things, the ten things I thought about today, the ten things I love but that also make me want to move to Canada or pull my hair out. But just ten? That's the impossible task. So I deflect.

"What's on your list?"

"For the record," he says, "things aren't so good between Molly and me."

"That sucks."

Not profound enough for you? It's heartfelt. Accurate. I mean, there's nothing you can say when someone's raked over by their relationship. To extend the analogy, Jack is getting his ass pounded by some pretty powerful waves as he fights to paddle out and catch a wave. And that sucks and we both know it.

The incoming wave is beautiful. The peak breaks to the left in the moonlight and there's room enough for both of us to ride, although we'll have to ride in opposite directions.

"Give me a list," he says again, his eyes on the wave. He wants to ride it, too. "Stop standing on the side of the pool holding your dick because you're too chickenshit to engage. Jump. You remember the night you lost your virginity?"

"Afternoon," I correct, "and you want me to think about another woman *now*?"

He ignores me. "That was all about your dick. Sure, you popped that cherry, but that was just sex. You've never had a relationship, so Maple is your first."

A relationship virgin? I suppose it's possible. I laugh.

"So you think I should give it up?"

He starts paddling toward the right side of the wave. "I think you should ask yourself why you're holding on to your cherry. Who are you saving yourself for?"

Is it PC? No. We're guys. Cut us some slack.

I think about it as I paddle hard toward the left side of the wave. Remember that list I made the day I met Maple? The things I was so sure I knew about her? It wasn't complete. I didn't know *her* then. All I had was a list of facts, which was like having the dots for a puzzle but no pencil. I didn't know how to connect them.

The wave's breaking in the center now and it's a thing of beauty. I explode onto my feet, pushing up off the board and finding my center. The night-dark ocean stretches out in front of me as I fly toward the beach, board skimming the wave.

I know so much more now.

1. Maple takes pictures so she can't forget.

2. Sometimes Maple hides behind her clothes.

3. Maple worries that she isn't enough.

4. She worries that she weighs too much and her partner won't be able to lift her—and that's a metaphor.

5. She loves to go barefoot.

6. She hums when she's thinking. Or sad. Or happy. Pretty much all the time.

7. She needs more puppies and kittens in her life. I don't know how she feels about babies, but I want to ask. I want to give her the family she dreams about, but I need to listen first. I need to hear what she wants.

8. She's run four thousand miles away.

9. She's amazing in bed, but she's equally amazing out of it.

10. I never want to stop this.

The wave peters out and I glide toward shore. It's that last one, good old number ten, that sticks in my head. Okay, I'm not exactly forgetting number nine, either, but I'm an excellent multitasker.

All I need is a plan.

And a plane ticket.

CHAPTER TWENTY-ONE

Maple
#meetmeinparadise #livingmybestlife #iaorana

Tahiti and me? It's love at first sight. When I stagger off the nine-hour flight from Los Angeles, the sky is dark and a rainstorm has just passed through. The tarmac beneath my sneakers breathes that wet, lush scent of asphalt into the air. And then when I breathe in, there are flowers. So many flowers.

The lines that form for immigration snake outside the tiny airport, but I don't care because there's drumming and singing, two sarong-wrapped, floral-shirt-wearing men banging out a primal rhythm as they sing that's echoed faintly by the ocean drumming on the reef close by. The unfamiliar words of a love song wash over me. I can't tell if they're happy or sad, but they're beautiful.

As is the dancer.

Did you think I'd miss her?

Barefoot, wearing a long grass skirt and one of

those ridiculous coconut shell bras, she dances joyfully, arms extended, feet moving in ancient patterns. Someone's dressed her up to match the postcards, but her long, dark hair ripples down her back as she moves, lost in her own world.

She's neither young nor skinny and most of her audience is jostling for position in the immigration queues, but she dances with undeniable magic. I stand there until the line's almost gone, watching, learning, smiling. My first instinct is to text Max a picture, which is when I remember that there are four thousand miles (and more) between us. I still take my phone out, though, checking to make sure that it's no longer set to airplane mode and that it's picked up the local cell phone service.

I have new messages from Lola and my agent.

But not Max.

Because we're not a couple. We were definitely nothing like the endless line of honeymooners or even the slightly lumpy American couple in khakis and polo shirts bringing up the rear of the line. They're bickering quietly, passing bags back and forth while they search for something. And whatever it is—a pen, the passports, the extra jackets she brought for the plane or the new camera he bought on impulse in the duty-free—they eventually find it and he slides an arm around her shoulders and she leans into him while they wait their turn. They look happy.

I mouth a thank-you to the dancer and move on. I have a job to do.

When I wake up the next morning, my hotel room's so close to the ocean that salt spray lands on my deck. Dark blue water rolls away in the bay, and a few miles away, on the other side of the fringing reef, there's a second jewel-green island almost within touching distance. It's almost enough to make me forget that I'm here alone and not celebrating a romantic anniversary with my man.

In fact, I'm not alone at all. I mean, not entirely alone. The athleisure company that hired me has also sent a small support team in order to guarantee high-quality content. I have a photographer, a stylist and an assistant/manager. The first two days are a whirlwind of jet lag and photoshoots on the black sand beach in front of our hotel.

I pose in various yoga outfits, Instagram my best tropical fruits, and do yoga both on the beach and by a mountain waterfall with a melodic, polysyllabic name. It's my dream gig. Everything I dreamed it would be.

Except that I can't stop checking my phone.

Over and over.

When we fly to Bora Bora, I'm almost relieved. This is the island everyone dreams about, a legendary place for lovers. And indeed, the airplane is absolutely stuffed with lovers. I've never seen so many honeymooners in one place. They're like octopi, flashing blinding diamond sets, touching, embracing and somehow entwined with each other no matter what the circumstances. And then there are the babies.

Yes, babies.

Honeymooners: pay attention. The tiny airplane that flies us from Tahiti to Bora Bora is like a bizarre Polynesian version of *The Love Boat*. Apparently, since there's just a clinic on Bora Bora, the local women fly out to Tahiti a few weeks before their due dates so they can give birth in a hospital—and then make a triumphant flight home with their progeny. They've got a huge cheering section when we touch down. It seems as if every auntie, uncle, nana, papi and cousin has crowded into the family boats and rushed out to the airport to say hello to the newest Tahitians in the world, tossing flowered leis over the mamas and the babies and then ambling away in a happy, loud, cheerful crowd. Someone breaks out a ukulele and sings, just because. I can feel my feet tapping, remembering bits and pieces of the dance I watched at the airport.

While I bask in the baby cuteness, my team disappears to claim our baggage (which is neatly laid out on a metal counter for us to grab) and to suss out the rumor that a celebrity guest has just arrived in the sleek private jet that's parked on the runway near the cheerful blue-and-white Air Tahiti plane. While they reconnoiter, I drink in the blue of the lagoon and the sharp, fierce mountains that stab up from the center. The airport's on a motu, which means it's surrounded by water and you have to take a boat to get off it. The passenger pickup zone is a series of small docks rather than the crowded, smelly concrete jungle of LAX and the other airports I've passed through.

And then the crowd thins out, the babies are whisked away, and I see him.

Max.

He's standing by a rack of creamy flower leis, watching me. He looks slightly anxious and a little frazzled. He also looks amazing, which (let's be honest) makes me mad. I feel stupid and needy—and rather desperate to run over to him and jerk his face down to mine and fuck his mouth in the middle of this airport of people.

Jesus.

Of course that's his plane.

He plucks a flower lei off the wooden stand and strides toward me. His forehead gets that little crinkle—he's got a plan and now he's executing it, so all's well in the Max-verse.

He stops when he's right in front of me and drops the lei over my head. He may also draw his hand down my face. Which is sweet. And hot. And totally provoking.

Do you remember how we met? And how I destroyed his laptop and my phone? He either doesn't—or he didn't learn. I smirk at him, giving him a taste of his own medicine. And then I reach out and shove him into the lagoon.

He lands in the water with a deeply satisfying splash. For a moment, the whole airport seems to freeze. I hear someone yelling and realize it's me.

"You don't call.

"Or text.

"Or come over.

"You WALKED AWAY FROM ME.

"You didn't want to stay."

It turns out that therapists the world over are right. It feels good to let it all out, so let it out I do. At full volume. It's too late to change the course of my relationship with Max, but the locals on the mainland are probably getting an earful. The Tahitians trapped at the airport with me look at me. They look at Max treading water. And then they point out the ladder, giggle and leave us alone. God bless a nation of laid-back, blissed-out locals.

When I finally dial back my volume, he's treading water and listening. I was stupid to up and leave without having it out with him. We'd never talked about the important things. But I also knew that I didn't want to hear all the reasons he couldn't or wouldn't or shouldn't choose me. So I held it together and left.

And now here he is MESSING UP ALL MY CAREFUL PLANS.

"What are you doing here?" It's not the suavest greeting in the world. I'm sure I'll think of much better lines in the days and nights to come because that's how it always works, isn't it?

"Waiting for you." He swims effortlessly over to the ladder and hauls himself up.

Water sheets off his clothes. His T-shirt's stuck to

his chest and the stupid, hopelessly romantic part of me wants to lick him dry with my tongue. It would take a long time. It's hardly feasible. But God…look at him.

Or don't look. Be strong. Bora Bora's tropical and even at barely noon it feels sort of like we're standing in an oven. A gorgeous, palm-tree-studded, sunshiny oven, true. Max will dry off and then maybe I can act normal.

"What do you want, Max?"

For a second he looks uncertain, but then he pulls it together. He definitely has a plan. "I miss you. We were good together."

"The sex was awesome," I blurt out.

Damn it.

My hookup king nods. Sex. That's how he connects with women. It's strangely impersonal in some ways.

"But I needed more than that," I continue.

He nods. "I figured that out." He holds out a blue box tied up with a very soggy velvet ribbon. "I brought this for you."

There's no way I'm taking it. Whatever *it* is.

"I don't need presents, Max. Those are things, and while they're nice, they're not what matters. You can't fix everything by throwing money at it."

He takes my hand and sets the box in it. "I flew here."

"In your private plane." I roll my eyes. Such a hardship.

"Yes." He's smart enough to look wary.

"It's a long way to come for a hookup."

"I thought we could renegotiate the terms of our relationship," he says.

My heart pounds as loudly as the Tahitian drums. "By giving me stuff?"

I know that works for some people and I'm not judging. When I was in high school, I fantasized more than once about a boyfriend who'd shower me with Victoria's Secret and roses. Later, however, I grew up and realized it was better to buy my own stuff. I also realized that I needed to learn to pick different men. Max is simply a gorgeous mistake and I need to move on.

He stares at me. "I made this for you."

Is he…blushing?

"Open the box," he growls.

He's definitely blushing. His face is the bright red of a hibiscus.

I open the box. Or what's left of it. It's a little soggy after its swim in the Polynesian lagoon. It half disintegrates in my hand, the sides falling apart once I tug the ribbon free.

I'm holding a plastic bag.

I shoot Max a look and he shrugs. "You said you had no idea how Dev could be so unconcerned about carting an expensive engagement ring around on a surfboard. You pointed out that he could fall in. I was listening."

I also worried about sharks, but now probably isn't

the time to bring that up as I just dunked him in the lagoon—and I know for a fact that Bora Bora's famous for its shark population.

"Did you get me a ring?" If he did, it's enormous—and not in a good way. The baggie's a quart-sized zipper bag.

He takes a step forward. "Do you want one?"

Do I?

I turn away and unzip the bag before I can have a heart attack and pull out—a phone.

Okay. So that's not entirely what I was expecting. I mean, it's nice and all, but as a romantic gesture it's definitely not in my top ten.

Max puts his arms around me and taps the screen.

Wow.

And wow again. If it had been a ring, it's safe to say that the bride and groom dance at our wedding would have been epic.

I stare at the naked dancing Max that fills my screen. He hovers by my side—I think he's making sure no one else at the airport can see. I watch the video again. And then a third time.

Max still can't dance, but he bobs and gyrates and slowly strips down to his birthday suit. In fact, I think he may have been influenced by that very famous Marilyn Monroe scene where she rasps "Happy Birthday, Mr. President."

"Maple?"

"Give me a moment."

"I'm dying here." I hear him swallow, and I look

up. The hibiscus red has faded and now he's looking a little pale.

"Before you can tell me this was a really bad idea and that my following you here is not okay, I just wanted to give you this and tell you something."

"Wait." I pause Dancing Max and lean back against Max's chest. "First tell me why you're pretending to be a Chippendales dancer."

He winces. "Because I thought about how we met and how you made a video for your boyfriend. You said you shared it with him because you trusted him and that's what people do in relationships, so—"

He stops.

"So this is you trusting me?" I don't know what to say.

"Yeah." His arms tighten around me. "I had a list. Of all the reasons I trust you."

"How many?" This is Max. We all know he counted them. Hell, he probably ranked them, too.

His mouth brushes my forehead. "There was only one that mattered—I chose to trust you. So I'm hoping you might make a few choices."

"Really?" I turn in his arms so that we're pressed up against each other, arms around each other. I slide the phone inside his (very wet) pocket. He's staring at me and there's something there in his eyes, something warm and sweet and very, very Max.

"Yeah," he whispers. "Do you want the list?"

"Always," I say gravely.

"Item one," he says, "I love you."

And then his lips find mine and for a long time, there's no more talking. Just kissing and his breath in my mouth and mine in his and hands going places they really, really shouldn't go, but no one seems to mind. He kisses my neck, the corner of my mouth, all my favorite places where he hasn't kissed me since the last time we were together.

"Is that it?" I ask when we finally break apart. "There's just the one item on your list?"

"That covers everything," he promises.

"I think you copied my list," I whisper back. "Because I love you, too."

I think there's about to be more kissing, but then he pauses. "Can I stay with you? And take that chance?"

I nod. "I do have a great hotel room. An overwater bungalow and everything."

He pulls back, his hands cupping my face. "Not just here. For the whole year. For as long as you want me."

I laugh and lean up to do some kissing of my own. "Are you hooked, then? No more hookups?"

He smiles at me, a dirty, perfect, absolutely Max kind of smile. "I love you, Maple."

He pulls me closer still, until I'd swear we were defying the laws of physics or biology, and I swear my heart beats double time because Max O'Reilly is two-stepping me around the Bora Bora airport while people laugh and clap (and someone breaks out a ukulele that does *not* help his rhythm).

"It's the only dance step I could learn in two days," he whispers apologetically. It's silly and awkward. And yes, there's some stumbling with the strong potential of falling. But we're also holding on to each other and I know in my heart that if we fall, we go together. And then we'll get up together, too.

And I tell him the truth. "It's perfect."

* * * * *

THE SEX CURE

CARA LOCKWOOD

MILLS & BOON

For the Benoit and Lockwood clans.

I couldn't do what I do without you!

CHAPTER ONE

Why was she even here? Harley Vega had been asking herself this question ever since the butler had let her into Wilder Lange's private office inside his massive multi-level Manhattan penthouse. Maybe she was just a glutton for punishment. Maybe she was a masochist and didn't know it. How else to explain why she accepted a one-on-one meeting with the man responsible for tanking her career?

She knew why. She was going to give the asshole a piece of her mind.

Harley didn't know what *his* agenda was but hers included letting the corporate shark know that he'd made the biggest mistake of his professional life, axing her sex advice column from *Femme,* a glossy women's magazine that had been in production for the better part of fifty years. She'd been called the world's most famous sexologist (had a PhD in human sexuality, for goodness' sake) and had been writing the sex advice column for more than seven years.

And then there was Wilder Lange, who bought her

magazine for a song, gutted the thing, put his name on it and declared himself the savior of yet another publication with a long and storied history. *Yes, saving*, she thought bitterly. Saving by cutting the page count in half and laying off two-thirds of its staff.

And what the hell did he even know about publishing? As far as Harley could tell, he was a full-time playboy. He seemed to spend all his time dating and dumping models and pop stars. A poster boy for an unhealthy sex life, a type-A commitment-phobe. One of them had even written a song about him. It was called something ridiculous like "Sex God." The dumbest song title she'd ever heard in her life! She paced, anger thrumming in her veins. She glanced around the study to get her bearings and tried to calm down. She noticed the chrome shelves in his study lined with antique books and first editions that at a glance seemed heavy on Dickens: *Great Expectations*, *Oliver Twist*, *Tale of Two Cities*. Not exactly the light reading she expected from a would-be sex god. She sniffed. They were probably all for show. Somebody probably told him that having antique books in his library would make him look sophisticated.

She glanced around the sleek modern library in the penthouse of this mirrored building on Fifth Avenue, as they sat far, far above the street noise and traffic, and marveled at the very vastness of the place. Everything seemed to be white and chrome, modern and sleek, except for the traditional paintings hung in various places and the antique pieces of furniture that complemented the room. The place felt like a bundle of contradictions that somehow worked: old and new, antique and modern. Either Wilder Lange was broadcasting hidden depths, or he'd hired an interior designer to do just that. Most likely the latter. Harley was sure the man never lifted a finger to do any real work his whole life. Hadn't he inherited the company from his wealthy daddy? Harley glanced outside the huge glass windows overlooking the whole of Central Park and the buildings surrounding it. Impressive view, she'd give him that. But that was all she'd give him.

Harley glanced at her watch. The man wasn't even on *time*. He was ten minutes late. Was reading him the riot act even worth the wait? Or was he assuming that because she'd been let go of her job, she had nothing but time on her hands? Well, she didn't, as a matter of fact. Since she couldn't write her column anymore, she'd need to work on drumming up more life-coaching clients, more people in need of sex advice to pay her bills. And, maybe, at long last, she could finally finish that couples' therapy book she'd been dabbling with over the last few years. Maybe if she finished it sooner rather than later, she might be able to land an advance. Maybe. She needed the cash. Her Brooklyn apartment sure as hell wouldn't pay for itself.

Forget this, she thought. She'd waited long enough. She grabbed her purse from the nearby burgundy leather chair and made her way to the door. Just then, the massive oak study door cracked open and Harley jumped, backing away from it only to see Wilder Lange stride in, all six foot four of him, oozing confidence and an easy charm. His broad shoulders seemed to brush the door frame as he passed and Harley Vega felt rooted to the spot. She wasn't short, at five six, herself. But he was so…tall. And… damn sexy in that well-tailored light gray suit. Since when were billionaire communications magnates so hot? She took him all in: his carefully combed dark almost jet-black hair, rolling back from his forehead in waves, strikingly dark eyes framed with thick lashes, his athletic build telling her that the rumors that he hit triathlons in his spare time weren't rumors at all. She seemed to remember one of her Google searches of the man told her he had Irish, German and Armenian heritage, but the combination right at this moment made her head spin.

"So sorry to keep you waiting," he said, easily, with just the right amount of contrition, and for a full second she just stood there, probably mouth agape like an idiot. What was wrong with her? As if she'd never seen a good-looking man before. She'd almost completely forgotten she was supposed to hate him.

Wilder flashed her his famous dimpled smile and she felt her stomach lurch. This could not be happening. Why hadn't any of the online photos of him done him any damn justice at all? He was just 100 percent sex, his charisma like an ocean wave crashing over her and temporarily stunning her senses. Now that damn song didn't seem so ridiculous after all. Women probably stood in line for their chance to worship him.

He closed the minimal distance between them, hand out for a shake. She took his massive paw and felt her own delicate hand enveloped by his. What was it they said about a man with big hands? Although, she knew hand size had very little to do with other parts of the anatomy. Still, her mind couldn't help but wonder. His hands seemed to be too strong for a businessman's. He exuded a raw kind of power, something primal, something that didn't belong in the expensive suit he wore. He looked the part of a rich tycoon, but the bent of his sensual mouth told her that looks were deceiving. Her hand felt tiny in his, and she was distinctly aware of the power dynamic, of how he held back his strength when he clasped her palm gently. She realized that she hadn't said a word so far, as she'd been too focused on the man's eyes. Sharp, mesmerizing and so very, very dark that she could only barely make out the outline of his pupils. "So nice to meet you. Thank you for coming."

Why was he being so nice to her? That was the shocking part. Why on earth did he seem *pleased* to see her when he'd just fired her from the job she loved? He had to have read her columns and found them lacking. Why else hadn't she made the cut? But he seemed damned pleased to see her, like maybe the man was *flirting* with her. He was, after all, known to be a famous womanizer. But then she thought better of it. *Get a grip on yourself, Harley.* This man might be sex on a freakin' stick, but he wasn't any friend and he certainly wasn't interested. Harley wasn't his usual model type. That was just her projecting her want on him. *Stop thinking with your clit and try using your brain.*

"Well, it's not nice to meet you," she said. "Can't say I'm excited to meet the man who fired me."

There. At least she wasn't going to swoon all over him now. She got a tiny bit of satisfaction to see the man's dark eyebrows raise in surprise. He probably surrounded himself with sycophants. *Get used to it*, she thought, *I'm not here to kiss your ass*. What was the point? Harley didn't beg. She wasn't going to plead for her job back. Her parents would drive all the way up from Miami to lecture her on not giving in. *Vegas are proud*, her father always told her.

"You are as blunt as people say, I see." A slow smile played at the corners of his mouth. Why did he seem *amused* that she was pissed off? That just made her...more pissed off. "And, technically, I didn't fire you. You were laid off."

"Right. Let me just tell my landlord that. I'm sure she'd be just fine with me not paying my rent. Seeing as how I wasn't *fired for cause.*" She'd gotten the second eviction notice today as a matter of fact. If she didn't pay her rent in two days, she was going to be kicked out. She stuffed down the temporary panic that rose in her throat. And then what? Maybe crash on a friend's couch. Except that most of her friends were at the magazine, and most of them were in the same predicament she was. She could go home to Miami. But that would be admitting defeat. Her mother never approved of her moving to Manhattan.

She hated the fact that her mother's prediction—that she'd be scraping by in New York—had come true. Sure, she was professionally successful, but living on her own in New York on a modest columnist's salary only worked if she got the salary. She'd been living paycheck to paycheck for some time.

She noticed the gleaming Rolex on Wilder's wrist. That man had never had to worry about making rent even once in his whole silver-spoon life, she thought.

"It was a business decision. Nothing personal." He motioned to an oversized leather chair near the corner window. "Please, Ms. Vega, sit." She hesitated. Did she even want to stay? Part of her wanted to tell him to go to hell and run out of his penthouse. Another part of her was curious as to why she was here at all. Even though he made her furious, she still wrestled with curiosity. What the hell was she here for? Maybe he planned an apology. An apology would be nice.

"Please," he added. He nodded at the chair, and she noticed how perfectly symmetrical his features were: eyes, nose, mouth. Fending off his charisma felt like a full-time job. Something about Wilder Lange made everything seem off center. It was the way he was looking at her, she realized, and more than that, the way his gaze made her feel.

Eventually, she sat in the leather chair, sinking into it and struggling to keep her skirt at her knees. She'd worn one of the outfits she typically wore to the office: dark pencil skirt, trendy spring top in a pastel pink that complemented her almond skin. She dressed conservatively, because she knew that people sometimes assumed a sex advice columnist would show up wearing garter belts and a bustier. Nervously, a hand went to her dark updo, as if reassuring herself her twist hadn't come loose. Then she wondered why she'd done that, why she cared so much about looking put together at this moment. She knew that somewhere deep inside her, she wanted Wilder to find her pleasing. That was a dangerous hope, a stupid one. What then? He'd be attracted to her and give back her old job? Harley wasn't here to bargain for her job. She wasn't going to trade favors with any man to save her career. No matter how powerful—or how damn delectable—he seemed.

Wilder sat at the edge of his massive desk, and she was well aware that he was hovering above her. Sitting, she still had to crane her neck to meet his eyes.

"Why am I here, Mr. Lange?" Her tone was sharp, annoyed. Good.

"Are you always so to the point?" He raised an eyebrow.

"Most of the time," she said. "I don't believe in wasting time." Unlike Wilder Lange, it seemed.

"Would you like a drink? Iced tea? Scotch?" He flashed a wicked grin. Harley felt ire rise in her. Why did she feel like he was the cat and she, the mouse? What he didn't know was she was no mouse.

She crossed her legs at the knee, and very much wished she'd brought a leather-bound ledger for notes. Anything that she might use as a shield against Wilder's penetrating gaze. She didn't know why she felt so…vulnerable. Since when was she ever intimidated by money or power? Never.

"Do you have tequila?" she joked.

"I do. Reposado? Blanco? Anejo?" he asked, as if he had an entire bar hidden under his desk. Hell, the man might.

"Extra Anejo if you have it." She might as well sample some of his expensive liquor. Might as well get something that would be worth the cost of the train to get here.

"Of course." He slid off the end of the desk moving with the ease of a man comfortable in his body. He walked to the small glass cart tucked away near the chrome shelf, produced a small crystal tumbler and poured two glasses of amber-colored liquid. He handed it to her and she took a small sniff. It smelled aged and expensive, the kind of sipping tequila her father would fawn over at special occasions. Her mother had always wrinkled her nose and asked for a mojito, her drink of choice.

Wilder slid into the seat across from hers, deftly opening his suit jacket button with one hand, revealing a very defined waist beneath, his bright white starched shirt lying flat against the belt buckle bellow his belly button. She was strangely glad he didn't offer a toast. She took a tentative sip of the drink and it felt like caramelized butter on her tongue. Definitely expensive. Definitely delicious. Nothing to slam here. This was meant to be enjoyed. Slowly. Her hopes of slamming the drink and stalking out of his office faded.

He watched her drink with that damn amused quirk of his lip twitching. She felt the urge to toss the drink in the man's face. But her father would never forgive her. Tequila this good should never be wasted. She took another sip, the tequila already doing its job as it warmed her belly. Meanwhile, Wilder wasn't talking. He was studying her. As if trying to figure out a puzzle. She wished he'd just get on with the damn meeting already, so they could part ways and she could get on with her life.

"Is it too much to hope for that you're giving me my old job back?" She meant it as a light-hearted joke, but realized she'd failed miserably in her delivery. She sounded needy. Desperate. Dammit.

He frowned. "I'm sorry, no." He shook his head.

The disappointment hit her harder than she would've thought. Why had she thought he'd give back her old job? A corporate shark like him didn't gut staff and then have second thoughts.

"I've asked you here because I need your help."

She laughed out loud, a blunt bray. "You need my

help?" She couldn't imagine with what. And also, footnote: what the hell was he thinking? What kind of gall gave him the right to ask for *her* help? He'd fired her and he was asking her for a favor?

"Yes, I do." His expression was entirely serious as he took a small sip from his glass. Her laughter bounced right off him as if he were immune to ridicule. Probably the zeroes in his bank account made him impervious to shame. "You give advice. I need... advice." He rolled the liquid around in his glass.

"*You* need advice?" Had she fallen into an alternate dimension? Did she find herself in the upside down? Why was one of the most powerful men in Manhattan asking her for advice?

"Yes." He met her gaze, his dark eyes deadly serious. "I need advice...about sex."

CHAPTER TWO

HARLEY FELT HER brain had short-circuited. Did the billionaire playboy subject of the pop song "Sex God" and the most powerful communications magnate in America just ask her for sex advice? She almost dropped her tumbler of expensive tequila all over his pristine white carpet.

"You need sex advice?" She was barely keeping the laughter from bubbling up in her throat. "You? Mr. *Sex God*?" She threw the song title at him like an insult.

"Yes." He glanced at the carpet, looking contrite. And…a little lost. This wasn't a joke. He was serious. The laughter in her throat died. Clearly, the man had a problem and was struggling to cope. The advice columnist in her made her pause. A million thoughts ran through her mind: was he not satisfying his partners? She looked at the dark-haired, devilishly handsome specimen before her. No, that couldn't be it. Most women would be able to satisfy themselves just fine by practically looking at the man.

What about sex addiction? That was probably far more likely, she figured. She imagined the man unable to control his baser desires, falling into bed with countless women, and suddenly the image of him naked, helpless against his own impulses made a tiny bead of sweat drip down the small of her back. Was that…turning her on? Good lord. This was the first man she'd ever met that she'd immediately imagined…naked. What was wrong with her? She knew about charisma, knew about the power of sexual pheromones, yet, she'd never truly experienced their raw power. Until right at this moment.

"I understand how ridiculous this might seem." He glanced up at her, appearing almost desperate. He needed help. That much was clear. He was also a man not used to asking for it, she guessed. And suddenly, she felt… God, did she feel *sorry* for the man? She could absolutely not allow any feelings of pity or any other feelings into her heart for this man who'd single-handedly destroyed the magazine she'd lived to work for. "I want you to take me on. As a personal client."

"But…you fired me." None of this was computing.

"You're damn good at what you do. I've read your columns. I think you can help me." He'd liked her columns?

"If I had a good column, why did you fire—"

"Lay off," he corrected.

"Kick me to the curb," she said. She gripped her glass a little tighter, that old resentment bubbling up in her. He wasn't going to get away with sugarcoating anything.

"It was business. Not personal."

"How can I not take it personally?" Seriously. Was she about to hear the professional equivalent of the it's-not-me-it's-you speech?

"You decide not to." He eyed her. Why was he so confounding? She was just going to *decide* not to have a grudge against him. As if it were that easy. She drained what was left in her glass. He stood, fetched the crystal bottle from the mini bar and poured her another round. She accepted it without a word, her head starting to buzz from the first pour. And from the proximity of the man.

"Tell me why should I even consider doing a favor for you?" This was the real question.

He cocked his head to one side as if the answer was obvious. "Well, because I asked."

Now, she laughed, full-throated and bent over her knees with mirth. He was funny, damn. And cocky as hell. She kind of liked that about him. She hated that she liked it, but there it was. "Normally, I don't take personal life-coaching clients." Except now she'd need to take them on. Lots of them, if she wanted to not be homeless.

"I've heard you do make exceptions. I'd like you to make one for me." He had such gall. And why did that seem so damn sexy? Or was it just the perfect lines of that expensive suit? Her mother's voice was in her head then: *Hear the man out. Don't be so stubborn you cut off your nose to spite your face.*

"I'd have to hear *what* you need counseling for."

He leaned back in his chair, the very epitome of charm and ease, except for the guarded look in his eyes. The man clearly used charm to keep people at bay. Well, Harley wasn't just any person. She took a sledgehammer to emotional walls and usually had a pretty strong bullshit meter.

"I need another round." He poured himself more tequila, as well.

Harley quirked an eyebrow. "Do you need another cocktail to talk about your sex life, Mr. Lange?"

Wilder looked at her, eyes alight with mischief. "It's you who might need another cocktail, Ms. Vega."

Harley laughed a little. Oh, how little the man knew her. "Trust me, there's nothing you can tell me that will shock me."

Wilder leaned forward, dark eyes bright. "Is that a challenge?"

She hated to admit it, but the man was already challenging her in ways she didn't like. "No. Just a simple statement of fact." She took a drink of the tequila, the warmth trailing down her throat to her stomach. "I'm curious about why the world's most famous playboy wants…or *needs* a sexologist?"

Wilder seemed frozen for a second, his expression completely unreadable, and she worried she'd offended him. Then again, why was she worrying about his feelings? Did she care about making things easier for Wilder Lange? Not at all. He was full of himself. So why did she also think he was the sexiest man she'd met in God knows when? Because she always liked men who were trouble, and Wilder Lange had trouble written all over him.

He laughed, a deep chuckle in his belly that she almost felt as a vibration through her whole being. "So, you've been reading about me, too, I see."

"It's hard not to." He was everywhere—magazines, blogs, even the evening news sometimes. Clinically, she could admit she was attracted to him, but attraction had never been an issue for her before. She could compartmentalize her feelings, tuck them away in a box on a shelf and then let her clinical, scientific self examine those contents at a later date in a safer environment. But she was having problems compartmentalizing with Wilder sitting before her.

She needed to get this meeting back on track. She cleared her throat. Enough of dipping her toe in the pool of sexual energy flowing between them. Harley knew it was there, and she also knew that as a professional, she could ignore it. People might be animals, with animal instincts, but they also had cold hard logic.

"So, if we can discuss what you'd like from me..."

"Just your attention, Ms. Vega." His grin turned almost wolfish then, the innuendo subtle, yet she caught it. Maybe she was wrong about the flirting. He seemed to be laying it on thick. Too thick, maybe.

He studied her, dark eyes sharp, missing nothing. "This is…well…not easy for me, Harley. Especially with the paparazzi always sniffing around."

"I thought you *employed* the paparazzi?" She knew he owned more than one tabloid.

"Just because I'm the boss, doesn't mean they won't report on me. Besides, they have competitors that I *don't* own. And I've made enemies in some places. Political ones." She'd heard about those, as well. He'd had a public feud with a powerful New York senator over FCC regulations.

"I guess you can't make an omelet without breaking some eggs," she said.

"Isn't it a little too early in the day to be quoting Ayn Rand?" Wilder asked her, a playful smile on his lips. So, the books on his shelf weren't just for show. He'd read some of them. Perhaps he *wasn't* the empty-headed billionaire she'd assumed he was. The more he talked, the more he seemed exactly her type—tall, dark, devilishly handsome and most likely with more issues than *Sports Illustrated*. She hated how much she loved complicated men, but there it was. Her Achilles' heel.

"Maybe." She shrugged. "Are you going to keep changing the subject or are we going to talk about what you need from me?"

Wilder barked a laugh. "Okay. But, before I tell you, I'll need reassurances that what we talk about here today will be confidential."

She slid one knee over the other, her fitted skirt

sliding up her leg. "Absolutely. I won't tell a soul." Wrong. She'd tell every single person she knew and then people she didn't. She had zero loyalty to Wilder Lange.

Harley was finding it hard to meet Wilder's gaze. He was looking at her as if she were an intruder in his territory, as if he were a wolf defending his pack's hunting grounds. She tried to figure out why she thought he was so predatory. He was just a man, sitting in a chair, but there was something about the set of his shoulders, the barely restrained power there. Also, beneath that lazy smile, the bright, intelligent eyes, there was a hardness to Wilder Lange. She thought he must be a man used to using honey to lure bees, of that Harley was certain, but she also sensed a rigidity in him, which would account for the fact that he'd more than doubled his father's empire. One couldn't be a fantastically successful businessman on charm alone. Charm, she suspected, was just one of his weapons.

"Just to be certain, I'll need you to sign this NDA before we get started." Wilder rose, and moved over to his oversized antique desk, where he slipped open a drawer and pulled out a document of about five pages.

Harley blinked fast. She didn't want to sign her soul away in some document. She was no lawyer. "Do we need that?"

Wilder crooked his head and handed her the papers and a pen. "Indulge me." His sensual lips bent into a friendly smile, one intending to disarm her. Clearly, he was a man not used to trusting anyone. Harley took the document and scanned it. From what she could tell, it was a typical nondisclosure agreement, except that while most NDAs lasted two to five years, this one lasted for the entirety of Harley's life. And she was not allowed to ever even admit to knowing, let alone treating, Wilder Lange.

"I can't admit I know you?" she asked, puzzled, as she glanced at him. There goes spreading this little tidbit of gossip all over social media.

"If these terms aren't reasonable to you, then..."

Harley glanced at Wilder. She could get up right now and leave. Why was she doing him any favors? She hated him. Hated what he'd done to her beloved magazine. Yet, she knew deep in her bones she couldn't walk away. Not yet. Harley loved nothing more than a challenge, and she suspected Wilder would be that and more. The set of his chin, those mysterious dark eyes, the protective rigidity of his shoulders.... Oh, yes, he would be a delicious challenge. And what did she have waiting for her back at home? An eviction notice and hours to scroll LinkedIn for want ads? Besides, curiosity was eating her up inside. She needed to know what problem was so dire that he'd called her to his home and asked for her help.

She took the pen and signed her name on the contract and handed it back to him. He took it, tucked the papers back inside his desk drawer and then took his place opposite her in the leather-bound chair.

"Now, what can I help you with?" she asked. The curiosity was literally about to kill her.

"I can't seem to..." He took in a sharp breath. "Well, I can't seem to have sex."

CHAPTER THREE

HARLEY LOOKED AS if he'd just told her he was an alien born in a different galaxy. Well, he guessed she hadn't been expecting that. Wilder, himself, was the last man who would've thought it could happen to him, either. But there was the sad ugly truth: he was thirty-nine and having trouble getting it up. No matter how beautiful the woman, no matter how amazing or tantalizing she might be, he was having difficulty even mustering up a baseline interest in sex. He was supposed to be in the prime of his life and yet he couldn't enjoy it. He'd tried the pills, and he'd had all the examinations, and every doctor or specialist told him there was absolutely nothing physically wrong with him. He was in the best shape of his life. His problem, they said, was all in his head.

"I'm sorry...you can't...?" she said, and then quickly tried to mask her surprise. She was so shocked she put her glass on the nearby glass end table. He, however, took another swig of his.

"I can't maintain an erection," he clarified. No use beating around the bush.

"Oh."

He gave her points for the professionalism and for not laughing in his face. He knew she was angry with him, had every right to be angry with him, and that's why she'd be the perfect woman to treat him. Because she wouldn't let him have a pity party like the last therapist he'd tried, who'd gotten him absolutely nowhere. Harley Vega wouldn't let him manipulate her, either. Of that, he was absolutely certain.

Wilder was more than certain she was the woman to cure him. He hadn't been this intrigued by a woman in…he couldn't remember when. Before their meeting, he'd watched dozens of her interviews, read a substantial amount of her advice columns, and he had wanted to meet her in person. She was a rare combination of a beautiful mind who wasn't afraid to say what needed to be said and a strikingly beautiful woman with curves that simply didn't quit. The tight pencil skirt clung to her athletic legs, and while the pink ruffled top hid her curves, the sheer fabric showed just a hint of flesh-colored lace beneath, a tantalizing clue of the lingerie she'd worn to this meeting. He was certain she probably didn't even know the lace showed. Her normally dark shoulder-length curls were confined in a tight French twist, revealing a smooth angular jawline that he had the sudden urge to stroke with his finger. Her light brown eyes were both warm and yet also…reserved. This was a woman used to keeping herself on a short leash, and that made him wonder why she felt she needed to grip it so tightly.

"I see." She was stalling for time. Trying to get her thoughts in order, he guessed. It's probably not every day the man who laid her off admitted to such a crippling problem. He would pause to feel humiliated, except that he didn't have time for that. He needed to get help, and he needed to get it now. "So, I guess you're not a sex addict, then?"

He barked a laugh. She was exactly the no-nonsense, pull-no-punches Harley Vega that lived in those advice columns.

"Is that what you thought?" he asked.

She nodded. "Can you blame me? You have a new girlfriend every week. And they usually write songs about your…" she cleared her throat "…abilities. While, also, I should say, talking about how you can't commit."

"I choose not to commit, there's a difference."

"Said like a true commitment-phobe."

He laughed. He couldn't help himself. Damn, the woman was blunt. Bold. Unafraid of him. She was just what he needed. "Surely, you don't believe everything you've read about me. I'm sure you know that public lives can be different than private ones."

She nodded, once. "Yes," she admitted.

"So, do you think you can help me?" he asked.

She kept her face a perfect mask. "It's a common problem," she said, which he thought was kind, even as she uncrossed her legs and recrossed them. He watched the hem of her skirt rise, revealing her perfectly smooth olive skin above her knee. He felt his breath catch a little and wondered what that was about. He was a man who surrounded himself with beautiful women on a regular basis, so why would a hint of skin even register with him? Yet, it did. She bit her full lip, concentrating on her next response and he found it unbelievably sexy. The tiniest of lines appeared between her otherwise perfectly manicured eyebrows. Harley was beautiful, but not perfect, he noted, her smile slightly lopsided, her light brown eyes almost too big for her face. Almost. He'd call them doe-like, if he had to use a cliché, but really they were just big and warm and cautious. It was the cautiousness that intrigued him, the guardedness in her otherwise warm and open expression. She wore little makeup, which Wilder respected. He preferred the natural look, no matter what the tabloids might say about him.

But before he could fully appreciate the view before him, his phone rang. It was his younger brother Seth. He was the oldest of Wilder's half siblings.

"I need to take this," he said, even as Harley rose to her feet to protest. He stood and moved to the other side of the study. "Hello?"

"You sitting down?"

"No. Should I be?" He glanced at Harley long enough to see a flash of annoyance cross her face. She didn't like being put on hold. But he'd not send his brother to voice mail. For him, family always came first.

"Maybe. I heard Mom is talking to Stuart. She's trying to get him to sell his shares in Lange Communications." In the background, Wilder heard a seagull cry. Seth was supposed to be somewhere in the Mediterranean, which was why Wilder was always going to take his brother's call. He never knew when it could be an emergency. "Stuart said no, but just wanted you to know she's trying to up her shares."

"Of course, she is. That's her full-time obsession for the last two years. Ever since the company became profitable." Wilder felt the tightness in his chest loosen a bit. He was always a little worried about any of his brothers and was glad to hear this was just a routine call about Lucinda and not something serious like a car accident or, worse, a sinking yacht.

"Not that she'd ever admit you saved Dad's legacy. She was livid when you got the lion's share of the stocks. But he knew you were the best man to run it. We all know that."

"I did what any of you would do."

"Dad's company would be bankrupt by now if any of us had tried to run it. You did something extraordinary. Give yourself credit."

Wilder felt a swell of pride in his chest. He'd spent most of his life looking after his younger brothers. He'd had to: Lucinda drank too much and while his father was fantastic—when he was home—the business kept him traveling around the world most of the time when he'd been alive. Sure, they'd had a parade of nannies through the house. The nannies had made sure they were fed and wore clean clothes, but none of them dealt with school bullies or helped with homework assignments or, at least for one brother, aided him in talking through his difficult decision to come out. Wilder had been the one who'd been there through it all, making sure the boys knew they had someone in their lives who wasn't going anywhere. They'd all naturally handed over the job of running their father's business to him, no questions asked. If pushed, he knew, all of them were relieved not to have had to deal with the burden. No matter what their mother told them about how Wilder wasn't fit to do it. They all knew he was the only one who could.

And Wilder took the responsibility because that's what Wilder did. He always did what needed to be done.

"And by the way, thanks for taking it on, so I didn't have to," Seth said. In the background, he could hear the ocean waves lapping against the boat's hull. Seth loved the water, preferring to spend his days on the family yacht far, far from family drama.

"You can repay me by winning that next yacht race," he said, smiling at the thought of Seth out doing what he loved, racing across the ocean, the wind at his back.

"Oh, I plan on it." Wilder could almost hear his

little brother smiling through the phone. Nothing gave the kid more joy than being on the open water. "Anyway, I hear Lucinda is very close to getting other shareholders to sell to her. So just be aware she's trying for a coup."

"I'm not surprised." Everything he worked so hard to build could be taken away from him if Lucinda got her way, which he didn't plan on letting happen. Not now, not ever. "Thanks for the heads-up."

Harley paced near him, impatience in every step, not bothering to hide the fact she was listening to every word. He supposed he should make this quick, now that he knew it wasn't a life or death emergency.

"Look, if the worst did come to pass…" Seth paused "…you could always opt out of the Lange legacy. You don't need it."

"I owe it to Dad. You know if Lucinda got control, she'd just liquidate everything. Immediately. All she cares about is money." He clenched his jaw, as he glanced at Harley who stood studying him, not bothering to hide that she was eavesdropping. That almost made him smile. He glanced beyond her to his father's books on the shelf. Dad had left him these and the penthouse. He'd left Seth his boat, and the other boys had gotten more cash than they could probably spend in their lifetimes. Lucinda had gotten much less and had spent the last seven years trying to get what she thought was her fair share. At least in death Dad had admitted that Lucinda was… less than deserving.

"Dad's dead. He can't care about the company anymore. You could sell. Especially now that you turned the failing company around. Start your own business. You don't need to be fighting Lucinda all the time."

Hadn't he been doing that his whole life? He wasn't sure he knew how to do anything else. Plus, he was closing in on forty. This was quickly becoming his own legacy. Not just his father's.

Harley Vega stopped her pacing, crossed her arms and tapped her foot impatiently. He'd wrap this up.

"Trust me, life is better away from her." Wilder could imagine Seth standing on the decks in the bright sunshine. He was happy for his younger brother, truly happy, but also felt a deep-seated envy. Wilder didn't know how to let things go. If something needed doing, he did it. Period.

"Say, did you give Harley Vega a call like I suggested?"

"I did." He glanced over at Harley and she froze. The impatience on her face changing to…curiosity. "I'm trying things out."

She took her seat once more, gazing out the windows of his study, waiting for him to end the call.

"Good. You deserve a happy ending, too, brother. Pun *intended.*"

"Ha. Ha. Very funny." Wilder rolled his eyes.

"Well, if you're going to be fighting off Lucinda at every turn, then you need to have a way to blow off some steam. I also think if you just got away from that nest of vipers for a little while, come out on the boat, maybe you'd get your mojo back."

"If I left, Lucinda would have me booted, no doubt, and take over the company now that it's finally turning a profit."

"Would that be so bad?"

"Just go sail your boat, little brother."

"Don't have to tell me twice." Seth paused. "Watch your back, Wild," he said. "And call me if you need anything."

"Will do."

Wilder ended the call and stared at his phone for a minute. He couldn't help but wish Seth was here, the brother closest to his own age, the one who'd watched his back countless times in school and in life. The bond between them ran deep, and after he'd come out to him in high school, the bond had grown deeper. Wilder had been even more protective of Seth. He had helped Seth talk to their father about it, who'd accepted the news without any judgment. Lucinda, however, had been a different story. She'd been raised by conservative parents, and thought being gay was a choice. No matter how often Wilder, Seth or their father would try to explain sexual orientation was something you were born with, she'd never accept that Seth's attraction to other men was something he couldn't control. Wilder was glad Seth was happy out there on the wild blue sea. He deserved that happiness. Wilder wondered if he would be happier out there, too. But duty called.

And right now, that duty was Harley Vega.

"Sorry about that," he said again. "It's one of my little brothers. He's abroad and I just wanted to make sure he's okay."

"Oh." She seemed to be considering this a moment. "And is he?"

"Fine," he said. "Not that he's really trying to stay out of trouble." Wilder laughed a little.

"Sounds like my sister," she said. The two exchanged a glance and for the first time she seemed as if she did not want to kill him. That was progress.

"So." She cleared her throat as she recalibrated, the warm moment cooling. He was losing her again. He needed to win her over. Needed to try harder. Watching her there, back ramrod straight, legs crossed at the knee, her almost-sensible pumps on, he felt a stirring in his groin. He nearly did a double take, as he glanced down at his lap. He hadn't felt *anything* there for months. Hell, more than a year, if he were honest with himself. Could seeing this woman's bare calves have this kind of effect on him? he wondered. Maybe he got off on therapy. Or maybe… he got off on her.

She studied him now, lacing her fingers together. "So, tell me about what's concerning you most. About…your issue."

What was concerning him most was how he was halfway to an erection, a thing he thought had left him for good. He took a deep breath and stared at Harley, who blinked at him, her pink lips full and halfway parted, and felt all of her laser-like attention focused on him. He liked it. Her attention.

"Well, I'd like to be normal." Hell, he'd just like to get back to his life. That was all. Right now on his phone he had a dozen playful and sexy missives from his crew of friends with benefits, women who were always eager and ready for a good time. Except he wasn't able to show them one. Not with his current predicament.

"There's no such thing as normal, really," she said. "There's just people and what they like and don't like. A normal amount of sex to one man is not the same for another."

"Yes, but I'd just like to have sex. Period." He felt like such a failure. He hated admitting defeat, and even worse than that, hated asking for help. He never asked for help in his life. Yet, he needed her help, whether he liked it or not.

Except that, right at this moment, he seemed *not* to have any problem with getting turned on. He shifted, crossing his legs to try to get his own growing hard-on under control, and almost laughed to himself about the irony of hiding his erection when he'd just told her he couldn't get it up.

"Are you having trouble getting hard…or staying hard?" she asked him.

"Getting," he admitted, though from the stiffness he felt growing in his lap, he doubted she'd believe him. "And maintaining." He swallowed, hard, and crossed his legs. That seemed to make things worse so he uncrossed them. Was it the woman's voice? It seemed every time she spoke, she was like a snake charmer, playing a delicate tune that only his cock seemed to fully appreciate. She was weaving a spell around him even now, her light brown eyes focused on him, her skin looking almost bronze beneath his study lights, her hands gently clasped in her lap. What he wanted to do was lean across the space between them and kiss her, feel for himself whether her lips were as soft as they looked. Hell, what he wanted to do was lie her down on the floor right now and taste *all* of her. The thought of finding her delicate pink—or would it be more mauve or magenta?—center set off a five-alarm fire in his brain, and his groin responded, growing harder even now. He casually put his hands in his lap, amazed to feel himself coming to life there. *Now, you pick the time to work?* He cursed his body, cursed the way the thing stubbornly refused to follow his orders.

"How long has this been an issue?"

The fact was, Lange's mind and his body had been at odds for quite a long time, but it was only in the last year that it had become a crippling problem. He thought back to his last disastrous date with that swimsuit model… Now, he couldn't remember her name, though she'd graced the covers of any number of magazines. How she'd patted his hand, a look of pity on her face, as she told him, "This happens to men all the time."

Except that it didn't happen to Wilder Lange. Not ever.

Except now it did.

"About a year ago, it started. It was on and off for a while, but now it's..." Every single time he tried to take a gorgeous woman to his bed. "Constant." He almost spat the word. He hated failure, wouldn't tolerate it in any other aspect of his life, and yet the one part of his life that was supposed to be easy, fun and uncomplicated—his sex life—he couldn't make happen.

"Have you tried medication?" she asked him, her voice clinical. So why did it affect him so much?

"I've tried them all." This was the sad truth. He'd had all the prescriptions, and none worked. His last doctor had suggested it was a mental block. He'd seen half a dozen traditional therapists, psychiatrists and psychologists, but none of them had gotten at the root of his problem, either. "I've got a complete clean bill of health. No infections. No STIs. No high blood pressure. No weight gain. Nothing physical that would account for the issue."

"Do you usually wear protection?"

"Always," he said, not sure what that had to do with anything. "What does that have to do with this condition?"

"Nothing. I'm just trying to figure out how reckless you are." She quirked an eyebrow.

"So it has nothing to do with my problem?"

"Probably not." A sly smile tugged at the corner

of her lips. Despite her struggle to be professional, she was enjoying this. Just a little bit. Well, he supposed he deserved it.

"And you? Do you?"

She didn't even raise an eyebrow. She wasn't easily thrown. "Yes, I do. And get tested every year. It's the responsible thing to do."

"I'm glad we're both responsible, then." He'd much rather talk about her habits, even if they were clinical, than his. "Do you always keep yourself on such…a tight leash?"

She studied him. "I'm not the one who asked you for sex advice, Mr. Lange."

He laughed at that. God, the woman was quick. Blunt. To the point. He loved it. Found it unbelievably refreshing. He was surrounded on most days by people who were eager to get so far up his ass they might as well have been giving him a colonoscopy. She wasn't going to let him get away with anything. That's exactly what he needed.

"Are you able to pleasure yourself?" she asked, which took him off guard.

He nodded, once. It was the last thing he wanted to talk about. It felt strikingly shameful. He'd been a man who up until a year ago was fighting women off, had his pick of any number of gorgeous, willing partners, except that now he couldn't fully enjoy them. Hell, he didn't even want to try. That was the worst part.

"How often?" She stared at him a beat too long

and his cock responded. He was on his way to full-blown readiness. He glanced away, focusing on the sprawling cityscape outside, and the big rectangle of green that was Central Park. They were so high above the park it could have been the view from a plane. Yet, he could still see the vague outline of the walking paths, where his mother used to take him almost every Sunday before she died. He felt the intensity of want for Harley slip away in that moment, as his past, a ghost intent on haunting him, made its presence known.

"Not that often." If he were honest with himself, he hadn't just lost the ability to get and stay hard, he'd also largely lost interest in sex. Maybe he'd overloaded himself. Running Lange Communications and being the patriarch of the Lange family was no easy task. He'd managed to keep the brothers on task and Lucinda away from the family coffers, but the fact was that he was starting to feel worn out. He'd used sex as his way of relaxing, as his way of taking something for himself, but now that he wasn't able to do it, he was starting to question everything.

Harley studied him, intently. He expected to see pity there, that horrible look he'd seen in the eyes of so many of the women he'd tried to seduce recently, the pity that slashed at him like a knife to the groin. He hated pity. Pity was for weak people, for pathetic people, and Wilder was many things, but he'd spent his life proving he wasn't weak. Or pathetic.

But Harley wasn't pitying him. And she wasn't studying him like a bug in a petri dish, either, thankfully. She was still a bit angry with him; he could almost feel the heat pulsing in her veins. He knew that was there, brimming just below the surface, and that's exactly what he needed. Someone who'd call him on his bullshit. And she was the woman to do it.

"Often, people can experience psychological blocks that impede... .certain natural behaviors," she said. "Stress can play a role, for sure, but so can past trauma. Is there anything that might have happened when you were younger that might be surfacing now?"

He looked away from Harley and back out to Central Park. He hadn't had the easiest childhood, but he was determined to leave the past in the past. There was nothing in his past that could hurt him, and he damn well wasn't going to rehash any of it here. If ever.

"No," he said. He was almost convinced it wasn't a lie.

Harley leaned forward, and he turned his attention to her in time to see the hint of the top of her left breast at the V of her shirt. He desperately wanted to lay his cheek there. "I think what can benefit you the most is simply talking about some of the challenges you are facing—and have faced—in your life, and I think you'll find that we can get you back to where you'd like to be. But you don't need me for that. You could get a therapist."

Disappointment hit him, cold and hard. No, he needed *her*, not someone else. "I've tried therapists. They don't work. They're afraid to be blunt with me."

"You just want abuse, then."

"Maybe. Something like that. I need someone to shake some sense into me." Now, he had something else up his sleeve. Some other bit of information he knew about Harley Vega. "And there's one more thing I need from you."

"What's that?" Her brown eyes studied him, wary.

"For the duration of treatment, I'll need you to live here. With me."

CHAPTER FOUR

HAD HE JUST invited her to *live* with him? She'd live with the man who'd fired her? The man she hated?

"No. Absolutely not." She shook her head. White-hot panic rushed down her spine. It was one thing to treat this intriguing man on a weekly basis. It was another thing to live with him and see him daily. Would she be able to stuff down her attraction for him under those circumstances? She wasn't even sure she *could* treat him or if she'd just be playing at being therapist. Also, she hated him. Hated everything about the corporate shark who gutted companies and left hundreds of unemployed in his wake. Maybe he did have an endearing relationship with his brother, but that didn't change who he was.

"There's more than enough room," he said. "You can live in the east wing."

East wing? Since when did a penthouse have *wings*? Then again, she guessed, this was no ordinary penthouse. It was, after all, three levels at least. "No. That's off the table."

"It's completely contained, with its own kitchen and other facilities. And my servant staff will be at your disposal, should you need them. If you'd rather have your privacy, that's fine, as well. And, obviously, I wouldn't burst in on you. We can set rules." Wilder stood then, too, even as Harley moved away from him to the windows, her mind crowded with a million worries.

"What kind of rules?"

"Any you'd like."

Would it work? Could she effectively treat someone *in his own house*? The idea seemed absurd. Since when did a life coach *live* with a client? And yet… why wasn't she dismissing it outright? Why was she even considering it for a second? She knew why. It was the damn money. She hated that the money actually meant something. That she might just need it.

"Why live with you? I don't need to *live* with you to treat you or coach you, or whatever it is you need from me."

"I want you to treat me exclusively. I'll need to have access to you when I need you. And I work long hours and need someone, well, someone at my beck and call." Of course, he did. Since when were billionaires reasonable? Since when did they respect other people's schedules and free time?

"You think I'll drop everything at two in the morning if you need a chat." She crossed her arms.

"Maybe." Wilder moved closer to her. Even without looking, she could feel him behind her, less than a foot away.

"It sounds like you want a security blanket. Not a life coach."

"Also, you living here would solve a second problem, which is that I can't afford for anyone to know you're treating me."

"Having a sex advice columnist under your roof might raise suspicion." Harley glanced over her shoulder at him, frowning.

"Believe me, women come and go in my penthouse. You won't raise suspicion."

"I'm not someone you're dating," she said, wondering if she needed to point out the obvious.

"Yet." His face remained expressionless and she was wondering if he was kidding or not.

Harley coughed. Was this why he wanted her to move in with him? Was he under the impression that therapy from her involved *hands-on* work? "I can't date you. Not if I'm coaching you. It violates every rule I've ever made for myself, and if you think I'll treat you by actually having sex with you, then you've recruited the wrong sexologist." She should've left already. She shouldn't even have stayed this long.

"I'm not asking you to move in so we can have sex, Ms. Vega. I'm simply protective of my privacy. That's all. Most of the time, paparazzi stalk me, and stake out the lobby of this very building. If you came regularly, eventually they'd know." He took a deep breath. "If I came to you, then they'd know."

"Getting help is nothing to be ashamed of." Harley met his gaze.

"No, it isn't. But I don't want my company's stock to plummet, either, on scandalous news that its owner is impotent."

"Would they really?"

"Of course, they would. They've dipped on much less salacious news."

She looked away from him, back out the window. She couldn't seriously be considering moving in with the man. What on earth kind of business dealings could sexual therapy throw a wrench in?

"Also, there's a third reason you should move in."

"I can hardly wait to hear this."

"You're being evicted, Ms. Vega. In a week's time, you won't have anywhere to stay, anyway."

She was struck speechless. "How did you know that?"

He gave her a sly look. "I trade in information, Ms. Vega. I made it my business to know."

So he knew how desperate she was, then. Knew she was facing rough times. Facing having to move back in with her parents in Miami by the month's end if she didn't change her circumstances and fast. She could do that, though. It wasn't as if she had *no* options. She just didn't have any good ones.

"Since it's my fault you are being evicted, I figured offering you a place to stay was the least I could do."

Well, he had a point there. It *was* his fault she couldn't pay her rent.

"How about we have a trial period?" Wilder sounded calm and confident. Of course, he did. He expected people to do as he instructed, no questions asked. "You can treat me for one week, living here, and then after one week's time, if you would like to leave, I'll pay you a full month's salary, anyway."

Harley's mind spun with the possibilities.

"If I do this, you understand that I am not a sexual surrogate."

"Sexual...surrogate?" Wilder looked confused.

"I don't have sex to heal people or help them work out their...issues." Not that she'd ever have sex with him, anyway. She hated him. Period. But she knew Wilder was a man used to getting what he wanted, and she needed to be sure he knew there was absolutely one thing he couldn't have: her body. No matter how charming the man's smile was, he had to understand she had rules that she didn't intend to break.

"I'm asking you to treat me," Wilder said. "Sex is optional."

"No, it's off the table." Harley had to make this perfectly clear. She could only agree to this if she set up rules. She didn't want a handsy billionaire who felt entitled to her body.

"That's your decision completely." Wilder shrugged,

indicating with a slight head nod that he'd respect her decision.

She was not quite sure if she felt relieved or disappointed. "So you'll respect my rules, then?"

He took a step closer to her and Harley craned her neck to meet his gaze, suddenly very aware of how broad he was, how very, very tall.

"I always respect women's rules. It's my motto that if you make the rule, you have to be the one to break it."

"I won't break my rules." Harley had no intention of changing her mind. No matter how charismatic Wilder Lange might be. Plus, she despised him.

"Sounds like you're challenging yourself now." Wilder flashed a bright white smile, all charm, all ease, and yet, she sensed that reticence beneath it all. A distance that he put between himself and others. It might just be at the root of whatever issues he was having. She itched to dig into his mind, figure out what made him tick. *Why?* she wondered. So she could know her enemy better?

"I'm not the one who's going to be challenged if I treat you," she said. She might not be a therapist, but she'd done enough coaching to know that really dealing with his issues meant getting a closer look at the ugly truths that most people kept hidden away. For Wilder Lange, she suspected he used that charming smile to lure people in and then somehow keep them at arm's length, all at the same time. "I'll take this job but only on the condition that you respect my therapeutic methods."

"Certainly." Wilder cocked his head to one side, the light catching the hint of red highlights in his otherwise nearly black hair.

"And I'm free to leave at *any* time, even before the full week is up, should I decide that my methods are not being respected."

"Of course. I don't plan to keep you prisoner against your will." Wilder looked at her as if she were crazy. And maybe she was. Why was she even considering doing this? Because she was losing her apartment. She didn't want to admit defeat and go home to Miami. Especially not when they were already strapped. Last year, her sister had recently gotten divorced and moved back in with her parents with two small children in tow. She didn't need to be another burden, not when her parents were dealing with their own. But even more than that, she had to admit to herself, she might be a little bit too fascinated with Wilder Lange.

"Okay." Why was her heart beating so hard in her chest? Why had her blood pressure ticked up a notch? "Then, we have a deal." She stuck out her hand. She was a professional and she could damn well act like one.

He grasped it in his, putting a little more pressure against her palm this time, and held it for a little bit too long. She sucked in a breath and realized she was holding it. Harley deliberately exhaled. She didn't like the man, but that didn't mean she couldn't treat him. And she'd have a free place to stay while she saved cash and figured out her next move.

"I'm glad to hear it." His voice rolled over her like melted caramel and as she watched his lips move, she realized that she was already looking forward to their first real session, when she could start unpacking the man's secrets and dive into that fascinating brain of his. She knew the excitement meant trouble. But she could handle it. She was certain she could. What could possibly go wrong?

CHAPTER FIVE

ONE WEEK LATER, Harley was already regretting her decision to move into Wilder Lange's penthouse, and she hadn't even unpacked yet. Not that she'd likely get the chance to do that, as Lange's impressive staff (a butler, a maid and one valet) worked to get her things tucked away in the largest guest bedroom she'd ever seen. The problem wasn't the accommodations. They were stellar. Her "room"—bigger than her entire Brooklyn apartment—had a giant mahogany four-poster-canopy bed to her right, a large flat-screen TV on the wall, an ornate antique dresser, a connected full bathroom, complete with a Jacuzzi tub, and, next door, its own "kitchenette," which was, Harley was sad to say, larger than her own small apartment kitchen. The fridge was also already stocked with the essentials. It stood nearby to the other gleaming top-of-the-line appliances, all of which looked as if they'd never been used. But why would they have been? Wilder had his own kitchen downstairs, and his own chef to cook for him. Why would anyone need to use this one?

She ought to be grateful for such lovely accommodations, but the fact was she was simply annoyed. Annoyed that a man like Wilder had such nice things and she'd been desperate enough to agree to living with him in the first place, so she could be reminded that he had everything and she had nothing. Well, not nothing, exactly. She had her furniture in storage and a Visa that was about to combust since she'd swiped the darn thing so often this month. She still couldn't quite believe a week ago she'd gone into his penthouse with the intent of giving him a piece of her mind, and now she was…moving in? The whole idea was absurd. So absurd, in fact, that she'd deliberately *not* told her parents or sister about it, because how would she begin to explain moving in with a billionaire? Besides, she was fairly certain that her NDA made it impossible to tell anyone where she was living or what she was doing for the next few months. She'd read over the damn thing the night before and she pretty much couldn't speak one word about Lange.

"Do you have any questions, Ms. Vega?" asked Jacob, Wilder's butler, an older gentleman with more salt in his hair than pepper who was dressed in a suit, and made her feel decidedly underdressed in her tank top, coral linen capris and flat sandals. Jacob had gone through all she needed to know about her swanky new digs, including how to turn on the lights, run the shower, set the temperature, request maid service and get the news and weather all by talking to smart device panels in her room.

"Uh..." Harley glanced around the room, which was both traditionally furnished yet distinctly high tech, and thought she had a million questions, but she figured she'd have to stumble through and figure out how to live in a room with smart devices and not light switches. "No, thank you."

"If you have any questions, don't hesitate to call us." Jacob nodded toward the panel on the wall with the video screen linked to every other room in the house, she assumed. She'd never stayed anywhere so modern and traditional at the same time. Again, she wondered about the old furniture, the traditional quilt on the bed juxtaposed with the cutting-edge tech. Each side seeming to be working for dominance in the room. Harley looked up in time to see that the maid and valet had made quick work of her small rolling suitcase, hanging up her clothes and putting her other items away in drawers before tucking the suitcase into the massive walk-in closet. Her clothes, she noted, took up about one-hundredth of the space provided. Resentment hung heavy in her gut. Why did Wilder Lange deserve such nice things? Why did he get this when he ruined so many lives with a click of his mouse or a single phone call?

"Thank you," she said, feeling awkward as the servants nodded in her direction and then quickly dispersed. She was glad to see a safety bolt on the door. At least she could lock it from the inside and sleep at night. Not that she expected Wilder Lange to slip into her room in the middle of the night. But, still, the bolt was reassuring.

Nonetheless, she was still starting to feel as if coming here might have been a mistake. First off, she was far more comfortable sitting behind her computer writing advice. She was far less comfortable sitting across from a man like Wilder Lange and telling him how she thought his body ought to work. It didn't help, either, that she wasn't in a relationship right now. In fact, *most* of her relationships had fizzled lately and she couldn't quite figure out why. It was the ultimate irony: *she* was the woman who was supposed to have all the relationship answers and yet she couldn't manage to keep a man in her life for more than three months before they ran for the door. Granted, she suspected why. She took things slow. Maybe too slow, granted, but that's where she felt comfortable. She didn't jump right into sex. She might be fine talking about vibrators and climaxes in her column, but she wasn't all that fine with taking off her clothes with a complete stranger. And anyone she'd known less than a couple of months, in her mind, was a complete stranger.

Harley glanced at her watch and realized that their first session, agreed upon in advance, was about an hour away. She felt jittery and nervous and figured a walk around the penthouse might be the best way to work out her nerves before the big session. She smoothed down her tank top, grabbed her bag and decided to head out of her room to get a layout of the place, and maybe, she'd admit, because she was a little nosey. She'd never been in a giant penthouse before. Who knew how the rich lived? Once in the massive hallway with the sleek pristine white carpet, she hesitated. Which way?

She'd already been to the right, since Jacob had led her there from the front door. So, left it was. She quickly found that Wilder's home was larger than most hotels, and it contained no helpful signs pointing guests to the lobby, but she did find a stairwell and decided to see where it went. She walked through room after room, a seemingly endless number of sitting rooms and lounges and, after peeking in a few doors, many, many bedrooms. Who needed this many bedrooms? He could sleep in a different one every night and not even dirty his sheets. What she did know was that she was impressed. Damn impressed. The man had *real* marble statues that looked like they were actually from ancient Greece, which they probably were. He even had a game room, she saw, complete with a pool table with *gray* felt. She'd never seen a pool table with gray felt before, and figured it had to be expensive. In fact, everything in the penthouse screamed money, even the sleek stainless steel doorknobs and light switch plates.

The current hallway she stood in was lined with vibrant modern paintings. No staid oil painting portraits of ancestors here. She made it to the end of the hall and went left, wishing she had a bag of breadcrumbs to lead her back to her room because she'd taken a number of turns and feared she might be lost. She wondered where Wilder's room was and then immediately felt warmth in her cheeks. Wilder Lange. She was still reeling from their first meeting, from the way his dark eyes seemed to read her mind. Today, however, she was bound and determined not to let attraction get in the way of the work she needed to do. How often had she coached her readers about controlling their impulses? Now, it was time to follow her own advice. Besides, what she needed to worry about was being able to help the man. She still disliked him, disliked his entitled ways and how he played God with people's lives, and part of her hated that she'd even agreed to help the man in the first place. But she knew why she'd agreed. She needed the money. And, maybe, a small part of her was holding on to the hope that, with her dazzling insights, he'd reinstate her old job. Okay, time to head back. The last thing she needed to do was get caught snooping around his place.

She took the right fork at the end of the hallway and found herself at a back staircase. This wasn't the staircase she'd used to get to this level, so she turned around and walked down the other fork and found an actual elevator at the end of that long hallway. How many ways up and down did this home have? Hell, how many *stories* was it? Did he own the whole building? Though, technically, he did, since his name was on it. The first fifteen floors were dedicated to his national news empire in both broadcast and broadsheet news. She shook her head at the size of the place, and wished she'd paid better attention when Jacob had shown her to her room. Only now she realized the folly of taking one wrong turn, as she wound her way through the house like she was in a hedge maze. She pivoted, and before she knew it, she found herself standing in the double doorway of a massive home gym, complete with mirrors, free weights, a treadmill and about a half dozen weight machines. She froze when she saw that one of the weight machines was occupied—by Wilder—who was pushing quite an impressive block of weight in a chest press. He sat with his back to her, shirtless, which showed off his impressive muscles that rippled with effort every time he moved. Harley realized she ought to turn quickly and head out, before she was caught staring at the man. It felt like the worst invasion of his privacy, and yet, she felt rooted to the spot, mesmerized by the twitch of the muscles in his back, as he pulled the weights back, his thick arms bulging with the effort. He let the weights go with a sudden jerk, the set complete, as the weights cracked together. And then he stood, disentangling himself from the machine and reaching for a nearby water bottle. The mirrored wall reflected the profile of his face, and at any moment, he could look up and see her standing there.

Now's the time to go, she told herself, and yet she watched as he lifted the bottle to his full lips and drank. He could turn around at any moment or turn to his left and see her in that mirror, and then what? She'd explain that she was simply admiring the view? She was snooping around his giant penthouse? Then again, it had been so long since she'd seen a half-naked man, she realized it was partly just a physical reaction to being so close to so much bare skin. She turned to go, but the movement caught his attention and he turned.

"Ms. Vega." She froze at the sound of her name. "I thought our appointment wasn't for another hour. And, I thought we agreed to meet in my study."

"Yes, er…" Was she about to admit to this man she was simply lost? "I was just…uh…" *Rudely poking around your ginormous penthouse.* "Taking a walk. I'll head back to my room."

She ducked back into the corridor.

"Actually, your room is the other way," Wilder called. Stricken, she quickly turned.

"Oh, right." She smiled, uneasily.

His dark eyes looked almost golden in the gym light. He eyed her, assessing. "Lost?"

Harley felt a little flame of heat flicker up her neck. "I was hoping it wasn't that obvious."

He grabbed a towel from the back of the weight bench and wiped his sweaty brow with it. The glisten of sweat on his firm muscled arms just made them even sexier, if that were possible. She was distinctly aware he wasn't wearing a shirt, and she was trying to avoid staring at his chest and the pronounced pectoral muscles. Damn the man was beyond fine. He was…just white-hot. Why did he have to be like a walking underwear model? How did he get his abs so cut? And why was she imagining what it might be like to lick that sweat right off his swollen muscles? She'd never imagined jumping into bed instantly with any man she'd ever met before. She was methodical, slow, plodding when it came to her own personal relationships. But somehow, Wilder just made her mind go directly to the dirtiest deed she could think of.

"Everybody gets lost the first time they stay." He smiled, flashing his perfectly straight, bright white teeth. "Even the governor did, when he stayed here."

Harley imagined the governor, an older gentleman with a wife and kids, probably wouldn't have been so flustered catching Wilder shirtless in his gym. Harley didn't know where to focus her attention. Everywhere she looked, she seemed to see Wilder's skin: in front of her and reflected back on the mirrored walls, all dimensions of him in view at once. *It's just a body,* she told herself. *We all have one.* Of course, few people had one as impressive as Wilder Lange. Harley had no doubt about that. She knew that few men had abs so distinctly rippled, or that V of muscle diving right into the waistband of his shorts. Why was it that *he* was half naked but she was the one who felt exposed?

"Well, glad I'm in good company," she said. She took a step backward. "I guess I'll be going to my room…if you can just point me in the right direction?"

He hung the towel on his neck and grinned. "I'll show you."

"No, that's not—"

"I don't mind. I'll drop you there, and then I'll go shower."

She thought of him soaping up his sweaty body in the shower and started to feel her palms go clammy. What on earth was wrong with her? She was acting like a sex addict herself. *Get a grip, Harley.* She didn't even like the man. Of course, she didn't need a doctoral degree in human sexuality to know that not liking a person had zero to do with physical attraction. There was such a thing as hate sex. Plenty of people had it. Now her head was filled with images of savage hate sex with the already half-naked Wilder Lange.

"Okay," she said, suddenly grateful the man couldn't read her mind.

Thankfully, he tossed the towel aside and grabbed his shirt, a blank gray T-shirt, and slid it over his head, pulling it down over his impressive chest. With more of him covered, she felt less…exposed, somehow, and more like her old sensible self. As he led the way, she reminded herself of the main reasons she disliked him and shouldn't, under any circumstances, think about him naked.

"Did the move-in go smoothly?" he asked her, typical small talk. She almost resented the break in silence. She was here to do a job and then leave, not to be friendly. She could listen to his problems and give him advice without *being his friend.*

"Fine," she said, curt.

"Is everything to your liking?"

"Yes."

"Do you always use one-word answers?"

"Yes," she said. With him, anyway. She was here to treat him, save up her salary and then get out. Hell, if she found another paying job before treatment was done, she'd book it out of there.

"You know we can be friendly. I don't bite."

"No. You just fire entire staffs. Gut historic publications. Take credit for turning them into lightweight airplane reading material."

"So I see you're still taking business personally."

"Hard not to." She glanced at him. She knew she was being petty, immature, even, but she couldn't help it. She had longtime friends who'd lost their jobs, friends who were having an even harder time than her finding work. She adjusted her bag, but as she did so, her elbow brushed his, and she felt surprised by the contact, by the warmth of his skin. She realized the hallway was entirely too narrow for her liking, and that they might well brush up against one another again. She wondered if she dreaded the contact or welcomed it.

"You know, making those decisions is not easy for me."

"You don't look like you're losing any sleep over

it." He looked well rested and deeply tanned, his bronzed skin flawless, the whites of his eyes pristine.

"I'm not heartless. I know my decisions can hurt people. But I cut the jobs so that I can save some of them, so that I can preserve what's left of the magazine. So it doesn't completely go under."

"By slashing half the pages of the magazine? Turning it into something completely without personality?"

He sent her a sidelong glance. "I turn it into something I can sell. So I can keep the jobs I can."

They turned down a familiar corridor. She remembered this from her first visit to the penthouse. They were nearing the study.

"And make a few bucks for yourself?" She was sure greed had quite a lot to do with it.

"Actually, I lose money on almost every print venture. The magazines and newspapers are pretty much black holes. I do it because I don't want to think of a world without those publications in it. I know my father wouldn't have wanted that. He was a man who read five newspapers a day and more magazines than that every week."

This was news to Harley. She just assumed corporate raiders did what they did purely for money. Could it be that she'd been wrong about Wilder Lange? Maybe she had been slightly hard on him. Would she rather see all her colleagues fired from the magazine? No, she wouldn't.

"Besides, my brother Seth always reminds me

to remember print. He loves a good old-fashioned newspaper or magazine in his hands, too."

"How many brothers do you have?"

"Three. Half brothers, actually, not that I see them that way, and all hell bent on causing trouble. Someone has to keep them in line. So it falls to me, since I'm the oldest."

Harley could hear how much he cared for them. They neared the entrance of her suite.

"Here we are." He indicated the door. "I'll be taking a shower then if..."

"Yes." She nodded. She knew he'd be going, but she wanted answers first. She wasn't ready to part company with him. "But...your brothers..."

"Yes?"

"You love them?"

He laughed. "I do. Even when they're a pain in the ass." He shook his head. "Don't let the money fool you. It can cause far more trouble than it solves."

"How so?"

"One brother wants to be a rock star. One wants to sail around the world in a yacht, stopping only so he can race other yachts." He shook his head. "And then, there's one brother who strictly does peace corps work, refuses to take a family nickel, even if it would mean finally getting the guy new shoes. Let's just say Thanksgiving is interesting. And I'm the one controlling the purse strings. Dad made sure of that. Their mother, however, is still furious about it."

"What about your mother?" Why was she suddenly interested in his personal life? Yet, the questions kept popping out of her. It was for the coaching sessions, she told herself.

"My mother was my father's first wife. She was a model, her background mixed. Part Armenian, part Irish. She died in a skiing accident when I was five. My father remarried when I was eight."

"That had to be hard." She hadn't expected Wilder Lange to have problems. She always thought of him as a spoiled heir to a fortune, but she was beginning to realize she'd made assumptions that simply weren't fair.

"It was."

Harley paused, hand on the doorknob. "How did you get along with your stepmom?" She almost felt him stiffen at the word *stepmom.*

"I'd rather not talk about Lucinda, if you don't mind."

He offered nothing more, and Harley could almost hear the steel door snapping shut. He'd shared about as much as he planned to about that, she thought. He turned and left her then as she turned the knob to her room and opened the door. She'd hit a sore subject, she realized, one that she'd need to probe deeper in their session.

CHAPTER SIX

WILDER WAS BEGINNING to regret sex therapy. First of all, it seemed to have nothing to do with sex at all, and everything to do with his past. He'd been through several "sessions" now for the past two weeks, and all he could say was that he was slightly disappointed. Harley was turning out to be much more like all the other counselors he'd ever met. Except, of course, he hadn't wanted to fuck all the other counselors he'd ever met. In fact, he hadn't want to fuck someone as much in his life as Harley Vega. He sat across from her, watching her study him beneath her librarian's reader glasses, her full and all-too-kissable lips pursed in concentration. He was sitting on the couch, and Harley, the chair, a notebook open on her lap. It was for taking notes, except she seemed not to be bothering this session.

She kept her legs crossed at the knee, and the coral sundress she wore had inched up, showing him more thigh than he'd seen before. He had a hard time not staring at the skin there, the delicate shape of her toned quadriceps. This was a woman who took care of herself. He wanted to talk more about her. Was she dating anyone? What did she like in bed and how could he get her into his? But she stubbornly refused to answer questions about herself. She kept the focus on him. He realized that most men would be glad to blather on about themselves for hours, but Wilder wasn't that kind of man.

At least the open hostility had faded a bit, now that she was starting to see him as slightly human. He understood, of course. He'd be upset, too, if he'd been let go from his job, but he was hoping she'd see that the magazine was dying, anyway. If he hadn't bought it, another raider would've, or it would've simply folded like so many other print publications in recent years. Long gone were the days when Lange Communications could sustain itself entirely on the sales of glossy global magazines. Now, it was all about cable companies, airwaves and internet. Sure, outlets still needed content, that hadn't changed, but everywhere was paying less for it than they ever had. Still, he didn't blame Harley for trying to hold on to a way of life that was changing.

And he knew she was tough. He'd done his share of research on her. He was a careful man. He knew her family was from Puerto Rico, that her parents came to Miami after a 1989 hurricane destroyed their home. She was born in Miami and went to school in New York, and had one older sister who'd married young. He knew that her father and mother ran a small restaurant and barely made ends meet. She'd come to New York on a scholarship to NYU and had stayed after graduation to make a name for herself. And make a name for herself she had. Not only had she been the youngest columnist ever hired by *Femme*, but she'd also been regularly featured in other magazines, and interviewed on countless daytime TV shows. He admired her grit, the fact she'd come from nothing and made something of herself. Most people thought he'd inherited a fortune when his father died, except that Lange Communications was near bankruptcy when he'd taken it over and had millions in debt. He'd single-handedly turned it around, made it profitable again. It had taken some doing. It was probably why Lucinda had been sniffing around for the first time since his father's funeral seven years ago.

"So, last time we talked a little about Lucinda," Harley was saying. He flinched at the name. The last person on earth he wanted to talk about was his stepmom. The evil stepmom of all stepmoms.

"I don't see what she has to do with anything," he said, feeling like a virus beneath a microscope. She was studying him clinically, when all he truly wanted was to take Harley into his arms and kiss the life out of her. He had never felt so drawn to a woman before. Never had trouble controlling his want. It was near impossible to ignore the obvious current between them, the hum of its power. Wilder knew how rare such chemistry was, such raw attraction that seemed to pull the need out of the deepest part of him. Sure, he found women attractive, and they him, but this was something else running between them. This was pure animal want. It was something even his wounded body seemed unable to resist.

It maddened him that she seemed to be able to ignore it. Worse than that, she kept subtly glancing at her watch, as if she were counting down the minutes to the end of the session. He'd gotten the impression that she had half a foot out the door.

"Why do you want to know so much about my childhood?" Wilder asked. "Aren't we supposed to be talking about sex? About...getting me back on track?" He glanced down at his lap, which seemed to be having no trouble being on track at the moment, not with Harley Vega watching him with her sharp light brown eyes. Not when she uncrossed her legs, and he saw the pale inside of one thigh.

"Sometimes, a past trauma can affect our sexuality. I'm just trying to rule out different possibilities. Plus, we need to get back to why you avoid relationships, why you prefer casual sex."

Wilder snorted. "That's no mystery. I prefer casual sex because it's damn fun."

Harley shook her head slowly. "No, it's destructive. Especially in your case."

"Well, don't hold back on me," he said.

"You told me to be blunt, so I am. You're running through women, trying to avoid your problems. It's absolutely obvious. You're not having fun. You're avoiding your issues."

"Avoiding my issues *is* fun," he remarked.

"You know what I mean." She glared at him, nostrils flaring slightly. God, he loved getting under her skin.

"So, let's talk a little more about Lucinda. Try to get at the real reason you can't commit to a woman. That might also be the real reason you can't…have sex right now. Your body isn't even able to make the commitment to have *sex.* Maybe if we figure out why, we can cure you."

"You're saying my dick isn't working the way I want it to because it's commitment phobic?" The idea was laughable.

"It's as good a theory as any." She stared at him. "So. Lucinda?"

Wilder didn't want to think about his past. He worked hard to lock it away, chain it away in the darkest places of his heart so it couldn't crawl out and hurt him. Instead of focusing on his past, he chose to focus on Harley's voice, which felt like raw honey, sweet and sticky. He thought about what other parts of her body might also be sweet, and about whether or not her skin was as soft as it looked. "How was your relationship with your stepmother?"

His spicy thoughts about what her bare, tanned skin would feel like beneath his fingertips cooled. Nothing like the mention of Lucinda to douse any thoughts of passion. He needed to change the subject. He knew what would cure him and it had nothing to do with talking.

"You sure seem interested in my childhood," he said. "Is it because you're trying to cure me, or you're interested in finding out more about me?"

A tiny little flame of a blush appeared on her chest. Interesting. Maybe he'd hit a nerve.

"I'm not." Her voice was sharp, annoyed. A little too annoyed and far too defensive. Ah, the crack in her armor. So she was intrigued by him, no matter how much she pretended she disliked him. Some of the questions she was asking weren't purely clinical; they were because she was curious about him. About his past. About what made him tick. So, the truth came out.

"You're not the least bit interested?" he challenged.

"Well," she began, carefully. "I have to get to know you if I'm going to offer you decent advice. That's what the last two weeks have been about."

"So this is all about the job, then. Nothing personal in it?"

She waited just the tiniest of beats before answering. "Nothing personal." Now, he knew she was lying. He could read people, always had, and she was definitely lying.

"Fine." He was starting to get frustrated. Maybe he'd been wrong about a sex advice columnist being able to jumpstart him, when so many others haven't. Maybe his problems weren't solvable. Yet, he couldn't quite shake the feeling that Harley *could* solve them. If she wanted to. He knew exactly how she could start. By putting her lips on pretty much any part of his body. Or all of it.

"So you're saying my inability to perform in the bedroom is because my father's wife was mean to me?" He never called her stepmom. To him, she would always be his father's wife.

"So, she didn't like you." Harley typed a bit more on her keyboard, but she kept her dark eyes focused on him.

"No, she didn't like being reminded that her husband had a life before her, no." That was the understatement of the year.

"That had to be difficult." She seemed genuinely grieved to hear that he had had a difficult childhood. Interesting. He thought she hated him.

"Does it really matter? Nobody has a great childhood, do they?"

"So, why not talk about it?"

"Lucinda drank a lot. She wasn't nice to me or any of my brothers. There, I talked about it." He leaned forward. "Can we finally talk about sex now?"

"Okay." Harley put down her pen and straightened her glasses on her nose. "Let's talk about it. How do you feel about sex, Mr. Lange?"

The way she said it, devoid of all interest, made him think of a doctor prescribing erectile dysfunction pills. This was not what he had had in mind.

"Don't make it sound so dull." Wilder was only half teasing.

"Sex is just sex. It's not dull or exciting all on its own. It should be *fun,* but only if we let go of the things holding us back. But we have to make sure we're not doing anything that's harmful to us, to our self-esteem. Harmful like one-night stands."

"One-night stands are beautiful works of art, they are definitely not harmful. Have you tried them?"

"We're talking about your sex life, not mine."

Hmmm. There was the defensive block-out again. What was the woman hiding? He badly wanted to talk about her sex life. So badly he could almost taste the curiosity in his mouth. He wanted to know what he'd have to do to get past that hard protective shell of hers.

"For the next five minutes, let's talk about your sex life. Not mine," he said.

"No. No way," she protested.

He sat up a bit straighter, guessing that she might take the bait. "But you realize you've been asking me the same questions for two weeks and I haven't given you any new answers." He'd been a black box. And he could keep it up forever if he wanted.

She bit her lip, considering, and then blew out a frustrated breath. "Yes, I noticed."

"Okay, then. You want to pry open this steel trap?" He tapped his temple. "Then, you'll have to play my game. It's just five minutes."

She narrowed her eyes, looking wary. Even after

two weeks, he'd done very little to win this woman's trust. And while she might not be *openly* hostile to him, she damn sure wasn't friendly. Not nearly as friendly as he'd like. That needed to change.

"I'm not the one who needs sex advice."

"No, but if you want to help me, then I suggest you give this a try. Otherwise, I can stonewall you all day, every day, for weeks, or even years on end." A little color drained from her face. So, it wasn't just his imagination: she was counting down the days until she could leave his penthouse, until this job was over. He didn't like that she found it so distasteful. Was his company truly so bad that she wanted to bolt at the first opportunity?

"You promise not to evade my questions?" He saw a glint of hope in her eyes. Well, that was something, he guessed. Even if the hope stemmed from her wish to try to get away from him as fast as possible. At this point, he'd take what he could get. He already knew he could be damn persuasive if he had an in.

"Promise," he said, and meant it.

"Okay." He saw a crack in her armor appear, then. Yes, just what he wanted. "I'll do it. Go ahead, ask me what you want."

Ah, the possibilities were endless, the temptations tantalizing. What would he ask her first? Perhaps what part of her body she liked touched the most? He'd been trying to guess at that since he'd met her. Or, maybe, he'd simply ask how she was managing to ignore the white-hot chemistry between them, the pulsing want that felt like a river of lava. He knew it wasn't in his head. Why was she resisting it so much? Maybe she had herself on a tight leash, he thought, because there was another person in the picture. Maybe she wasn't free.

"Are you in a relationship?" he asked her. Might as well get that out of the way.

"No." Annoyance flicked across her face. Touchy subject, then.

"Do you want to be?"

"Maybe," she said, eyes wary.

"Do you tend to be a relationship person…or a casual sex person?"

A little bit of pink colored her almond-toned cheeks before she crossed her arms and turned her back to him.

"Relationship person," she said, but her voice was low, reticent. She was hiding something. She wouldn't meet his eyes.

"Are you sure?" he prodded.

"Well, technically…" She cleared her throat. "I've never had casual sex. But my study of it suggests it's not what will give people the most satisfaction. So, I prefer relationship sex."

Now, he felt blindsided. She was thirty. How had she never had a hookup?

"Wait. You've never had casual sex? No one-night stands. No casual vacation sex. No ongoing friends with benefits. All the sex you've had has been in a committed relationship?"

She nodded. "Yes. So?"

He realized, by the flicker of insecurity in her eyes, that she was sensitive about it but also defensive.

"Well, I mean you are a sex columnist, but you've only had relationship sex?"

"Yes. And I have my degrees. More than any others in my field."

"Right, because sex is all academic." He shook his head. "So, this relationship sex, you think it's prepared you to understand…all kinds of sex?"

"Of course. I've had two partners who were—"

"Wait." He held up his hand, not quite sure he'd heard correctly. "You've only had two partners?"

He wasn't sure how many he'd *thought* she'd had, but two was…well, mind-bogglingly low. That damn secret would stay with him. He wasn't going to tell anyone. Yet…he couldn't quite believe it. Only two?

"So, these two partners," he said, trying to tread softly. "Who were they?"

Harley let out a frustrated sigh. "The first was my college boyfriend. Dated him for seven years, but then we broke up. I wanted to get married, but he didn't." There was a whole lot of heartbreak in that single sentence, Wilder knew. He could feel it in the tight, controlled way she talked about it. "The second was a year-long relationship that ended about a year ago. He got a job in California, and I wasn't willing to move."

"So, you've never had casual sex."

Harley seemed to realize too late her mistake in being so honest. “So?”

“So, you’re telling me that casual sex is evil, but you don’t really know because you’ve never had it.” Wilder leaned forward, clasping his hands together.

“I don’t have to *do* something to know it’s bad. All the research says…”

“Research isn’t doing. How can you truly know that you’re giving good advice to your readership when you’ve never even had a one-night stand?” Wilder stood now, spreading his hands.

“I can tell drugs are bad without doing drugs,” she said. But he could tell that she was shaken, unnerved.

“Right. But you wouldn’t know how great a high is, would you? The temptation a drug addict might fight if you hadn’t been there yourself? You’re writing with certainty about something you’re really not certain about at all.” Wilder moved a bit closer to her now, closing the distance between them slowly, ever slowly. “Aren’t you even the least bit curious about casual sex?”

“Maybe.” Harley’s voice was so low he wasn’t sure he’d even heard her correctly. Harley turned away from him, toward the floor-to-ceiling glass windows overlooking the Upper East Side. He stood behind her, tantalizingly close, but with his arms at his sides. He saw every ragged, unsettled breath she took with each rise of her shoulders.

He knew he had her now. Knew that her curiosity would do the rest of the work for him.

"What if casual sex isn't what you think? What if it's actually hotter than you know? What if it's… exactly the right thing to do sometimes?"

She remained still, thinking. He could almost hear the gears in her head move, almost sense the inner conflict inside her.

"I think we can make a deal, Ms. Vega," Wilder whispered, voice low in his throat, so close to her that he could kiss her neck. "I can talk to you all day, but that's not going to cure me."

She stayed still, studying the skyline. "It's your body I want," he said. "It's your body I need. It's your touch that can cure me, Ms. Vega. You know it and I know it. And it's damn time we stopped pretending, because now I know that there's something I can give you, too."

She stiffened. "What's that?"

"Experience," he said. "And sex you'll never forget. But it will tell you once and for all if you're right about casual sex. I'll do everything I can to prove you wrong."

"You're going to teach me about casual sex?" She looked stunned.

"I promise to show you everything you've been missing."

CHAPTER SEVEN

LATER THAT NIGHT, Harley paced the inside of her room, unable to sleep. It had been hours since the session with Wilder Lange, but her heart still felt like it was racing. Her emotions raging in her chest. Sometimes, she'd feel outraged: how dare he assume *he* was the one who should teach her about sex? That she even needed to be *taught* about sex. She knew plenty about sex and human sexuality. Hell, she'd written a dissertation on it. She had a PhD, a *doctorate* for heaven's sake, in human sexuality. She was a sex doctor, technically. She was probably the most informed sexologist that existed in North America, maybe even the world. And *he* was going to teach *her* about sex? The gall of the man.

And yet…

Yet, she wasn't entirely sure she'd tell him no. That was the scary part. She was actually considering his offer. Casual sex. Even if it was just once. The whole deal. She was *seriously* considering it. And she knew it had everything to do with the fact that she'd never in her life been interested in a one-night stand, until the day she met Wilder Lange.

Hadn't she been imagining ripping the man's clothes off since the first time she'd laid eyes on him? Hadn't he lit up her arousal centers immediately?

"This is crazy," she told her empty room, and the little kitchenette. "This is insane." She couldn't seriously be considering falling into Wilder Lange's bed. She'd told him she wouldn't sleep with him. Hell, she wasn't even sure she *liked* him. He was still the man who'd gutted her magazine and laid her off. He was still responsible for the loss of all those jobs. But why did the images of sliding her naked body against his keep running through her mind? Why did she keep thinking about him shirtless in the gym, wondering what the weight of his body on hers would feel like?

No. She couldn't be seriously considering this. She'd never done anything so reckless her whole life. Not just casual sex, but sex with someone like Wilder Lange. He probably had so many notches in his bedpost he didn't have any bedpost left. And he was full of himself. And entitled. And…completely infuriating. She couldn't believe she was thinking about jumping into his bed like some romance novel virgin desperate to learn new techniques from a powerful master. No. She was a modern, educated woman who didn't actually *need* a man for anything. Sure, she'd only had two partners her whole life, but wasn't that plenty enough to know about sex? She'd had deep, meaningful relationship sex. She knew what sex was. Knew the difference between good and bad sex. She'd had plenty of actual sex. Did the number of partners even make a difference?

Yet, it was true she'd never had sex with a stranger, never casually fallen into someone's bed without knowing their middle name and pretty much everything else about them. Never followed the path of lust to see where it led just for the heck of it. And wasn't that part of her problem now with finding a relationship? She just wasn't comfortable jumping into a bed casually. Actually, she realized that she wasn't comfortable jumping into bed at all unless she'd known a person for a while. Her college boyfriend she met in high school and had had a secret crush on him for years before they finally did the deed. Her second boyfriend had been a work colleague she'd known for a year as friends before they went out on a first date.

Maybe her lack of experience with casual encounters was part of her problem now. Part of the reason she couldn't properly date anyone, her secret shame. That she gave relationship advice but couldn't seem to maintain a relationship. Could Wilder be *her* cure?

Then there was the crazy idea that somehow *she* could cure him. She knew, clinically, that she couldn't solve his problems. That despite his desire for her, impotence was a complicated puzzle, and he'd need to work on fixing himself. She couldn't just swoop in and save the day. Human beings just didn't work like that. And yet…and yet…wasn't she tempted to try? Who wouldn't want to be Wilder Lange's savior? Who wouldn't want to be the one woman on earth who could stoke his fire of desire? All the models and the sexy pop stars he could have, and he wanted her.

The power felt delicious. Heady, even.

She was supposed to hate him. Now she was just trying to convince herself he wasn't such a bad guy because she wanted his body as much as he wanted hers.

God, she didn't know what to do. She itched to pick up the phone and call her sister, her best friend and the one who held no punches when it came to relationship advice. Of course, normally, Harley was the one telling her sister what to do with her life. Besides, it was too late to call. It was nearing midnight. Not to mention there was that damn NDA she'd signed. No, she'd have to figure this out on her own. She grabbed her notepad and began furiously scribbling two headers: *Pros* and *Cons*.

She ought to be logical about this after all. Pro: she'd get experience she could use to give other people advice. Con: she might regret it. Pro: she might regret it if she *didn't* do it. Con: giving in to baser instincts never usually had good results. Eating a whole pint of ice cream, for instance, never made anyone feel better, did it?

After she'd scribbled more pros and cons, she stood up, frustrated, feeling that the walls of her big suite were somehow closing in on her. There's no way she would be able to sleep now, not with thoughts of Wilder Lange in her head, of the temptation of exploring his body and finding out what all those other women he'd taken to bed had found so bewitching. She tucked the pen and pad under one arm and headed out of her room, figuring just a walk down the long corridors of his penthouse would clear her head. Maybe after a walk, she'd feel clear-headed or, at least, able to look at her problem logically. Plus, her whole body buzzed with a kind of excited nervousness. The very idea of inviting Wilder into her bed made her nerves thrum with excitement. Too much excitement.

She walked down the long, darkened corridor, lit only by ambient lighting in the floor, which seemed to be motion activated. Whenever she took a step, a new lowlight would flick on. She almost felt like she was living in a spaceship. Everything was so impossibly high tech. Remembering her wrong turns from the first time she wandered out of her room, she almost laughed. Now, two weeks later, she'd more than gotten her bearings. She'd definitely steer clear of the gym and the wing where she knew Wilder's master bedroom suite was located. Harley just needed to walk. Let out the nervous energy buzzing in her veins.

It was pent-up sexual energy, she realized with a shock. God, the irony. It had been too long since she'd had sex with anyone, even herself. Well, no wonder Wilder had her in a tailspin. She ought to go back to her room and take care of it with one long soak in the bath. But, no. She wasn't going to do that. She feared that thoughts of Wilder would invade her me-time, completely defeating the purpose. No, she'd get rid of all this energy the old-fashioned way: a brisk walk. Then, maybe, at long last, she could think clearly. She thought about heading to the rooftop deck, maybe taking a look at the stars. She knew the deck existed: Jacob, the butler, had mentioned it. What had he said? Second stairwell all the way up? She was wearing her pajamas, a tank top and cotton-striped bottoms, and in her bare feet, but she knew the early June weather was warm, and, she figured, might as well try to get some fresh air. She felt claustrophobic all of a sudden, trapped inside the air-conditioned penthouse. Being outdoors would do her good.

She found the second stairwell and followed it up, glad to see the green light on the control panel near the door. That meant the alarm was off. Good. She pushed open the door and a warm breeze came over her, as she stepped onto the huge rooftop patio. She'd never been outside on a roof so high above the city before, but it was surrounded by tall ten-foot privacy walls. The rooftop deck had to be at least eight-thousand-square feet alone. It was divided into sections, too: the lounge area with a full couch and chairs and colorful potted plants, and then at the edge, a single lap pool and an adjacent Jacuzzi, lit blue against the night sky. The other lights were off up here, but the blazing city lights from Manhattan offered even more light than the full moon overhead. She glanced up, rubbing her bare arms, as she looked at the stars she could see, faint against the city sky but there nonetheless.

"Beautiful," she whispered. She stared in awe at the sky. *Should I do it?* she silently asked the stars. Should I sleep with Wilder Lange? Could he teach her things she didn't know about sex? Were there things that books couldn't tell her? Maybe it would make her a better columnist. Maybe it would make her a better lover for *future* boyfriends. Or maybe it would be the biggest mistake of her life.

She tried to squash her insecurities. She was a smart and talented woman. She'd had two boyfriends and they hadn't complained. Except, she thought sourly, they had left her. The hollowness of their rejection still stung. Her first boyfriend hadn't wanted to marry her. The second had picked a job over her. If she'd been a sex vixen, then maybe they wouldn't have been able to say no.

What was she even thinking? She didn't care what men thought of her. She liked who she was. She didn't need any sex coaching. Did she?

Then, suddenly, the rooftop door swung open with a clatter. She jumped in surprise, her bare toes slipping a little on the wooden decking, as she glanced up to see Wilder Lange, bath towel hung casually around his bare neck, wearing nothing but swim shorts. God, he was pure sex. There was no other way to describe the man. Ripped muscles, smooth tanned chest, tall and lean with angles on him that seemed best suited for an underwear ad in Times Square. Dark thick hair and just the hint of matching hair at the center of his chest. Looking at him now, she was beginning to wonder why she was even *debating* whether or not to sleep with the man. Look at him. Powerful, magnetic, experienced and so very, very confident. A sex god if ever she saw one.

"Harley." He raised his eyebrows in surprise as he glanced over her outfit. She wasn't wearing a bra and the night air had made her nipples rise. She crossed her arms across her chest, cursing herself for not having the forethought to wear a shirt with more coverage.

"I'm sorry. I didn't expect you here." Would he think that she was accepting his offer? That she was hoping to run into him so they could get it on? And what if she did…? What if right at this moment she slipped out of her clothes and walked over to him? Would he take her—here, on this rooftop deck, on the sectional outdoor couch just feet away from them? She blinked away the image and tried to tell herself to stop being ridiculous. That wasn't going to happen.

"You sure about that?" There was laughter in his eyes, and in the quirk of a smile at the corner of his mouth. His luscious soft mouth. How soft was it? She wanted to find out. That nervous energy in her body ramped up then, and she felt shaky. Jittery. It was probably the cool night air. Probably not the way the man was looking at her right now. Like a midnight snack he'd been craving.

"I'm sure. I just needed some..." *Sex.* She almost said sex. What was wrong with her? She knew what was wrong. She did want sex. No...she *needed* sex. With him. Where had that thought come from? But then she knew. It came from looking at his bare chest. From feeling the pent-up sexual energy between them, the hum of mutual want. She'd never before been so fixated on a man. Never in her life felt like being so reckless as when she was standing in front of him. "...fresh air," she finished, though she could feel her cheeks grow hot. She almost wanted to slap herself. She was literally playing the role of the blushing virgin. And she was no virgin. Not by a long shot.

"I see." He grabbed the loose towel by its ends, and studied her. "So, you're not debating my offer."

"What? No." She laughed, nervously.

"You're not up here because you can't sleep because you're thinking about sex with me." His mouth curled into a slow smile. How could he read her mind like that? Was she that obvious? Was she that easy to read? She took the pros-and-cons list in the pad from under her arm and pressed it against her chest.

"No," she lied.

"Really? Must just be me then. I can't sleep because I was thinking of you. Thought a cold swim would settle me down." He nodded at the lap pool behind her, the single-lap rectangular pool at the edge of his rooftop deck. Wilder took stock of the notepad. "What do you have there?"

"Nothing," she lied once more, her face growing hotter. The idea of the pros-and-cons list seemed immature, silly, especially faced with the man himself. In his presence, she forgot every single con she ever wrote. Hell, what was she even debating about? Wouldn't he be the perfect man to fuck? To experiment with? They were both adults and…

Suddenly, he took the notepad. Swiped it right out of her hands.

"Hey, wait…" She lunged for it, but he was too fast. Too tall, too strong. The towel around his neck dropped to the deck as he dodged to keep the pad away from her. He scanned her list. Then he quirked an eyebrow and began to read out loud. "Pro. More sexual experience." He glanced at her. "Con. Might regret doing it." He glanced at her, realizing exactly what he'd found. "Trust me when I tell you, darling, there's absolutely *nothing* you could possibly regret. Except not doing it sooner."

"I…" Oh, God. She wanted to drop through the floor. She'd never been so embarrassed in her whole life. Why had she brought the list with her? Hell, why had she even made it in the first place? "Give that back to me."

"Pro. He's sexy AF." He glanced at her, raising one eyebrow. "The truth comes out, then."

"Give that to me!" She jumped for the notepad, but he held it up higher than she could reach.

"Con. He's an egotistical asshole and sleeping with him will just make him worse."

"Ouch." He put a hand over his chest but didn't seem actually all that hurt. She lunged for the notepad, but he deflected her. "Pro. Curious to know if Wilder's reputation from that one song 'Sex God' is accurate."

He glanced at her. "Oh, I am *definitely* a sex god. Have no doubt about that." He studied the list as she desperately tried to get it. "Pro. Been thinking about sex with him since we first met." His eyes grew wide. "You *have*?" He let out an exaggerated gasp. "*Harley*. I'm shocked." He held the list high above his head. "Con. What if I'm not as good as his other lovers?"

"Wilder!" she cried. She swiped the list out of his hands. He let her take it. "Give me that. You weren't supposed to see that."

"It's all right. I'm glad I did." He laughed a little, a sound that she felt in her toes. "And for the record, I know already you'll blow all the other women I've ever slept with out of the water."

This was unexpected. "Why?"

"Because I've never wanted any of them like I want you." He reached out and took her hand then, her free hand, and she felt the electric current of his touch. Her throbbing embarrassment of having her damn list read out loud faded. The touch made every other thought in her brain flee. She felt rooted there, immobile, frozen by his dark eyes and impossibly thick lashes, that straight strong nose and those sensual lips. How she wanted to taste them. She'd been a fool to try to convince herself otherwise. He was still holding her hand and the air between them had changed, become hot with the lack of oxygen, with the lack of space for words, and now was all about the silent message between them, the message their bodies sent to one another, older than words. Older than anything.

"Wilder." She said his name, that was all, but it was also everything. It was consent, it was desire, it was her surrender. In that one word, she finally admitted to him and to herself the impossible attraction between them, the wave of desire that bound them together, like a tide taking her out to sea. He'd read her list. Knew she'd been wanting him since she first laid eyes on him. There was no need to lie. Not to him or herself.

She'd told Wilder she wouldn't have sex with people she treated, but the fact was, her desire had nothing to do with healing Wilder, and had everything to do with what she wanted. She wanted him. More than she'd wanted anyone.

She couldn't fight the attraction anymore. Didn't want to. Didn't want to put up barriers to something that felt this inevitable. She'd known from the very second she'd met him that this was coming. She'd known it in her bones, even if her mind had fought it all this time.

She took another step closer to him, but he remained still, hope in his eyes, hope and something else, want. He wanted her, and the power that gave her made her feel light-headed. Made her feel almost invincible. Her body knew what she would do next before her mind caught up. Her body had known this was her fate long before. He stood, watching her, cautious, his eyes never leaving hers as she reached up on her tiptoes and kissed him

CHAPTER EIGHT

HARLEY'S MIND HAD shut off. Her body was in control now, her body who knew this was what it wanted, to hell with the consequences. She was kissing Wilder Lange. She hadn't planned it. She'd just done it. Maybe it was a hate kiss. Because she hated that he'd read those pros and cons, hated that he now truly knew how much of a spin he'd put her in. She could tell herself that, and maybe part of her would believe it, but even she knew that she was kissing him because she wanted to. She'd been fantasizing about what his lips would feel like since she'd first laid eyes on the man. She'd been fighting the urge to touch him every single moment they'd spent together. Hadn't she glanced at the clock during their sessions the last two weeks, counting down the minutes, because she was having trouble concentrating on what he was saying because the man looked so damn fine?

And now she felt just how much she'd underestimated him. The way he was kissing her right now told her he knew absolutely everything he needed to know about sex. She'd only kissed three men her whole life, and so she wasn't one to know based on experience, which she knew was ridiculous. Knew it was something that even her most avid readers didn't know. But she never thought she'd needed a dozen partners in order to know what good sex was. Or a healthy relationship.

Yet, Wilder Lange made her think that maybe, she'd been wrong. The way he was kissing her now, the way his tongue moved in her mouth, the way his hands dipped to her lower back and pulled her entire body into his, told her that she'd never been properly kissed before this moment.

Before now, she'd never realized that a kiss was… well, so damn hot. Sure, she'd kissed her boyfriends, but that had never revved her up, taken her to these kinds of heights before. She'd never understood that even a single kiss could be so mind-blowing, that a person could lose all reason. Her body felt like it was melting in the best possible way. And there she was, devouring the man's mouth, unable to get enough of his tongue, thinking, *I have not lived. Not until this single moment.*

Which didn't make any sense at all. None of the research on human sexuality prepared her for this moment. She was supposed to hate this man. She wanted to hate him, except that now she had her tongue in his mouth and she liked it. She liked it too damn much. Her body pressed hotly to his, his bare chest against her tank top, yet, still she cursed the clothing that kept them apart, the friction that rubbed between them. She wanted skin on skin. More than wanted—needed it. Her leg went up his side, and he caught it expertly with his hand, the only barrier now between their hot centers was his swimsuit and her flimsy pajama bottoms. Oh, how she could feel him. Feel the flesh there, the flesh growing harder. For her.

He didn't seem like a man who had trouble having sex. On the contrary, he seemed like a man who knew exactly what he wanted and planned to get it. Harley broke free and realized she'd been practically grinding against the man, her body having taken over completely, her baser instincts in control. This had never happened to her before in her life and it scared the hell out of her. She'd been attracted to men in the past but this was…this was something else. Pure, unadulterated lust. And it was far more powerful than she'd ever imagined it could be.

"What am I doing?" she asked Wilder, as if he'd know why she decided to kiss the man she'd vowed never to *like* much less *lust* after.

"You're kissing the hell out of me," he growled, and then he pulled her closer and she lost her breath. Full, flush against him, she felt his taut, muscled chest, his flat stomach and his cock against her belly, growing ever bigger, ever harder through the thin fabric of his swim trunks.

The realization shocked her. He wanted her.

Hadn't she just heard that he couldn't do this? Yet, it was clear, his anatomy worked just fine.

"You do things to me that other women don't," he growled. "God, I want you." Then he kissed her, hard on the mouth, and she was once again thrown into the ocean of desire, the waves crashing against her one after another as his tongue found her again and again. She felt dizzy with it, the want, the lust bubbling inside her, and yet, she couldn't understand what was happening, why it was happening. It had never been this way for her before. Did that mean casual sex *wasn't* all bad? Did it mean that relationship sex wasn't torrid, wasn't passionate? Did it mean she'd been wrong with all the advice she ever gave her readers?

She pulled away from him, gasping, the cool moonlight bathing his face. The intensive look in his eyes at that moment made her feel a rush of blood flow to her core. She was still holding onto him, and yet, his gaze was like a vice grip she couldn't shake. He bound her to him with a single look. He brought her hand to his lips then, and laid a soft kiss on the back of it. The touch of his lips against her skin felt like a bolt of lightning rushing through her nerves, up her arm and all the way to her brain. Her breath suddenly caught in her throat. This wasn't just lust, she realized, as a grinding want for this man's touch took hold of her, it was a need, burning in her, a need to touch him, to be touched by him.

These thoughts were wrong. She knew they were

wrong, but she'd never felt such a strong cocktail of need and want, and the way he was looking at her, the knowing look on his face, made her want to wrap him up in her arms and tell him to show her what she'd been missing her whole life. She knew, looking at him, that he guessed exactly what it would be like. A match to gasoline, a fire that would burn out of their control. He reached out with his free hand and traced the curve of her cheek, and all coherent, logical thought scattered in her mind like raindrops on a car's windshield. The feel of his finger tracing her face was all she could concentrate on as her breath caught.

"You're beautiful, so very beautiful," he said, voice low and hoarse. "My body reacts to you as if we've met before. As if I've known you my whole life. Do you feel my body calling to yours? Do you feel it?"

The question was bold, and she should tell him that she felt no such thing. That theirs was strictly instinct, just bodies acting on chemistry and pheromones. Hadn't she studied all of that? Hadn't she read about human attraction being a cocktail of evolution and hormones? But all that would be a lie. Standing beneath the stars with this man, she realized that whatever it was between them wasn't just chemical. Her body opened for him like a flower, and she could feel even now the draw to him, as if his body were a primal call she couldn't ignore. Not with all her years of training, not with all the professional, clinical barriers she'd put up in her brain. He cut through them all. She barely knew him, but that didn't matter. Their bodies knew each other, it seemed, their bodies knew what their minds didn't: that they needed to be together.

"Yes," she croaked. "Yes, I feel it." At a later time, she knew she'd chastise herself for encouraging Wilder. Because she felt right then that she'd stepped over a line. Crossed a barrier she'd vowed never to cross. Wilder moved closer, and her body already knew what he intended, even if her mind was slow to catch up.

He put his free hand on her lower back and tugged her to him. She went, as if locked in a tractor beam she couldn't escape, and then her body was pressed fully against his, and she could see exactly what he meant by the effect she had on his body. She could feel him pressing into her belly, his full hardness, his undeniable want for her. The knowledge singed her brain, lit up all her nerve endings, made her own body pool its heady want between her legs. She felt herself grow wet as she stood, pressed against him, his dark eyes full of desire for her. He studied her lips, and she his, and all her professional reasons for keeping her distance seemed to melt between them, burned in the heat between their bodies.

He dipped his head lower, ever closer, his lips mere inches from hers.

"You can fix me, Harley." His voice was gruff and low, and his body told her he spoke the truth. Could she fix him with her body? Could she cure him of all his past ghosts by letting him touch her, letting him explore her deepest places? The very idea was foolish. She knew it, and yet, her body thrummed with a different kind of truth. A different answer altogether.

She opened her mouth to protest, but he dipped downward, his warm breath on her neck and he kissed her there, softly at first, gently, running his soft lips up her neck and to her earlobe. The gasp came out of her mouth before she could stop it, the delicate touch on her sensitive skin like a lightning bolt straight to the center of her, awakening her deepest parts, the parts of herself she'd tried so long to keep dormant. The want in her hummed with its own life, as he nuzzled the delicate skin of her neck. She clutched at him so she wouldn't fall, as she felt the back of her knees go weak. His tongue flicked out, and she gasped, sucking in air as if she were suffocating.

She moaned. The sound husky, full of want. Not the least bit professional. She had to grab the reins, pull herself back on course, and yet she was spiraling out of control, her brain only able to process his lips on her neck. He was moving downward, ever downward, to the V of her neckline, the line where her breasts came together. She could feel his breath there, too, as he kissed her gently, inhaling her scent, and her fingers dug deeper into his arms.

"I want you," he murmured into her chest. He rubbed a hand over one of her nipples, bringing it to attention through the thin fabric of her tank top. She moved one hand downward, curious at first, to feel him there, feel his growing want for her, her need to see if it truly was real. If he was hard for her. God, she felt the rush of power, it was reckless and dangerous and seductive. She did this to him. She made him want. The feeling made her delirious. He looked up then, dark eyes on hers. She could have this man, here, right on the rooftop in the middle of Manhattan. She could take him inside her, she could learn from him, she could let him take her to places she never knew she even wanted to go. She knew it. And so did he.

"So? What do you think of my proposition now?"

She wanted it. It felt like fate since she'd walked through the door of his glamorous penthouse. She'd be kidding herself if she thought otherwise. It had been written in the stars. A white-hot desire as powerful as the one they shared wouldn't be ignored. He knew it. She could tell by the way he was looking at her now that he already knew she was his. His hands moved downward and cupped her ass, powerful, knowing, and his hands spoke to her body with a kind of directness words could never achieve. They promised that he'd please her. And she knew in that moment the sex would be off the charts amazing, because forbidden sex always was.

And yet...she shouldn't be doing this. She shouldn't be. It wasn't right. It violated every promise she'd made herself, every bit of advice she'd given to readers hoping to avoid toxic men. Because Wilder Lange was the poster boy for toxic. He was commitment phobic, cocky and made no apologies for using sex to avoid bigger problems. Jumping into his bed could be amazing. Or it could be devastating. What happened after the white-hot casual sex? What happened when she cured him so he could hop into the bed of another model? Then what?

Hadn't she told her clients a million times before that they controlled their own destinies? That no desire was too strong to overcome or to properly steer to a healthier target? Here she was, drowning in her own desire, making her words moot. She pulled back, though, to suck in a breath, to try to get her bearings, even as her knees felt like they might give at any second. Wilder glanced at her, the surprise on his face mirroring her own. Neither one of them had expected such an explosive kiss, it seemed, neither one was prepared for the unstoppable avalanche of desire that welled up between them, the hum of the electricity.

The power of it took her completely off guard. It unnerved her.

"I can't..." What was she even going to say? *I can't do this?* More like, *I can't stop myself from doing it.*

"I'm not going to push you where you don't want to go." Wilder took another step back, and his arms fell away. "I don't want this unless you do. Period."

She felt surprised by his intent to get consent.

She shouldn't have been. Hadn't she been ranting about consent—mutual consent—in her column for years? Hadn't she denounced the alpha, rip-your-clothes-off, courtesy-be-damned arch type? Now that she was faced with Wilder, though, with his white-hot sexuality, with him challenging her to take what she wanted, she realized he wasn't going to give her an out. He was going to make her claim what she wanted.

And then she swung open the rooftop door to his penthouse and, without a word, disappeared inside.

A stab of disappointment stung her. She did want him. She wanted him badly. And that was the whole problem.

CHAPTER NINE

WILDER FELT THE water rush over his head the next morning as he glided through his single-lap pool on the other side of his enormous penthouse. The glass walls looked out over his rooftop deck. It was as if he was sliding along the edge of the rooftop, since the only thing separating him and a seventy-story drop was a glass partition. He loved that lap pool, because to him, it felt like he was swimming on the edge of the world.

A white lounger sat on the other side of the pool room, with his shirt and towel draped on it. The pool was where he went when he needed to clear his head, but this time, it didn't seem to work. All he could think about was the soft feel of Harley's lips, the ample curves of her body, the way she seemed to be made for him. Everything about her turned him on, from her dark curls and high cheekbones to her slim ankles and polished toes. And then there was that fascinating mind of hers. But he didn't believe in trying to persuade women to cross boundaries they didn't want to cross. In his experience, women knew exactly what they wanted and usually asked for it. Men who didn't understand this didn't deserve a woman's company. He knew she had rules, and she had to be the one to break them. Not him. End of story.

The cold water rushed over him as he took yet another lap. He'd need to swim to London and back if he'd ever hope to forget about the feel of Harley's lips on his. Leave it to him to be off women for nearly a year and then be head over heels for the one woman who'd already told him she wasn't going to sleep with him. He'd always been attracted to the forbidden. He loved breaking the rules. Of course, if she did…then what? He still wasn't in the market for a serious relationship, and after he'd seen his father and Lucinda's disastrous marriage, wasn't even sure he wanted to try. He'd been asked about whether or not he wanted a family, but he already had one—his brothers, and they were enough to take care of.

Even if they were grown.

Looking after them since he was eight had kind of purged him of the need to settle down. He'd been settled down since he was in elementary school. And Harley was the kind of woman who didn't do things casually. He knew that. Could see that from miles away. There was a reason she'd never had a one-night stand. He'd never met a woman who took sex so seriously before. Hell, he'd never met a woman with a doctorate in human sexuality, either. Yet, the scariest thing for him was that the thought of a relationship with Harley didn't seem so outlandish after all. The moment she'd walked into his life he'd started to wonder if maybe he did need someone. He was drawn to her, to her mind and her body. But what did he know about serious relationships? He was the king of casual, and that was how he'd keep it. The very fact that he'd even *think* about something more, about the possibility of more, just spoke to the lust he had for the woman. It was clogging up his brain, confusing his own logic, making him second-guess himself.

And it was all because she had an effect on him that no other woman had. It was that simple. He couldn't shake the feeling that *she* was the cure for him. He knew it was unreasonable. Laughable, even. Yet, the thought just stuck there, unmovable. Did it matter if the cure was temporary or permanent?

And he also knew he could cure her, too. Because he'd come to see she was stuck. She might not even know it yet, but she seemed trapped—in this place where she was keeping herself from casual sex because—why? Because she feared it would negate all her advice columns? Or because she feared she'd like it? He badly wanted to find out. He pushed through another lap in the pool, wondering if he was losing his mind.

He thought about what she'd said about past traumas. Could Lucinda's drunken rages have led him to not being able to have a full life now? He'd always thought that the abuse he'd suffered at her hands had made him stronger. He'd always worn his scars as a source of quiet pride. He'd survived and he'd protected his brothers. He had nothing to be ashamed of. Lucinda was the one who ought to have regrets. So why was she reaching out from the past and haunting him still?

He grabbed the edge of the pool and came through the surface, gasping for air. He shook the droplets of water off his hair and ran a hand down his face and then dove back in for another lap. Harley Vega was getting under his skin. Dredging up his past, churning his thoughts from his past to his present, twisting him in knots. That very morning, he'd desperately tried to distract himself with work, but after hours of answering the backlog of emails (What was his decision on hiring a new news director? How about next year's budget?), he was still focused on Harley Vega. Two opposite thoughts battled in his mind. Part of him wanted to avoid Harley and all her prodding questions about his past, but another part of him yearned to be in her presence even now, her body seeming to call to his from across his massive penthouse. He knew the woman could feel the chemistry between them, the way their bodies silently talked to one another. He knew she was tempted—more than tempted to accept his invitation to his bed. He'd felt her desire in their kiss last night, when she'd finally—if only for a brief second—let go of that tight leash she kept herself on. He knew in his bones that one night with Harley would very likely cure him of his little problem, and might also help her, too. She was a woman who spent too much time in her head, too much time trying to think about sex logically, when in his experience, there wasn't anything logical about sex. It was all primal instinct. All base deliciousness. Reason had no part in it.

Wilder reached the edge of the pool at the end of his lap count, and sucked in air, his chest heaving as water rolled down it. He grabbed his thick fluffy white towel from the chaise lounge at the water's edge and patted his face with it and then pulled himself out of the pool just in time to hear his phone ping with an incoming message. He dried his hands and picked up his phone in time to see Seth's name flicker across it.

Lucinda is getting more shares. Just a heads-up. Someone is selling, but I don't know who.

He shut his eyes and dropped the phone on a nearby chair. It felt like the company was slipping through his fingers. He'd need to figure out how many shares Lucinda had, how close she was to gaining a portion of control, but he also knew it would be hard to figure it out. Whoever was selling wouldn't want him to know, wouldn't want him to counter. This felt strangely personal, though, as if someone was betraying him. He thought of the board members, the shareholders he knew personally and tried to figure out who might be open to advances from

Lucinda, but came up empty. No one liked her. No one that he knew trusted her.

He thought about his twin brothers. Would they sell? Seth said Stuart had said no. Would Liam sell? No. He wouldn't. Would he? Wilder shook his head in frustration. The very fact he was even considering one of his brothers betraying him just underlined how out of control he was. They'd never undermine him like that. Not after all he'd done for them. No. This was probably Lucinda's strategy all along. Start rumors and let the brothers start fighting amongst themselves and then swoop in when they were all distracted and try to take the company over.

The muscles in his jaw clenched a bit. He needed to focus on business, but he also had to clear his mind to do it. He couldn't be obsessed with Harley Vega's mouth when he had to go to battle. What he needed was the cure Harley could give him. He needed to be fixed, once and for all, so he could move on and deal with real problems. He'd give Harley another week. One week. Either she'd help him, or he'd figure out a way to stop obsessing over her. Either way, time was running out.

And in the meantime, he'd get to the office and figure out who the hell was selling shares behind his back. He hated to leave, but he needed to get a handle on this situation and fast.

Harley was dreading the counseling appointment today with Wilder Lange. After the white-hot make-out session on the roof the night before, she didn't trust herself to be with him alone and not think about what his lips felt like on hers. Because she'd decided that… Well, she hadn't decided. She wanted to jump into bed with the man, but she didn't trust the instinct. Didn't trust her own motives. She was the kind of person who moved methodically, with purpose. She didn't make decisions quickly. Hell, she barely made decisions at all. Hadn't her first boyfriend teased her that she could spend an hour debating whether or not she wanted a bagel or toast for breakfast? But her methodical nature meant she could work out problems, help people see parts of their relationships they turned a blind eye to. She looked at all angles and she didn't jump into anything hastily, and never with both feet.

Was that so wrong? She didn't think so.

She waited for him in his study and glanced at her watch. He was five minutes late. Where was the man? She was here, waiting for their session at the normal time. Who knew where he was? Had he taken offense to her not jumping into his bed the night before? Well, that's just not how she operated. And she'd let him know that the second he walked through the door.

She stared at the door and waited.

And waited some more.

Where was he?

Wilder Lange, the walking enigma, the black box that kept all his inner thoughts and emotions wrapped up deep inside himself. She thought of those big broad shoulders and that squared-off jaw that seemed determined to get exactly what it wanted. How would her body react when she saw him? Or worse, when he opened his mouth? The real danger, she knew, wasn't that she was attracted to his body. She was increasingly intrigued by the man's mind.

Sure, he had every advantage: wealth, power, prestige. Everything she'd read said he could be a ruthless businessman, but to hear him talk to his brother, she also knew he was a loyal family man, someone who clearly loved and cared for his brothers. Many wealthy families fought over their inheritance, but not the Lange family—at least not the brothers—and Harley thought that had everything to do with Wilder Lange. He'd surprised her in any number of ways. Yes, he was an egotistical, entitled jerk at times, but he was also, surprisingly...levelheaded and selfless. If he were truly the villain she'd imagined, why would he care for his brothers? Why not write them all out of the will? How often had she heard about families fighting over money? Yet, the Lange brothers were steadfast in their loyalty to Wilder.

She was loyal to her own family, knew she'd do anything to help them and had even sent money home to Miami after a hurricane knocked out power for a week and her parents had no income from the restaurant. She'd never walk away from that responsibility, no matter what. She sensed that same loyalty in Wilder. Still, she wondered about the relationship he'd had with his stepmom, and how that had shaped his worldview. Wilder was hiding some intense memories, of this she had no doubt, but getting to them would be a very different kind of challenge. She knew people put up their own defenses to avoid their pain, but Wilder's heart seemed to have more security than Fort Knox.

The door to the study opened then, and her stomach lurched. Here it was. She'd figure out if she could stay in the same room with Wilder Lange, if she could keep her libido under control. It would be the ultimate test. Butterflies ricocheted around her stomach. Why was she so damn nervous? Then, as she was debating to herself, Jacob, Wilder's butler, poked his gray head in the study.

"Ms. Vega, I'm sorry to report that Mr. Lange won't be attending today's session," he began. "He begs your pardon, but urgent matters at the office require his full attention."

Harley felt a cool prick of disappointment at the back of her neck. He wouldn't be at the session today. Hell, she might not even *see* him today. That hadn't factored into her calculations, not at all. She hadn't even realized how *much* she'd been looking forward to seeing the man. How much she'd been counting on it. Until the moment when she realized she wouldn't be seeing him.

"When will he be back?" She hated that she sounded like she cared. After all, she couldn't very well expect the offer of casual sex to be at the top of his to-do list, could she? He ran a Fortune 500 company, with thousands of employees. Hell, he was probably buying and gutting another magazine right at this minute. She knew the thought was unfair and unkind, but she didn't care. Because the fact was she'd been on the verge of accepting his offer. Today. That was the truth of it. But he wasn't even here to take her up on it.

"I'm not sure, Ms. Vega. He didn't say."

Did this have something to do with the fact that she hadn't jumped into his bed at the first opportunity? That she'd cut their make-out session short the night before? That when he snapped his fingers she hadn't jumped? Surely, that wasn't it. Yet, part of her worried she'd missed her chance with Wilder Lange. He could have any woman he wanted after all. What if he found a replacement? Someone else who lit his fire?

It was just her ridiculous insecurities running around her brain. She knew that. Clinically, she knew there was no basis to any of them, and yet…

"Thank you, Jacob," she said, and slipped her notebook back into her bag. "I guess that means I have the afternoon off."

Just last week, she would've been overjoyed to be off the hook for a session, an afternoon free to leave the penthouse or do whatever she wished without being the subject of Wilder's moodiness. But, now… Now, when she finally *wanted* to see the man, he disappeared.

* * *

The afternoon, next morning, next evening and next full afternoon went by with no word from Wilder Lange, except his profuse apologies for not having time for a session, messages all sent through Jacob. In fact, he hadn't even returned to the penthouse, opting to grab a few hours of sleep at the office, where he also kept a full change of suits. More apologies through Jacob came, and more promises of makeup sessions without any real dates or times attached.

The apologies and promises rang false in Harley's mind. He had to be deliberately avoiding her. But why? Sure, she imagined, he was a busy man with all kinds of pressing decisions to be made at work, but she couldn't help but take his absence personally. Plus, the longer he stayed away, the more she started to worry that she'd missed her chance. That his offer to bed her had an expiration date that she didn't know about.

Then she told herself that she couldn't have imagined the chemistry between them, couldn't have imagined the spark on that rooftop, which they'd nearly set ablaze with a single kiss. No. That was real. That had to be real. But maybe it hadn't affected him as much as it affected her. What if… Well, what if he'd changed his mind? What if he'd found her kiss wanting? She simply couldn't believe that. Her gut told her that he'd felt the desire as hot and heavy as she had.

Harley threw down the book she was reading and

sighed. She felt like she'd been trapped in his penthouse for the last two days, in this enormous, well-heeled prison. Sure, she could leave if she wanted to, except she'd pathetically hung around. Hoping he'd be back. Hoping they could pick up where they'd left off, hoping she might, at last, scratch the itch that had been burning in her belly ever since Wilder Lange invited her to his bed. Because the longer he stayed away, the more she desperately wanted him. She knew, logically, it was just reverse psychology. She didn't want him, until he was no longer there. A simple principal, and yet, profoundly effective.

Harley glanced at her watch. It was nearing eight in the evening and she hadn't had dinner yet. What had she been hoping for? That Wilder would miraculously appear and take her out? The thought was laughable. Hadn't she signed an NDA where she couldn't even admit to knowing him? It's not like they were going to go on a public date. And, hell, that's not even what she wanted. What she wanted was a private date. Naked. In his bed.

She realized how desperate she sounded. She also realized that she'd flip-flopped in her thinking at least a dozen times in the last two days: swinging from desperately wanting to have sex with the man to hating his guts and vowing not to give in to her baser desires. And she'd be fine with that, except, of course, for that damn kiss. It haunted her dreams, woke her in the middle of the night, came to her when she soaped herself in the shower. He'd turned something on in her, something she couldn't turn off.

She could still feel his lips on hers, still sense the electric shock that rode up her nerve endings and straight to her brain. The striatum, to be exact, that's where lust lives. That's all this was—lust clouding her good judgement. Lust activating the striatum, the same part of the brain where food cravings lived. She just craved him like she would chocolate. It was all just electric pulses in the brain, she reminded herself, things that ultimately she could control. She didn't have to stuff her face with chocolate any more than she'd need to kiss Wilder again. She was the master of her body. Not the striatum.

But right now, her striatum was demanding food. Namely, dinner. She could warm up a frozen dinner in her kitchenette. Or order a pizza. But neither sounded appetizing. She could go out, but what if Wilder came home? What…if? Then again, maybe he should come home to find it empty, and her gone. Just because she'd agreed to this job, didn't mean she'd agreed to be his prisoner.

She was feeling better already as she stood and walked to her closet, plucking out a pair of skin-tight jeans, a bare-shouldered halter and gold dangling earrings. She let her hair down and put on her highest heels. She was *going out.* She'd already scooped out a few social media feeds of friends nearby. They were out, having drinks at a local bar, and she'd surprise them. She'd have wine with her girlfriends and forget all about the Wilder Lange horror show.

Just as she was putting on bright red lipstick, puckering her lips at the brightly lit mirror of her bathroom, a soft knock sounded at her door. Jacob, no doubt, here to tell her most likely that Wilder wouldn't be back tonight, either. Or hell, maybe he'd tell her he was gone for the week.

Harley swung open the door and was surprised to find Wilder standing there, wearing another gray suit, a darker one, with a pinstriped tie. He'd come from the office, she guessed. He reached up and loosened the knot of his tie. The symmetrical perfection of his face hit her like a punch to the stomach. Why did he have to be so damn fine? Even when she was angry at him, she still could register the man was off the scales sexy. How was she supposed to keep her thoughts lust free when he looked like a walking heartthrob? There were those electric pulses in her brain again, the ones demanding that she sample, just one more time, the man's lips. God, the temptation was strong, a craving like none other she'd felt before. But, wait. No. She was angry with him. Annoyed.

"Yes?" There, her voice sounded clipped, restrained. Good.

His eyes widened in surprise as he took in her skin-tight skinny jeans, stiletto heels and halter, along with the gold bangles on her wrist and the earrings. His gaze rested on her bright red lips. She'd also put on extra mascara, not that he'd gotten that far. He was staring at her lips as if he craved them. The heat of his attention warmed her from the inside.

"You look good enough to eat." His voice was low, a hum in her belly. "Where are you off to? A date?"

His voice sounded slightly pinched. Was that… jealousy?

"You told me I couldn't be a sex columnist without getting more experience, so…" She shrugged one tanned bare shoulder. "I'm going to get some more experience. The first man who offers. I'll just jump into his bed."

Wilder looked like she'd punched him in the face. All the color drained from his cheeks. He loosened his tie further, as if it was suddenly choking him, showing the hollow of his neck. She suddenly wondered what it would be like to kiss him, right there, below his Adam's apple. Maybe even, she thought devilishly, lick him there. Lick him…all over.

"I'm kidding," she said, delighting in the relief that flooded into the man's eyes. "I don't do that. Pick up men in bars."

"Good." The relief was evident in his voice. "The only man I want you to sleep with is me."

"Hard to do when you're not around." She tapped one toe on his carpet. She felt impatient. She had plans, plans to go out, and she wasn't going to be derailed. Wilder couldn't just make her wait around his penthouse and expect her to jump up, happy to see him when he finally returned, like some Labrador retriever.

"I know. I'm sorry. It was a work emergency. Lucinda was trying to steal the company from me. She was trying to figure out a way to get controlling shares."

Harley felt a little bolt of panic. "Did she?"

"No. But, I had to… Well, I had to keep an eye on things. To make sure. I had to twist a few arms." He let out a long breath. "Turns out it was some of my own executives, if you can believe it." He shook his head. "They don't like me propping up the magazines. They think it's bad business, since those takeovers don't make a profit. I just had to convince them that profits aren't everything."

She laughed, deep in her throat. "You're pretty persuasive, if I recall." Then she had a flash of memory: his hands on her ass, the way he'd grabbed her possessively, promising to teach her all about sex with a stranger. Yes, the man was damn persuasive. She was beginning to see his logic. How could she write about sex if she *didn't* have that much experience? And, she had to admit, he wasn't all egotistical billionaire. As she got to know him better, she knew he was a dedicated brother, a business owner who did care about his employees, or at least saving the jobs he could save. She'd overheard countless business calls where he'd been stuck between a rock and a hard place. She was still a little resentful about *Femme*, but she was beginning to understand his reasoning better. All the barriers to saying yes to him were falling, one by one, in her mind.

"I'm sorry I disappeared on you. Believe me, it wasn't my plan." He flashed her an apologetic smile and her stomach twisted. Perfect smile. Easy charm. That magnetism in his dark eyes, his perfectly combed, thick nearly black hair rolling back from his forehead in perfect waves. Why did he always look so damn delectable? "I'd like to make it up to you by offering you dinner. Would you join me?"

Her first instinct was to shout no. She was dressed up, ready to go out, sip wine all night with her friends and forget all about Wilder Lange. Except now the man was standing right in front of her, tie askew like some ruffled dark-haired James Bond. There was no forgetting about him. Besides, her stomach was in rebellion from hunger, and the half smile on Wilder's face made it seem as if no was simply an impossibility.

Not to mention, there were other parts of her anatomy other than her stomach that were casting a vote to stay.

"I..." She hesitated.

"The cook is making steak medallions and mushroom risotto. If you say no, it'll be a wasted steak." He moved a little closer, touched her fingertips with his, the jolt of contact zapping her to attention. What were the reasons she didn't want to stay? She forgot them all in that instant, as he carefully picked up her hand and kissed it. "You'd be doing me a great favor if you do join me. I've had a long couple of days. I could really use the company."

She could see that, his bone weariness. She could see he needed her. How she loved to be needed.

"And I just want to see a friendly face."

She laughed at that. "*I'm* a friendly face in your world?"

"As crazy as it sounds, yes. You are." He let her hand go. "More than you know."

Now, she was truly torn. He really needed her. Not just her body, it seemed, but also her mind. She was curious about how bad the two days had to have been for him to want to open up. Since when did he ever open that vault around his mind and let her in?

"I want to thank you, too, for being so patient with me. If I overstepped any lines, I apologize," he said, and it seemed heartfelt. "I was thinking about what you said about past and trauma. I think… I just think you were on to something. About my past."

And there it was, the bait for her brain. Her body wanted his body, but her mind… Well, her mind wanted to dig up all his dirty secrets. She wanted to find out how Lucinda now plotted against him. Why she did it in the first place. The nugget hung there, the temptation to find out more about this enigmatic billionaire. Of course, this is where it could get dangerous. This was where those electric pulses in the brain moved from the craving centers to the more complex, thoughtful, deep bonding centers of the brain. This was where true connection happened.

Still…if he were open to talking more about his past, then they could make real progress with his issues. And she wanted to do that. She wanted to help him heal so she could get the heck out of his penthouse, and far away from the troubling thoughts and feelings he drudged up in her. Yes, maybe dinner was the way forward.

Was she really so scared of her own desires that she didn't think she could handle a single meal with the man? Surely, she could. Besides, she'd never eaten a meal cooked by a private personal chef, and it would no doubt be amazing. And a simple meal didn't mean she'd have to sleep with the man. That, of course, was only if she wanted to.

"All right," she said, trying to ignore the little flicker of excitement in her own chest. She was already looking forward to a night alone with Wilder Lange a bit too much. She'd have to control her feelings if she wanted to get out of the night unscathed. The question was, did she want to be unscathed?

CHAPTER TEN

HARLEY FELT UNDERDRESSED for the massive dining room she found herself in. The dining room was practically bigger than her whole Brooklyn apartment and she wondered, again, how anyone could afford this much real estate in Manhattan. The cost of the penthouse must be mind-boggling. She tiptoed on her sky-high stilettos, noting that even in her tallest shoes she came nowhere near to Wilder's height. The man was a pure wall of muscle, muscle in a six-thousand-dollar suit from Barneys. He pulled out her plush dining room chair and then sat kitty-corner from her at the end of the sleek table that sat twelve, easily, not far from the big silver chandelier in the middle of the white-and-chrome room. Harley glanced down at the many pieces of cutlery on either side of her gold-rimmed plate and struggled to remember what her mother had taught her about fancy table settings. *Outside, in,* she thought. She eyed the far fork and picked it up to delicately take a bite of her beet salad in front of her. Harley tried not to worry about the tiny fork laying just north of her plate. She had no idea what to do with that.

"This is…" Harley struggled for the words "…formal."

"I don't eat in this room very often," Wilder said. "But I asked the chef to make something special tonight. To make up for my bad behavior. So that meant breaking out the good china."

"I doubt you have any bad china." She eyed the white plates with the no-doubt-actual-gold rims.

He grinned, a bright white dazzling smile and his dark eyes lit up a bit. "Do you like wine, Ms. Vega?"

"Occasionally," she said.

"Red or white?"

"Red."

As if poised with an ear to the door, a servant came then, and filled their stemless wineglasses with a big bold red. From the look of the label, the wine was as old as the table, or more so.

"A good vintage," he told her, as he inhaled, his nose poised on the rim of the glass.

She did the same and inhaled a fruity bouquet of rich goodness before she tasted the complex juicy wine. She swallowed and thought this might be the best wine she'd ever tasted. Probably one she could never afford. She felt herself suddenly relieved to have the wine. She was uncharacteristically nervous and thought the wine might help calm her. She tried to do a quick scan of her feelings and realized she was genuinely nervous to be alone with the man, in a setting where she couldn't use her notepad as a shield. Maybe she should've gone to meet her friends. Maybe this had been a mistake.

"Amazing," she said, taking another sip.

"Glad you like it." A warm fuzzy feeling filled her stomach, and she wondered if it was the wine already or the half smile on Wilder's face.

"So what happened? With Lucinda?"

"She's trying to steal the company from me. I had to be at the office to stop a few of the sales going through," he said, frowning. "I had to call in a few favors, but I think I've stopped her for now."

"Why is she so determined to take the company?"

"Greed. Pure and simple," he said. "That, and she's hated me my whole life. Can't stand to see me successful." He swirled the ruby red wine in his glass. "She tried to take the estate and the business from me. She's still trying. She doesn't believe I'm a…rightful heir. Because I came from his first wife." He shook his head, sensual mouth thinning into a grim line. "It's always a battle. It has been since my father married her when I was eight and everything changed."

"How so?" Harley felt like she was treading on dangerous ground.

He laughed, but it came out sounding thin and brittle. "Once, when my father was on a business trip, I failed to finish the broccoli on my plate. For that small offense, Lucinda locked me in a closet for one week straight. Wouldn't even let me out to use the bathroom. Made sure the servants didn't, either."

Harley felt as if she'd been punched in the stomach. "That's child abuse."

"That was the idea," Wilder said grimly, taking another deep drink of his wine, as if even talking about her reignited all that old pain. Harley's heart welled up with empathy. She tried to imagine Wilder as a scared little boy, having just lost his mother and now dealing with a stepmother who not only didn't care for him but actively sought to hurt him. "And believe me, the abuse got worse."

Harley wanted to comfort him, wanted to wrap her arms around him, but instead, she forced herself to remain in her seat.

"My father was furious when he found out. Cut his business trip abroad short and came home. After that, it was pretty clear that when he was in the house, I was safe, but when he wasn't, all bets were off." Wilder shook his head grimly.

"I'm sorry that happened to you." Harley's voice sounded hoarse to her own ears. The anger at his unjust treatment growing inside her.

"That's the first time anyone's said that." He glanced at her, dark eyes suddenly intently focused on her. "Granted, no one knows about Lucinda except my half brothers."

"How do they feel about it?"

"They weren't immune from the abuse, either. At least, not until I got big enough and she got scared of me." Wilder shook his head. "I made sure she never did anything to those boys again."

"What about your father?"

Wilder hung his head. "He didn't want to believe it. He lived in denial."

"Did you try to tell him?"

"Most every chance I got. He blamed the alcohol. He kept trying to find her treatment centers, but they all failed. Sometimes, she was better when she was on the wagon. At least, less psychopathic. But, eventually, she always went back to drinking. And her old habits came back."

"I'm sorry." She reached out and grabbed his hand. He froze for a moment, but then squeezed her hand back. She almost felt as if she could sense his pulse in his hand, the thrumming of his heart. He shook his head as if to free himself from the bad memories. "I don't usually talk about this. With anyone."

She felt giddy at the compliment and even more at the fact that he'd shared a secret with her, one he didn't share with anyone who wasn't family. She was making progress; she was lifting the veil. And the more she dug into his brain, his heart, the sexier the man became. She noted again how striking he was, how he could be a poster child for attractiveness of a scientific scale, his features perfectly symmetrical.

"You're staring at me," he pointed out. His shirt was now unbuttoned to the third button and the white sleeves rolled up to his elbows. He'd discarded the tie and jacket, but somehow he still seemed sexy as hell. Maybe more so. His dark hair a little ruffled, stubble on his chin.

"I'm not."

"You're a terrible liar."

"I was thinking that your features are symmetrical." She took another sip of her wine. Why had she said that?

"I hope that's a good thing." A teasing smile flitted across his face.

"It means…that you're healthy, according to scientific research on symmetry and genes and…" Despite the fact she was talking about science and theory, Harley felt her cheeks grow warm. What about the presence of this man made her lose all her bearings? "…and that you're good-looking."

"You think I'm good-looking?" Now, his grin turned wolfish. The man already knew he was off-the-scales attractive. All he needed was a mirror to figure that out. "What was that pro again? That I'm sexy AF?"

"Don't forget the con."

"Oh, I haven't. As I recall, you wrote more of them. Somehow, trying to convince yourself it's a bad idea. Just goes to show that you actually really want to do it."

She took another gulp of her wine and suddenly her palms felt clammy. What was she doing? "I haven't said yes, yet."

"No," he admitted. "Not yet." His dark eyes were

playful. She almost felt uncomfortable under the weight of the stare. She cleared her throat.

Then, his phone, somewhere in his pocket, dinged, a notification of an incoming message. He tugged it out, glanced at the phone's face and frowned. She wondered what message might lay there. Business-related? Personal? The thought of one of his many girlfriends messaging him while they had dinner sent a little wave of annoyance through her. She noted the feeling and tried to talk herself out of it. She shouldn't be annoyed by the man's love life. She was here to help him get back to it. She needed to focus on that. Not on the fact that the man's full sensual lips looked kissable in the soft light of the dining room. That he looked every bit the part of a man in control: of his life, his wealth and his position, and a man who broke hearts in his spare time. He tucked his phone away silently and focused on her again.

"Everything okay?" she asked.

"Fine," he said, but offered no more. Was the veil coming down again? Was she losing her window into his mind?

"So, before we talk about your..." she swallowed "...proposal, I think it's my turn to ask you questions."

"Go on." There was a challenge in his voice.

"Are you...seeing someone at the moment?" She told herself she asked the question in order to further his treatment. Not because if she planned to jump into his bed, she wanted to make sure she wasn't betraying someone else.

He cocked an eyebrow. "No." She felt relief flood through her, and she hated herself for it. This wasn't the way to be professional. A hint of a smile tugged at his full lips. His dark eyes studied her. "Does that please you?"

"It makes me feel better that you offered me casual sex." She coughed. "And how many lovers… have you had?"

She almost didn't want to know the answer. But she thought it was only fair. He knew she'd had two. How many had he had?

"I've lost count," he said, as the maid, Vanka, whom she'd met the day she moved in, came into the room, carrying two small plates of salad. She was a tall thin woman in her fifties, with a perfect streak of gray in her hair. The first course, Harley guessed.

"You can't have lost count."

He shrugged one mischievous shoulder.

Harley stared. "Ballpark, then. Twenty?"

He shook his head. "Higher."

"Fifty?" He shook his head again. "One hundred?" Harley's throat went dry. "Two hundred."

He shook his head. "I don't think you really want the number."

"Two hundred and fifty?" Now, she was darn near flabbergasted.

"You're getting closer." He grinned. "But, remember, I *do* believe in casual sex. I'll tell you this. It's lower than twenty thousand."

"The number Wilt Chamberlain claimed? Are you serious?"

"I said it was *lower.*" He laughed. "How about we just say *a lot* and leave it at that? Besides, I thought *you* agreed that numbers—low or high—didn't matter."

He took a bite of salad and so did she, as she mulled over Wilder's revelation. Well, Harley thought numbers didn't matter, but if this man had literally been with hundreds, or even thousands of women, how could she hope to stand out? Did she want to? Oh, who the hell was she kidding, of course she did. She wanted to rock the man's world.

She took another bite of salad, only to have Wilder put her on the spot.

"Have you given more thought to my proposition?"

"Yes." It was all she could think about if she were honest.

"Why don't we stop playing around? I know you want to do it. You know I want to do it. What's stopping us?" Wilder didn't even blink an eye. He didn't even break a smile. There was no hint of a joke in his manner.

"That's quite bold of you." Could the man see right into her brain? Why did he always seem to be one step ahead of her?

"I didn't get where I am, Ms. Vega, by being timid."

His dark eyes never left hers, and she was very much aware that the two of them sat alone at this massive table in this large room. The servants that seemed to be ducking in and out constantly were suddenly nowhere to be found. "What I know is that you've been debating having sex with me. That little pros-and-cons list…"

She blushed at the memory of him reading her uncensored thoughts.

"But what I don't know is if you're trying to convince yourself *not* to do it…or…to do it." He shook his head slowly. "My point is that if you're fighting with yourself over it, why not…just stop fighting?"

"Because I'm supposed to be treating you. It's unethical for me to sleep with you."

"Yes, but you're not a doctor. Or a therapist." He finished the last of his small salad, watching her intently. "And I'm not one of your advice column readers looking to be in the next column, either. So where's the true conflict?"

"Because you're…" He wasn't her patient exactly, since she wasn't a licensed counselor. "Because you're paying me…"

"For a consultation. The sex has nothing to do with that. The sex," he said, and paused, a smile tugging at the corners of his sensual mouth, "that's just for fun. To see if this thing between us is as real as I think it is."

"It's not that simple," she said, feeling a bit too vulnerable beneath the weight of his heavy gaze.

Every time she let herself by tempted by him, she felt so out of control, so… wild. If she were honest with herself, truly honest, she didn't trust her own judgment anymore, not when it came to him. "The point is not to indulge in the attraction. People are attracted to other people all the time, but they don't act on it."

Even as she said the words, she could feel a hardness at the center of her chest, the want that was growing in there, heavy and hard, like something alive, something dangerous, something with a mind of its own.

"Sometimes, actually, they do," he said, and she knew he spoke from experience. "Besides, we've already acted on it, haven't we? I can still feel the delicate skin of your neck beneath my lips. The taste of your lips." He picked up his wineglass and gently pressed his lips to it, and she remembered the feel of them beneath her earlobe. The living want inside her shuddered, sparked alive with his words, a thing whose hunger was only just beginning to be known.

She felt it, too, and she knew he could tell. Harley couldn't look at his face now. She feared he'd see the living thing in her eyes, the living, breathing desire in her that was threatening to take control of her. If he even touched her now, she felt the monster would be let out. And then she didn't know what might happen.

A small silence fell, and Harley glanced up only to find Wilder considering her. She wondered what he was thinking in that moment, and if the want in his chest was as strong as hers. Then she hated herself for caring. What was it about this man—this complex, wounded man—that drew her in so completely? He might be able to read her, but Harley had no idea what he was thinking from one moment to the next.

Vanka came in once more—she'd magically made herself scarce when talk had turned a bit too flirty—carrying two piping hot plates of food, each with a small filet and a side of mushroom risotto, topped with baby greens. They fell silent as the maid gently set the plates before them. The food smelled delicious, but Wilder barely moved to touch his.

She cut into the delicate beef and put a bite on her tongue. She wasn't anywhere near hungry anymore, not with Wilder staring at her like that, and her stomach tying itself into a series of knots. But she badly wanted a distraction. Eating seemed like the easiest. She chewed and the beef melted on her tongue in warm perfection.

"Mmm," she murmured, the amazing flavors overcoming her palette that was more used to quick meals like store-bought salad kits or pizza. "This is amazing." She took a bite of risotto and she swore she nearly fainted from the creamy goodness of it. How could food even *be* this good? She was mystified as she scooped another delicate forkful in her mouth. Maybe, with this amazing meal, her appetite would come back and she'd forget that Wilder was looking at her as if she were on his menu.

When she glanced over at him, he was simply watching her, making no move to touch his own food. He shifted uncomfortably in his seat, almost as if… But surely not. The very act of her eating dinner couldn't arouse the man, could it? She was imagining things.

"Your cook is amazing," she said.

"I know," he said, simply. He stared at her for a beat, and his attention made her feel warm. "I insist on the best." Somehow, the statement should have been cocky and egotistical, and yet when he said it, it was simply a statement of fact. The food was fantastic. "That's why I want you."

"You haven't had me yet. How do you know I'm the best?"

"Call it a hunch." He finally took a few bites of his own meal. After a brief moment of silence as they both ate, he took his napkin from his lap and dabbed the corners of his mouth with it, his almond skin looking a shade darker beneath the lowlight from the ceiling and the flickering candles of the table. "Let's be frank."

"Okay," she agreed, tentatively.

He nodded once, brisk. His manner had become increasingly businesslike, even as Harley felt a growing pull to the man, an increasing desire to touch him. She put down her fork and put her hands in her lap. She reminded herself these were strictly chemical impulses, a cocktail of hormones, nothing that she couldn't bend to her will.

"How long before…before you think I'll be cured of my…" he sucked in a breath "…issue."

Harley felt put on the spot. She knew he was a man who expected answers—no, demanded them—but she didn't have a good response. "These things can take a lot of time, or a little," she said. "But in your case…"

He seemed to brace himself for bad news and Harley hated that she was the one who'd be delivering it.

"I'm just not sure," she said. "I think we could try doing some visualization exercises and maybe we'll see some progress."

"I need to be cured in a week." His tone left no room for argument, even though Harley had quite a lot of arguments to make.

"I can't guarantee that." Harley felt the muscles in the back of her neck tense. He was asking what could be impossible. "You need to be fully open and I don't even think we're there yet."

"I know what would cure me," he said. "You. In my bed. Tonight."

CHAPTER ELEVEN

WILDER TOOK AN insane pleasure in watching Harley Vega blush from the roots of her hair down to the front of her chest. She froze, wineglass halfway to her mouth. At least she hadn't already taken a sip. Otherwise, she would've spit it out all over his expensive white linen tablecloth. She wasn't a virgin, nothing anywhere close by the way she'd kissed him a couple of days ago, but she was so easy to tease. And the way she was blushing right now and chugging her wine told him she *wanted* to be in his bed. If she wasn't seriously considering it, then she wouldn't have kissed him. Hell, she wouldn't be sitting at his table right now in those sexy heels and those skin-tight jeans that he wanted to peel off those muscled legs, inch by delicious inch.

"I—I can't cure you," she stuttered, not meeting his eye.

"How do you know if you don't try?" He leaned back in his chair and pushed up the sleeves that threatened to roll down his arms. "Look, I'm a businessman. I'm used to making deals. We can help each other, Harley. You know we can."

She stared at him, eyes unreadable in the darkened dining room. He felt a flicker of anxiousness in his stomach. He hated not being in control, hated not knowing what was coming next. Would she rebuff him? He was always a man who prided himself on knowing people, and knowing exactly what they would do next, and yet, Harley left him a bit off balance.

She took her napkin from her lap then and placed it gently beside her knife. She took a deep breath, her ample chest heaving. "Okay," she said, surprising him by completely surrendering. "I accept your proposal."

"You do?" Few people could shock Wilder Lange, but Harley had done it.

"With a few rules. One, you don't have sex with anyone else while you're having sex with me."

"Okay." Technically, he *couldn't* have sex with anyone else. Hell, didn't even want to. That would be a promise easily kept.

"And, two, you don't tell anyone about us. Or about the fact that I only have had two partners before you."

"I think that NDA you signed technically means that you can't, and neither can I." Anticipation bloomed in his stomach. He wanted her. Now. On this dining room table. He imagined all the dishes clattering to the floor. He wasn't quite sure if he'd even be able to make it to his bedroom.

"And if it's more than one time…"

Wilder licked his lips. "It will *definitely* be more than one time," he said.

"I get to say how often. When. And when we stop."

"Of course. Lady's choice. Always."

"And if anything makes me uncomfortable, we stop. Immediately."

"Absolutely. I'd insist on it."

"Okay, then." She stood up and licked her full red lips. "I'm ready if you are."

Wilder had never had a woman so matter-of-factly tell him she was going to fuck his brains out. It instantly made him hard. *This* was what he needed. Not talking endlessly about his past, or traumas or anything else. He just needed Harley. In those skin-tight jeans, hugging all her delicious curves, as she walked over to him in her sky-high stilettos. He'd never seen a woman so sexy in all his life. She came to him, and he pushed away his chair from the table. She straddled him and his breath caught. At that moment, he wondered if there was anything at all he could teach her. Anything about anything.

He put his hand on the back of her neck and pulled her down, he needed those thick red lips, needed them now. He could barely help himself, being so close to her, smelling her, sensing her full lips so close to his. He promised himself it would simply be a taste, a little nip, nothing more. He pressed his lips to hers, gently, expecting at any moment for her to stop the contact, to pull away from him. He was testing her boundaries, and he knew it. Yet, her lips were more amazing than he remembered, soft, but firm at the same time, knowledgeable, and made to fit his. He broke the kiss.

"Are you sure about this?"

"Yes," she said, pupils wide and dark. Then she kissed him again, aggressive. Decisive. Sure. And then, like a miracle, her tongue flicked into his mouth, the best thing he'd ever tasted in his life. His want for her roared to life then, as if it had been holding back, testing the waters. Now it was a living, breathing thing inside him, something that needed to be fed. Now.

They devoured each other, there was no other way to describe it, tongues and lips, whole, as his hands roved down her back and hers clutched the back of his neck. He knew he'd awakened something in her as well, something beastly, something she had no desire to control. She grinded against him in his chair, and he felt her warmth pressing into him beneath the fabric of her jeans, and his brain nearly exploded. The chair was suddenly too confining, too rigid. He needed room to move. Wilder picked her up then, easily, as he stood, and her legs wrapped around his waist, their mouths still hungry for one another, insatiable. She tasted like red wine, and the promise of a cure. Yes, he knew it, knew it in the very nerves of his body that she was what he needed. He realized it had been so long since he'd even been able to have a woman this way. A year? Had it been that long since he'd been inside another woman? Since he'd even been able to be inside? His body had failed him for so long, he could barely remember. Now, it strained with urgency against the fly of his suit pants, ached to be free. To be in Harley where he belonged.

But he couldn't do it here. In the dining room. Not where they could be interrupted. He planned to take his damn time with her. Planned to explore her body all night long, planned to try every position he could remember. He'd show her that she needed him, and what he could give her, just as much as he needed her. He stood, easing her off him and pulling away from her kiss. Her lipstick was deliciously smudged now. He'd done that. He took pride in it.

"Come," he said, not caring that his napkin had fallen to the floor or, hell, that his steak was half eaten. He was ready for dessert. She took his hand, and he led her out of the dining room, down the lowly lit corridor to his room, his master suite, where he could have her and they'd not be disturbed. Where he could take his time, where he could taste every part of her body.

His whole self had been wanting this since the moment he'd first saw her picture, since he'd first picked up a copy of *Femme* magazine. He'd wanted her before he even met her, and that meant the urgency of this moment nearly drowned him. He walked quickly and she hurried behind, wordlessly.

He shoved open the door of his bedroom, not bothering to flick on the lights. They came up by themselves, automatically, as soon as he said, "Bedroom lights." That was his code for low light, romantic light, the perfect setting for undressing a beautiful woman. It was low enough to be romantic but light enough so that he could see it all. And he wanted to see all of her. Every inch.

He pulled her to his bed, and then he stopped, grabbing a condom from a side table's drawer before turning to kiss her again. Yes, the taste of her. So perfect. So made for him. She pulled back, then. He watched as she slowly lifted her tank top. Beneath, she wore no bra. Nothing, just gravity-defying breasts and milk chocolate nipples. He took them in, appreciating the sight. Next, he pulled her close, put his mouth on one and then the other, making her moan. Yes, the first of many moans tonight. He'd make sure that she'd feel pleasures she'd never known before. He planned to worship her. Show her that sex between near strangers could be the hottest possible. There was no need to hold back, no need to worry about what the other person was thinking. No, this was the time where he could make all her fantasies come true. Even the ones she hadn't admitted to herself yet.

He tossed the condom wrapper on the bed, and she eyed it, but said nothing. He pulled away and she began to unbutton his shirt. Slowly, button by button, and the wait was nearly too much. He wanted to rip the damn thing off, buttons be damned. He wanted to be inside her *now,* by God. Wanted to be consumed by her. She got the shirt off, and then she went for his pants. He could barely contain himself now. But she was still so methodical, so infuriatingly slow, as she reached for the fly of his pants and then…he was free. Completely free, and decidedly hard. He'd almost forgotten how this felt, how it made him wild and needy. She stroked him, slowly, almost reverentially, and he thought he might come then and there.

No. But he couldn't. He needed to wait. Needed to calm himself. Needed to be in her first. He glanced at her and saw wonder in her eyes, awe, even. He'd been with hundreds of women, but had never been treated like this, as if what he had was precious. He knew he was on the north side of average, knew women typically were satisfied, but most women barely looked at him at all. Weren't interested in the male anatomy, but not Harley. She held his thickness in her hands and stroked him as if she were trying to memorize the lines of his cock. He grabbed her wrist then. One more stroke and he was done for.

"You don't seem to have any problems that I can see," she said.

"No," he growled. "Not with you."

He laid Harley down on his king-size platform bed and it was his turn to undo her jeans. Her tight jeans that he loved rolling down her legs. He kissed her, inch by inch, as he revealed more skin. She arched her back into his kisses. And then he tugged at the edges of her underwear and then she was free of them, too, all beautifully bare for him. He loved every bit of her tanned almond-colored skin. He could barely contain himself now, as he rolled her over on her back and she spread her legs for him, her mouth finding his once more. Her tongue teasing him, beckoning him to taste her.

He broke the kiss then and knelt then before her, because he planned to do some worshipping. He kissed the inside of her thigh, as he pulled her to the edge of his bed so that all he could see was her, all of her. She glistened in the low light of his bedroom as he spread her lips with his hands, and found what he was looking for, the swollen knob of her clit.

"Wait," she said, sitting up. "I don't know..." The look of panic on her face melted something in him.

"You're amazing. I don't care whether or not you showered," he said. He was a man who wanted to explore every inch of a woman. He wasn't squeamish. Wasn't afraid. He loved tasting women. And he would damn well taste Harley. He'd been imagining devouring her just this way almost since the first day they met. He would not be denied now.

She still seemed timid, and so he pushed her knees farther apart. She let him and he dipped down, kissing her clit first, gently. Then he lapped at it, just a little tease, and then he worked his tongue, faster and slower, responding to her body. "You taste so good," he told her and her body relaxed a bit. *That's right*, he thought. *This is what it's supposed to be like. You should be worshipped just like this every day for the rest of your life*. "Tell me what feels good," he commanded, breaking from his work. He dipped down and licked her once more. "Fast?" He flicked his tongue. "Or slow?"

"Slow," she murmured, so softly he almost didn't hear her. He knew, even if she didn't, that sex was all about personal preference. What pushed one woman over the edge, completely turned off another. He knew it was about getting to know each woman, and he badly wanted to know Harley's every want. Before they were done, he'd become an expert on her. Hell, he'd get his Harley Vega PhD. She groaned, and her hands came to his hair, grabbing a handful. He knew he was doing something right.

"Faster," she told him after a bit. "Yes. Faster still."

Her wish was his command. A few more seconds and she tightened her grip on his hair.

"There," she breathed, almost strangled. "Right there." Her back arched and every single muscle tensed. He knew the signs, knew what was coming, as Harley griped his hair harder. He didn't mind. Because she let out an amazing shout, completely free, not caring who heard. It was like another being had taken control of her, something had been ripped loose inside, something primal and perfect. He stood, swiping at his mouth with the back of his hand, her juices on his chin. Delicious. Just like her. She lay before him, legs spread and breathing hard.

"We're not done yet," he promised her.

"I…" She sucked in a breath. "I've never come like that."

"So hard?" he asked her.

"No." She sat up on her elbows. "Like…with a man…" She glanced downward.

"You've never had a man go down on you?" Wilder froze. What the hell? What kind of men had she dated?

"No. I have. But…" She shifted uneasily. "But they never made me… I mean…" A blush crept up her neck and down her bare breasts.

"Never made you come." Now, he got the picture. Still, he was stunned. How had they *not* made her come? Sure, he'd had women who'd had difficulty, sometimes a couple who only came in very certain positions, and sometimes only with the help of a vibrator, but Harley was not one of those women. He breathed on her and she came. If a man knew even a little bit about how to please a woman with his mouth, she'd come for him. That meant that the men hadn't even really tried. "That's a crime," he said and meant it.

"I didn't realize it was so good." She fell back, almost exhausted, her face flushed pink in the afterglow. "I mean, I read about it, but…"

"You can't find out everything in books." He held

his own cock in his hand now, finding it hard and ready. He took the condom wrapper and ripped it, slipping the latex over himself. "And that was just the first course."

"What?" She sat up, surprised. "No. I… I mean, I never come more than once."

Now, he was completely bewildered. Were the only two men she slept with the worst lovers of all time?

"Do not tell me you've never had multiple orgasms."

He rubbed against her, finding her deliciously wet, amazingly ready, and he almost lost his control right then.

"N-no," she said, squirming a bit beneath his touch. "No, I haven't."

"This changes tonight." He teased her a bit more, as he studied her beautiful bareness. Still unable to believe that two men had made such terrible mistakes with such an amazing woman. It was like hitching a thoroughbred to a plow. Not something that would ever happen under his watch. But right now, he couldn't think about other men, other lovers. He was all about her soft skin, the smell of her on him, lighting up all the primal parts of his brain. He just wanted to be in her. Fill her. He needed her, more than he'd needed anyone in his whole life.

She'd be his cure. She'd be his answer. He set himself up on his elbows, breaking the kiss and stared into her dark eyes. He waited for her to tell him no, that they'd gone too far. He waited, but no counter came. She was panting beneath him, lips swollen from his kiss. He could wait no longer, looking at her nakedness, feeling the hunger in himself for her. He met her gaze and that took him over the edge. Then, as if his body had a mind of its own, he plunged forward, finding her snug depths, and she gasped, arching upward, her fingernails digging deliciously into his back. This was exactly where he needed to be. He realized that he'd been looking for this place his entire life.

CHAPTER TWELVE

HARLEY'S NEED WAS a monster unleashed, and could not be contained. It clawed itself out of her soul and into her brain. She simply could not stop feeding it. Not with Wilder deep inside her, moving slowly at first, and then decidedly faster, he fit in her as if she were made for him, as if this was inevitable between them. And maybe it was. She'd never in her whole life had sex with a near stranger, and yet, here she was, flat on her back in a bed she'd never seen before, wanting nothing more than Wilder to go deeper and harder. Hell, she'd never even *come* twice during one sexual encounter her whole life. She counted herself lucky if she came at all with the two boyfriends that were more about finishing themselves than making sure she was completely satisfied. As a sex advice columnist, she knew the ridiculousness of it. But she'd always thought that if she just talked about her needs enough they'd be met. But now she realized no amount of talking with her ex-boyfriends would have made them *want* to make her come. That was something that Wilder was showing her right now. How much he wanted to bring her pleasure, how much he wanted to make sure she came as hard, as fast and as often as possible.

And that undid something in her, unleashed something. Pure animal want. And now that he'd helped her take off her leash, she wasn't sure she'd ever want to go back. Now, she worried, her need, her want might just burn her alive.

She tried to reason it out, except her brain had shut off. It couldn't function with the monster of desire shouting in her ear, the monster that needed to be fed. They were finally, at long last, skin against skin, and Wilder was staring at her, right at her, in a way that was both sexy and beyond intimate. He was deep inside her, yet it was the look he was giving her now, the hot desire in his eyes that felt even more intrusive somehow, even more...personal than his body. He wanted her. Wanted her in every way. His eyes told her that he'd have her, too, devour her, pleasure her, worship her. And in that moment, *right* at that moment, she worried that none of this would ever be casual. Not for her. Maybe she simply wasn't built for it, but the way Wilder was looking at her right now, part of her was falling in love with him.

This was probably a mistake. She realized that now, her logical brain, but the desire in her didn't care. The monster in her, newly unleashed, just wanted more of Wilder. More of his mouth. More of his hands. More of his cock. She wanted his come, too, hot, and thick and deep inside her. She wanted to get rid of the condom, which seemed absurd. Beyond absurd. Dangerous. The very thought of that made her gasp in his mouth, lift her own hips up to his and meet him thrust for thrust. She wanted to make him lose his will, lose his control. She wanted to milk him in the most primal way. She would come. She would come hard, and fast and dirty. She let out a primal cry when she came, the monster inside her letting loose at last, wild, and hungry and free.

And then he thrust deep inside her and he, too, came with a bellowing cry, primal and monstrous. He collapsed on her, the weight of him delicious on her chest. They panted together, breath coming hard, on the bed. Eventually, he pulled out. And then he cursed.

"The condom broke," he said, meeting her gaze. She glanced down and saw, yes, the thing had split, nearly in two. She'd never seen that before, but how many columns had she written just about this? How often had she counseled panicked readers to go find Plan B at their local drugstore?

She sat up, abruptly, worried that somehow her wanting his come had made this happen. Now, he was in her, deep inside her. He was a part of her, just as she had wanted, and yet, she saw on his face that he wasn't happy about it.

"That never happens. I'm sorry."

"It's okay," she said and meant it.

"No, it's not okay." He seemed to be beating himself up. In that second, she wondered if he regretted having sex at all. Surely, he'd had a broken condom before. Surely, with all those women, this must've happened before. The burning desire in her cooled. The monster in her retreating back into the darkness where it lived.

"I should've asked. Are you on…?" The normally silver-tongued, quick-witted Wilder seemed to be at a loss for words.

"Yes. I'm on the pill," she told him, sitting up, realizing that he was worried she might be pregnant, and that the frown on his face told her he wouldn't be thrilled at the prospect. After all, an accidental pregnancy for a wealthy man could be very costly. Yet, why did it irk so much? What was she expecting? Him to want to give her a baby? Want to have a happy family together? They'd only just met. This was supposed to be casual sex. Casual sex should never end in a pregnancy. Otherwise, it wouldn't be casual anymore, would it? She was being irrational. Unreasonable. She was acting like she was in a relationship when she wasn't. Because this was the first time that she'd just had sex with someone she had no intention of falling in love with. She wasn't even sure how that worked.

They could have no real relationship. So this shouldn't be that hard.

"I'm sorry. We shouldn't have…" He was still talking but she wished he'd stop. Because it reminded her that this was temporary. And she wasn't sure she wanted it to be temporary. Because sex with Wilder Lange had been some of the hottest, most amazing of her life. She didn't want it to end. But it would end. She'd made a deal with him. Casual sex, nothing more.

She glanced under a nearby chair and ottoman but couldn't find her underwear anywhere. No matter, she had others. Harley needed to get out of this room, compose herself before she did something stupid like cry.

"Harley." His voice was filled with concern, and she hated it. He was handling her, placating her, now that he'd gotten all that he wanted. Now that he'd challenged her rules and she'd immediately caved for him.

"I think I'd better go..." She backed away from him, unable to meet his eye.

"We should talk about this."

She almost wanted to bark a laugh. That was *her* line. She was the sexologist. The one who always insisted on talking everything out. But she couldn't talk about this. She barely even understood her feelings herself.

"We've done enough for tonight," she managed, and pulled on her shirt.

"Wait. Harley." He grabbed her wrist. "Is everything okay?"

"Fine." That was such a lie. She pulled down her shirt. If she could only find her underwear. If only she could get her cold hard reason back. Why was she acting like a little girl? Pouting, almost. Because why? He didn't want to give her an accidental baby? She was being absurd.

"It doesn't seem like you're fine." He locked eyes with her with an intensity that demanded the truth. Except she wasn't prepared to give it to him.

"I… I am. Just… I'm embarrassed." The lies were coming thick and fast now. "That I told you about not coming… About…my past boyfriends." It was an excuse that sounded as good as any.

"That? Please. I was glad to show those guys up." He laid back on the bed and put his hands behind his head. "They should've treated you better."

True, she guessed. Although they stuck with her for months. Wilder wasn't willing to promise even that. What was wrong with her? She wanted to shake herself. She was being stupid. She was acting like she'd wanted an accidental pregnancy. Which she didn't. Not at all. So why would she be angry with Wilder for worrying about one? What was he supposed to do? Look at the broken condom, and get down on one knee and propose marriage? The thought was crazy. But she had these feelings in her now, feelings that made no logical sense. She wasn't sure she liked them. She had to stop acting like a teenager. She was a grown woman with control over her feelings.

"Come back to bed. I have about a dozen more positions I want to try." Wilder spread out his perfectly sculpted body on the bed. She was tempted. God, was she. He grabbed her wrist.

"But if this is casual, I mean. I won't sleep here, so…"

"Why wouldn't you sleep in my bed?"

Because sleeping is the most intimate thing you could do with another person, she wanted to shout. Because it's where you are both most vulnerable, asleep, unconscious and naked, and…

"Because it's casual."

He tugged on her arm, pulling her to the bed. "Casual doesn't mean we can't sleep together. Share the same bed."

"It doesn't?" Now, she was confused. What the hell did casual mean if not sneaking out of someone's bed after the deed was done?

"You have so much to learn, grasshopper." He pulled her on top of him and she went, inhaling his scent, dizzy with it. She wanted to stay. Wanted to let him make her come again.

"Come on. It's time for another session. I want to make you come with my mouth again."

She hesitated. Her knees felt a little weak. The monster she thought was sleeping woke once more. "One time should be enough, though."

"One time is never enough," he said. "That's the first lesson I'm going to teach you."

Wilder was spent. He'd fallen asleep sometime around dawn and slept like the dead. He woke slowly, to the delicious weight of Harley's head on his arm. She was breathing heavily, and the light was starting to come in through the curtains. Was it noon? Later? He had no idea. What he did know was that he'd made Harley come half a dozen more times, exploring her body in a way she'd never been explored before. The woman hadn't even done a *reverse cowgirl,* which boggled his mind. Who were these talentless hacks out there calling themselves men? Who were the two men she'd given herself to? They ought to be hauled out of bed and shot. Or at least publically humiliated.

Harley knew her way around his body, for sure, but she'd been systematically cheated out of decent sex. It was a crime. Thankfully, he'd done a pretty decent job of rectifying that in one night. And planned to keep on rectifying it for the next many nights.

Because, hallelujah, Harley *was* the miracle cure he thought she was. His body *worked.* He knew men took that for granted every day, but for Wilder, it had been a worry at the back of his mind for so long that he wasn't sure he was even normal. Wasn't sure he was even a *man.* He'd been questioning his own manhood for more than a year. Hell, he'd been questioning his *sanity.* He'd had his pick of gorgeous women—models, actresses and more—all eager to please him, eager to do everything he wanted, and yet, he hadn't wanted any of them. As horrible as it sounded, he felt like a man at an expensive restaurant that couldn't muster up enough appetite to eat anything on the menu.

But then Harley Vega walked into his life. And he knew hunger. Boy, did he. He felt like a starving man. He'd never had a woman like he'd had Harley last night: manically, in every position he could think of, again and again, as if he'd never tire of her. Because he wanted to devour every inch of her, because he was starving for a meal only she could provide. He'd been so damn excited to be aroused by someone that he simply hadn't wanted to stop. He'd come again, and again and again, a record for him as a nearly forty-year-old man. Harley made him feel like he was twenty once more. Like he couldn't imagine losing a hard-on ever again in his life. That had been the most amazing, thorough, delicious sex he'd ever had. Harley had been an amazing lover, sensitive, selfless, hot. And seeing her face light up with delight as he showed her things she'd never seen, well, that had just been the icing on the cake.

It made him feel needed. Wanted. Necessary. Manly. There wasn't any other way to describe it. He felt whole, and strong, and that had everything to do with Harley Vega. His thoughts filled with her skin, the smell of her, the *feel* of her, and he itched for another round. The idea was ridiculous. They'd nearly chafed themselves raw the night before and he was ready for more. Harley had saved him, of this he had no doubt, but he needed her to save him over and over again.

He shifted a little, his arm having fallen asleep beneath Harley's head. She moaned a little and rolled into him, burying her face in his chest. At that moment the feeling to protect her came on so strong, it felt like a blow. He felt possessive in a way he'd not felt with another woman. This woman had saved him, and he'd saved her back, and she was his. He knew, of course, that a person didn't belong to another person, but as he pulled her in tighter with his arms, he didn't care. He wanted to protect her. Wanted to keep her coming today and all the days from now on. The feeling was an unusual one. He wasn't sure what to make of it. Usually, when a woman slept in his bed, even for a few weeks at a time, typically the longest his relationships went, he never felt attached. Not like this. Not like he wanted to take care of her, make sure she never wanted for anything, most of all the pleasure she deserved.

A knock came on the door. Before he could call out, Jacob entered with the usual tray of his morning espresso and yogurt, which he placed on the bedside table before he opened the curtains. Then, Jacob saw the figure of Harley. He took the tray and instantly backed out. No doubt he'd send in Vanka in fifteen minutes with *two* coffees and an assortment of coffee cakes. This is what Jacob was trained to do when Wilder had company spend the night. Hell, he had it down to a science. Coffee, scones and then the door. How often had Jacob had to actually see women off? Into cabs or Ubers while Wilder sprinted off to work? But he didn't feel like doing that this morning. He knew Lucinda wasn't done with her coup, but he didn't want to leave his bed. Or Harley's side. For once, he wanted to stay right where he was and inhale the flowery scent of her hair.

Harley stirred, though, yawning and sat up. She blinked at him sleepily and smiled. Her hair was a mess, her mascara smudged a bit and her lips were swollen from kissing. A faint pink remained on her cheeks, though. He'd never seen her look more unkempt—and more damn beautiful ever. That was the look of a satisfied woman. He felt a kind of perverse pride in that.

"Morning, sleepyhead," he said and dipped down to kiss her nose.

"Morning," she murmured and then kissed his bare chest. A delicate gesture that sent a shiver straight down his spine. "What time is it? Is it even morning?"

He picked up his phone from his nightstand and glanced at it. "Technically. It's 11:50."

"Oh, geez. We slept in."

"That's because we were busy, very late."

She laughed, and he felt her belly's vibrations in his own. "Yes, we were."

He sat up a little and so did she. Her eyes roved around his massive bedroom. They were surrounded with one of the most impressive views in Manhattan. They were high above the other people, so no fear of spies, and outside the city sprawled out in all directions. A kind of steel manmade landscape that never ceased to take his breath away.

"That's an amazing view," she said, sounding awestruck.

"It should be."

A knock sounded at the door. She stiffened in his arms, eyes warily trained on his door.

"Don't worry," he told her. "It's just breakfast."

The door creaked open and Harley, for her part, ducked under the covers, hiding half her face. Vanka, wearing her uniform of a white suit, came in, carrying the silver tray of various kinds of pastries, a silver pot of coffee and two cups. Down to a science. He almost laughed. It had been a year since he'd had a woman in his bed, but his staff was so amazing that they knew what to do.

"Thanks, V," he said and the woman gave him a nod and a smile. The servants knew of his problem. How could they not? They had ears and eyes everywhere. But no one had ever mentioned it, though the satisfied gleam in her eye told her she was happy for him. He had no doubt the servants were probably celebrating. What an insufferable bastard he'd probably been this last year, unable to let off steam, constantly worried that he'd somehow lost his man card. When, as it turned out, all he really needed was the right woman. He gave Harley a squeeze, but noticed she was still stiff and quiet, waiting for Vanka to set down the tray and leave. She placed the tray at the foot of the bed and then turned to leave, quietly and discreetly. He made a mental note to give all of them bigger bonuses this year. They deserved it.

"She's gone," he said and Harley emerged, again, dark curls in a riot over her head, and swiping at a smudge of mascara under her left eye.

"Do you always have breakfast in bed?"

"It's a perk of being a billionaire." Harley sat up and blinked at the tray, her eyes silently counting the two cups and two plates of pastries.

"How did they know…?" Then her cheeks flushed a deeper pink. "Oh, God. Were we that loud? Does *everyone* know? Jacob even?" Harley buried her face in her hands. He found her modesty completely adorable.

"They're discreet. And their NDAs are even stricter than yours. Besides, I trust them all with my life. They've worked for me for decades." He reached for a coffee cup and poured Harley a cup. "Sugar? Cream?"

She shook her head.

"Ah." He appraised her with care. "You're just like me. You crave unadulterated coffee." He handed her a cup of steaming hot black coffee and she took a tentative sip.

He could see that Harley was still coming to terms with the idea of having other people so personally connected. He'd almost forgot that for most people, servants weren't an automatic asset.

"Don't worry. It's their job to anticipate my needs. And they don't judge. Believe me, once, Jacob came in and saw two completely naked—" He stopped, mid-sentence, because Harley looked stricken. What the hell was he doing talking about other women with her in bed with him? God, he'd lost all his manners. He was a complete ass. "I'm sorry. I didn't mean to…"

"No. That's okay." She sent him a weak smile. "We're casual, right?" The way she said it made him think she was trying to convince herself more than him. And why did the word bother him so much? That's what this was, of course. Casual. No strings. A mutually agreed upon exchange: she craved experience and he needed her to jumpstart his body. It was the perfect agreement. So why wasn't he happy that she'd reminded him of it?

She took a deep sip of her coffee and looked away from him. He could feel an awkwardness settle between them and he didn't like it.

"Well." She stretched and set down the coffee on the tray. "I guess I'd better head back to my room."

Now, panic struck him. "Why?"

"Shower, dress. You know. What people are supposed to do with themselves on a Friday morning. And don't you have to get into the office?"

"I'm taking the day off." He hadn't realized he was until right that moment. But he wanted to spend the day with Harley. The weekend, too. He wasn't done with her. Not by a long shot.

"Oh. Well. I still should shower."

"But the thing is, I have the best shower in the

house." He nodded to the open door across the room to his huge white-marbled bathroom, complete with Jacuzzi tub and walk-in shower. The damn thing had more showerheads in it than tile practically. With that thing, no angle went uncleaned. "Besides, I have to ask, have you had shower sex before?"

"I actually have had shower sex," she admitted.

"Well. I guarantee you. It's not like this."

CHAPTER THIRTEEN

WILDER HAD BEEN right. Sex in the shower with him was *not* like the one awkward time fumbling with her college boyfriend, when they'd knocked over the body wash and also lost hot water halfway through. They'd had to race to the finish, so they could escape the cold drizzle inside the tiny and less than pristine tub in his college apartment with the faded, mildewed shower curtain sticking to their legs. No. Sex in the shower with Wilder was a completely new experience. First of all, the shower itself was the size of her bathroom in her own place, and it had a bench, six different showerheads and an endless supply of hot water. He applied rich smelling soap on a soft loofah and rubbed her from head to toe, careful to give her most tender spots extra care. He soaped her nipples and she moaned, unable to help herself. They were tender from all his attention the night before, and he seemed to instinctively know that. He was gentle, but the touch still excited her.

In fact, she wasn't sure if it was the spray of water or her own slick want between her legs.

She couldn't believe that she still wanted Wilder, even after all the many times the night before, but here she was, devouring his mouth beneath the hot water of the pizza pan–size showerhead, the water and his hands delicately stroking her naked body. Her heavy breasts were lifted up by his hands as he seemed to weigh them with a gentle squeeze. She pressed her wet body to his, amazed again at how quickly he came to life, how he seemed to be hard and full instantly, ready for her. That nearly tilted her over the edge, just their two bare bodies in the shower. The anticipation was killing her. She wanted him in her, she wanted him in all the ways he'd have her and she wanted him now. He turned her around, and she went, pressing her hands against the glass, her back to him, and he followed the ridge of her back down across her ass with the soft soapy sponge and she nearly went wild. The monster of need in her grew savage in its desire, as it clawed viciously inside her, wanting out.

Palms flat against the glass, she felt vulnerable, exposed, but ready for him. Each nerve ending of her body vibrated with anticipation. Yes. This is what she needed. His body. His attention. His everything. She felt him big, and hard and heavy against the curve of her backside. He was ready for her, and he was bare, the hot water dripping from him, down her hips and the backs of her thighs. She wondered, fleetingly, about a condom, wondered if he had them stashed here, too, in the shower, where he probably took hundreds of other women. How many other women had stood where she was standing, palms against the glass, legs spread-eagle, waiting for him to enter her? To make her his? She banished the thought. Now was not the time to be jealous. Now was the time to want. Just pure, unadulterated lust. She'd deal with jealousy later.

She reached behind her and felt the long thick length of his cock, finding it without latex, just his smooth, perfect skin. She squeezed it, hard.

"I want you," she told him, voice rough. "I want you like this."

Because that's all she'd ever wanted, she realized. Him inside of her, skin on skin. She knew it was risky. Hell, she'd never had a stranger before, much less one who wasn't wearing a condom. But she was on the pill and she already knew they'd both been tested for STIs. What was the true risk after all? But in that moment she didn't care. She wanted him in the basest possible way, and she wanted him now. He hesitated, and for a devastating second, she thought he might turn her down. Instead, he gave a single, deliberate thrust and was inside her, moaning with the pure pleasure of it.

"Yes," she moaned, feeling as if she'd won some kind of victory as he began to move, slowly at first, as if he were delicately exploring every centimeter of her. He pushed against her, and her breasts flattened against the cold glass, sending a sensation of new delight through her body. The cold glass, the hot steam around them from the shower and his hard hot body behind her, pressing against her, burying himself in her deepest places. This wasn't just shower sex. This was fucking amazing sex. How had she lived so long without having sex like this? Is this what truly amazing sex was all about?

She suddenly felt silly for trying to give advice about a thing she realized at this moment that she'd truly known nothing about.

"Harley… God, I can't…" And in a hard thrust Wilder came inside her, hot and heavy and seemingly endless. *Yes*, she thought. *This is what I want, you in me.* She felt pride that he couldn't hold it, that somehow she'd been so much that he'd had no choice but to explode. She almost felt that she'd stolen the come from him and that made her smile. Who was the teacher after all, she wondered. "I couldn't hold it. I tried, but you tore that out of me," he murmured in her ear. She almost didn't care that she herself hadn't come, that her own body was still taut with want. She'd be satisfied with the fact that she'd made him lose control. How often had he made her wild with desire? Dizzy with need, and now she'd done the same.

"But now it's your turn," he said, and turned her around slowly, kissing her as the hot water of the shower trickled down between her breasts.

"Mine?" she asked him, surprised. She couldn't imagine he'd get on his knees and use his mouth. After all, he'd drown. But he seemed to have a different idea. He reached for the small gold-handled handheld spray, untangled its cord from the wall. He pressed a button on the side and a small spurt of water came out. He grinned. "Time for another lesson," he promised her and her body tingled with anticipation. What was he going to do with that?

He gently sprayed her neck and then the rounded top of her breasts, before landing on her nipples. She groaned with the delicate pleasure of the soft water running down her chest. He flicked the head of the mini showerhead and the pulse of the water changed, from soft to hard. She gasped and arched her back into the spray. She'd never had a shower with a handheld spigot, never been in one where the massaging channels were so varied. Then he pulled her against him, so her back was against his stomach once more, and began slowly moving the showerhead down her body. It felt like a hundred fingers on her at once, a hundred delicate massaging touches. He went slowly, deliberately, rinsing what was left of the soap off her body, and then he hovered between her legs. She spread her legs a little wider and he pointed the water there, the deliberate massaging stream, and it felt like a hundred delicious tongues.

"Do you like this...?" He clicked the setting to soft. "Or this?" And then to hard, a deliberate pulse.

"That one," she said, feeling the vibrations exactly

where she needed them, her legs spreading of their own will, her pelvis arching into the stream. Her want grew, her need growled inside her. God, how he could make her want. He gently moved the small head in time with her own hips and then, suddenly, the water stream overtook her. Pushed her over the edge and she was crying out, gripping at the smooth shower wall, desperate to hold onto something, fearing she'd drown in her own pleasure.

"That's it," he murmured in her ear, his voice smooth like melted chocolate. "Lesson complete."

The next two months passed in what Harley could only call simple perfection. Eventually, Wilder did go back to work, but they settled into a routine where he'd come home to her at night and on the weekends and show her things she could never have imagined. She realized that what she didn't know about sex could fill her dissertation and more. She dove into her "graduate" studies in a way she'd never done before. She was the eager student, he the teacher, and she loved every damn second of it.

Their arrangement was crazy, impossible, even. She was a professional woman with a PhD in human sexuality, and yet, still, there was so very much she didn't know. Not about sex. Not about how it truly worked. He showed her that every day. They barely slept, they sometimes ate, but they absolutely devoured each other's bodies in all the ways possible. Harley never wanted it to end. She also felt herself falling harder for Wilder. With each amazing come, each new discovery about his body or hers made her fall even deeper.

She knew this was supposed to be casual. Told herself that the day would come when they would part ways, and that this was not a man to fall in love with, but she also knew that she was in so deep already, that when he did rip off the Band-Aid, she'd be devastated. So, she made herself a cozy little nook of denial in her brain. She refused to think about parting with Wilder. Refused to think about what would happen the day she woke up and he didn't want her in his bed anymore. When he was at work, she busied herself looking for jobs, revamping column ideas and finishing the first few chapters of a couples' advice book that she hoped to pitch to publishers. The advice book almost wrote itself. Hell, every night she plowed through hands-on research with Wilder only to add in *another* chapter about spicing up your sex life in her new book. She kept herself busy, and she kept herself focused on her career, when she wasn't focused on Wilder's magnificent body.

And she never ever once talked about the future. She didn't want to know the answer. Didn't want to hear Wilder tell her that eventually their "agreement" would end. Eventually, he'd take his amazingly rock hard body and move on to another woman. Because, she reminded herself, that's what she was here for. She was here to jumpstart him, to help him get back to his old life. Not start a new one.

Even as she knew she was falling in love with him, she knew she couldn't admit it: not to him, not even to herself. Wouldn't that mean she'd failed the ultimate test? Wasn't the final lesson in all this how she could do casual?

Wilder sat at his desk in his corner office and frowned at his computer. He glanced at the clock. It was already six o'clock, and he wanted to be home. With Harley's legs wrapped around him. But, no. He was stuck here, furiously answering emails and dealing with another mess Lucinda had made. She'd failed in her bid to take over Lange Communications, but now she was threatening to report them to the FCC, to try to get one of her cronies on the board to investigate them for being a monopoly. Or, more likely, it was her senator friend at work. She'd bought him with hefty donations to his campaign. Lucinda just never quit. It was infuriating and exhausting. If it wasn't one tactic, it was a hundred others. If she won with the FCC, then the government might demand they break up into smaller companies. He was sure her play was to snatch up one of the smaller ones. Apparently, she'd given up hope on the entire pie, and was now just eyeing a slice.

He'd be damned if she'd get it.

Wilder had no doubt they'd win. Lange Communications was no monopoly, but it would be a protracted battle. And being scrutinized by the Feds was never good. Or cheap.

He could feel the walls closing in on him again, and he was suddenly so deathly tired of fighting Lucinda. A faint headache pulsed behind his temples. The woman was a walking migraine. He clacked away on his keyboard, sending out instructions to his attorneys. He thought of the coming weekend, of all the ways he could intensively relieve his stress with Harley in his bed.

His phone dinged, announcing an incoming text message.

Home soon?

Harley had read his mind. He wanted to be home, more than anything. He wanted to be there now. But he had at least another hour's worth of work. Maybe more.

An hour. Tops.

Then he got a better idea. What they needed, he thought, was a little getaway. Where he couldn't be dragged into work, or trapped there.

But...what would you say about a new lesson? Have you ever had vacation sex?

He waited for her response.

Only once. In a tent at a campground.

He shook his head. Having sex in a sleeping bag while fighting off mosquitos was not the vacation sex he had in mind.

Doesn't count. You need a lesson in real vacation sex.

Her answer came fast.

Then why don't you teach me?

CHAPTER FOURTEEN

HARLEY KNEW SHE was beyond help, the second she'd stepped off his helicopter that landed on his massive estate in Aruba. He'd flown her in his private jet direct, and the helicopter had whisked them off on a tour of half the island before landing on his gated estate near the shoreline, surrounded by blue-green water. Her whole body vibrated with anticipation. She was going to enjoy this next lesson. Hell, she enjoyed them all. Just when she thought he couldn't possibly teach her any more, there he went and surprised her. The man was a bottomless wealth of sex, a walking Kama Sutra. But he ought to be, with the long list of partners to teach him. She pushed that thought away. She wouldn't think about the other women. When she did, her stomach felt tight. Tight with jealousy.

Which she did know was foolhardy. She had no right to be jealous. He'd told her in straight terms he didn't want commitment. She could also see that he'd been a man who'd avoided emotional entanglements all his life. Breaking through the walls he'd built around his heart wouldn't be easy. Actually, she knew *she* couldn't do it. He had to be the one to take a sledgehammer to them. He'd have to want to do it and he wasn't ready for that. Would he ever be ready for that?

Could she even seriously think about trying to have a real relationship with him? What happened when they had an inevitable hiccup? When Wilder ran out of new things to show her? Or when he inevitably had a setback? He saw her as a cure for his impotence, but long term, the same psychological troubles that plagued him the first time would return. He'd need to unpack some serious emotional baggage not to suffer any setbacks. She couldn't be a cure for him. He'd have to be a cure for himself.

"Penny for your thoughts?" Wilder asked her, as the two lounged on deck chairs on his massive patio overlooking the blue-green sea. In front of them was a small square-shaped pool, crystal clear water that sat still, looking like a pane of glass.

"I was just thinking about how this feels like we're running away," she said, shading her eyes from the bright sun above them.

"That's because we are," he said. "And, of course, this is *all* about new lessons."

"Indeed." She laughed. God, she loved his lessons. Could spent a lifetime learning from him. Actually, wished she could. She glanced at his bare chest, thick with muscle. His body was a work of art, and she could stare at it all day. The monster in her was always ready to come out. The one she wasn't sure she could control. Or, hell, that she even wanted to control anymore. "So, why are we here?"

"What do you mean? It's all about the formal education of Harley Vega."

"And about Wilder Lange avoiding some stress at home. Or work." She eyed him above her sunglasses. She stretched out on the armless lounger beneath the warm Caribbean sun and the cloudless blue sky.

Wilder stared at her a beat and then laughed. "You don't pull any punches, do you, Ms. Vega?"

"No, I don't, Mr. Lange. I think you know that about me by now."

A teasing smile tugged at the corner of his mouth. "Oh, I know that and so much more." Wilder grabbed her chair and scooted her closer so their legs were touching. He planted a long deliberate kiss on her lips. Harley pulled away first.

"Do you?" she asked him, a little breathless.

"I do," he said, grinning. And then he rolled on top of her, so his bare chest was against her, the only fabric between them her thin yellow bikini. He shifted his weight and Harley could feel his want, stretching the fabric of his swim trunks. The monster in her, the one that seemed never to be satisfied, came to life then, a flicker of movement in her belly. Her lips found his and their tongues entwined together. She hungered for him, for his taste, for the feel of him inside her. Harley told herself to tread lightly, told herself that what they had wouldn't—couldn't—last, and that the more she invested of herself in him, the more she'd be brokenhearted down the road.

He moved away from her then, sliding off her body and standing up.

"Time for a new lesson, I think." He tossed his sunglasses down on the lounge chair. "Have you ever had swimming pool sex?"

She shook her head once. "Never really had the chance."

"Well, then. Let the lesson commence." He held out his hand and she took it, as he led her deliberately to the pool. They stepped into it, the small rigid steps near them leading them into the cool water. Once they were waist deep, Wilder pulled Harley into his arms and kissed her again, open-mouthed and hungry. The water slid between their bodies as he pulled her close, and she felt the heat of his hard-on even through the swim trunks and the water. He moved her to the edge of the pool, facing away from the house. When he pulled back, his eyes seemed to devour her.

"What's the first part of the lesson?" she asked him, trying to catch her breath.

"The first part is this." He reached back and untied the bottoms of her string bikini. They floated up to the top of the water, a triangle of yellow fabric. "The second part is..." He reached down and his fingers found her beneath the water. She glanced around, almost reflexively checking to see if they were alone.

"No one is here," he said. "But even if they were, they can't see below the water." His finger traveled inside her and she gasped. He kissed her again and it felt as if she'd melt straight into him. She wasn't sure where his lips began and hers ended, just that kissing him was the best damn thing she'd ever done in her life. And then there were his fingers. His amazing fingers. Exploring her, heightening all her senses, making the monster in her howl.

Distantly, she heard his smart-watch ping, the sound of an incoming message. He was hardly ever unplugged, but then again he had a corporate empire to run, so it's not as if she expected him to completely disconnect. On the flight here, he'd kept his nose buried in his laptop. There was a delicate deal in the works to buy a German broadband company. She figured the message had something to do with that. But she also felt as if she should rise to the challenge of trying to distract him from work. He needed to relax, too. He glanced at the face of his watch and frowned. While he read his messages, she reached down and felt the front of his swim trunks, hoping to slip her hand down the waistband. When she did, however, she found he wasn't ready.

Surprised, she began to massage him…but nothing.

At her touch, he stepped back from her, sending

waves across the pool. He glanced down, and even reached for himself. But whatever he tried failed.

He cursed and glanced at her, an apology on his face.

"It's okay," she said, reaching for him, but again, he pulled away. Soon, he was hefting himself out of the pool, dripping from head to toe, as he moved away from her to the towels folded on the chairs. She knew this might happen, feared it would. He hadn't really dealt with his issues, thinking he'd been cured when he hadn't. And despite all her training, all the research she'd done on human sexuality that told her people couldn't fix other people of their shortcomings, she'd also come to believe she might be the cure. She wanted to be his remedy. But now, she saw that she wasn't. "We need to talk about it."

"It's just me. Just my damn body. It doesn't work." Wilder punched the stack of towels in frustration.

"Let's talk about it. We can work through this."

He shook his head, water droplets flying. "I need a minute." Wilder retreated into the house, leaving Harley waist deep in the pool, wondering if he planned to come back.

Wilder's body had failed him again. He couldn't believe it. He wanted Harley Vega more than he'd ever wanted any woman in his whole life, and yet, he was having issues—again. He felt less than a man, less than a human being. How could this happen? Her kiss ignited a powerful want in him, and yet his body seemed determined to douse that flame. Why? How could he have a real relationship with Harley if his body wasn't going to cooperate? Would he be doomed to platonic relationships with women for the rest of his life?

He angrily dried his hair with a towel, having retreated to his bedroom to get his bearings. It's what he always did if this happened. Retreat, compose himself and then pretend it never happened. Hadn't he been doing that for the past year?

Of course, this time, a text message from his corporate attorneys. Lucinda had succeeded in persuading the FCC to investigate Lange Communications. That was enough to completely take the wind out of his sails. In that second, he'd felt the whole weight of the world on his shoulders, and then…his body had just shut down. Like it usually did. His mind running in a million directions, none of them to fun places, and all of them away from the beautiful woman in his arms.

He needed to focus on *her*, and then maybe he could get a hard-on. But, no, there was the company…and Lucinda's endless efforts to steal the business out from under him. The weight on his shoulders felt heavier than usual. If he weren't careful, he'd slip into a pity party, one where he'd lament the fact that he was always the responsible one, always the one doing the work no one else wanted to do, that he was literally tearing himself down in order to hold the family up. But Wilder didn't have time for pity parties. They were a waste of time and energy.

Besides, he had no excuses. He knew who was to blame: himself. He never should've invited Harley here, never should've promised her a good time when he damn well knew that he might not be able to deliver. Sure, they'd had the best two months of his life, but hadn't he feared that it was all somehow temporary? That the demons that haunted him would raise their ugly heads sooner rather than later?

He had no idea what was dragging him down, why his body was so determined to fail him, but he knew there was this weakness lurking in him. He felt horrible that he'd disappointed Harley, embarrassed that she'd seen him that way. He wondered if she'd flee now, if he ought to give her the opportunity to leave, to go back to New York. The worst part was that he had really and truly thought he was cured. But now he realized if an amazing woman like Harley—a woman who affected him so deeply in so many ways—couldn't cure him, then how could he ever hope to get his libido back? How could he ever hope to be normal again?

Then again, he was being stupidly selfish. Yes, this was a problem, but it was an issue other men faced. It wasn't as if he had cancer, or a fatal disease. There were starving children in the world, so who cared if he could get it up or not? He was being silly, immature and weak. Maybe that's why his body was having such problems. It was all a mental failing on his part. He was weak, that was his problem.

He angrily finished drying himself with a towel and grabbed a dry shirt from his dresser and he yanked it over his head. Then he stepped out of his wet swim trunks and into dry gym shorts, stabbing his legs into each hole. Maybe Lucinda had been right about him all these years, maybe he was a failure. How often had she screamed that at him in a drunken rage? That he was doomed to fail, that he would never live up to the Lange name, that secretly his father was embarrassed by him? Sure, she'd always waited until his father was gone to make such accusations, but even these many years later, they still affected him. Hell, Lucinda even now was winning.

A soft knock sounded on the door.

"Yes?" His voice came out gruffer than he intended.

"Can I come in?" Harley's voice came softly through the door. He wanted to tell her to not bother, that there wasn't anything she could do. He'd come to realize for the first time that he was truly alone, that his dysfunction was a problem that might never be solved. But he also knew that would make him sound like a toddler, and he was a grown man. Despite what his body might think.

"Yes," he answered and turned to face the door. She stood in the open frame in her bikini top, her hair wet and a towel slung around her waist. He wondered, fleetingly, if she'd put her bottoms back on, or if they were still floating in his pool. She looked amazing, as usual, gorgeous, and he wondered why his body refused to respond. It must be willfully blind. He took a deep breath and braced himself. Would she be angry? Disappointed? Amused? He'd faced them all with other women who'd seen his failure in action. Instead, she walked straight in and wrapped her arms around him. He froze, not sure what to do. She squeezed him hard, and then pulled away.

"We're going to talk about this," she told him, her light brown eyes flashing with determination.

"What if I don't want to?"

She shook her head. "I don't care. We're going to talk about it. Now." She pushed against his chest. "Take a seat."

"With that tone, I don't think I can argue." He sat. She sat next to him, her toweled legs against his.

"First of all, not being able to…get in the mood—" she nodded at his lap "—isn't a big personal failure. It happens sometimes. We don't all live in romance novels where the hero is always ready all the time."

"But I should be able to do it. I want to do it. You're the most amazing woman I've ever met, and I think I'm…" He almost said *falling for you.* What the hell was he doing? This was casual. This wasn't anything more than that. Was he falling in love with his cure? The symmetry of it seemed poetic, and yet, he was a man who lived in reality and reality told him there was no way that a woman who knew of all his weaknesses…his shortcomings…could ever truly love him. How could Harley respect him now? "Anyway, you're my cure. And now I've somehow ruined it."

"I was never your cure."

"I don't understand. Of course you were." How else to explain the last two amazing months? He'd never had sex so remarkable in his life, and that had everything to do with Harley Vega.

"No. I was a distraction." She sighed and sat down next to him. "If you want my opinion, the reason this is happening is Lucinda."

"How?"

"She was an abusive, overbearing figure in your life. And she was a woman. And she undermined you then and now. When you looked at your watch in the pool, was it something about Lucinda and the company?"

He nodded.

"I thought so. I also think she's preventing you from having serious relationships."

"I don't get what you mean." His relationships were *his* choice. Not hers. She wasn't controlling his life. Not now, not ever. The very thought that she was somehow reaching into his personal life, hell, into his bedroom, and mucking things up made his blood boil.

But Harley wasn't finished.

"I think you're using sex to project strength. Virility. But more than that, you deliberately leave broken hearts in your wake. Publically. You're the one doing the rejecting. I think that's because you were rejected by your stepmother, and you want to make sure everyone knows that's not going to happen to you again."

Wilder felt exposed. Could she be right? But surely he didn't give a damn about Lucinda rejecting him? Why would he ever want her approval? And yet....yet...maybe something in it was true. "You're saying that because I had an evil stepmom, I'm seeking revenge on all the starlets and pop stars I can get my hands on? It sounds like I'm an asshole."

"I don't think you do it knowingly," Harley said.

"So that makes me an oblivious asshole." Wilder didn't like where this conversation was headed. He didn't use the women he dated. He was completely upfront about how he wasn't planning on settling down, about how marriage was not in the cards right now, if ever. All of them had told him that was fine with them. He often thought some of the broken hearts were just convenient for their careers. He never *intended* to hurt anyone. That was how he operated.

"No. It makes you a person with past scars that haven't been dealt with—yet." Harley reached out and touched his knee. He felt the shock of the contact, the warmth of her hand. It was a kind gesture, yet all he could think of was the current between them, the circuit that wasn't closed.

He stood. It all felt so overwhelming and so damn close to the truth in his core. Was he haunted by Lucinda? He thought he'd long since made sure she could never hurt him again, but was she doing it, now *in his own head?* Were his memories doing her dirty work for her? He hated the thought. But hadn't he feared this could be true? So close to his fortieth birthday, he'd begun taking stock of his life in a way he'd never done before. And thoughts of Lucinda, of his childhood, had been popping up. Yet, getting older should have made the memories seem further away, not closer. Suddenly, he didn't want to think about it anymore. Didn't want to think that he was damaged, that he might not ever be right. And maybe Harley wasn't his cure, because there was no cure to be had.

"Maybe you're right. Maybe you're not my cure." He walked away from her but glanced over his shoulder. "Maybe this isn't working out after all." She looked ashen suddenly.

It wouldn't be the first time he'd thought he was rehabilitated, but it turned out it was all just a silly mirage.

"Wait." She stood as well and moved to him. The fact that she seemed so perfect then, so beautiful and fragile and strong all at the same time unnerved him.

"No," he said. "You're right. You're not the solution. I was dumb to think so."

"I think you can cure yourself," she said. "And I can help you." A small flame of hope lit in his chest. "What do you think about switching roles? I think I have a lesson to teach you."

Wilder sat in the oversize chair near his king-size white oak bed in his vacation home, watching her move slowly in the dimmed light of his master bedroom suite.

"Don't move," she warned him, and his heart ticked up a notch, his breath catching in his throat. "You can only move when I say you can."

He wasn't the kind of man who took orders—he gave them. He wasn't a man used to surrendering power, wasn't used to not being in the driver's seat. He'd had many women in his arms, many in his bed, a blur of faces he could hardly remember, famous women, beautiful women, but none of those mattered now as she stood before him, clad only in her now dry yellow bikini. He drank in her body with appreciation, the tanned muscled arms, the lean legs, the delicate lines on her body that he'd grown to know so well over the last two months. His hands itching to move, because his fingertips knew how soft her skin would be. He had to fight to remain still. Slowly, achingly, she untied the back of her bikini top, the knots coming lose. His anticipation built as he watched her drop the top to the floor, baring her chest. Her beautiful, perfect nipples rose in the air-conditioned air, seeming to defy gravity.

His body burned for her, to take her, to make her his, to feel every inch of her skin, to feel her shudder with the pleasure he planned to give her. He wanted to take her to places even she'd never been before. He knew, deep in his soul, he would. Wilder wasn't finished with his lessons, but today, this night, she was going to teach him.

All he wanted was her. She would heal his wounded soul, she would be the elixir he'd needed his whole life. He was the man who had everything but understanding, and now, her dark eyes—those eyes that seemed to know him so well, that ferreted out all his secrets—drew closer. She untied one yellow knot on her hip, then the other, and dropped the bottoms on the floor. His legs tensed. He was going to stand.

"No," she warned him, shaking a single finger. "Stay put. You aren't the teacher. I am."

She stood before him, bare, miles of her bronzed skin. He wanted to move, and his fingers twitched. But she simply shook her head, slowly, maddeningly. He was her prisoner. He wanted nothing more than to reach out and touch her. Follow the line of her hip with his hands, feel the warmth of her body. He was the man who had everything: power, money, women, and yet even with all his wealth, he knew now, sitting before this woman, that none of it would ever be enough. That hole in him, that hole that seemed never able to be filled might finally devour what was left of his soul.

But she was his salvation. She was the one who'd make everything right. She stepped forward and picked up her bikini top and her bottoms and then moved tantalizingly close to him. He sat rigid in the wooden chair, arms gripping the rails. She leaned in, and he could smell the coconut sunscreen on her neck and then he reached up, cupping one bare breast in his hand. He couldn't help it. They were there, so tantalizing, so perfect. But she slapped his hand softly, a quick act of discipline. He released her and held the arm of the chair again.

"Bad, bad, bad," she taunted him, clicking her tongue in disapproval.

She slipped her string top under the chair's arm and tied it tightly against his wrist. Her touch as she grazed his wrist finishing the knot was electric, and he felt the bolt run all the way down to his toes. He worked to keep his hands steady, gripping the hard arm of the chair. She used the bottoms for the other wrist. And then he was bound to the chair. Bad boy, indeed. He was being punished. He couldn't imagine a worse punishment then being so close to this beautiful woman and unable to touch her bare skin. She offered warmth and the promise of pleasure, and more than that, everything he'd ever need.

"I'm in control of you now," she said. "You're going to be mine." He nodded. "No one else enters this room, enters your head. Nothing but me."

She'd turned off his phone and even the home's Wi-Fi. There would be no distractions. Not that he wanted any. He felt powerless, and he kind of liked it. She was giving him permission to let go, not to think about all the pressures in his life. She stood before him, beautifully naked, and he couldn't imagine wanting to be anywhere else. He loved the idea of her taking control. This was perfectly delicious.

She dipped down and kissed him, her tongue flicking against his. He strained against his wrist restraints. He knew he could break them if he really tried, but the fact was he didn't want to. This was too damn good. Harley knelt slowly before him, his gaze taking in her beautiful curves, and then, she was working the fly of his shorts. He was halfway to hard, he realized. That was an improvement over the pool, and yet, he worried still. Worried his ghosts would come and snatch away his desire.

"This is mine," she said, eyes sparkling with mischief as she held his cock in her hands. "It's mine to do with as I please." Her voice alone made him come to life, made him stiffen with want. Yes, he thought. I want to be yours. All yours.

He thought he'd hate giving up power; he thought that was the worst thing in the world. After all, hadn't that been what he'd been battling against all his life as he fought off Lucinda's claims on the company? But maybe, sometimes, letting go was the answer.

Hadn't he been trying to teach Harley this very lesson? That letting out her desires could be a healthy thing? Here she was teaching him the same thing. He relaxed into his wrist restraints then, happy to give over control for once in his life. Because he knew it was the right thing to do. And because he trusted Harley. He wouldn't have done this with anyone else. He could only do it with her. He might need to be his own cure, but she was the one who would help him find it.

"You take care of your father's company. And of your brothers. And everyone else." She met his gaze, on her knees, working him with her hands. "But who takes care of you?"

Then she knelt down and licked his shaft, one gloriously perfect sensation. And then he was in her mouth. Her wet, willing and so very talented mouth. He almost came right there, almost couldn't hold it. She was damn good at that. No doubt about it. She knew what she was doing. Harley took him, deeper and deeper, more urgently, and as she picked up the pace, he knew there was no way he'd last. No way he could hold out. She had control of him, and she was riding him hard to the finish. He came with a primal shout. He came and came and came, a river of all the things he kept bottled up inside him, all the pressure, all the worry, all the pain of his past. He was going to let it all go. And he did.

When Harley pulled away from him, a satisfied smile on her face, he felt spent. Felt as if he'd finally put down the burden of past pains, of current pressures, of everything that had held him back. All because he'd let this woman tie him to a damn chair. The pupil had become the master. Now, she should teach him.

"That was one helluva lesson," he said.

"There are more to come," she promised, and he felt himself stirring again. She reached up and slowly untied him, pulling on the string of her bikini.

"Good."

CHAPTER FIFTEEN

WILDER SPENT THE next week in tropical paradise learning that he had the power within himself to fight his demons. That was what Harley taught him, by showing him that letting go *was* what he needed to do. He'd been hanging on so tightly that he'd actually been hanging on to the pressure and negativity and the running reel in his head of Lucinda telling him he wasn't good enough, wasn't smart enough to be the heir to his father's company or the patriarch of the family. It was that undercurrent of insecurity that had been at the root of his sexual shortcomings. Once she'd shown that to him, it felt as if a lightbulb had gone off. Now, he was confident that he wouldn't have a relapse, and hell, even if he did, he knew exactly what to do. He'd never felt more in control of his life.

"You saved me," Wilder told Harley as they woke in his penthouse bed the morning after arriving in Manhattan. He couldn't avoid work forever, but he was confident he could face Lucinda's attacks now.

And an FCC investigation wasn't the worst thing in the world. The company would survive. And he knew he was capable of running it. He'd come this far.

Harley moved against his chest, wrapping her arm around him. "You know I'm not your cure. I thought we've been over this."

"No. You showed me how to do it myself," he said, kissing the top of her head. "And for that, I'm forever grateful. These last two months have been amazing."

"Actually, it's been almost three now." Harley sat up, studying him with her light brown eyes, the hint of a worry there. He knew her so well. Knew there was something on her mind.

"How do you feel about that?" he asked her, tentatively.

"How do you feel about it?" So, she was turning the tables, avoiding the answer. He was getting even better at reading her, especially when she had her defenses up. He wondered why she was defensive. Was she getting tired of him? God, he hoped not.

"It doesn't feel like it's been three months." For him, it had all gone by in a blink of an eye. He couldn't even remember the last time a relationship had lasted this long as he'd usually grown restless and bored, eager to move on to the next. Not with Harley. All he could think was how much he didn't want to let her go, how he wanted this day, and many other days, together, to stretch out ahead of them.

"No, it hasn't." She seemed like she wanted to ask him something more but was hesitating.

"Come on. Spit it out. I know when there's something on your mind."

She considered him, looking pensive. "I don't know. But tomorrow is your birthday..."

He'd almost forgotten. He was turning forty tomorrow. It should have caused him complete consternation. He'd been dreading the birthday for the last year. But somehow, with Harley in his life, he seemed more at peace with getting older. With facing his eventual mortality. It didn't seem so scary. Not anymore.

His phone on the nightstand dinged then, announcing an incoming message. He looked at the face of his phone and realized too late that it was a risqué picture from one of his friends with benefits, Andrea, whom he hadn't heard from in nearly a year. But she always remembered his birthday. Always texted him on his birthday and the major holidays.

Happy pre-Birthday Day! she texted. *Want to unwrap your present?* And with it, a picture of her in a sexy thong and nothing else.

Another man might have been intrigued, but he wasn't. He had zero interest in Andrea or anyone else. Not when he had Harley in his arms. He deleted the photo, but not before Harley saw it.

"Who's that from?" She sat up.

"No one."

"I thought you agreed not to sleep with anyone else while you were sleeping with me. Even though this is casual, that was one of the rules." Harley looked…well, hurt. She looked betrayed.

"I'm not sleeping with her."

"Why did she send you that photo?"

"Because I *have* slept with her. But I'm not *currently* sleeping with her. She always sends me a birthday text."

"But you might. Sleep with her in the future. After…" Harley bit her lip. Was she going to cry? What on earth was happening? How had this morning gone so wrong so fast?

"No. I don't want to sleep with her." Why were they arguing about Andrea? He couldn't care less about Andrea. She was a sexy blonde, and they had a good time together, but he wasn't going to marry her. Wasn't even going to call her his girlfriend. Hell, he hadn't even seen her in more than a year. "Why are you upset?"

"I'm not upset." Harley hauled herself out of bed and yanked on her jeans. "I just… I just guess I don't understand what we're doing."

"We're having fantastic sex. I'm teaching you. You're teaching me." Had any of that changed? Did she want more? Of course, he suspected she did. Part of him knew she'd always had a problem with casual. But if she did, she damn well needed to tell him. Maybe he needed more than casual, too. But he'd sensed she was as skittish as they came. She needed to *admit* for once in her life that she needed someone in it. "I did not sleep with Andrea while we were together. I don't want to."

"Great."

"Isn't that what you wanted?" He pushed the cover aside. "If it's not, if you want something else, tell me."

"Why? We have a deal, don't we?" She grabbed her shirt off the floor and yanked it over her head. A deal she never should have agreed to in the first place.

"For a sexologist, you sure hate talking about your own damn feelings," he pointed out.

"That's *why* I'm a sexologist. So I can talk about *other* people's feelings. Not mine." There was a great deal of truth in that, he thought. The most truthful thing she'd said so far this morning. Wilder sat up in bed.

"You need to talk to me, Harley. Tell me what's wrong."

"No. I don't." She shook her head as she buttoned her jeans. "I think I need to… I just need to go to my room."

"You are all about the flight. Not fight." He'd seen it countless times. "You're always trying to run away from me."

"I can't do this anymore."

"Can't do what?" Amazing sex? A perfect partnership where each person seemed to get what the other needed before they even opened their mouths? Pure perfection?

He swung his legs over the side of the bed, but just as he did, the maid knocked and came in, carrying a tray of breakfast for two. He whipped the sheets over his nakedness, just in time to see Harley move past her and out the door.

CHAPTER SIXTEEN

It took Harley no time at all to pack the few things she'd brought to Wilder's penthouse. She'd been an idiot to stay for so long. Of course, she'd get emotionally involved in three months. She knew the science. Three months was a hell of a lot longer than an hour, and an hour plus thirty-six in-depth personal questions were enough to make most people fall in love. Most men said *I love you* within the first eighty-eight days. Women, 134 days. Still, she knew she'd been playing with fire, all that dopamine and oxytocin running through her system after those many, many climaxes, and then, of course, there was just the fact that no matter how hard she worked at it, Harley couldn't do casual. Nothing about her relationship with Wilder Lange felt casual.

And that was why she needed to leave. She couldn't stay here and watch him go back to his playboy life and his revolving door bedroom. Sure, logically she knew that one stupid picture on his phone didn't mean anything. She knew he wasn't cheating on her, knew instinctively that of course he'd kept his promise. She didn't doubt his loyalty. She knew logically that the tornado of jealousy inside her was baseless. So what if a beautiful woman sent him a picture? He hadn't asked for it. Besides, she knew that a man like Wilder Lange would always be fending off the advances of beautiful women. He was rich, he was gorgeous and he was damn near perfect in every other way.

If she analyzed her feelings clinically, she knew the problem was that now they were reaching a point where she'd need to ask him to give up every other beautiful woman that wanted him. Fight against all those evolutionary instincts men are born with, all for her. She'd need to ask something of him, something that she wasn't sure he was ready to give her. And that terrified her.

She'd almost rather not ask than ask and be rejected. That was the hard truth of it. She felt the coward. She wasn't nearly as brave as she'd like to believe she was. Adrenaline buzzed in her brain and her flight impulse was set to high. She needed to flee. She needed to escape and then figure out what she'd do next. Harley had worried about this from the start, worried that he'd been too much her type, too alluring in too many ways. She felt like she owed a big swath of her *Dear Harley* clients an apology. Not just for breaking her own rules but for not truly understanding their own impulse control issues. How often had she sat at her keyboard and lectured a client about reining in their desires? About how they could control their wants? When they had told her they couldn't help themselves, hadn't she said, *It's in your control*, and believed it?

Yet, with Wilder over the last three months, she'd been completely out of control. Reckless. Not just with her body, but with her heart. And it wasn't his fault, either. Every choice she made had been hers—even though none of it felt truly in her control.

The fact was she'd wanted Wilder Lange the moment she'd met him, and she'd known he wanted her, as well. And despite her weak protestations, her lip service to her professional code, her liking to think of him as an enemy, part of her had been hoping she'd have him in the most carnal way possible. She'd known, really, that if she'd stayed beneath his roof this would happen. She'd told herself she could be objective, but part of her had always known sex was a danger. And when it came right down to it, she hadn't even fought against it. In some ways she could handle that, she guessed, handle the misstep of simple sex. But, the fact was, she'd been falling for him, too. Hell, she might have just fallen in love with him at first sight in that damn study.

Such a thing sounded impossible, especially to her clinician's mind, yet she knew it happened. Hadn't she read research about how people can "feel" in love in a fifth of a second? And she'd spent far more time with him than that. Harley zipped up her suitcase and then froze. Where would she even go? She didn't have an apartment. Didn't have a place to live. She'd have to call a friend, or worst-case, head home to Miami. She pulled the suitcase off the bed and extended the handle, wheeling it to the door of her room. Then she swung open her door. She nearly ran into Wilder Lange. Harley jumped back as if she'd been struck.

"What are you doing here?" she asked him, heart thudding in her chest. He looked even more delicious than he had yesterday—dark hair swept back, eyes watchful. He'd thrown on a T-shirt and shorts.

"I could ask you the same thing." He nodded at her suitcase. "I hope you're not leaving."

Her grip on the bag loosened slightly. "I think I should. I need to think."

"You can think here."

Could she? She couldn't think with Wilder around, standing in front of her like this. She couldn't think about anything except the feel of his hands on her body.

"I don't think I can."

"But you saved me."

She shook her head slowly. "No. You saved yourself."

"You did save me. Or at least showed me how to save myself. You were the only one, Harley. You were different."

She hated how she soaked up his words, beamed with pride, almost, about how she'd been able to rouse him when other women hadn't. Who wouldn't want to be the only woman who could stir desire in a powerful man like Wilder? The power went straight to her head, but she also knew that it was a false truth. She wasn't the one who made him do *anything.* She dropped the handle of her suitcase and retreated deep into her room, standing by the big bay window that overlooked Manhattan.

"It's not me who's making you better," she said, shaking her head.

"It is." Wilder sounded resolute as he found her again by the window, putting both his hands on her shoulders and turning her to face him. "You showed me the way, Harley." He gently stroked her chin and she felt her will being tested. She wanted more than anything to wrap her arms around the man, hell, to rip off his shirt and have a round two right now. But where would that get them? Deeper emotional attachment, an attachment she couldn't afford. Not with this man.

"Why not stay longer? Why end it now?" he asked.

The idea of lying in Wilder's bed, not thinking about anything but how wonderful being there felt, was exactly what the monster of need in her wanted. He was a man haunted by his past, and she was a woman who didn't know how to do casual and was already in love with the man.

"Because..." She was in too deep. But could she tell him that?

"You have to tell me what's on your mind, Harley," he said. "You have to tell me what you want."

She knew that. But it was so hard to tell him, impossible to tell him that she'd fallen in love with him. She felt afraid. Afraid he'd laugh in her face, afraid he'd break her heart into a million pieces. She knew she had to tell him, but she couldn't. Her mouth didn't seem to work and the words stuck in her throat.

She shook her head.

"You have to tell me, because I think I already know what you're going to say. I know you don't want to end it." She glanced up at him, feeling worry tighten her throat. Could he see through her? Did he know her true feelings? "Tell me you don't want me. Tell me and I'll let you go." She couldn't tell him that because she did want him. More than anything. He stared at her, dark eyes full of promise. "I know you're not satisfied. I know you can't be satisfied. Not with just these last three months. They've woken something in you, just like they've woken something in me. I can feel the want in you." He grabbed her wrist, and she felt her rapid pulse beneath his thick thumb. The monster coming to life once more, wanting to have its fill. "Tell me you've had enough and I'll let you go."

She shook her head, slowly, once, not trusting herself to say a single word. Her throat felt dry and her hands itched to touch him. "I want to hear you say it." His words left no room for argument. Her heart kicked like a rabbit in her chest. Blood rushed between her legs, and she felt swollen and sore. And while she had all her clothes on, she somehow felt bare. Vulnerable. This man could read her better than any man had read her before. Somehow, he seemed to know about what was in her. What was ready to be unleashed.

"No, I didn't get enough." How could she? The monster in her was never satisfied, not when it came to Wilder Lange. The monster couldn't be satiated. Even now, it was coming to life inside her, warming her thighs, making her nipples beneath her sheer bra tingle.

"I didn't get enough, either. I want you. Not just today. Not just tomorrow. But for as long as you'll have me."

She started at this, shocked. "You do?"

He nodded. Wilder walked her backward and she went, knowing all the while that they were headed for the bed at the far end of the room, the giant four-poster canopy. He wanted her? Wanted her for more than just a day, or a week or a month? Her heart sang with the news.

"I know you want that, too."

She nodded, fiercely.

Wilder moved his hands now down to her hips even as her butt hit the edge of the bed. There was something amazingly sexy about being pinned there, between the bed and Wilder, his big body pressed against hers.

"Good, because I've fallen in love with you, Harley Vega."

She could feel the impact of his words at the very core of her being. She couldn't believe it might be true. "I love you, too."

"There." He stroked her face. "It's about time you admitted it."

And then he leaned in and kissed her. The monster of want, once sleepy, now came fully awake in her chest, as her tongue lashed out and found his. God, the man tasted so good. Like something sweet and salty, like caramel and forbidden fruit. And he *loved* her. He had fallen in love with her. His hands moved down the front of her shirt, and suddenly, he'd pulled it up and over her head, and there she was in her skirt and a sheer bra. He dipped down then and flicked his tongue over the fabric, her right nipple standing at attention, a light brown against the ivory lace. She groaned, unable to help herself, as she tangled her hands in his hair. He moved to the other side, his soft, warm mouth on her and sending an explosion of want running through her.

"I love you, Harley. I want no one else." He moaned the words against her chest, and then she was flat on her back on the soft bed. He was tugging on her skirt, easing it off her legs as quickly as he pulled. He whipped off his own shirt and stepped out of his cargo shorts and for the first time she saw his fully naked body. Caramel-colored, fully chiseled, a man who took pride in his appearance. He was beautiful, like no man she'd ever been with. Perfect on the outside, and slightly broken on the inside. She loved him, all of him.

"I love you," she said. Would she ever tire of saying it? The words just fanned the flames of the monster. She slowly lowered one bra strap and then the other, unfastening the front clasp until she was free. He grabbed one breast and nuzzled the other with his nose, flicking out his tongue and gently licking until her nipple stood at attention and she arched her back with want. He growled, like a starving man, and tugged at her underwear until she was bare beneath him.

He dove into her, licking her liquid center, devouring her like a man who'd never known true want before. She felt worshipped, as his tongue dipped deeper and deeper inside her and then flicked over the bundle of her nerves swollen with need. His tongue sent her flying over the edge, and in seconds, she'd grabbed a handful of his hair, shouting as her body wracked with her climax. She'd never come like that, so hard, so fast, so completely without warning. And she remembered, he was the one who'd shown her just how amazing a come like that could be.

"God, I love to make you come," he groaned, sitting up and wiping his glistening mouth. She lay on the bed, panting, legs parted as he climbed up on top of her, his cock thick, and heavy and ready. "This is what you do to me. Do you see what you do to me?"

She nodded, reaching out and finding him with both hands. He let his head fall back, his mouth slack as she worked him, up and down with long, measured strokes. His erection was impressive, big and unwavering, and she could barely even imagine him impotent. The very word just didn't fit him. Not this powerful man in this immensely sexy body. His mouth found hers and she could taste herself on his tongue, salty and sour, and that reminded her how he'd made her come, how he'd given her no choice in the matter. His delicious weight settled on her and she spread her legs for him, knowing she craved it, knowing the raging monster of want in her would get its due.

And then he thrust inside her, and both of them froze, groaning with the pleasure of it. She felt taut and stretched to her limits, and yet, despite it all, wanted more. And more. She wrapped her legs around him, even as he broke free of the kiss, his dark eyes on hers, as he moved deeper and faster. She met his gaze, and it felt like she was seeing right into his soul, right into his wounded childhood, into the man he'd become, and how far he'd come in treating himself. How much healthier he was.

Then he was off her in an instant, rolling her over to her stomach and pulling her to the edge of the bed. Her feet met the floor, even as she laid, stomach against the comforter. He took her from behind, a little rougher this time, a little deeper, more urgent. She could hear the slap of his skin against hers, the primal sound of two animals driven by instinct. Then, just when she wasn't sure if she could take any more, she found herself coming, hard, and she choked on her own cry, even as Wilder came as well, in a final hard thrust followed by his own guttural shout.

He fell on her back, and she could feel her sweat and his mingling, their chests desperately sucking in air. Her body had never felt so used and so wonderful at the same time. She'd never come that hard back to back, never in her life. Her brain felt like scrambled eggs. The monster want within her had been quelled—for the moment, and as it receded, her brain switched on. Wilder had told her he loved her. Everything in her world was going to be different now.

"So, we're not casual anymore?" she asked, sitting up on her elbow.

"I don't think we were ever casual." He reached out and smoothed her hair.

"We weren't? But you said..."

"I would've said anything to get you into bed. But I always knew there was something different about you. Always."

She pulled away from him, feeling stunned. "Really? But wasn't the whole point that you needed to teach me about casual sex? What was all of that?"

"Well, I needed to teach you about sex. Your education was appalling for a sex advice columnist," he teased. She reached over, grabbed a throw pillow and thwacked him with it.

"Hey," she warned, hitting him again.

"I'm kidding. Really. I am." He held up his hands in defense. "You taught me the most important lesson," he said. "That I've been letting my past dictate my future. That stops now. And now I want to make a different deal with you." He reached out and pulled her to him, so they were nearly nose to nose.

"What's that?" She felt wary.

"I want to teach you the lesson of me loving you forever."

"What?" She arched back from him, scanning his eyes for any sign of a joke.

"I think I've loved you from the moment I met you," he said. "And this isn't casual for me, either. I don't want another woman. All I want, all I've ever wanted, is you."

"I love you, too."

"Good. I want you to marry me." He gazed intently at her.

"Marry you?" Harley had never been more stunned in her life. She rolled away from him and stared at the ceiling, her heart pounding, activated by a nervous thrum of barely contained energy. "*Marry* you?"

"Yes," he said, and nodded. "Tonight, if you'd like. Or tomorrow. Or next year. But I want you to be my wife." His sensual lips curved into a teasing smile. "Do we need to write a pros-and-cons list?"

She glared at him. "No. No you don't."

"Pro. I'm sexy AF." He lifted one finger, then

another. “Con. I’m an egotistical asshole. Pro. I’m madly and completely in love with you…”

“Con. I’m madly in love with you, too,” she pointed out.

He laughed. “That’s no con.”

“Kiss me, you fool. Before I change my mind.”

“Is that a yes?”

“Yes. Hell, yes, it’s a yes.”

And he pulled her close and kissed her.

EPILOGUE

A year later

HARLEY LAY OUT on the deck of her brother-in-law's hundred-foot yacht, letting the warm Mediterranean sun beat down on her bikini-clad body. Wilder lay beside her on deck and a bottle of chilled champagne sat between them in a sterling silver cooler.

"This was a good idea for a honeymoon," she said, reaching out to hold Wilder's hand.

"The only problem was prying Seth's hands off his baby for a week." Wilder grinned. "It took a lot of persuading."

"I bet it did." Harley still couldn't believe the amazing turn of events in the last year. They'd planned a wedding, gotten married just the week-end before. Her family had gone wild over him, but then she knew why. He was impossible *not* to love. At least, once they got to know him. Also, he insisted on giving them a loan for their restaurant to completely renovate it from nuts to bolts. Since its reopening, it had landed on every Miami food critic's hot-ten-places-to-eat list. Harley had also had the chance to meet his brothers, all of whom were so very different, and very contrary to him, and yet…they all carried a certain amount of Lange swagger. Lange Communications had been cleared of any wrongdoing by the FCC, and Harley had, at long last, finished her couples advice book and landed an impressive advance, the book due out in mere months.

Wilder deserved some credit. In addition to his hands-on lessons, the advance sales shot through the roof as women across the world would want to know how Harley had managed to tame one of the world's richest playboys. She could've told them the secret was simple. He'd fallen in love. Real love, for maybe the first time in his life. And so had she.

"I just want to thank you again, Mrs. Lange," he said, glancing over at her as he squeezed her hand.

"Why, *Mr.* Lange?"

"For making me the happiest man on earth." He looked around at the rolling ocean waves. "Or, technically, at sea."

He reached over and kissed her then, gently at first, with love, and then the kiss turned more passionate as he cupped the side of her face. She felt that old familiar need flare up inside her again. In the last year, she'd learned another powerful lesson: that relationship sex *could* truly be as hot and incredible as any casual sex. Furthermore, she'd come to understand nearly daily that previously she'd been settling for mediocre sex, when she could have been having amazing sex. The heat she felt for Wilder hadn't cooled. Not even a little bit.

She glanced at the massive diamond on her finger, which caught the bright sunlight. How she loved this moment. Hell, she loved all moments with Wilder. They were perfect. All of them.

Wilder broke the kiss. "And thank you for... curing me."

"You know I'm not your cure," she scolded him.

"It's been a full year since any relapses. I'd call that a cure." He flashed her a bright smile as he adjusted himself on the lounge chair. She still, sometimes, couldn't believe he was really hers, that such a beautiful and sexy man wanted *her* when he could have nearly anyone he chose.

He glanced around now, a sly look crossing his face that Harley knew too well.

"I think it might be time for another lesson," he teased.

"Oh, really? And what's that?" Their noses were nearly touching as he reached out, pulled their armless lounge chairs together, so their legs now touched. He reached for a nearby blanket and tossed it over them, even as the deck rolled with the waves of the water.

"Have you ever had yacht-deck sex?" he asked, a teasing smile blooming on his face.

"Well, now, let me see," she said, gently rolling on top of him. "I've had below-decks-yacht sex. Bath-

room-yacht sex. Bed-yacht sex. Wheelhouse-yacht sex and…" She ticked off the various kinds on her fingers.

"Is that right?" Wilder frowned. "Well, then, sounds like you've done it all—"

"Nope." She pretended to think. "I haven't had yacht-*deck* sex. Not yet."

"Well, then, little pupil." He reached for her bare waist beneath the towel and pulled her closer. "Shall we start the lesson?"

"You sure *I'm* the pupil? I seem to recall that last night I taught *you* a new trick. With that toy you bought."

"You did?" He nuzzled her nose. "Does that *really* make you the expert? I'm not so sure…"

"You seriously think I have nothing to teach you?" Now, Harley was starting to get offended.

"On the contrary, I think you have *everything* to teach me," he said and kissed her so hard, she was almost sure she might not mind another lesson. Or two.

* * * * *

MILLS & BOON

MODERN

Power and Passion

Prepare to be swept off your feet by sophisticated, sexy and seductive heroes, in some of the world's most glamourous and romantic locations, where power and passion collide.

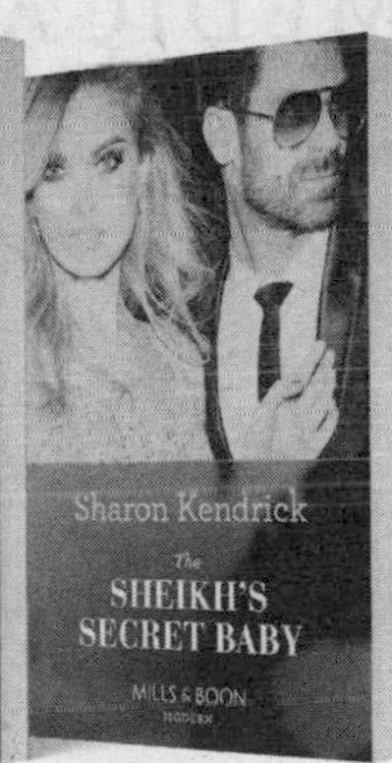

ght Modern stories published every month, find them all at:

millsandboon.co.uk/Modern

LET'S TALK
Romance

For exclusive extracts, competitions and special offers, find us online:

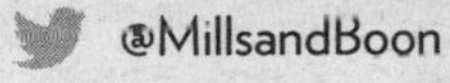

@MillsandBoonUK

Get in touch on 01413 063232

For all the latest titles coming soon, visit

millsandboon.co.uk/nextmonth